# WHERE
# **PEACE**
# IS
# **LOST**

**ALSO BY VALERIE VALDES**

*Fault Tolerance*

*Prime Deceptions*

*Chilling Effect*

# WHERE
# PEACE
# IS
# LOST

a novel

## VALERIE **VALDES**

**HARPER** Voyager
*An Imprint of HarperCollinsPublishers*

WHERE PEACE IS LOST. Copyright © 2023 by Valerie Valdes. All rights reserved. Printed in the United States of America. No part of this book may be used or reproduced in any manner whatsoever without written permission except in the case of brief quotations embodied in critical articles and reviews. For information, address HarperCollins Publishers, 195 Broadway, New York, NY 10007.

HarperCollins books may be purchased for educational, business, or sales promotional use. For information, please email the Special Markets Department at SPsales@harpercollins.com.

Harper Voyager and design are trademarks of HarperCollins Publishers LLC.

FIRST EDITION

*Designed by Alison Bloomer*
*Splatter illustration © lalan / Shutterstock*

Library of Congress Cataloging-in-Publication Data has been applied for.

ISBN 978-0-06-308593-0

23 24 25 26 27  LBC  5 4 3 2 1

*To those who light a candle instead of cursing the darkness,*
*and to those still looking for a match*

# WHERE
# PEACE
# IS
# LOST

# CHAPTER ONE

**K**el hung upside down from the side of the enormous xoffedil she'd been climbing and reconsidered her life choices.

The creature thankfully hadn't noticed her distress; if it did, it might reach back with its long, tentacled proboscis and try to yank her off. This might tear out a clump of its fur and make it violently angry, sending it charging into the forest with Kel in its furious clutches. Or it might rip Kel's leg off at whichever joint was weakest, and she'd probably die of shock, pain, or blood loss long before anyone noticed she was missing.

Or it might eat her. Or all those things in no particular order.

None of the options appealed, but admittedly, nor did being stuck with her booted foot going numb while leaves and branches slapped her face and arms with every step the creature took through the trees. Above her—or technically below her—a slash of lavender sky flashed in and out of view, flanked by walls of vegetation as the xoffedil lumbered along its path. Birds hummed or whistled deeper in the green, occasionally taking to the air with a scream, and insects clicked their carapaces and rattled their wings in defiance of the predators lurking in the underbrush, eager for a crunchy snack.

With a grunt of effort, Kel wrenched herself up by bending at the waist, then fumbled for the rope wrapped around her ankle. Her muscles strained as she pulled until she was vertical, climbing further up to ease the tension on the knotted loop. Wrapping a length of the cord around her wrist a few times, she reached down and bent her leg, grabbing the loop and tugging it over her boot's heel. All this work to scale the creature for a few fistfuls of kexeet—the valuable rainbow moss growing on its shaggy fur.

The xoffedil trumpeted, and Kel jerked in surprise, nearly losing her grip. In the distance, a similar call replied. Oh spirits. The giant hexapod wasn't out looking for food; it was trying to find a mate.

A series of new potential methods of dying spread out before her like a feast in the village. Xoffedil were extremely vigorous in their reproductive activities. Kel had to get away before the two creatures reached each other.

Abandoning all hope of a profitable harvest, Kel clambered up the xoffedil's flank as fast as she could. She reached the spot where she'd attached her anchor line to its fur, decoupling the elaborate series of clips that spread her weight around. The more she moved, the more likely the creature would notice her presence and try to rid itself of an unpleasant pest. If she lost her grip on the way down, she could easily fall to her death. If she survived the four-story drop, she might be crushed by a foot the size of an armed transport.

If this were simple, everyone would do it, Kel thought. And the price of kexeet would be much lower.

Slinging the anchor line and clips diagonally across her back, Kel climbed sideways toward the creature's nearest thigh, its swaying gait making the task more difficult. Knots in the fur served as natural hand- and footholds, but she paused between movements to avoid attracting attention, slowing her down. The xoffedil trumpeted again, the answering call closer now.

Kel sped up, halving the distance to the middle leg. She could do this. Just a little farther. Not for the first time, she wistfully considered how much easier this would be if—

A flash of movement caught her attention: the xoffedil's whiplike tail, heading right for her.

Kel dug in like a tick and clung to the creature's side. The thick tail slid down, its natural curve scraping the fur to the left of her while leaving her untouched. She relaxed her grip and breathed a sigh of relief, the xoffedil's musky scent filling her nose and mouth.

Then the tail came back up from underneath and flicked her into the air.

For a few stunned moments, Kel flew, higher than she had in years without a flitter. The top of the forest canopy stretched in front of her like a richly woven carpet, shades of green mixed with purples and reds and oranges that might be fruit or flowers.

And then she reached the apex of her flight and fell toward the trees.

Death by falling had always been one Kel expected, even welcomed more than a sudden shot through the head or a blade through the heart. And after everything, perhaps she deserved to die alone. To her surprise, though, she found she wasn't ready to accept that fate.

Years of training and instinct kicked in, once she overcame her first impossible impulse. Kel relaxed her limbs, tucking her chin close to her chest and covering her face, knees bent. She hit the canopy, vines and twigs catching at the ropes and clips slung across her back even as they whipped her legs. While she might slow her descent by grabbing a branch, she could also break or dislocate an arm, so she resisted the urge.

The density of the vegetation thinned as she plunged into the dim light of the understory. Below her, a sun-dappled assortment of shrubs, ferns, and moss-covered saplings fought for supremacy over the ground. In other circumstances, she might have better control over where she landed, but now she was entirely at the mercy of gravity. Down she went, mentally preparing herself for a hard landing, hoping she'd be able to execute a maneuver she hadn't practiced in years—

The ropes on her back went taut and yanked her to a halt, burning her skin and pressing sharply against her chest and underarms. She dangled long enough to draw a shuddering breath and assess that she had about two stories left before she hit dirt. Whatever branch had caught her sagged beneath her weight, then snapped, sending her once again plummeting to the forest floor.

The shock to her feet on landing quickly dissipated up her legs as she rolled awkwardly sideways, finally coming to a stop flat on her back after two full rotations. The branch, still attached by her ropes, missed her by a handbreadth. Above her, only the barest gap in the canopy existed to indicate where she'd entered, and she had no doubt it would be gone within a month. The plants cared little for the passing of humans, and kept their own counsel.

Kel inhaled tentatively, wary of bruised ribs. Her only pains were external, skin and muscle and dull aches in her joints that would no doubt worsen. She was lucky. If she told the villagers the story of what had happened today, when she brought them the kexeet, they'd probably tease her about the poor quality of her bird impression. Or they would say the planet had offered her its protection and she should be honored. And yet, despite her previous desire to continue living, she had trouble feeling good about it.

*Where we fall, may peace rise.*

Old memories Kel avoided came rushing back, and she lay there staring up at the dark underside of the trees feeling miserable and alone. A bug crawled across her arm, then fluttered away, its translucent wings catching the light like colored glasteel. Eventually, grudgingly, she sat up and untangled herself from her ropes, then stood, then began the long walk to her borrowed flitter, wounds new and old aching in her flesh and bones and soul.

A TENDAY AFTER HER XOFFEDIL MISHAP, KEL SAT CROSS-LEGGED ON THE small covered porch in front of her house at the edge of the swamp, mending a tear in a spare shirt, when the insects and birds around her fell silent. She didn't get many visitors, and they usually called out their approach from a distance, to let her prepare for company. The last time she'd been surprised, the poor man who'd come to warn her about an impending storm had left with a wrenched arm and her most profound apologies. He'd spread the word, more for everyone else's safety than hers.

Still, one person persisted in attempting to sneak up on her.

"Lunna," Kel said, calmly continuing her work. "You'll be sorry if I stick my finger."

"How do you always know it's me, Friend Kel?" Lunna asked, emerging from behind a tree. Their coppery hair fell over their shoulder in a single braid interlaced with colored threads, loose wisps framing their narrow, freckled face and bright blue eyes. They wore their usual brown tunic over a long-sleeved shirt, with comfortably loose pants tucked into knee-high boots. Also as usual, they brimmed with barely contained excitement, though it seemed to be overflowing today.

I don't always know it's you, Kel thought. Every time she guessed it was Lunna, part of her whispered that it could be someone else, and her presumption would mean her death.

"You have news," Kel said instead. "Go on, before you burst like an overripe stinkmelon."

"You could at least pretend to be interested," Lunna said, flinging themself down on the wooden floor next to Kel.

Kel pretended a lot of things, to her shame, but not this. "Well?"

Lunna grinned back, then leaned forward conspiratorially. "There's been a sighting. A Pale war machine."

Now Kel did stab herself with the needle, hissing in surprise and pain. "A war machine?" she asked, sticking her bleeding thumb in her mouth.

Lunna nodded. "One of the really big ones. Bigger than a xoffedil."

Flashes of memory assaulted Kel. She sucked her thumb hard.

"Where is it now?" she asked.

"Still in the Parched Fields, I expect." Lunna stroked a puffy weed that grew in a crack between two boards. "My parents sent me to tell you there's an all-villages meeting to decide what to do about it. In Esrondaa, tomorrow night."

Esrondaa was the only true city in southern Loth, where the spaceport was located. A meeting there meant thousands of people from dozens of villages cramming into the open-air amphitheater where such business was conducted. Anyone was allowed to attend, but many would simply give their opinions to some chosen representative to pass on in their place.

Kel didn't make a habit of involving herself in local politics, even though she'd been living on Loth for almost five trade years. The locals knew their own business better than she did. Still, every time there was a meeting, Lunna or someone else from their village, Niulsa, was sent to invite her. Every voice mattered, they always said. Kel had believed that once, too.

This time, though, she might actually go to this meeting. A Pale war machine was no trade or farming discussion. While Loth wasn't an official territory of the Prixori

Anocracy and hadn't been among the planets caught up in any recent wars, the Pale had exerted political pressure to be permitted to set up a temporary base in the northern part of the continent. They had promised to withdraw after their war at the time ended, and for the most part they had done so.

Unfortunately, they'd left a few things behind. Always at war somewhere.

"Has someone been notified?" Kel asked.

"What, like the Pale?" Lunna asked.

"Yes," Kel said. Best to report it and stay well away.

Lunna's bright expression dimmed. "That's why we're having the meeting. It was reported right away, but the Pale say they won't send anyone."

"Impossible." The war machines were dangerous. They couldn't be left roaming about.

Lunna shrugged. "They said it's low priority and they'll take care of it when they can. Something about resource allocation? You could have lit a cookfire with the flames coming from my ma's eyes."

Kel felt pretty heated herself. That settled it. She was definitely attending the meeting. Perhaps the people who contacted the Anocracy hadn't explained the problem adequately. She needed more information and, if necessary, she had to ensure none of the locals attempted something foolish—like trying to stop the machine themselves.

"I should pack," Kel muttered, staring down at the half-mended shirt in her hands.

"You'll go?" Lunna asked, clapping their hands in delight. "Oh, bring me, please? My parents said I could go with whoever went, but Leader Thrim already conveyed her regrets, and her counsel. I think they assume no one else will want to go."

They likely didn't want Lunna to go, Kel thought, but didn't want to oppose the request outright. At twenty-two trade years old, Lunna was entitled to make their own choices; even so, they would always be a baby to the people who'd raised them.

Even Kel sometimes saw the fresh-faced eighteen-year-old they'd been when she first met them, instead of the adult they'd matured into. At their age, Kel was already somber and star systems away from the planet where she was born. Lunna, by contrast, retained a youthful brightness and optimism, still lived at home, and had responsibilities to their family and the village.

Perhaps Kel should discourage them with a carefully placed nudge?

"Don't you need to finish repairing the village's fabricator?" Kel asked. "Before your family leaves for the trade fair?"

"We won't be leaving until the war machine problem is solved anyway," Lunna said. They tilted their head in thought. "Now that you mention it, I do need to get a new belt and print head. Can't fix the fabricator without them, and the only supplier is in Esrondaa. It's a perfect excuse!"

She'd hoped to convince Lunna to stay, not give them a bespoke reason to go. "You're safer here," Kel said, knowing how weak it sounded.

"I can choke on a bone anywhere," Lunna retorted. Their tone became wheedling. "You shouldn't travel alone, either. You know I love seeing the spaceport, and I know all the villages and paths between here and Esrondaa."

"So do I."

"Please," Lunna begged, their blue eyes wide with longing. "I'll keep asking until you agree. I'll . . . I'll stand outside your window and make fyoo calls all night so you can't sleep!"

Kel snorted a laugh. "Threats? Not bribes?"

"You won't take bribes," Lunna said dismissively. "And anyway, we both know I won't do it. I might lure a real fyoo here, and then I'll have to stay home until I get the stench off."

"True," Kel said. "And you'll have to clean the stench out of my home as well."

Lunna's laughter rang out, loud enough to send a flock of birds—probably not fyoo—winging into the sky. They leaped to their feet and gave their lips a perfunctory flick of goodbye with two fingers.

"I'll be here at first light," they said, nearly skipping down the path through the trees.

"Talk to your parents," Kel called after them. "Be sure you're not leaving them floating in the swamp without a pole." Until Lunna made good on their grand plan to travel the stars someday, they couldn't simply flit away without a care.

Kel had worked hard to earn her quiet life here after the war. Part of that meant ensuring she followed village customs as best she could, and didn't cause anyone trouble. The last thing she needed was to draw attention to herself.

Which she would be doing by traveling to Esrondaa. She would have to be careful there. Keep her hair covered. Let Lunna do the talking. If it seemed like the Speakers were going to make a poor decision, she'd figure out some way to intervene.

With a sigh, Kel returned to her mending. She had planned to try another kexeet harvesting trip soon, and instead she'd be making a journey that could prove far more dangerous. But at least she would have an extra shirt to bring with her.

TRUE TO THEIR WORD, LUNNA ARRIVED JUST AS THE SUN ROSE, ITS RAYS peeking between the high arching roots of the mangrove trees and shimmering across the surface of the water. Kel had gone for her usual run and now waited in the same spot on the floor as if she hadn't moved all night, except a pack sat next to her, heavy with supplies. While they should reach Esrondaa within a half day, swamp and weather willing, she didn't want to be underprepared.

"Morning!" Lunna called cheerfully. "Ready to go?"

Kel ran through her mental inventory once more. Sleeping tarp, bedroll, rations, shirts, pants, underclothes, socks, sandals. The daily pills that made local food edible to people like her who hadn't been modified. Her raincloak was crammed through a side loop so she wouldn't have to open her pack to get it when it rained. She'd strapped a machete to her thigh, more for vegetation than defense, and her long walking stick was propped against the wall next to her front door.

She'd also spent half the night arguing with herself over whether to bring other items, ones she had hidden years earlier under the foundation of her one-room house. If she had them, she would be tempted to use them, she told herself, and that would reveal her presence to anyone with the knowledge to recognize what she was, so it was better to leave them behind. Better not to take the chance of being found by her enemies. Better to leave the past buried, quite literally.

But if she didn't have them and needed them against the war machine, what then? Would not having them be more dangerous? Could innocent people be needlessly harmed when her intervention might have saved them? She would have to suffer that burden on her conscience with all the rest, and that load was already heavier than the pack she would carry to Esrondaa.

Was it weakness or strength that drove her to preserve her anonymity? Was it fear, or the last frayed strands of her honor?

In the end, Kel wriggled into the narrow space underneath her house, ignoring the bugs and mold and muck that smelled faintly of bad eggs, and retrieved the container that held the last vestiges of her old life. Her sword stayed where it was; few people on this planet carried such a weapon, so it would immediately call attention to her. She also left her uniform, its fabric impermeable and comfortable in virtually any climate, but eminently recognizable. She did take her ellunium bracers, which she could easily hide under her shirtsleeves; anyone who happened to glimpse them might mistake them for decorative cuffs or some similar adornment.

It was the best balance she could think of between secrecy and preparedness. And if the worst came to pass, she had one other skill to rely on.

Lunna's easy laugh interrupted her musing. "I thought it

was a simple question," they said. "I should have known you would give it a great deal of thought."

"It comes of being older," Kel replied. "I know what it's like to run off with my boots half laced."

Lunna laughed again. "You're not old, Kel," they said. "You're just broody as a hen. Come on, I want to be there before I'm the one who's old."

Kel picked up her pack and slung it across her back, then took up her staff and trailed after Lunna. When she reached the tree line, she paused and looked at her small house, at the carefully laid wooden beams and fitted slats, the roof covered with broad palm leaves and sealed with tar, the wide porch where she'd sat and watched the rain come down in sheets year after year, dreaming of other places and seasons.

She tried to tell herself this was just another journey, no different from traveling to the xoffedil territories or any of the villages beyond Niulsa. But none of those trips had involved the Pale or their war machines. None had come so close to trailing their cold fingers along scars that still itched and burned and startled Kel with a pain like fresh wounds.

The wind picked up, sending clouds overhead scuttling across the brightening sky and bringing with it the smell of coming storms. No sense delaying the inevitable, Kel thought. She turned away and left.

# CHAPTER TWO

Despite dark clouds dumping buckets of warm rain on them, turning the roads into rivers of mud, Kel and Lunna arrived in Esrondaa just after midday. Rows of colorful outer buildings made of wood and mud bricks and recycled metal sheets gave way to mosaic-covered concrete and tinted glasteel, the structures growing taller and closer together in clusters around communal gardens or buildings or intersections. Passenger transports cautiously nudged their way through the groups of people walking or riding from place to place, and unicabs darted around all of them with a recklessness born of skill and experience. Volunteers carried long poles with bags of fruit picked farther afield, or set up fireboxes where the day's catch sizzled over open flames, while vendors pushed umbrella-covered carts full of handmade or fabricator-printed goods around the perimeters of the parks.

At the center of the town, the largest of the gardens grew in carefully managed quadrants, nearly as big as all of Niulsa.

Some of the trees, vines, and ground plots were currently laden with almost ripe fruit, berries, and vegetables, while others waited for their natural turn to bud and bloom. Still others had already been harvested by robots or people, the food arranged for easy access in nearby bowls and boxes, or sent to a factory for processing and distribution. Insects drifted between the flowers whose sweet scents perfumed the air, humming serenely, oblivious to the emotions of the humans around them.

Along with dozens of other people, Kel and Lunna ate a late meal sitting on a broad wooden bench near one of the public water dispensaries, the sun drying their damp clothes with the help of a warm breeze. Kel even splurged and bought them each a crispy flat bread from a street vendor, the buttery top sprinkled with sugar and chopped nuts.

The meeting wouldn't be held until the sun went down, so they had plenty of time to rest and relax—except Lunna wouldn't allow it. With an energy that belied their journey, they dragged Kel first from one shop to the next, delighted at the variety of items on display for barter or the infrequently used local currency called scales. They bought the necessary parts for the fabricator, bargaining earnestly and cheerfully. Then they went to the spaceport, a tall spire stretching higher than any other buildings or trees, to see the landing platforms and the interstellar communications hub and anything else that was publicly accessible. They tried to beg a ride on a flitter from one of the attendants, who gently rebuffed them, which is how Kel learned that flights across the planet had been grounded due to the war machine. An overreaction, maybe, since the machine's scanning radius was about twenty standard marks, but if some curious soul decided to fly nearby to catch a glimpse, it could interpret them as an enemy unit and act accordingly.

Better safe than scorched, Kel thought. At least road and water travel were still possible, even if they took longer.

Their proximity to the port also meant she saw an unfamiliar starship land. Loth didn't get much traffic, far as it was from galactic trade routes, and the Pale had apparently decided it was too poor in coveted resources for them to conquer and strip-mine. Only the kexeet that grew on the xoffedils held any interest for them, since that was unique, and locals used it to make a particularly fine, beautiful cloth. Kel had heard complaints that inferior artificial imitations were starting to flood the market, but it hadn't driven down prices yet.

The ship looked like an interstellar transport, big enough to have a warp drive but small enough to land instead of staying in orbit and sending down a tender. The shape was more squat than sleek, curved wings tucking themselves against an oblong body. It was painted a utilitarian gray speckled with small blue and gold dots that might be shapes, if Kel were able to get close enough to examine them. She was more familiar with military craft than civilian ones, but she thought it might be Chonian, which meant the captain could be from a Pale-occupied planet or a border world. Likely not one of the Pale themselves, though; the Prixori Anocracy had their own shipyards and preferred styles, which tended toward unnecessary extravagance and the bone-white hulls that gave the empire their more colloquial nickname.

Odd timing for them to arrive now. And surprising they were allowed to land at all, given the flight bans.

Kel talked Lunna into having their evening meal just

before the meeting began, then the pair joined the crowds heading toward the amphitheater. The large structure was as round as a bowl, rising three stories up and one down into the ground, with ramps leading to tier after tier of seating or spaces for wheeled or hovering chairs. Instead of a ceiling, an energy curtain kept the rain out, but the clear, balmy night made it unnecessary. Floral and spicy and green scents from the nearby gardens drifted in on the breeze, mingling with sweat and perfumed oils and the sharp, minty salves that drove away the most obnoxious insects. The dim glow of small lights affixed to the floors cast the assembled faces into shadow, so the processions entering the building appeared strange and mysterious—marching masses of disembodied legs, Kel thought with amusement. But as soon as they cleared the entry tunnels, the setting sun chased away the darkness, and two thousand people, give or take, took their seats to hear about the danger the Pale had inadvertently brought to their thresholds.

Lunna paused in their perusal of the assembly, leaning closer to Kel. "Are you going to say something?" they asked.

Kel shook her head, gripping her staff more tightly. Lunna had discussed the concerns their parents wanted raised along the way, and Kel thought they were reasonable—mostly worries about evacuation criteria, mutual aid needs, and destruction of habitats. They were likely to be mentioned by someone else before Lunna got a turn to speak. Kel had always been more inclined to listening than talking anyway, so she leaned against the wall behind her and settled in to do just that.

A few stragglers were still making their way inside when a platform at the center of the amphitheater was illuminated by a large, bright spotlight. An older woman limped across the stage, leaning on a cane, wearing a simple belted dress in a red fabric that complemented her coppery skin. Her white braided hair was threaded with green and purple and gold, among other colors, arranged to signify her personal pronouns, birth village, marital status, and position in the local government: Speaker for Esrondaa, which meant she had likely prepared a statement on behalf of the city's council and anyone who had given her their thoughts in advance.

"Be welcome, friends," she said, her husky voice amplified by some hidden receiver. "Our water is your water."

"Our sky is your sky," the assembly replied in unison, raising their cupped hands.

"I am Speaker Yiulea," the woman continued, "and I am sorry to meet you all in a time of fear and uncertainty. As you were informed, a Prixori Anocracy war machine was discovered approximately two days ago, by an ecologist retrieving soil data in the Parched Fields. Specifically, this is the SIARV-417 Mark 3, commonly known as a demolisher. It is approximately five trunks tall and three times that length, and weighs over ten thousand stones."

Gasps and mutterings went up among the crowd, from people who perhaps hadn't been fully aware of the sheer size of a demolisher. The biggest creature they routinely interacted with was the xoffedil, and those were mostly viewed from afar unless they were being climbed by kexeet harvesters.

And that's just one of the Pale's land units, Kel thought bitterly. They have battlecruisers as large as Esrondaa.

Speaker Yiulea lifted a hand and the chatter lessened. "The demolisher will reach the Gounaj Gulch in seven days, and at its current pace, if it is not stopped, it will reach the Verdwell Basin in ten days."

The xoffedil breeding grounds were in the Verdwell Basin. The scattered whispers now turned to exclamations of dismay and outrage. Some people sprang to their feet and gestured emphatically, while others commented to their neighbors or absorbed the information in stony silence.

"Ten days!" Lunna said, shaking their head. "What will it do when it gets there?"

Nothing good, Kel thought.

As if she'd heard Lunna's question, Speaker Yiulea said, "Our understanding of Prixori defensive programming suggests the demolisher will not attack the xoffedil unless provoked, but what it considers to be provocation is unclear. Even if it did not begin an assault, its mere presence will almost certainly destroy the breeding grounds, given the damage it has already done to the land from its passage."

"Stop it, then!" someone yelled, loud enough to be heard over the crowd.

"If you have a comment," Speaker Yiulea said calmly, "please save it for when we open the discussion after I conclude my remarks." She waited for the noise to settle from a boil to a simmer, leaning on her cane with a poise that made Kel smile wistfully at the memory of someone like her.

"The Prixori have been contacted," Speaker Yiulea said finally. "Their representatives were apologetic—and yes, we spoke to more than one—but they assured us they could not spare anyone to deactivate the machine immediately. We have been added to their support queue and will be helped as soon as possible."

"What does that mean?" came another shout.

Speaker Yiulea ignored them. "The most important thing we can communicate to you now is: do not go anywhere near the demolisher. We have already sent out warnings, but we want to emphasize this again. If the machine believes itself to be under attack, it will retaliate overwhelmingly."

Once a demolisher went into attack mode, it would remain in that mode until every designated enemy on sensors was killed. It would pursue anyone marked as hostile, and in its pursuit new villages might fall within its range. Kel summoned up a mental image of southern Loth. From the Gounaj Gulch, the demolisher could potentially reach Handeen and any surrounding homesteads. If it left the canyon to chase a perceived enemy, anyone attempting to flee Handeen could lure it farther east and south, turning more homes and villages into targets.

"We must also consider the defensive capabilities of the Prixori base in the north," Speaker Yiulea continued. "We were told it does not contain any long-range weapons systems, but under the circumstances we must assume it could also pose a threat and plan accordingly."

That was new to Kel. As far as she knew, the base didn't have such weapons. If it did, though? The damage wrought by a demolisher was nothing compared to the prospect of long-range missile bombardment.

Tens of thousands of people were in danger, not only from the ecological, social, and economic collapse that would come if the xoffedil lost their breeding grounds so late in the season, but also possibly from direct attacks. Perhaps more importantly to the Lothians, the planet itself had rights, and they were its designated protectors, caring for the land as the land provided for them.

All it would take to set off the carnage would be a single mistake by a single person with more curiosity than sense.

"I wish I could see the machine," Lunna breathed. Kel closed her eyes in dismay at the thought of a dozen Lunnas wandering the plains and mountains and forests, courting disaster.

Speaker Yiulea knocked the end of her cane against the floor sharply, once, twice, then fixed the crowd with a critical eye. "We will now begin discussion," she said. "Press the panel on your seat if you wish to speak. If you cannot reach the panel, ask your neighbor or hail an attendant and you will be assisted. Refreshments are available at the kiosks outside or by request. All voices are equal, and all will be heard."

"All will be heard," the crowd repeated.

Four more people joined Speaker Yiulea on the platform, their hair and clothes suggesting they were also Speakers from Esrondaa. Questions and comments immediately flooded in, but so far it sounded like they were aware of the full scope of what they faced. That was one fear quelled, because Kel hadn't wanted to speak up at all, much less to convey information about Pale weapons and tactics. She might then be asked to explain how she came to know such things, and she'd never been an especially good liar.

As she listened, Kel's thoughts returned to the grooves they'd been tracing in her mind. Why had the Pale refused to send help? Surely they had forces near enough to this system that it should be a simple matter to give someone the order to shut down the wayward machine, if it couldn't be done remotely. Could their resources be stretched so thin that they genuinely couldn't spare even a single ship? It was possible; their empire was vast, and as Kel had been told before, the expansion of their territories couldn't possibly be sustained. Not that it had stopped them yet.

Another question resurfaced from the depths of her anxiety: why now? If this was one of the units left behind by the forces who evacuated years earlier, why would it suddenly activate on its own? Or had someone intentionally turned it on and set it loose?

It's not looking for you, Kel told herself. The universe doesn't revolve around you. If the Pale wanted you dead, they'd send a Dirge. Which they won't, because you've honored the treaty.

As the hours passed, the arguments settled into two camps: those who wanted to wait for the Pale to dispatch assistance, even if that meant evacuating villages to safer areas and risking the land and the xoffedil habitat, and those who wanted to figure out a way to shut the demolisher down without Pale intervention. Most of the people supporting the latter option lived in the villages closest to the demolisher's expected path, or relied on the xoffedil for their livelihoods, while those willing to wait were from the east, the far south and the northeast, well outside the expected range of the machine's weapons—though not the base's missiles, if they indeed existed and could be deployed as the Speakers feared.

Kel wasn't sure where the council's preferences lay. Speaker Yiulea's responses were carefully neutral, answering questions with as much straightforward, unembellished fact as possible. Occasionally she deferred to a colleague, or paused to confer with the others on the platform, or offered a wry joke meant to ease tension without disrespect. But the woman's face was a closed book, and so Kel listened and hoped their final decision was a wise one.

While Lunna initially offered spirited commentary on the proceedings, over time they grew bored and listless. First they took breaks to relieve themself, then to peruse the refreshment offerings, then to stretch their legs by wandering the perimeter of the building. Kel promised to keep their seat safe—as if anyone would be rude enough to take it—and to wait for them if the meeting ended with them still out and about. In exchange, Lunna brought Kel chilled juice in a citrus-flavored edible cup that stuck to her teeth, as well as gossip they'd picked up along the way.

The moon loomed high overhead and the rush of people waiting to speak was down to a trickle when Lunna returned from their latest excursion, blue eyes wide and mouth half-open as if their brain had overheated and they needed to vent their thoughts. They threw themself into their seat, hands gripping their knees as they leaned closer to Kel.

"There are offworlders outside," they whispered conspiratorially. "I heard them talking about the Pale."

"What did they say?" Kel asked.

"That the Pale will never send anyone to help us," Lunna said. "That we're fools to think they will, and we're wasting our time talking about it."

Maybe they knew something no one else did, Kel thought. But how? And why were they here? She wasn't a suspicious person by nature, but life had taught her wariness.

Lunna turned their attention back to the proceedings,

slouching in their chair. The person speaking finished, the next was called, and suddenly Lunna straightened again and pointed.

"That's them!" Lunna said. "The ones from outside."

The two people standing in the spotlight were, indeed, clearly from off-world. The woman's springy black hair formed a soft halo around her dark brown face. She wore a garish short red cape with a high collar, tossed back over her shoulders to reveal bare arms and a red chestplate with a gold bird emblazoned on the material. Her black pants were tight enough to show off a shapely figure, tucked into boots that reached nearly to her knees. A pistol was strapped to one thigh, another in a shoulder holster under her arm, and Kel got the impression more weapons were hidden in less visible locations.

Her companion, staying in the shadows behind her, was just as out of place. A mop of silvery hair fell across his tan forehead, obscuring his narrowed eyes. His boots were shorter, clothes looser, and he dressed more plainly in a dark gray tunic over black pants. His posture was like a soldier told to stand at ease but fundamentally incapable of complying. He also wore a pistol on one hip, but his more striking weapon was an enormous sword slung across his back. Difficult to use in close quarters, more suited for clearing crowds or combating foes larger than humans. War machines, for instance.

For both of them to be so blatantly armed was rude by Lothian standards, where rules of hospitality meant safety and protection for guests, and carrying weapons in social spaces implied lack of trust. Or worse, threat of violence.

But was the rudeness accidental, or were they projecting intentional personas?

"I'm Captain Savaelia Vyse, of the CS *Brazen Solace*," the woman said in faintly accented Lothan. "I'm here to solve your demolisher problem."

The murmurs that had begun as soon as the spotlight shifted grew louder, but Speaker Yiulea slammed her cane on the ground and the crowd quieted again.

"Could you explain your position in more detail?" Speaker Yiulea asked. Her face betrayed nothing. Tradition dictated anyone could be heard, but that didn't mean she wouldn't shut this down if it became a problem.

"I know you've already contacted the Pale—excuse me, the Prixori Anocracy," Captain Vyse said, the disrespect in her tone so slight as to be easily deniable. "They told you they would send someone as soon as possible, but that's a soft lie. Loth is too far from major trade routes for them to waste the resources, and the Prixori never do anything if they don't stand to benefit. The earliest you can expect someone is with the next seasonal flotilla."

That was months away. The war machine could decimate the population in that time, wreck huge swathes of forest, even drive the xoffedil to near or total extinction. Kel's nerves sent needles up her arms as the people around her erupted into distraught, angry discussion.

"You seem very certain of this," Speaker Yiulea said with a faint smile.

"It's simple logic," Captain Vyse said, shrugging. "You're not under their direct control, so you must not have resources worth plundering. The outpost here is only sporadically staffed, which means they don't consider you a useful way-point or training ground anymore. They trade with you just enough to keep you beholden to them, but not so much that they rely on you. It's a lovely planet, but you're basically one of their storage sheds. They couldn't care less if you live or die."

The uproar in response to that drowned out anything else she might have said, and even Speaker Yiulea's composure fractured enough to allow a frown to mar her features.

"Can you support your contention with more than conjecture?" Speaker Yiulea asked finally.

"Yes," Captain Vyse said, straightening her gloves. "I have a contact in their bureaucracy who reaches out to me with problems like yours. Suffice it to say, if either of us thought other help was coming, I wouldn't be here."

Now the Speakers behind Speaker Yiulea muttered among themselves. Crude of the captain to announce this publicly; better to discuss it with the leaders quietly and let them come to some accord without all the attention. Or was that the point? If Captain Vyse swayed the crowd, the Speakers would be more inclined to agree to her demands.

"What is your proposal?" Speaker Yiulea asked.

Captain Vyse paused dramatically. "I have a device," she said, "that will deactivate the demolisher."

"Give it to us, then!" someone yelled. A chorus of agreement followed, but the captain shook her head.

"I'm the only one who can operate it," she said. "Which I will do, for a modest fee."

Kel's suspicions once again flared. It was too convenient; a problem manifested out of nowhere, and then the solution arrived soon after, while everyone was worrying themselves into their graves. She suspected the council members were thinking the same thing, despite the forced neutrality on Speaker Yiulea's face.

"And if we choose not to pay your fee?" Speaker Yiulea asked.

Captain Vyse shrugged, her cape flaring slightly. "You have more options than you might realize. You can still wait for the Prixori to come, or keep petitioning them until you're enough of a hassle that they want to shut you up. You could hire a band of mercenaries skilled at defeating demolishers and hope they don't die or run off with the job half done. You can see if someone from Indastral or the Kaolaras Collective might help." She smirked and dropped her voice to a stage whisper. "You could try to contact the Defiants, and risk the Prixori finding out and branding you sympathizers."

A murmur of unease rippled through the crowd at that suggestion. It was one thing to be beneath the Pale's notice; it was quite another to oppose them openly or covertly, as the Defiants did, without the backing of one of the larger coalitions.

"That we cannot do," Speaker Yiulea said firmly. "What are your terms, that we might put the matter to a vote once open discussion is concluded?"

"Five hundred domins," Captain Vyse said. "You refuel my ship and replenish my stores with two weeks of nonperishables for two people, plus cover supplies while we're planetside. Anything of mine breaks or gets lost on duty, you replace it with equivalent or pay the cost."

Speaker Yiulea's eyes narrowed pensively. "We would require an inventory to ensure you do not mysteriously lose items you don't possess."

"Naturally," Captain Vyse said. "And I assure you, I have no intention of breaking my weapons on purpose." She patted the pistol at her hip and grinned.

The deal was more than fair, to Kel's surprise. Five hundred domins was no pittance, but neither would it be a hardship. Perhaps that was part of the enticement if this were a swindle? If the fee were too high, they might be rejected outright; too low, and they would seem suspicious. Well, more suspicious. And they no doubt expected the leaders to negotiate, which would decrease the price further.

The pair of offworlders returned to their place to await the outcome of the vote. Captain Vyse seemed unconcerned, a confident half smile lingering on her lips. Her companion was more stoic, even grim, his eyes scanning the assembly as he stood with his back against a wall. Kel had a feeling he knew where every exit was, and the fastest way to reach them.

Well, so did she. That was simply good planning.

"Do you think they'll take the captain's offer?" Lunna asked while the next person spoke.

Kel considered her reply. "Assuming she has the device she claims, it would be the safest solution for everyone." And Kel wouldn't have to get involved. The relief she felt at the prospect of returning to Niulsa still shrouded in anonymity shamed her.

What if the pair weren't what they seemed? As the moon sank lower in the sky and discussions wound to a close, fear of duplicity or sabotage gripped her like a xoffedil's proboscis. Could she retreat and leave something this important in the hands of two strangers? Would the council be so trusting? They might, or they might prudently enact multiple plans to ensure the best outcome. But what if someone provoked the demolisher into attacking before it could be deactivated?

So many variables and unanswered questions, so many paths to failure and death. Kel's heart sped up as she considered the possibilities. She calmed herself with breathing exercises until the vote began, listening even as she scrutinized the Lothians' potential saviors.

The silver-haired man looked in her direction, and Kel wasn't sure whether she imagined their gazes meeting across the distance. She couldn't even tell what color his eyes were. His face didn't move; was he studying her as she had been studying him? He didn't turn away until the vote was finished, and Captain Vyse touched his arm.

The vote had indeed favored them. The pair made their way toward the platform while the rest of the assembly began to file out, to return to their homes or wherever they were staying in Esrondaa for the rest of the night.

"Come," Kel told Lunna. She climbed down the ramps and approached the group of people milling around the platform, eavesdropping or trying to talk to the Speakers directly. Lunna, for a change, simply followed quietly, though their blue eyes regarded Kel with curiosity.

Captain Vyse and Speaker Yiulea exchanged polite gestures as they apparently concluded their discussion. As Captain Vyse turned to leave, Speaker Yiulea stopped her.

"A moment, please," she said. "We are assembling an escort to see you safely to the demolisher's location."

"Thank you, but no," Captain Vyse replied with a smile. "I have a bodyguard, and we'll move faster by ourselves."

The so-called bodyguard crossed his arms over his broad

chest, looming impressively. His hands were gloved, like his captain's.

"You misunderstand, I believe." The furrow in Speaker Yiulea's brow was barely visible. "You cannot expect to navigate between here and the demolisher alone."

"I'm quite good at reading maps," Captain Vyse said, her smile widening a fraction.

"It's not a question of losing your way. With the flitters grounded, you'll have to travel by swamp and land."

"We could travel partway by the—what did you call them? Flitters? Land outside the demolisher sensor range and go the rest of the way on foot. I know you're worried about long-range weapons, but a base this small and isolated isn't likely to have them."

Speaker Yiulea shook her head. "You may think us paranoid, but our trust in the safety of the Prixori technology has already been shaken. We will not risk inviting the wrath of automated systems with the capacity to reduce the continent to ash. Perhaps you wish to rethink your commitment when faced with a journey of nearly a sennight rather than hours?"

"No, but I'm rethinking my price," Captain Vyse muttered. "Fine, no flying. We take the scenic route."

The Speaker continued. "Between villages, there are many dangers—"

"I've been through worse, I'm sure."

"—and in our experience offworlders do not fully understand our laws governing the protection of the land."

The captain's hesitation was so slight, Kel almost didn't catch it. "We will take every precaution to comply with your laws."

"We must provide you a guide, at least?" Speaker Yiulea's voice was tinged with exasperation. Kel wondered whether she really wanted a spy to send back regular reports. Practical.

"We work better alone, I assure you." If Captain Vyse smiled any wider, Kel thought, she'd look murderous instead of reassuring.

"I'll guide them!" a voice called out.

Captain Vyse and Speaker Yiulea turned in unison to look at Lunna, who surged forward and clung to the platform's edge with both hands.

"I know the swamps and forests," Lunna said eagerly. "Been down the roads plenty of times, and the water trails. I'm an excellent skimmer pilot, and I know how to fix them if they break down. I can defend myself, too."

Kel wanted to grab Lunna and haul them back, possibly hide them under a chair or in a closet. Instead, she held her tongue, waiting for the inevitable polite dismissal. Surely the Speaker wouldn't allow this. The stakes were too high to trust a random villager and a pair of offworlders to—

"You're Ylrosa's youngest, aren't you?" Speaker Yiulea asked. "Her hair always was a flame in the sun."

"Second youngest," Lunna replied. "She's taken me with her to Handeen every dry season since I was old enough to swing a machete. You know she trained me well."

Kel's urge to retreat increased. "Lunna," she said quietly. "Shouldn't you confer with your family about this?"

"I'm sure they'd support me," Lunna replied, eyes innocently wide. "They won't be able to travel to Handeen until the problem is solved, anyway, so they won't miss me."

Kel doubted that, and moreover she suspected they

wouldn't be best pleased at one of their children leaping head-
long into a dangerous situation. "But perhaps someone else
could—"

"As my father says, who can do a thing should do it,"
Lunna interrupted. "And I can do this. I wouldn't offer if I
couldn't."

"Oh yes," Captain Vyse said, her eyes narrowing. "I'll
take this guide. I expect they'll suit our needs perfectly."

Kel squeezed her hand into a fist, then relaxed it. Of
course the captain would be happy to have someone apparently young and potentially malleable. Or she intended to slip
away and ditch them at the first opportunity. The Speakers
could make an armed escort a condition of employment, but
they'd already held firm on the travel requirements. If they
pushed too hard and the offworlders left . . .

"Very well," Speaker Yiulea said curtly. "If they say they
can do it, they can. But we must send at least one extra guard.
We will have a volunteer momentarily."

Lunna pointed at Kel. "My friend can go! She's amazing
with a staff and blade. And she's a kexeet harvester, so she's
good at climbing."

Kel's frustration flamed and shriveled into ash as all gazes
shifted to her, including those of Captain Vyse's companion.
His eyes were green as a new leaf, and keen as sharpgrass.

Speaker Yiulea sized her up in a glance, possibly seeing
more than Lunna did, more than Kel might like. Had she
been a Speaker when Kel came to Loth? She could be remembering Kel's suspiciously timed arrival, if so, with forged
identification papers and a life story as porous as a sponge.

"Can you fulfill the role of a guard for this journey?" she asked.

Kel could say no, and perhaps Speaker Yiulea would change her mind about accepting Lunna's offer. Or Lunna would reconsider—no, that was utter nonsense. Lunna was so excited they were fit to burst. Oh spirits, what would she tell Lunna's parents if she showed up in Niulsa without their child? Especially if the mission failed and the machine went on a killing spree through southern Loth. She couldn't allow that to happen.

But could she stop it?

"I can," Kel said.

"She's done it before," Lunna added. "Traveled with my family to Handeen, I mean, and others from our village, as extra protection. She knows what to watch for in the swamps and forests. She and I can get this all patched and sealed quick as a whistle."

"Will you go, then, friend?" Speaker Yiulea asked, her face a mask of calm.

"Please say yes," Captain Vyse added, grinning like a cat with a trapped bird. Her impassive companion said nothing at all.

"I will go," Kel said. She winced at Lunna's yell of triumph, which sounded, for a moment, precisely like the memory of a shout of terror, from long ago on another world.

# CHAPTER THREE

The sun skimmed the tops of the trees outside Esrondaa the next morning, lightening the deep indigo of the sky into pale lavender with not a single cloud to ease the heat. Kel made no attempt to hide her approach as she and Lunna caught up with Captain Vyse and her companion, well down the road to the docks on the southernmost shore of the Grass Lake. She had expected them to try leaving without their agreed-upon guide and guard, as had Speaker Yiulea, who had discussed the logistics of the trip privately with Lunna and Kel before they rested at the Speaker's home for the night. What Kel hadn't expected was how early the pair would rise. Ship time conflicting with planet time often caused sleep issues, and she underestimated the captain's commitment to completing her mission quickly and quietly, thinking instead that the offworlders would prioritize rest over haste.

The campaign was in its early stages yet, with each side gathering intel and making decisions based on what they knew of the other. This simply meant Kel had to revise her opinions for future engagements and take appropriate countermeasures.

Captain Vyse stopped and gave a cheery wave, as if she wasn't the slightest bit sorry she had been caught trying to slip away. She'd exchanged her flamboyant red cape for a light brown shirt, loose-fitting enough to hide any weapons beyond the pistol tucked under her arm. She still wore her gloves.

"Good morning!" she called. "Glad you bedslugs came along finally. We're making good time so far."

"Oh yes!" Lunna replied. "We were worried when we heard you had already gone ahead without us, because you wouldn't know what kind of boat to borrow and how to ask properly, and what if we couldn't find you because you took the wrong road to the docks?" Their smile was infectious, and Captain Vyse laughed, either in delight at Lunna's naive assessment of the situation or how earnest they were about it. Maybe she thought Lunna was being facetious, like she was.

*Keep watch over them,* Speaker Yiulea had asked. *If they try anything harmful or deviate from the task, contact me immediately. Loth relies on you.*

Kel fell in beside the silver-haired man, who wore either the same clothes as before or ones exactly like them, right down to the gloves. Lunna and Captain Vyse took the lead, and were soon chattering away like a pair of nut-hoarding mrilli—mostly Lunna, with prompting from the captain, who seemed amused by her new guide's enthusiasm.

"You must call me Savvy," she said after Lunna respectfully referred to her as "Captain Vyse" for the tenth time. "All my friends do."

Kel suppressed a snort.

"Oh, thank you, Friend Savvy!" Lunna exclaimed. "I am honored. Friend Kel and I do not have different familiar names, but if we did, you would be welcome to use them."

"So you're Kel?" Savvy asked, glancing over her shoulder.

"Yes," Kel replied.

"Kel what?"

"Garda."

"My second there is Darennir Tanseith," Savvy said. "But I call him Dare, and so should you. So there, now we've all been properly introduced."

Kel glanced at Dare, who looked like he'd bitten something sour. Perhaps he didn't like people using his nickname so freely.

"You live in the same village as Lunna, Kel?" Savvy asked. She stayed ahead of them, not slowing her pace, but Kel sensed she was listening carefully.

"Near it," Kel replied.

"And Lunna said you're a kexeet harvester?"

"Yes."

Savvy flashed her a smile. "I asked someone about that last night. Sounds dangerous."

Kel shrugged noncommittally.

"Don't be humble, Kel," Lunna said, turning to walk backward as they spoke. "It's a difficult task. Harvesters are quick and strong. You have to track the xoffedil without scaring them into a stampede, then climb them without falling, then scrape the kexeet off before you're brushed away like a biting fly."

Kel thought of her most recent expedition and winced internally. Her ribs still ached, but the rope burns had healed.

"That does seem quite impressive," Savvy said. "And Lunna said you can fight, too?"

"If I must," Kel replied evenly.

Savvy laughed, a throatier sound than Lunna's. "I suspect it won't be necessary," she said. "Dare will happily take care of us all, won't you, hmm?"

"If I must," he said. Kel raised an eyebrow at him, but he didn't spare her a look. Was he mocking her?

It was the first time she had heard him speak, now that she thought on it. His voice was low, raspy, as if he didn't use it often.

"Friend Dare isn't prone to fits of birdsong, is he?" Lunna asked.

"Strong, silent type, that's him," Savvy said. "He talks to me, at least."

"Like Kel and me," Lunna said. "My ma always says if my eyes are open, my mouth is running. She says I talk enough for ten people, but my whole family's like that. I go visit Kel when I want quiet company. She's like a soothing tisane."

Kel hadn't realized that. She felt strangely honored.

"Dare's more like a swig of flamewater," Savvy joked.

"What's that?" Lunna asked.

"High-proof alcohol," Savvy said. "It's lit on fire before it's served. Burns like ship fuel on the way down."

"You are meant to blow it out first," Dare observed sardonically.

Kel chuckled, and Dare flashed her a congenial smirk.

Those ended up being the last words he spoke until they reached the docks twenty minutes later, though Lunna and Savvy kept up a running dialogue.

The Grass Lake was more of an inlet, eventually spilling into the inaptly named Endless Swamp that spread across much of southern Loth. Blue-green waves lapped at grass-covered mud that gave way to bushes with long roots, then to slim trees and their taller brethren on more solid ground. The land was utterly flat, far from the foothills of the Cloudrise Mountains and the gulch that split them like an ax wound in a tree. Most of the local fishermen had been up and on the water even before their merry band departed Esrondaa, and some visitors had left to take word of the council's decision to their villages, so only a few craft remained tied to the wooden piers or flopped onto the shore like the sun-craving throllax. A bored-looking attendant sat inside a rickety wooden building, playing a solitary game of Knocks with sun-bleached tiles. A sign proclaimed it the place to check in if one wished to borrow a communal craft.

Lunna approached him, gesturing at a skimmer with two benches that could be covered to function as a low cabin. The man's leathery face was sheltered by a broad-brimmed straw hat like the one Kel wore, but his incredulity showed in the angle of his mouth. As Kel waited for Lunna to secure their transportation, she scanned the road they'd just traveled for any sign they'd been followed, then searched the lake for boats that seemed out of place for the time of day and season.

"We're not lying, you know," Savvy said.

Kel cast a sharp glance at the woman, who tugged at her gloves. A nervous tic?

"It's clear you don't trust us," Savvy continued. "And neither does your council. But we really do want to help, and we'll do our best." She searched Kel's eyes. "We know the Pale quite well. Their methods, their priorities. They'll delay until they see some advantage to themselves, and then they'll swoop in and take over. That may even be someone's plan. We won't know until we finish the job and see what happens."

I know something of the Pale, too, Kel thought, but she simply nodded.

"Are you a refugee?" Savvy asked.

"I am," Kel replied. It was what she'd told the locals, so she saw no harm in saying that much. She had no intention of spilling every detail of her life like Lunna, though.

Savvy offered her a sympathetic smile, then winked at her companion. "You were right, Dare. I owe you a domin."

Kel raised an eyebrow at Dare, who gave the barest shrug. In the sun, the green of his eyes was lighter, clear as glass. He wasn't wearing a hat or visor, and he might regret his dark clothing since they would be out in the heat and sun for most of the day, but it was none of her business. Her job was to get these people where they needed to be, see the machine was stopped, then ensure Lunna made it home to Niulsa. Worrying about the comfort of her charges, who were full-grown adults with their own minds, was not her problem.

But how precisely had Dare figured out she was a refugee?

Savvy clapped her gloved hands and rubbed them together. "The Pale's awfulness is our gain, at least."

Before Kel could divine what she meant by that, Lunna waved them over. They all stepped onto the skimmer, which sank a little deeper into the water, gently tugging at its moorings. The craft was flat-bottomed and about ten paces long by four wide, with a slight curve at the bow, a gunwale just high enough to stub a toe, and two waterproof benches that doubled as storage. Lunna had already shoved their pack inside one, and Kel followed suit. A rolled-up tarp roof rested beside another; it would barely reach her knees if she stretched it across the benches and secured it to the appropriate cleats, but it would make a covered space between wide enough for everyone to share. In front of the benches was a clear deck area of about two paces; behind them were the low pilot's chair and controls for steering and engines. At the very back of the boat, two circular rings as tall as Lunna would propel them forward with air whenever it was clear enough; otherwise, they'd use the long push poles latched on to the deck, or the pair of oars fixed to the back of a bench.

Savvy and Dare also stowed their gear, the former retrieving a snack first, which Kel took as a hopeful sign that the spacer was immune to water sickness.

Lunna slid into the pilot's seat. "Everyone ready?" they asked.

After a chorus of affirmatives, Kel untied the mooring. Lunna started up the surprisingly quiet engines and guided the skimmer away from the dock, expertly steering it across the gently wind-whipped crests of the lake. Occasionally, they veered to one side or the other, presumably avoiding unseen obstacles beneath the surface, but the motions were never sudden or jerky. No one lost their balance, and no one slipped overboard—not yet, anyway. Kel tightened the string under her chin so her hat wouldn't fly off, though even if it did, the cloth she wore underneath should hide her hair.

Kel hadn't traveled on the water in almost nine months, not since the last time she went to Beelea for a festival at the insistence of Niulsa's then leader. He wanted all the help he could get to ensure their small flotilla reached their destination, as even the most careful traveler might fall prey to the dangerous creatures lurking above and below the water. Loth had a few bandits, people who chose to live cut off from society by their own rejection of justice, but they rarely attacked anyone outright. Or at least, they hadn't until recently.

They soon left the Grass Lake and entered the Endless Swamp, trees closing in around them like the walls of the buildings in Esrondaa. Curls of hairlike moss hung from gnarled branches, and drifts of broad-leafed flowers and algae bloomed on the water's surface like patches of grass on land. Birdsong echoed in the distance, silent in their immediate vicinity due to the low hum of the engines. Here the water was fresh, not brackish as it became where it kissed the western coast, and scented with growing things as well as the rich decay of peaty soil.

"Lucky it hasn't rained yet," Savvy said. "Does this boat have an energy curtain?"

Lunna shook their head. "When it starts coming down, we hook the tarp on and you can duck underneath."

"It'll be a tight fit for all of us," Savvy said, a slow smile spreading across her face.

Dare snorted but didn't speak.

"Oh, don't worry, Kel and I will stay outside," Lunna said innocently. "We're used to the rain. Did you take your food pills? And have you put on your pest repellent yet?"

Savvy wrinkled her nose. "The smelly salve? Is it really necessary?"

"It will be," Lunna said. "The biters get thick in the swamp, and there are these little gnats that swarm like anything. Even I won't talk as much because I don't want bugs flying in my mouth."

With a sigh, Savvy retrieved her pack and pulled out the salve container. She and Dare took turns administering the stuff to each other.

"At least it improves your natural aroma," Savvy told Dare.

Dare snorted again, not rising to the bait. Kel wondered how much of Savvy's impishness was natural, and how much was feigned or exaggerated for the present company.

Their progress continued, the sun arcing northward, its rays sparkling on the surface of the water where the trees didn't cast shadows. Sometimes the vegetation thinned and spread out, other times it closed in tightly enough to form a viridescent tunnel. Savvy asked questions about the area, especially what kinds of dangers lurked around them, and Lunna gleefully explained about the pockets of noxious gas that could pop at any moment, or the acid-skinned herbivores that floated about slurping up algae, or the poisonous glowing bugs that emerged at night, or the predators that folded their long legs underneath them and hid among the arching roots of certain trees, then leaped up to snatch birds from the air.

Savvy told her own stories about other planets and their flora and fauna, to Lunna's immense delight. They were hoping to leave Loth with the next seasonal ship, to find work as a pilot or mechanic on Uchoren Station, and they soaked up all information about the wider galaxy like a drying cloth. Kel recognized many of the places mentioned with varying degrees of familiarity, and felt wistful about not contributing to the discussion. She had stopped herself from regaling Lunna with her own tales over the years, so she wouldn't reveal too much about her past and invite unwanted questions.

Perhaps she'd been trying to keep the memories at a distance out of selfishness as well. Dredging up the names and faces of those she'd lost was akin to wallowing in the thick muck that accumulated around the trees and shorelines. Certain people swore it had healing properties, but to her, it was a cold mess.

"What tongues speak you?" Savvy asked in faintly accented Zeopran, startling her from her thoughts.

Kel stared at Savvy as if she didn't understand. If she hadn't told Lunna anything in five years, she wasn't going to let Savvy goad her into sharing after a few hours.

"What language was that?" Lunna asked. "It sounds like rasples taste. Tart and crunchy."

"Zeopran," Savvy replied. "I can teach you a few phrases, to pass the time." She switched to Vojali. "Maybe no one else knows where you came from, but I intend to figure it out. I think this game is fun, you know."

Do you? Kel thought. Her expression remained fixed, blank as a new scriber.

"I like to win," Savvy said in Oyaric. "If I continue to try, you'll shit the cot eventually."

Such a charming turn of phrase, Kel thought. Savvy did have an impressive command of languages, though, she had to admit. Was there any chance she spoke Stellan? No, she was more likely to know Dominari.

"Will you ask where the nearest toilet is next?" Dare asked Savvy in Vethonian.

"Suck an inflamed testicle," Savvy replied in the same language.

"Oh, that was lovely," Lunna said. "What does it mean?"

"It means 'I'm getting thirsty,'" Savvy said.

Kel choked on her own saliva and started to cough. A slow grin turned up the corner of Savvy's mouth as Kel spat into the water.

"Bug," Kel said.

"I'm sure," Savvy replied dryly.

The low background hum of the engines cut out, and the skimmer slowed.

"Friend Kel," Lunna called. "We've got some clingers. Could you pole while I take care of them?"

"Sure." Kel pulled one of the guide poles off the side of the boat, lowering it into the water to test the depth. Deep enough that she'd be underwater if she went overboard, but not by much. The currents flowed generally east or southwest, so she couldn't stop pushing or they'd drift in the wrong direction. Unlike the rivers to the north, these flows were gentle enough that she didn't have to overexert herself.

"Dare," Savvy said, "why don't you use your big sword to help with the vines? It'll go faster." She made a whooshing noise and waved her arm in a chopping motion.

"I'd rather not get it wet," Dare replied coolly. He didn't bother looking at her.

"Hard to avoid the wet around here," Lunna said, occasionally pausing for breath as they hacked at the vines stuck to the hull just below the air rings.

"I'll manage," Dare said.

Lunna huffed out a laugh. "Didn't mean it as a challenge, Friend Dare. More that there's no sense fighting the inevitable. I told Kel the same when she got here. You live with the planet or against it, and one way's more miserable than the other." They grinned at Kel. "I can say wise things sometimes, too, yeah? When I'm not rambling about whatever's in my head."

Kel smiled and continued poling.

"Ah, but you're delightful," Savvy said, shading her eyes as she stared in Lunna's direction. "Dare can be charming, too, when he wants to be. Otherwise he's a stick-in-the-mud like that one Kel is using."

"A closed mouth catches no flies," Kel murmured.

A chuckle made her look over just in time to catch Dare smirking before he turned away. She'd thought no one could hear her. Spirits, what a voice he had. Went straight to low places.

The dart of a shadow across the deck caught her eye. A bird, except they'd been avoiding the vehicle and its noisy passengers. Another shadow passed, then another. Circling. Kel confirmed her suspicions before she slid the pole out of the water, then took a deep breath to center herself.

"Take cover," she said. "Bladebeaks." If they were careful, the problem would be a mere nuisance.

Without a word, Lunna stopped their task and sheathed their machete, pulling the tarp over the benches. "Come on," they said. "Hide!"

The hiss of gunfire behind her startled Kel. She turned, mindful of her pole, to glare at Savvy.

"Got one." Savvy kept her pistol raised, scanning the sky. "Hard to tell how big they are from a distance."

As if that single shot had opened a locked door inside her, Kel was flooded with a sensation she'd never thought to experience again: the intense, all-consuming urge to protect. It was both utterly strange and agonizingly familiar, like the taste of a childhood meal, or the scent of a long-dead loved one. She straightened and threw her shoulders back, her grip on the pole tightening.

*Where peace is lost, may we find it.*

"You should get under cover," Kel said, forcing her voice to be quiet and calm. "Blood makes them frenzy." And Savvy had already hit one. Hopefully it had gone straight into the water.

Savvy ignored her, while Dare drew his sword and thumbed the trigger that collapsed its sheath into the hilt. Its black finish absorbed light rather than reflecting it—futhite alloy, which meant it could cut through the deck if he wasn't careful, especially in a space this tight. His face was flat, calm, as if his emotions had drained out of him, an expression she'd seen often enough on soldiers to recognize it as battle readiness. Kel longed to simply issue orders, but she doubted either offworlder would take them, and who knew what they'd think of her if she fell into old habits.

Blessed stars, the hardest part of being a bodyguard was dealing with a disobedient body.

Kel pulled her hat off, letting it hang on her back from its string as she peered at the sky. A dozen of the bright red creatures wheeled above the skimmer, with more farther away, waiting. They favored fresh meat, but were happy to steal it after it stopped moving.

Two more shots from Savvy. One bladebeak flapped awkwardly away, clearly injured. The other dropped to the deck, a splatter of purplish blood slowly spreading around the corpse.

The rest of the flock went wild. With cries as piercing as sonic awls, they dove from one blink to the next, so fast Kel couldn't think, could only react. She whirled and dodged, avoiding razor-sharp beaks and talons—and Dare's huge sword. More shots rang out from Savvy, while Dare's blade sliced cleanly through some targets and batted others aside. The skimmer rocked as they moved, but Kel and Dare compensated. Savvy gripped the pilot's chair to keep her balance.

With each swing of her pole, Kel knocked a bird from the air. Some she flung into the water, others she launched into the trees, still others recovered and flew off drunkenly. One made it past her defenses, and she didn't realize she'd been cut until her forehead began to sting and swell.

As the number of bodies increased, so did the amount of blood and ichor around them. Kel had to be careful not to step wrong and slip onto Dare's sword or over the side. That thought gave her an idea.

"Dare," she shouted. "Dump the corpses overboard. Savvy, cover him."

He had ignored her request before, so she braced herself to do it if he didn't. Blessedly, he resheathed his blade and fixed it to his back, then grabbed the carcasses and flung them away. The water around the skimmer purpled, and gradually the volume of bladebeaks attacking the boat decreased as the birds went for the easier prey bobbing temptingly nearby.

A larger shape appeared underwater a few lengths away, approaching from the left. Kel shoved her pole in the mud, pushing as hard as she could. The craft slid forward and she pushed again, ignoring the ache in her arms and burn in her forehead. The bladebeaks continued to circle and dive around the bloody patch of water, cannibalizing their brethren with shrieks of triumph. The dark shadow on the swamp bed moved toward them, hidden by the churn of gore and muck. Kel gave one last, desperate shove, hoping they were far enough away to be safe.

From beneath the tea-colored water, the vast maw of a slurx rose up, swallowing a half dozen birds in a single gulp. Any bladebeaks still on the surface desperately took to the air, screaming their rage. Those still tearing into their meals were unaware of their doom, or struggled futilely to disengage their talons. The slurx consumed them all within moments, and Kel held her breath, praying their boat wouldn't be next.

A few large burps bubbled up and dissipated. The slurx turned in a circle, then retreated in the direction from whence it had come. Overhead, all sign of the bladebeaks was gone, save for the echoing cry of the flock in the distance.

Kel surveyed their surroundings one last time. No other visible threats. She inhaled sharply, blood and sweat trickling down her face, then exhaled. Savvy scanned the sky, while Dare stood next to the covered benches, examining a long slice along the outside of his left arm. He turned away as soon as he realized Kel was looking.

"Lunna," Kel called. "Please get the medkit."

Lunna's head popped out from beneath the tarp. "Oh no, Kel, your face!" they exclaimed.

"Looks worse than it is," Kel said. The cut stung, as if to make a liar of her.

Savvy pursed her lips, looking around the skimmer. "What a mess," she said. She knelt and examined a stray feather stuck to the boards, but prudently didn't touch it.

Kel used the pole to guide the skimmer as Lunna stowed the tarp and retrieved their small box of healing patches and wound paste.

"Help Dare first," Kel said, gesturing at him with her chin.

"I can take care of myself," he replied curtly.

"Bladebeaks secrete a mild toxin," Kel said idly, staring at the blood-soaked deck. "It has to be treated with a specific cream."

Dare grunted acknowledgment, but still waved Lunna away.

Kel stoically endured the cleansing pad and the burn of the antitoxin, but when Lunna tried to move the cloth covering her hair, she reflexively caught their wrist and leaned away.

Lunna blinked in confusion. "I only wanted to check," they said.

"It's fine," Kel said, releasing their hand. "Just patch me."

Lunna did, uncharacteristically quiet, and Kel pulled her hat back on over the cloth. The woven reeds brushed against the bandage-covered part of her forehead, but the painkillers had numbed the skin.

"I'll finish clearing the clingers," Lunna said. They patted Kel's shoulder. "You were very brave. I knew you would guard us well."

Kel gave her young friend a half smile and a nod, despite the ache in her chest.

Dare wrapped a pressure bandage around his wound, covering most of his upper arm. He resumed scanning their surroundings for threats, but when he noticed Kel's scrutiny, he narrowed his eyes.

"Fancy moves for a refugee," Savvy said quietly. Her smirk chilled Kel despite the wet heat suffusing the air.

Kel shrugged and turned her back on the offworlders, hoping her fear and worry didn't show on her face. Let them think what they wanted. The odds of them figuring out the truth from a single fight against local wildlife were not high.

And I didn't use my bracers, she thought with relief. She hadn't even been tempted. Maybe she could see this mission through and go back to Niulsa with everyone safe and no one wiser.

# CHAPTER FOUR

They reached Oalea at sunset, Lunna jumping off the skimmer to tie it to the moorings while Kel stowed the pole and ensured everything was secured and ready for them to disembark. Lunna helped Savvy climb onto the dock, for which they received a smile that made them blush. Dare waited for Kel to finish and grab her pack, then both of them trailed after their respective charges.

Oalea was bigger than Niulsa but smaller by far than Esrondaa, painted wooden homes arrayed around the docks in rough semicircles that spread like ripples to the edge of the village. Late as it was, most people had already dispersed for the evening meal, so the docks were empty and quiet. A single guard watched the collection of boats gently bobbing in the water, offering them a polite thumb to the chin as they passed.

"Why the guard?" Dare asked.

"Bandits," Kel said. She didn't elaborate, and he didn't ask. They made for the local guesthouse, which also served as a gathering place for anyone inclined to seek amusement and company with or after their dinner. Like most guest-houses on Loth, it was run by the local council, and had sleeping quarters, a kitchen that supplied basic meals, a common room with ceilings tall enough to let the heat rise, and gentle yellow lights affixed to the walls and beams overhead at intervals. This place was decorated with large paintings of the local wildlife, which Kel remembered were made by the spouse of a village mechanic.

There was also a combox in its own private room, which could connect to any other combox on the planet, or relay recorded messages off-world. By law, Loth didn't allow things like satellites or relay towers, which were deemed harmful to the wildlife and thus the planet itself. Instead, networks of carefully buried cables linked the various villages, and off-world messages went through a single facility in Esrondaa.

One of the many reasons Kel had chosen to settle on Loth: more privacy and quiet.

Two long tables and benches took up the center of the room, with smaller round tables and seats surrounding them. Many of them were already occupied, by local villagers and others who had either made better time from Esrondaa or were heading south, drinking mushroom wine or savoring slices of warm bread, chilled fruit, and spiced nuts. All heads swiveled to watch the newcomers enter, responses varying from more polite thumb salutes to cold stares.

Once everyone was seated, Lunna leaped back up to ask the attendant for four meals and drinks, then waited for the bowls to be brought out of the kitchen in the back. Kel took the opportunity to use the combox, sending a brief message to Speaker Yiulea that they'd reached Oalea and all was well. She noted the bladebeak attack in case someone coming through after them had to deal with the birds in the same area. She didn't elaborate on how the creatures had been fought off.

Kel hadn't realized how much she missed eating something besides raw fruit or mashed boiled tubers with whatever else she could scavenge or catch. Some of the ingredients were the same as what she made herself, but there was more variety, and the preparation methods were much more sophisticated.

I've never been a good cook, she thought ruefully. I didn't have to be before. What's my excuse now?

She could have let someone in Niulsa teach her, but that would mean spending time with them, and they would want to get to know her. She couldn't risk it.

As excuses went, that sounded flimsy, even to her.

Once they finished their meal, the long tables became the site of a rousing game of Oracles and Omens, with two teams casting their tiles and trying to tell wilder, more elaborate stories to bluster their way to victory. They offered to let the newcomers join in; Kel and Dare refused, while Savvy took up the challenge and dragged Lunna in with her. The next thing Kel knew, Savvy was teaching everyone how to play Nova Cubes with a set she'd pulled from her pack, then coaxing them into gambling with her for scales or domins, the Pale credit chits she'd brought with her since they tended to be easy to exchange.

"Do you want to play?" Lunna asked Kel at some point.

Kel shook her head, biting back further comment.

To her surprise, Dare asked, "You don't gamble?"

"No. Did you think I would?" Kel eyed him over the rim of her cup, more curious than offended.

"No," he said. "But I was prepared to be wrong."

Kel's lip curled slightly. "Your captain cheats."

Dare snorted. "She likes to win early, so when she starts losing, everyone is too smug about it to wonder."

Kel considered that. Why would Savvy choose to lose on purpose? What satisfaction did that give her? She listened to the conversation among the players, mostly amiable discussions of their daily lives, the seasons, the harvest, the catch. The latest machine that needed repair or replacement. She closed her eyes and let the currents of it pull her in, let her thoughts float and filter whatever drifted through. Savvy's flirting was interspersed with teasing questions, some light and carefree, others more astute and pointed. Pumping them for information with a touch as gentle as a breeze off the lake, and yet, she didn't have to lose money to achieve the same ends.

One of the women complained about how her skimmer had been stolen by bandits, and the others plied her with comforting sentiments and assurances that she'd have another boat soon. The thieves were becoming more brazen, supposedly because of their new leader, though how anyone heard such rumors when the outcasts rarely entered villages, Kel didn't know. Loth had some of the most permissive restorative justice she'd seen, but the few rules they did have were strict.

Perhaps the remaining relatives of the bandits were still sympathetic and helped them despite the prohibitions, or perhaps some people cared more about the goods bartered than where they'd come from. Regardless, skimmer parts were hard to come by, fabricated as they were using the limited metal supplies brought in by offworlders during seasonal trade. That made the boats a popular target.

As Savvy made an offhand remark to the woman being consoled, Kel returned her attention to Dare. "Does she do it out of kindness?" Kel asked.

Dare tilted his head in assent.

"No one here needs charity," Kel said, brow furrowing. "They take care of their own."

"And refugees as well, apparently," Dare said, his green eyes darker in the dim light. "Not every place is alike, however."

Kel glanced at Savvy, who threw back her head in laughter. "It pleases her to please them."

"Yes." His expression softened, and Kel wondered if he and the captain were more than merely comrades. The way Savvy flirted, Kel had assumed not, but Savvy might mean nothing by it, and Dare might be used to it.

Kel had little practice at flirting. She'd had her share of deep feelings, love of every kind, but she had always been devoted to her work. It left little time for other pursuits.

Well, she had no work now. All she had was her solitude and her secrets.

Another bold laugh from Savvy, followed by a whoop of triumph from Lunna. A few villagers snapped their fingers against their palms and hooted, while others clapped or slapped thighs and grinned. The skimmerless woman had won a throw, apparently, and was now recounting how perhaps her luck was turning.

Other times and places flitted through Kel's mind like birds with sharp beaks, and she stared down into her cup.

"We should rest," she said.

"Yes," Dare replied.

Kel finished her drink and collected their dishes, taking them to the attendant. He showed her to the sterilizer and watched to be sure she placed them inside correctly, then absently flicked his fingers from his lips in farewell and returned to his perusal of some old scriber.

It took Kel two tries to get Lunna's attention, and when she did, her request that they sleep was met with dismay and wheedling. Kel reluctantly walked away as they continued socializing, settling into her seat again with a sigh.

She had lost her touch. She couldn't even manage a single rambunctious fresh-face anymore.

She'd known someone who had a way of phrasing suggestions that had others leaping to act, or offering observations that prodded people into making choices that led to his desired results. His mind had been all twists and turns, his tactics often questionable until the final outcome became clear. She'd never learned that skill, though more and more frequently she wished she had. Then maybe she'd trust herself to interact with her neighbors, instead of withdrawing for fear she'd make a mistake, say or do the wrong thing and cause trouble.

"There are many refugees throughout the galaxy these days," Dare said suddenly.

Kel dragged herself from her morose thoughts to study his profile. He was watching Savvy and Lunna, pointedly not looking at her.

"Yes," she said.

He inhaled and exhaled before speaking again. "It's nothing to be ashamed of," he said. "Many lives have been taken or disrupted by the Pale. Even great armies have been laid low by their ruthless forces."

Kel considered his words with a growing sense of relief. He thought she was embarrassed at being a refugee, perhaps assumed she'd been part of some ill-fated pocket of resistance somewhere.

He'd also said more to her in the last few minutes than he had for the entire day.

Another cheer went up from the gaming table, with Savvy giving a theatrical groan and Lunna rubbing her back consolingly.

"Savvy will pry," Dare continued. "She means well, but you don't need to humor her."

"Why are you telling me this?" Kel asked, then winced. "I apologize. That sounded prickly. You're being kind."

Dare gave a dry chuckle and looked up at the ceiling as if examining the beams. "Don't let Lunna hear you say that," he said. "I have a reputation to maintain."

"Of course," Kel said. "Don't worry, I won't clean the mud off the stick."

They fell silent again, but Dare smiled his close-lipped half smile, and some of the tension in Kel's shoulders eased.

Time passed, villagers peeled off and left for their homes, and eventually the crowd thinned to a handful of regulars. Savvy announced she needed to go make offerings to the gods of luck after such a night, putting away her cubes and thanking everyone remaining for their hospitality. She tossed an arm casually around Lunna's shoulder, guiding them back toward the table.

"Have you sent your report yet?" Savvy asked Kel, winking.

Kel blinked in confusion; she'd had that dream more than once, that she hadn't filled out some form or sent some vital message, and frankly she welcomed it compared to other nightmares that plagued her. But she realized what Savvy meant.

"I'm only to send word of problems," Kel said. "Otherwise it's simple updates."

"Proof of life kind of thing?" Savvy asked. "Good to know."

Kel pressed her lips together, wondering why she'd let that slip. Had the relaxed atmosphere made her less guarded? Or Dare's attempts at camaraderie? No, she'd fended off Lunna and others for years. Savvy was simply a more skilled and unscrupulous interrogator.

She wouldn't let it happen again, she promised herself. Lunna might not be able to put a lid on the bubbling of their pot, but Kel should know better, and would do better. Even if it meant returning to the near-total silence she'd lived in for years.

Lunna led them to one of the sleeping rooms, which contained a dozen two-tiered beds, about half already taken. Lunna opted for a top bunk, while Savvy took the one below them.

"So I can keep an eye on you," she said with a smirk. Lunna laughed, but Kel thought perhaps Savvy was being more honest than they realized.

Dare sat down in front of the door, resting his sword across his lap and closing his eyes. Kel, who had planned to do more or less the same thing, considered how to approach negotiating with him for a rotation.

"Dare, what are you doing?" Lunna asked.

"Guarding," he replied.

"What?" Lunna asked, startled. "Who would harm us here?"

"No one," Savvy said soothingly, gaze shifting to the Lothians already abed. "Don't worry about Dare, he can sleep anywhere. He enjoys this sort of thing."

"Kel?" Lunna asked.

Kel shrugged. Couldn't be too careful under the circumstances. They still didn't know why the demolisher had activated and started on its particular trajectory, and it was entirely possible someone had heard of their intentions to stop it and would try to intercept them.

"I'll take second watch," she said.

Dare cracked one eye open to glare at her. "That isn't necessary."

"First watch, then."

He closed his eye and ignored her. She was definitely losing her touch.

"Why don't you flip for it," Savvy said. "I won't be able to sleep knowing you're cross with each other."

Kel won the toss and picked first watch. Dare grumbled his way into the bed closest to the door, which Kel had been planning to take, so she figured they were even. She opted for one near the window instead.

Kel listened to the steady breathing of the room's occupants, and the hum and buzz of the creatures just beyond the walls. One day of travel done. With luck, the rest would be uneventful. She made a mental note to check on Dare's injury in the morning, since he'd fussed about accepting the antitoxin. At least the slurx hadn't caught them.

Why were Savvy and Dare doing this? Kel wondered. For the money, perhaps, but they weren't charging an outrageous amount. Surely there must be more lucrative options for someone with their own starship?

Perhaps they were Defiants? Kel didn't know much about the group or their tactics; plenty of people subjugated by the Pale turned to rebellion, and the Defiants were the most notorious. The most organized, too, if one believed the stories. Sometimes she wondered if they were even real, or merely part of a propaganda effort to give the vast empire some ill-defined but tangible adversary they must constantly battle to maintain peace and order.

If anyone could be a Defiant, anyone could be an enemy. And for the Pale, that meant anyone could be jailed for an indefinite period, put to work in their labor camps or locked up on one of their prison ships.

Or murdered by a Dirge.

Enough, Kel told herself. Either you'll learn more about these offworlders, or you won't, and either way they'll be gone inside of a week if all goes to plan.

Halfway through the night, Dare rose to relieve her, and she crawled into her own bed. Taking a few deep, cleansing breaths, Kel began to relax her body from the feet up. By the time she reached her neck, she slipped into dreams of snow-white birds with blazing red eyes, their beaks and feathers matted with blood.

THE REST OF THE NIGHT PASSED PEACEFULLY. KEL SHORTENED HER USUAL morning run, partly because she hadn't rested enough, partly because she didn't want to delay their departure. Dare scrutinized her when she returned but didn't ask where she'd gone. Savvy wasn't so restrained.

"Doing a little light reconnaissance?" Savvy asked.

Kel shook her head. "Just running."

"Oh?" Savvy grinned. "You should take Dare next time. He loves to run. He does laps around our ship every day."

Kel raised an inquisitive eyebrow at Dare, who shrugged and nodded.

"Tomorrow, then," Kel said, and went to clean up. Her skin felt more flushed than normal, and the water from the tap a little colder.

Breakfast was delicious and filling, a grainy porridge sweetened and spiced and covered in nuts and berries, and they each took an extra fruit for the journey. Savvy thanked the morning attendant and praised the place effusively; they said they'd pass along the compliments to the local Speakers.

Given the discussion of bandits the previous night, Lunna brought out an ancient-looking jammer from a storage nook under one of the skimmer's benches and cranked it up, then set it in a groove near the controls. The constant subsonic hum set Kel's teeth on edge, but it would theoretically keep anyone from using sensors to track them, and deflect the piranha drones bandits used to disable boats. There was no way to get rid of proximity warnings—that was a necessary safety feature—but at least those were limited to a smaller radius.

Not for the first time, she considered how much faster and more easily this all would have gone if they could have taken a flitter to Handeen. Then the only dangers would have been birds that flew at certain altitudes and bad weather. Alas, wishing wouldn't change the world, so there was no point in wasting her energy on it.

While the previous swamp path had clingers that accumulated to slow the skimmer down, this next stretch to Beelea had patches of sharpgrass that could tear holes in the hull. Every dry season, villages sent out cutters to trim back the nuisance in a narrow band, like a water-road for the boats to travel safely, but it wasn't the time yet. Kel stayed in the prow of the craft and watched for the long spikes of the plant, pointing it out to Savvy and Dare when she spotted some so they would know what it looked like.

"Just like your eyes, Dare," Savvy joked. "Green and stabby."

Kel thought his eyes were nice, but as she'd made the same observation to herself during their first encounter, she stuck to her renewed vow of silence.

A storm kicked up about an hour into the journey, which slowed their progress and drove Savvy under the tarp. Visibility was limited to a few poles ahead of the skimmer, the rain coming down in thick strands and ricocheting off the trees. Cup-shaped flowers, their stems grafted to branches and trunks, filled with water that trickled out like tiny waterfalls, the ripples of their spilled contents vanishing among the many circles created by the impacts of other drops. Only the most intrepid insects and wildlife ventured out, the rest content to wait until the deluge had passed before resuming their activities.

Lunna stayed at their seat, controlling the steering and engines, their red hair damp even under the hood of their raincloak. Kel kept to the prow, her straw hat partly shielding her eyes; sharpgrass didn't care about the weather, so she couldn't abandon her post. Dare remained in his spot on the deck, his pants soon drenched beneath his coat. He looked, Kel thought, like a wet cat, his silver hair pushed back from his forehead and a scowl marring his features.

Eventually the weather passed, leaving a more pronounced smell of green things and peat. Savvy emerged from under the tarp, stretching and picking her footing carefully across the deck.

"Amazing how every planet's rain smells different," she said.

Kel hummed noncommittally. Not every planet had rain, but she knew what Savvy meant.

"Are we likely to see more bandits after a storm?" Savvy asked.

Lunna shook their head. "They'll just as soon ambush you when it's pouring as when it's sunny. Not that I've ever had to fight them off, mind, it's just what I hear."

"Why do you even have bandits here?" Savvy asked. "Anyone can get free food or shelter when they want it, unless I'm mistaken."

"Yes, they can," Lunna said slowly, leaning back in their seat. "We all do our part. That doesn't mean people don't fight, though, or decide they're being treated unfairly, or do something unwise in a hot moment. Lots of things can happen. Laws get broken."

Savvy plucked a blue flower off a low-hanging vine and sniffed it. "Seems a bit of a leap from doing something wrong to becoming a bandit, though. Plenty of outlaws are just trying to get by, not hurt other people."

"Maybe that's true in other places," Lunna said. "Here we try to settle things reasonably for everyone involved. Even if something extreme happens . . . I mean, people do really bad things sometimes. Like murder. You can't take that back, or pay reparations enough for the value of a life. But for most people, even killers, there has to be a way to atone."

Savvy tossed her plucked flower overboard and turned a smile on Lunna. "So the bandits are people who did something so bad they can't atone?" she asked.

Lunna shook their head. "They're people who refuse to accept justice. They decide they'd rather live in the wilds, or go off-planet if they can manage."

"I suppose you think they've brought it on themselves, then," Savvy said.

"Well, yes," Lunna said, puzzled. "They could come back anytime they wanted. But they don't. Some people go off quietly by themselves, but the bandits? They attack, and steal, and make a lot of trouble, because they didn't get their own way."

"Sometimes justice isn't so just from the perspective of the criminal," Savvy said.

"And some people are like spoiled children." Lunna stuck out their bottom lip.

They speak so earnestly, Kel thought. It wasn't that they

were wrong; it was more that beyond these villages on Loth, with their councils and Speakers and gatherings, the situation became infinitely more complicated. And yet that wasn't it, either. Not more complicated, just more difficult to persuade disparate groups to work together, and to equitably enforce the rules they had mutually agreed upon. And when basic needs weren't accounted for, when groups like the Pale were causing so many profound problems, people did what they had to do to survive.

"Anyway," Lunna continued, "the real problem is the Defiants."

Kel turned to look at them and raised an eyebrow. Dare snorted, and Savvy's eyes widened as her hand flew to her chest.

"The Defiants?" Savvy asked. "I thought you didn't have those here."

"Oh yes," Lunna said. "They showed up around Beelea a few seasons back and started causing trouble. It was one thing when it was just regular bandits—there were so few of them, and mostly they stole stuff when no one was watching. Maybe they'd go after a slowboat here and there. But the Defiants set up a camp and organized them. Started coordinating attacks."

Savvy looked at Kel for confirmation, and Kel frowned, brow furrowed. She hadn't heard much about it, which wasn't surprising given that she lived alone and didn't gossip. Presumably Lunna had learned something between their most recent visits to her house, and hadn't had the opportunity to share. It explained why Speaker Yiulea was so vehemently against enlisting the Defiants' aid, on top of concerns about the Pale finding out and retaliating. It didn't make any sense, though. What would they have to gain from setting up as bandits on Loth, of all places?

Savvy and Dare held a silent conversation with their eyes and hands, ending when Savvy gave a subtle shake of her head.

"Hopefully we won't run into them," Savvy said. "But if we do, we have our big, strong warriors to protect us."

Lunna nodded, grinning. "Dare does have a very large sword, doesn't he?"

Savvy took one look at Dare and burst into laughter. Kel flushed as Lunna asked what was so funny, returning her attention to the search for sharpgrass.

# CHAPTER FIVE

**M**any of the buildings in Beelea were on stilts above the swamp instead of on dry land, the irregular lapping of waves against pilings barely audible over the staccato rhythm of footsteps. Wooden platforms and bridges served as plazas and sidewalks, with a few arched or high enough off the water to allow boat access beneath. The public docks were on the outskirts of the village, while the guesthouse was farther inward on land; inconvenient to travelers, but it had been built first and the village had spread around it. One couldn't always predict the direction a plant would grow.

A combination of problems awaited them, none avoidable. One was the advent of a particular crustacean migration period that came twice a year. This meant virtually every surface—from pilings to platforms to walls and even roofs—was covered in green-shelled creatures with segmented legs, pearlescent eyestalks, and large pincers. They latched on to anything within reach and refused to let go, a tactic one would think evolution would have discouraged. However, given that it made virtually everyone try to avoid them as much as possible—which was not easy, since they were everywhere—perhaps evolution wasn't entirely irrational.

The other problem was an influx of people, many returning home from the assembly in Esrondaa, but some from villages in the path of the demolisher. Some stayed with local family or friends, some camped out on dry land or slept on their boats, but many had packed into the guesthouse, which was consequently completely full. Cots and bedrolls had been pulled out of storage so the common room could be turned into a spillover sleeping area, and the local council was coordinating efforts to find volunteers to take in anyone who absolutely wouldn't fit. More volunteers had also been recruited to prepare extra meals for the weary, scared travelers, some of whom planned to stay in the area, while others were excited or resigned to continuing to Esrondaa until the whole situation was resolved.

Two lines stretched from the front of the building in opposite directions, one extending around the corner, while the other was shorter and moved faster. The first was for people who wanted to eat inside and were waiting for a spot; the other was for the counters set up to serve people outdoors since the inside tables were full. Savvy declared she enjoyed dining in the fresh air and immediately went for the shorter line, and soon they were all savoring a stew thick with chunks of the local crustacean menace.

"Can we sleep on the boat, do you think?" Savvy asked Lunna.

Lunna shrugged. "The covered area fits all of us if we don't mind touching. The foredeck is fine if you don't move much in your sleep. Wouldn't want to wake in the water. We'll also need to put on extra biter repellent."

"Ah." Savvy stared down into her bowl, her cheerful demeanor fading into a forced neutrality. "I suppose the crabs will find us there, too."

"Oh, definitely," Lunna said.

Kel took pity on Savvy. "Lunna and I can stay in the boat, you and Dare can get beds." Even as she said it, she remembered how the pair had tried to give her and Lunna the slip not two days earlier. But now that she'd made the offer, it would be insulting to take it back.

Savvy brightened immediately. "It's worth a try. We can add ourselves to the list and see how it goes. Worst case, we end up on the boat anyway."

"I'll stay with the skimmer," Dare said. Savvy saluted him with her spoon as Kel tried to read his expression. He took another bite of his food, pointedly not looking at her.

Well, at least that way she could keep an eye on him, and she couldn't imagine Savvy running off without him.

"I'm sure the fresh air will do you good," Savvy said. "You've been cooped up on our ship rebreathing your own foul breath for too long."

"I can never tell which end your smells come from," Dare retorted.

Savvy laughed and nudged Lunna with her shoulder. "You see what I put up with?"

Kel rather thought they were putting up with each other.

"How long have you two been partners?" Lunna asked.

Savvy's eyes narrowed fractionally. "Oh, I'd say about . . . four years now?"

Dare nodded fractionally, still concentrating on his meal.

"How did you meet?" Lunna asked.

Savvy's grin widened. "Ah, that's a funny story—"

Dare cleared his throat, and Savvy pantomimed sealing her lips shut.

"Oh, come now," Lunna protested. "I can tell you how Kel and I met."

Kel sighed inwardly but decided there was no harm in it, though Lunna was inclined to exaggerate as a rule.

"Let me guess," Savvy said, tapping her lip with one finger. "She saved your life from some huge predator in the swamp and you've been friends ever since."

"How did you know?" Lunna asked, eyes wide with surprise.

Savvy turned her grin on Kel. "Did you jam your staff in its mouth sideways?"

"Oh no, it was much more exciting!" Lunna exclaimed. "It all started when I was trying to pick a big cluster of waternuts from a tree. I'd gone out by myself because I had a fight with my older brother, who told me it was too dangerous to go alone, so of course I had to prove him wrong. The branch with the nuts was plenty high, but the more of my weight I put on it, the lower it sagged, and it was more slippery than I expected . . ."

Kel finished her food and sat with the bowl in her lap, listening to her friend weave the tale. Funny how at the time all she'd worried about was saving a life, despite all the promises she'd made to herself about keeping a low profile and not attracting attention. Nearly five years later and she still hadn't learned her lesson, apparently, since she was on this journey instead of ensconced in her house. Or perhaps there was no lesson to learn; she would always try to do what was most right in the moment, no matter how hard she fought the inclination.

The real challenge, of course, was in knowing what was right.

"And then Kel said, 'Just don't do it again,'" Lunna said. "And I said, 'Of course I won't, I already got the nuts!'"

Savvy's laugh was loud enough to draw a few looks from people nearby, perhaps wondering what anyone had to laugh about at a time like this. That was often the best time for it, though. Grimness never kept anyone alive, but laughter could bring them back from dark places and give them the strength to keep going.

Lunna rested an elbow on one knee and propped their chin up with their hand. "So when did you two decide to become coupled?"

Dare choked on his mouthful of stew as Savvy launched into another fit of laughter. Kel pounded his back, marveling at how red his face had gotten. He held up a hand to stop her and she leaned away.

"You sweet thing," Savvy said. "He and I aren't lovers, we're just partners. He's extremely not my type."

Kel would have said Savvy didn't have a type, given how much flirting she'd done in the scant time they'd known each other, but she supposed that was leaping to conclusions. Maybe more of a hop than a leap.

"Oh, I'm sorry, I hope I didn't offend." Lunna put their hands to their own flushed cheeks, as if to cool or hide them.

"You might have offended Dare," Savvy joked. At Lunna's crestfallen expression, Savvy said, "I'm teasing. Dare knows I'm the best thing ever to happen to him, but not like that. And that's only so far; he has a lot of life left in him, and who knows what surprises may yet land in his lap. Tall, dark, and sexy ones, even."

He shot her an exasperated look, and she winked at him.

Kel stood, bowl in hand. "Does anyone else want me to take their dish?"

Lunna handed theirs over, followed by Savvy. Dare scraped one last bite into his mouth, then did the same. With that chore complete, they settled in to wait on lodging, Savvy keeping a wary eye on the crabs skittering across the walls around them.

People from near and far wandered the wide roads of the village. Kel watched them, her hat pulled down just low enough to hide some of her face. The colorful clothes and braids of the locals reminded her of other places and times—of soaring buildings like rainbow needles rising from a sea of green; of homes clustered together like iridescent bubbles in a pale pink sky; of a stretch of red stone split like a geode to reveal a dazzling city of amethyst and dark azure sinking into the earth.

She was surprised the memories were coming on her now, rather than when she was alone. Perhaps she was more aware of her loneliness when surrounded by others. Perhaps she'd grown adept at chasing the intrusive thoughts away, but her methods weren't ones she could engage in here and now. While Lunna wouldn't blink if she jumped up and ran into the nearby forest, Savvy and Dare might not be so understanding. And she was supposed to be protecting them, guarding them, which she certainly couldn't do if she wasn't around.

Perhaps that was the problem: what she was doing now was so close to her old life, it was like being pressed against a locked door, knowing what waited on the other side, but unable to throw it open and step through. It was just familiar enough, just tantalizing enough, to make every scar on her skin ache with phantom pain.

She absently rubbed her bracers, hidden beneath her shirt. Her shoulder blades itched, too. Kel ignored the sensations and returned to her perusal of her surroundings, glad that she would be sleeping on the boat tonight, away from the crowds. She had a feeling she wouldn't have been able to rest otherwise, her thoughts were so loud.

IN THE END, SPACE WAS FOUND FOR LUNNA AND SAVVY AT THE VILLAGE Speakers' office, and they agreed to take shifts sleeping and watching each other's backs. Kel couldn't decide whether their potentially nonexistent enemy would be more or less likely to attempt something with so many other people around.

Kel and Dare headed back to the docks where the skimmer was moored. With the crowds settling, the roads and wooden paths that wended from the guesthouse to their destination were quieter except for the crabs. The sun was almost gone, its last rays casting a warm golden glow on the rooftops as the sky flamed to orange and magenta. The scents of food and sweat and floral perfumes were replaced by peat and night-blooming flowers, and instead of chatter and the constant drum of footfalls, there was now the gentle gurgle and splash of water and the creak of the boards as they moved and settled.

Dare, she noticed, made little noise as he walked, and they'd quickly fallen into step with each other, their pace brisk but not hurried. Kel observed him with the occasional sideways glance. He smelled like the sanitizing towels they'd been given to clean themselves, since the bathing facilities were overwhelmed. Underneath it was something else, something besides sweat, but she couldn't put a name to it. She found it oddly familiar, and wondered whether it was artificial or natural.

Blessed stars, what did she smell like? She'd never noticed unless she was ripe, and never thought to ask anyone. Her few lovers hadn't volunteered the information, aside from the occasional compliment after she'd washed up.

Why was she thinking about that, anyway? Perhaps because of Lunna's awkward questions earlier.

The shadows lengthened around them as they reached their skimmer and climbed aboard. Kel reapplied her biter repellent and Dare followed suit. After gently relocating the crabs skittering across the deck, she took out her bedroll and readied it for whenever it was her turn to sleep. Dare did the same. She laid her staff nearby and pulled out her machete. The blade was one of the first things she'd bought on Loth, and it had held up well to years of use on wood and vines.

Dare's sword was fancy enough to have a retractable sheath that kept it miraculously in place without straps or cords, and futhite alloys didn't require excessive attention to keep them in good condition. It stayed on his back as he stood near the prow, gazing into the darkening swamp as if he could still see into its depths. He could, for all she knew; his eyes might be prosthetic, or genetically modified. She'd heard stories of some of the Pale's standard alteration techniques, as well as more tense, quiet debriefings of their experimental procedures. And they were far from the only people to deal in such things, for good or ill.

"Do you prefer blades or staves?" Dare asked, his gaze still trained on the trees.

Kel preferred not to discuss herself at all. Should she lie? Lies had to be remembered and tended to grow heavy, like extra weight in a pack. Surely a simple preference didn't reveal too much.

"Blades," she said.

He didn't speak again for some time, continuing his vigil as she paced around to the back of the benches, eyeing the rest of the docks and the paths that led further into the village. Dim green lights winked from the walls of buildings, small and unobtrusive, no brighter than the chattering glowbugs that awakened with the sunset. The air was still, not even a faint breeze to relieve the thick heat, which was barely lessened by the sun's gradual absence.

Kel returned to the front of the skimmer. "Do you want first watch, or should I take it?"

"When are bandits most likely to strike?" he asked.

"I wouldn't know," she replied. "Their tactics may have changed if some Defiant newcomer is leading them."

An unreadable expression flashed across his face, but

Dare smoothed it away and shrugged. "Then we can flip for it again if we must."

Kel retrieved a scale from her pack. One side of the local coin was marked with a stylized tree with a fish at its root to symbolize the swamp and its denizens. Other scales depicted different things: overlapping triangles for mountains, triangles and rectangles for forests, or a semicircle rising from a flat line for the vast oceans to the east and west of the peninsula. Each shape was simple, but the interior was printed with a complex pattern that was difficult to reproduce without the proper equipment.

"Winner takes first watch," Kel said, then tossed it. "Call it in the air."

"Shaped," Dare said.

It landed on the deck and they both hunkered down to see it. Shaped. Kel nodded and retrieved her scale, then opened her bedroll and climbed inside, flipping the netting up to protect herself from any bugs or biters bold enough to brave the repellent. The crabs she'd simply have to ignore.

"Sleep fast and dream of peace," Dare said.

"You as well," Kel replied. It had been ages since anyone had wished her a good night of any kind.

To her surprise, Dare snorted in amusement. "So you aren't one of Indastral's soldiers."

Ah, that was a test. Sneaky.

"What would an Indastral soldier have said?" she asked.

"Rise fresh and make it so." Dare returned to the prow of the skimmer, passing Kel's bedroll as he did. In the distance, a bird trilled. Twice, thrice. No answer.

Kel heard the sharp intake of breath that signaled more speech to come, but Dare held it longer than she expected, as if hesitating.

"I don't suppose you would simply answer my questions if I asked them," he said finally.

"Would you answer mine?" she asked in reply.

"Fair enough," he said. "I'm not . . . I do not mean to pry. I'm fairly certain you're not a Pale soldier, but you could be hiding it well. Or the Speaker gave you special orders and you're waiting for an opportunity to overpower us and take the control chip."

Not much she could say to that. Protesting her innocence would be a waste of effort, and any arguments might sound more rehearsed than genuine. Good to know the control device was a chip, though.

"I'm not a Pale soldier," she said. "Speaker Yiulea asked me to keep her updated and share any problems that might arise. You two are the only hope we have of saving a lot of people, not to mention my own livelihood. If it were up to me, we'd be traveling in a flotilla with more guards for safety, but your captain was adamant. I'm worried that you're a pair of swindlers, though I would hope you'd have better opportunities that didn't involve heat, rain, and crabs crawling into your bedroll."

"Too true," Dare said, his tone tinged with amusement.

She rolled over onto her side, pillowing her head on her arm, and decided to risk another joke. "If I was planning to stab you, I'd do it in the front instead of the back. You're wearing too much armor, and your sword is in the way."

Dare glanced over his shoulder at her and gave a low, throaty chuckle. His green eyes flared with an inner light, but it dimmed so quickly she wasn't sure it was real.

"I'll have to be sure I stay behind you, then," he said. "Certainly watching your back is preferable to being stabbed in mine."

The way he said it . . . was he . . . no, that couldn't be an innuendo. Unless . . . ?

Hush, fool, she told herself. It doesn't matter. He's an offworlder and you're on a mission. He'll be gone inside of a sennight.

For some people, that would be a benefit, but that wasn't how Kel was built. Her life might have been easier if it was, but maybe it wouldn't, and anyway it took all kinds.

Before she could formulate a reply, a cry went up from farther down the docks.

"Fire!" someone yelled. "Quick, help!"

Kel scrambled out of her bedroll as Dare turned in the direction of the shouting. More voices took up the call, and sure enough, a ragged cloud of smoke rose from a flickering glow that seemed to be spreading.

"Should we—?" Dare asked, but Kel was already moving. She didn't know how many refugees slept on their boats, but most of the crafts were made of treated wood—resistant to flame, perhaps, but not fireproof. The houses were more of the same, this far away from Esrondaa or the mountains. And depending on the type of fire, water might make it worse rather than putting it out.

She checked the bench crate, finding a chemical extinguisher pack inside. It was risky to take theirs if the fire made it this far, because they might need it for themselves; but if she used it now when the fire was still small, hopefully it would stop the problem before it started.

She also rummaged through her pack and grabbed an extra hair covering, wrapping it around her face to filter her breathing. By the time she leaped onto the wharf, the smoke had gone from blowing to billowing, and the screams had worsened. Flames licked the air, higher and higher, and bells sounded throughout the village to alert people to the danger and bring volunteers to help. While she ran toward the problem, others ran away from it, fast and fearful, staggering and coughing.

"Stop, fool, it's a grease fire!" someone yelled. Kel winced. Someone must have been throwing water on it. That explained the spread.

Or did it? How had the fire started in the first place? Surely the refugees knew better than to light a cookfire on the wharf. Then again, some people made poor choices, especially if they felt desperate. Maybe they'd arrived late and missed the meal service at the guesthouse. Maybe they were simply careless.

It didn't matter. What mattered was putting the fire out.

A loose chain of people formed, moving buckets of mud from one of the small tree islands in an attempt to smother the flames. Each offering of flung muck hissed and spurted as it landed, settling into a steaming pile that sometimes bubbled from the sheer heat. The liquid occasionally sent the grease flying instead, and some of the precious mud had to be used to deal with the spread. As more buckets were added, the process went faster. Soon Kel was splattered all over, especially on her boots. Her eyes watered, her skin and throat and lungs burned from the heat and smoke, and her mouth tasted of ash and sulfur despite her face covering.

Finally, the volunteers arrived with a large chemical sprayer. With so little wind, the smoke was slow to clear even as the fires sputtered out. But just as relief began to cool Kel's cheeks and forehead, a new cry began.

"Bandits!" someone shrieked. "They took my skimmer!"

A stampede started as every boater who'd rushed to help with the fire scrambled to check on their own craft. More cries arose from farther down the wharf. Kel joined the crowd, careful not to shove anyone in her haste. Had Dare stayed with their skimmer? She hadn't noticed him among those fighting the blaze, but smoke made it hard to see.

It felt like ages before she reached the end of the wharf. To her horror, their skimmer was moving off in the water, far enough away from the dock that she couldn't make the leap if she tried. Even if she swam for it, she'd never be fast enough to catch it.

A flash of motion caught her eye as footsteps pounded against the wood. Someone ran toward her, brandishing a machete, their face covered like hers. Kel moved reflexively, sidestepping and grabbing their wrist with one hand as they swung. She dug her fingers into their wrist until they dropped the weapon with a cry of pain, then she kicked it away. It spun and fell into the water.

Her opponent tried to writhe out of her grasp, but she wrenched their arm behind them and shoved them to the dock, kneeling on their back. The sound of more footsteps thumped behind her, and she glanced over her shoulder.

Someone else with a mask and a sharpened stick, meant for striking or stabbing rather than cutting. They thrust the pointed end at her face and she simply leaned out of the way, then grabbed the weapon with her free hand. One sharp twist and she yanked the stick away from them.

And yet Kel was still on the floor with one knee in her first opponent's back, and the newcomer pulled a knife from a sheath at their hip. Parrying was a fool's game, but Kel did her best, struggling to maintain her control over the person underneath her as she evaded the knife-wielder's blade. After enough failed stabs and being struck on the knuckles and wrist repeatedly, they finally pulled back and ran instead of continuing to engage.

No other enemies presented themselves, but Kel waited as patiently as she could, breathing steadily to calm the racing of her heart. How long had it been since she'd fought a human? And yet her training had come back to her as if it were days rather than years.

Where peace is lost, may we find it, she thought. The last remnants of smoke from the fire swirled around her, rising into the night sky like an unheard prayer.

## CHAPTER SIX

Dare found Kel still pinning her quarry to the wharf since she didn't have any means of binding their hands. Ash smudged his tan face and he smelled faintly of blood, either his own or someone else's; hard to tell because his shirt was dark, and the only lights were the dim ones outside some of the buildings and marking each pier. His sword was on his back, and he crossed his arms as he regarded the scene before him.

"Is this one of the bandits?" he asked.

"They won't talk, so I assume so," Kel replied. A more astute one might have lied and said they were a villager or a refugee, but this one had gone still and silent instead. She had no idea what they were punished for in the first place, but they'd chosen to become an outcast instead of facing the alternative, so she couldn't imagine it was a minor transgression.

A pang of remorse and solidarity slid through her. Hadn't

she chosen exile as well? And she'd thought her reasons were just. Who was she to judge this person's lot?

"We must retrieve our skimmer," Dare said. He hunkered down in front of the subdued bandit and grabbed their chin, forcing them to look at him. "Where is your base of operations?"

The bandit tried to wrench their head free from Dare's grasp, but he simply tightened his grip. In response, the person spat on Dare's shirt.

"Easy, friend," Kel said. "This doesn't have to be violent."

"Says the one who took my weapon and sat on me like a mother bird," the bandit replied.

"You're alive, aren't you?" Dare asked. "That's more than I can say for some of your associates."

Kel's stomach clenched in dismay. How many of them had Dare killed? They might be criminals, but that didn't mean they deserved death.

"If you think I'll tell you anything," the bandit grumbled, "you're a fool. Suck bog, Pale lover."

Dare stiffened as if struck. His eyes flashed like before, so quickly it could have been a trick of the light. But what light? Kel was so distracted wondering about it that she almost didn't notice his free hand reach for the hilt of his sword.

"Dare," Kel said, her tone a warning. "We need them to find the skimmer. Or we can get another skimmer. It isn't worth their life."

"Is it worth the lives of all the people here?" Dare asked. "My pack is on that skimmer, and without it, we cannot complete our mission."

The bottom fell out of Kel's stomach. Did he mean the control chip for the demolisher was in his pack? Surely he would have kept such a thing on his person. Perhaps it was too bulky or fragile.

Regardless, he was right: they needed to get that pack, and to do that, they had to find where the bandits were taking the stolen crafts.

A flurry of footsteps approached. Kel stayed on the bandit to keep them restrained, but Dare shot to his feet and drew his sword, the sheath retracting in a blink. Before Kel could beg him not to kill anyone—anyone else?—or even see who was coming, he lowered his weapon and sighed wearily. The footsteps slowed, and a familiar figure sauntered past the nearest mooring light.

"Everything all right here?" Savvy asked, hand on her hip.

"No," Dare replied. "This fool's accomplices stole our boat."

"Oh no!" Lunna exclaimed from behind Savvy. "It won't be easy to find another one, with so many people using them right now."

"Ah, but do we need that one particularly, Dare?" Savvy asked, as if sensing the true problem.

"We do," Dare replied.

Savvy hummed in displeasure, staring down at the bandit, who ignored her. She tapped one booted foot against the boards, crossing her arms and pursing her lips as if deep in thought. Whatever it was she decided, she flicked her fingers in a series of signs at Dare, who nodded imperceptibly and moved to stand a few paces behind her.

"Lunna," Savvy said, "would you mind retrieving our

things from the Speakers' office? I think we might need them. Imminently."

"Right, yes, I'll be quick." Lunna raced off into the darkness, the noise they made blending into the rest of the cacophony in the distance.

Savvy waited until Lunna was gone before proceeding. "Kel, my friend," she said. "I believe there's been a misunderstanding. Would you be so kind as to help this poor individual stand?"

Kel furrowed her brow. What was Savvy playing at? If this bandit escaped, they'd be out of options entirely.

"Please," Savvy said, her tone a little sharp.

Keeping hold of the bandit's arm, Kel carefully eased off their back and hauled them to their feet. Now that they were beyond the heat of the fight and fire, she could study them more carefully. A half head shorter than her, with shaggy dark hair left unbraided to show they had rejected their village. They shifted their weight as if preparing to run, but Kel squeezed their arm a little more tightly to suggest they reconsider.

"You have a name, friend?" Savvy asked them.

"No," they replied.

"Well, that's fine," Savvy said. "If you don't want to talk, it'll be easier for you to listen, won't it?"

They didn't answer. Dare snorted, whether from humor or annoyance, she wasn't sure.

"You may not know who I am," Savvy said. "But I know you're one of the Defiants. Am I right?"

"Maybe," they said, their sullenness yielding to hesitation.

"I certainly hope so," Savvy continued, stepping a fraction

closer. "You see, I happen to be a Defiant as well, and I'm here on a secret mission to handle a local Pale problem."

The bandit relaxed further, and Kel loosened her grip. "They sent you to take care of the war machine?" they asked.

"Yes," Savvy said. "Unfortunately, the solution to that problem was on my skimmer, and one of you stole it."

"No!" the bandit exclaimed, stiffening again in Kel's grasp. "We didn't realize. You should have sent word to Hegrun, warned him you—"

"It wouldn't be a secret then, would it?" Savvy asked, giving the bandit a charming smile. "Hegrun is in a different cell from mine, anyway. And don't go saying his name aloud . . . Someone might hear you."

The bandit's mouth snapped shut almost audibly.

"Now," Savvy said, casually flipping a knife that had suddenly appeared in her hand. "My associate, the one I sent away? They don't know we're Defiants. They're a local villager, guiding us to Handeen. When they get back, I'm going to make a big show of explaining that I'm pretending to be a Defiant to get you to bring us to your camp, see? So just play along and everything will be fine. Think you can do that?"

"Yes, of course." The bandit swallowed nervously. "How will we get to the camp, though? We'll need another boat. After this much time, I'm sure I've been left behind."

"Leave that to me," Savvy said, tapping her chest with the flat of her knife's blade. "Can you find your way in the dark? Need anything special to signal any guards?"

The two proceeded to discuss the minutiae of the approach as Kel's mind raced. Were Savvy and Dare really Defiants? She didn't think so, but she could be mistaken. The story sounded convincing, and had certainly earned the trust of the bandit. She didn't know enough about how the Defiants operated to guess at the source of Savvy's knowledge, whether it was firsthand or secondhand, whether she had a full understanding of their procedures or was simply guessing enough to fool one person.

The bandit seemed local, but Lunna had said the Defiants were offworlders. Their leader—Hegrun, they'd said—might not have shared enough information about Defiant protocols to make Savvy's lies obvious as such. Assuming they even were.

Assuming the offworlders were Defiants, which they might not be, either.

Oh, this net had gotten tangled. Kel hated when that happened. She always tried to unravel such problems slowly and carefully, but sometimes all anyone could do was take a knife to the knot and deal with the cut ends.

Where peace is broken, may we mend it, she thought, then pushed the litany away.

By the time Lunna returned, Savvy and the bandit were chatting as if they were old friends. Kel couldn't believe a single person could say so much while revealing so little. And yet Savvy did, teasing information out as easily as a fisher cast a line and pulled it in. Dare, meanwhile, simply loomed quietly nearby. She wondered how often he'd played the same role in a similar farce, and how much of it was even acting.

With a sly grin at the bandit, Savvy led Lunna aside and proceeded to deliver a whispered version of her plan to pose as a Defiant so they could get the skimmer back. Lunna caught on quickly, and despite some fervently muttered concerns, they promised not to reveal the ruse. Once they finished chatting, Lunna ambled past Kel and gave her a wink that anyone could have seen from ten marks away. Kel couldn't resist winking back, but otherwise kept her expression neutral.

This was, perhaps, not the best way to get the control chip back. They might instead send a message to the village Speakers and arrange a larger attack party. But that would put more people in danger, and if the Defiant leader realized the camp was being assaulted, the conflict could escalate. The bandits could escape in the very skimmer that held the missing chip, and then there would be no way to track them. Even if the boat had a locator beacon, surely it would be disabled or jammed.

But this plan relied on Savvy—and the rest of them— convincing this Hegrun person that at least two of them were Defiants. That could go wrong in a lot of different, bad ways, too. Kel linked her hands behind her back so she wouldn't rub her bracers for comfort.

IT TOOK SOME TIME TO GET ANOTHER SKIMMER, TIME THEY DIDN'T HAVE TO spare. Lunna had to appeal to the local Speakers while they were still dealing with the wharf fire, and of course they wanted an explanation of what the boat was for, and then Lunna had to let Savvy take over because they were a terrible liar. Finally the Speakers acquiesced to the request, once they understood who was making it and why.

Their new craft was in better condition, made of some composite material and recently painted, with an even wider bench area that had a retractable metal roof. Because of her cover story, Savvy stayed just behind Lunna to guide their driving, while the bandit stood next to her and gave directions to their meeting place.

Navigating in the dark required more care and attention, so they had to move slowly. The moon brightened the sky, but the trees cast long shadows, and moss hung from lower branches to brush the surface of the water like pale green curtains. While some of the dangers of the swamp went to sleep, others awoke, hungry and ready to hunt. The air had cooled only fractionally, still thick with moisture that slicked her exposed skin, and the hum and rattle of insects rose and died based on the skimmer's proximity and the motions of the creatures who ate them. Occasionally, a far-off splash would signal something larger and more dangerous, but thankfully the bandit didn't send them in that direction.

They eventually reached the meeting point to find it empty; as expected, the others had moved on. Fortunately, their guide knew how to get back to the camp from there. Unfortunately, the trail took them deeper into the swamp.

Kel did her best to keep track of where they were and which directions they'd been moving in, but she hoped Lunna was paying even closer attention. Navigating back out would be a nightmare, made worse if they had to do it in a hurry, with bandits in pursuit. As it was, they crawled along, slow as the glowing worms leaving iridescent trails on leaf and bark.

Fatigue dug its claws into Kel, but she pushed it away, sitting near the front of the skimmer with Dare. Every so often, his eyes brightened and dimmed. It happened quickly, and she still wasn't sure whether it was a trick of the light, but she was starting to believe more firmly that he could consciously control it.

Dare stiffened, his attention sharp as a shiv. Kel heard the camp before she saw it, the sounds of people speaking in low voices and moving about quietly still louder than the ambient levels of natural noise. The bandit guided them around a few tree islands, their roots filled in with mud. Lunna turned off the engines and merely steered with the rudder while Kel poled the skimmer back and forth.

A muted glow appeared near ground level, close enough that Kel was impressed at how well it had been screened from sight. No sign of smoke, which meant no fires, which meant either they weren't cooking or they used something other than fire for that purpose. She couldn't imagine they stole enough to survive without supplementing their stores with things they could pick or catch, and some of those needed to be cooked for safety if not flavor. She knew that from personal experience, sadly. And any offworlders would need the daily pills that made the food digestible in the first place.

The bandit camp was a large island formed from clusters of mud trees, easily a dozen of them. Single and shared tents were erected for shelter, surrounding a central gathering area big enough to accommodate everyone. Around the tents, clawed branches and sharpened tree trunks formed a rough palisade, camouflaged to look like the surroundings from a distance. It was more difficult to hide the various boats they'd stolen, six that she could see.

Guards awaited them, brandishing an intimidating combination of guns, spears, and blades. Kel kept her hands still on the pole, calm, rather than gripping it more tightly.

"Hello, the camp!" Savvy exclaimed, pitching her voice just loud enough to carry. "Not the friendliest welcome I've had, but you've been busy tonight and I assume you're all ready to drop."

Whatever the bandits had been expecting, Kel didn't think that was it. They exchanged looks varying from confused to angry, but didn't lower their weapons.

The one who'd guided them said, "It's fine, they're with the Defiants." But they shifted nervously, possibly from being on the ugly end of so many sharp things.

"We're on a mission," Savvy said, her posture relaxed. "You took something of ours, and we need it back. We're happy to trade skimmers with you and be gone before you can whistle."

"Now, that would be inhospitable," said an oily voice from the back of the group. The bandits moved aside, revealing a light-skinned older man in a burnished metal chestplate, part of its surface—and one of his arms—obscured by a dark green cape. Kel had seen his type across the galaxy: strong enough to pick fights with swagger, weak enough to resort to knives in the back. He wore dark pants and heavy boots, greaves just above them, and his arms were protected by scratched plasteel bracers and spaulders. His hair was hidden by a helmet with the blue-tinted visor currently lowered, no doubt giving him better night vision at a minimum, and possibly additional information like heart rates and body temperatures.

Kel hoped her own faster heartbeat could be mistaken for nerves rather than the unease that accompanied subterfuge.

"Hegrun, I presume," Savvy said, and the man inclined his head. "I'm Captain Savaelia Vyse, of the CS *Brazen Solace*. As I was explaining to your people here, you've inadvertently interfered with a Defiant mission."

"Oh, have we?" Hegrun replied, not sounding the least bit repentant. "And what's the current passcode, Captain so-called Defiant?"

Savvy raised an eyebrow. "We don't have passcodes."

A look Kel couldn't read flitted across Hegrun's features. "Of course we don't," he said. "I was testing you. Anyone can claim to be a Defiant, after all."

"Ah, yes," Savvy said, nodding. "Very smart."

Kel kept her mouth shut and her expression neutral.

"So, this mission of yours," Hegrun said. "I expect it's not quite secret, if you're sharing it with all of us so easily."

"Not at all," Savvy replied, grinning. "We didn't tell the Esrondaa council we were Defiants, of course, since the locals are . . . unfriendly about such things. But we were sent to deal with the demolisher problem."

Murmurs kicked up around Hegrun and were immediately silenced with an imperious wave of his hand.

"You may have noticed," Hegrun said, "we live in the middle of a swamp, outcast from the villages. We hadn't heard what was going to be done about the machine yet."

"I'm going to shut it down," Savvy said. "Once that's done, another team will be arriving to pick up the demolisher and take it off-world for reprogramming. But I need the control chip I left in my pack. It's on one of the skimmers you took."

A slow smile stretched Hegrun's lips. Kel didn't like the look of it at all.

"You can control a demolisher?" Hegrun asked.

Savvy chuckled. "If only. No, I can't control it, I can only shut it down. The chip I have is more like an emergency override than a command key. The next team will handle the rest."

Kel wondered whether that was true, or merely a deflection. Either way, Hegrun's smile vanished.

"I see," he said, his enthusiasm like a fire dampened by mud. But another look replaced it, something craftier. "You say a team will be picking up the machine once your mission is complete?"

"So I was told," Savvy said slowly.

"I think we need to discuss this privately," Hegrun said, glancing around at the bandits who lingered, their weapons long ago lowered or put away. "While I trust all of these people with my life, I don't want to jeopardize any active missions unintentionally with my line of questioning."

Savvy once again raised an eyebrow, then shrugged. "It doesn't look like a big island, but if you have a private place . . ." She gestured at Lunna and Dare. "You two find the skimmer with my pack. My aide comes with me."

Aide? Kel thought, realizing Savvy meant her. But why?

"Sure," Hegrun said amiably. "Miza, with me. Someone take the others to the boats."

A huge man peeled away from the crowd and stood just behind Hegrun, who led them all toward a large tent set a short distance from the rest, at the far end of the island. Kel cast a glance back at Dare and Lunna, who were being guided in the opposite direction, toward the makeshift docks hidden by foliage. Hopefully, Dare would find the right skimmer and retrieve his pack. Once he had that, all they needed to do was escape.

The inside of the tent didn't look much better than the outside. Dirt tracked in by boots, impermeable bedroll shoved against one wall, and a battery-powered lantern resting on a handmade wooden table that was little more than a carved stump. The most well-kept thing inside was the array of weapons laid out carefully on a cloth that might have been a raincloak. A plasma rifle, two burst pistols, two machetes, two small knives that looked about the right size to tuck into a boot, a brace of throwing needles, a bundle of flares, and even an ugly-looking plasteel scythe on a chain as long as her arm. That and the machetes were likely local, but the rest had definitely come from off-world, like Hegrun.

How many Defiants had he brought with him, and why? Kel wondered. What could they hope to accomplish here by rounding up outcasts and leading them in raids against villages?

Unless they weren't Defiants at all, as she had suspected. But even if they weren't, her questions remained. And while they were inside the tent, she needed to watch those weapons.

"Miza, the hummer," Hegrun said.

Miza's gray-streaked beard glinted orange in the lantern's harsh glare. He pulled out an audio disruptor, a small device shaped like a two-pronged fork wedged into a pyramid, and set it carefully on the bedroll. With his thumb, he swiped it on, and the machine immediately began to emit a high-pitched whining sound just beyond Kel's range of hearing, as if a swarm of biters hovered outside the tent waiting to attack.

"Haven't seen one of those in a while," Savvy said.

Neither had Kel. This was an older model than the ones she had used, but she suspected it worked fine for their purposes. It would prevent anything quieter than a shout from being heard for a distance of at least a few paces from the tent.

"Now," Hegrun said in Rekari, his gaze sharpening speculatively. "Captain Vyse, if that's your real name."

"Real enough for legal forms," Savvy joked back in the same language. A standard trade tongue in rim space, which told Kel that both Hegrun and Savvy spent enough time there to bother learning it.

Hegrun chuckled and leaned in. "I'll level with you," he said. "I'm not one of the Defiants."

Savvy's eyes widened in shock. "What? You aren't?"

Hegrun shook his head. "No. And despite your very fine story, I don't believe you are, either."

# CHAPTER SEVEN

Kel's fingers slowly eased toward the machete on her hip. Miza saw her movement and shifted his weight, one of his hands already in a pocket that could hold any number of weapons. Hegrun held Savvy's gaze, and she held his, for so long the air seemed to spark, until she tossed her head back and laughed.

"Well," Savvy said, tugging at her gloves. "What have we here, then? Do we keep our Scram pieces hidden or light up the board?"

"Not Defiants, then?" Hegrun asked, grinning and slapping his knee. "I knew it. Bleeding hearts they might be, but no way they'd send two of you'n to the ragged end of nowhere for a job."

"Oh, maybe they would," Savvy replied. "If they thought they'd get a demolisher out of it. I'm betting they have people who can reprogram one of those monsters and make it work for them."

Hegrun shook his head. "Maybe, but Pale tech's a real

cruncher. Nice if you can get it, but it's so crammed with spy-bots and such, you might as well build your own."

"Not my starship, not my hull breach," Savvy replied.

"So why are you really here, then?" Hegrun asked, leaning back with his arms crossed.

"Same reason, different approach," Savvy said. "We've got a Pale contact who feeds us jobs like this, cleaning up their messes here and there." She rested an elbow on one knee, the picture of calm ease. "The control chip didn't come cheap, but we'll make more on this than we would on a standard supply run to the border worlds, or on trying to smuggle something through Pale space."

"Not licensed, then?" Hegrun asked.

Savvy laughed. "Come on, you must know what a Pale license costs. And they charge you every trade year."

"And the price goes up every time." Hegrun glanced at Miza, then back at Savvy. "You could always go privateer."

Savvy hesitated for the second time since Kel had laid eyes on her. Then she smiled and shrugged. "I looked into doing that once," she said. "But they said my starship is too small. They want larger cargo vessels, or gunships with more firepower than my old wreck."

"They do," Hegrun said. He tapped a finger on his biceps, arms still crossed. "You may not be Defiants, but are you aligned with them? Just curious, mind," he added, though his eyes behind his blue visor had narrowed. Kel didn't like that look, or what he might be thinking behind it.

"We're aligned with ourselves," Savvy said, still smiling. "Whatever buys the fuel, am I right?"

"Too true," Hegrun said, his shoulders relaxing a fraction.

He shared another look with Miza, this time a longer one, then lowered his voice. "You sure your friend here is trustworthy? She looks native, if you know what I mean."

Kel straightened. She'd dressed to blend in with the villagers as soon as she was able to, and had never stopped, except for her shoes. She favored boots over sandals, for which she'd been teased by Lunna. And unlike a true local, she didn't braid her hair, instead keeping it short and hidden by cloth and a hat.

"Oh?" Savvy asked, looking at Kel with well-feigned surprise. "You mean Kel? No, she's not local. She's my aide, I told you. We met years ago, on Zeopra. Dare's the big lump with the sword, he's our muscle. The only local with us is Lunna, and I told them I was going to pretend to be a Defiant to get our skimmer back, so they'd play along."

Hegrun stared openly at Kel now. Thankfully, she'd long ago learned how not to squirm under such inspection. All she had to do was stay quiet and wait until they left with what they had come for.

"Zeopra, you say?" Hegrun asked in stilted Zeopran. "What you were there doing?"

"We were—" Savvy began.

"Not you, Captain," Hegrun interrupted in Rekari. "I was asking your aide."

Kel replied in Zeopran. "Refugee."

"From where?"

"Not your business, with respect."

Savvy flashed a smile at her, reverting to Rekari. "Same as she told me. Not one to mince words, our Kel. Smart as a slap to the ass, though."

Unexpectedly, that made Kel smile. She'd been accused of many things in her time, but intelligence was not the first among them. And being referred to in a possessive way was oddly pleasant, reassuring, after being an outsider for so long.

Don't get used to it, she told herself sternly. This is all temporary. And you just let slip to her that you know both Rekari and Zeopran.

Whatever Hegrun saw in her expression seemed to allay his suspicions. "I have a proposition for you," he said finally. "If you can get me and my crew off this rock, I'll see you're well compensated."

Kel's smile faded back to careful neutrality, but inside she frowned. Who was this man?

"Is that so?" Savvy asked, raising an eyebrow. She glanced at Miza, who revealed nothing. "You know, I spilled my guts, and you tried to pull Kel's out, but you haven't said why you're all here. In the swamp, no less, instead of one of their guesthouses."

Hegrun waved a hand dismissively. "It's a long, sorry tale," he said. "But the end of it is, our ship was taken from us and we were stranded here on Loth a while back. We haven't managed to retrieve it yet—the ship, I mean—but we're working on it. If you could fly us to, say, Vethonia, there's some folks who would pay you for getting us back into civilized space."

Civilized space. Only one of the Pale or their allies would call it that, and Vethonia was Pale occupied. Kel's skin prickled. These people weren't Pale themselves, or they wouldn't have been stuck here for so long. Privateers? Had they reactivated the war machine? No, Hegrun would have balked at their mission if that were the case. He'd seemed excited by the prospect of controlling a demolisher, not concerned that his actions would be undermined.

"That's an enticing offer," Savvy said, running a finger along her chin in thought. "After we deactivate the demolisher, we'll be leaving the planet anyway, so might as well make a few extra domins out of it. Can you meet us at the spaceport?"

Hegrun's expression flattened out again. "No," he said. "We're . . . not welcome in the big town. But there's an old Pale base up north that should suit."

Far north. How was he planning to get there? Kel wondered.

"How many in your crew?" Savvy asked.

"Twelve," Hegrun said.

Savvy wagged her head from side to side. "We can't fit so many, not all the way to Vethonia. My ship is kitted for four, fills up at six, and half of that is taken by my own crew already."

Kel didn't like this. She hoped it didn't show on her face, because there wasn't much she could do but play along. Had Dare found the missing control chip yet?

The flap at the front of the tent opened, revealing an unknown face with a sour expression. An outcast, if Kel judged correctly.

Hegrun answered with narrowed eyes and a curt nod. "What is it?" he asked in Lothan.

"Heard the young one of them talking," the newcomer said. "They think this is a setup. That they're pretending to be Defiants to get their boat back." A scowl raked across Savvy and Kel, like claws on tree bark.

Savvy shifted closer to Hegrun and dropped her voice. "That's the local I told you about. They don't like Defiants here, so I had to think fast. Told them this was all a ruse." She grinned at him. "Like I said, I really do need that control chip, or I don't get paid. I don't need the same boat you took, I just need a skimmer that will get us to our next port."

"You do come up with a lot of pretty stories," Hegrun said. "Makes it hard for a man to know which ones to believe, in the end."

"It's easier than raiding a village and starting fires, I imagine," Savvy replied. Her smile took the venom out of her words, if not the sting.

Miza murmured something directly into Hegrun's ear, looking at Kel as he did. Hegrun flicked his fingers at the outcast, who seemed puzzled by the dismissal but took the direction, leaving the tent. The faint sound of the hummer whined in the silence that followed.

Hegrun leaned back, arms once again crossing. "It occurs to me that maybe you've gifted me a valuable opportunity. Some leverage to negotiate for the return of our ship."

Savvy raised an eyebrow. "Is that so? You didn't mention who took your ship, or why."

"It was confiscated at the port," Hegrun said, a frown pulling his mouth down. "After a misunderstanding."

"Big misunderstanding, I suspect."

Pieces of the story started to come together in Kel's mind. Hegrun or someone on his crew must have broken the law, then gone on the run rather than deal with the local authorities. Their ship was impounded and they couldn't get back to it, so instead they'd set up with the outcasts who were amenable to engaging in a little vengeful thievery and violence. Had he intended to eventually attack the spaceport to get the ship back? He'd certainly built himself an armed gang that might manage the feat, and they seemed loyal. Would they feel the same way if they knew he wasn't really with the Defiants?

How many other lies had he fed them?

"Here's the new plan," Hegrun said, his grin turning into a leer. "You give me that control chip, and I hold you hostage until the backwater fools in Esrondaa give me back my ship. Then I let you go back to your very important job, and everyone is happy."

That didn't sound happy to Kel, who took slow, deep breaths to steady herself. In the storm, the calm eye. Above the storm, clear sky.

"Wish I could say that works for me," Savvy replied, her smile tinged with an emotion Kel couldn't read. "Unfortunately, we're on a tight schedule, so we don't have time to deal with the extra travel and negotiations."

Miza took a step forward as Hegrun barked out an ugly laugh.

"You think you have a choice," Hegrun said. "That's precious. Even with that big sword your bodyguard is carrying, you're outnumbered ten to one. More if I don't count your native, who looks like they wouldn't fill a bird's stomach."

"Are you threatening me with violence?" Savvy pressed her gloved hand to her chest dramatically.

"I'd hardly call it that," Hegrun replied. "If you resist, well. Any injuries you sustain would be your own fault, then, wouldn't they?"

Kel continued to breathe slowly and rhythmically. She had always been taught, always believed, that violence was to be avoided unless it was in self-defense or for the protection of another who was incapable of self-defense. The intent was not to harm, and if harm occurred, it was the fault of the aggressor. But in this, Hegrun was the aggressor. He was the one making threats, and Kel had no reason to believe he wouldn't carry them out. To blame someone else for the injuries he was suggesting he would deliberately cause . . . Such a perversion of her own ethos disgusted her.

Even so, she couldn't bring herself to act first. To hurt him before he hurt Savvy or Dare or Lunna. Her body burned with need and shame and regret, with the memory of the schism among her own people and the death it had wrought. More and more she thought she had picked the wrong side. And now they were all dead or hiding, and the harm could not be undone.

"It would be inconvenient to break a nail on your face," Savvy said, spreading her gloved fingers wide and examining their tips. She looked up at Hegrun through her lashes and smiled.

A moment later, Hegrun slapped at his cheek just as Miza did the same to his neck. Biters? But no, the hummer should have kept them away, even if one had snuck through the netting across the tent's entry flap. Kel stared at them, watching for signs of aggression, preparing to defend Savvy if they reached for weapons or called out for help.

But instead, Hegrun's visor-tinted eyes unfocused and rolled back into his head. He slumped over, and a heartbeat later, Miza joined him. Kel watched closely until she was sure both were breathing regularly, their skin color unaffected. Tranquilizers, not poison? Still risky, depending on the exact formula.

"Well," Savvy said in the silence. "I only have a few more of those, and I'd rather not carve my way out of here like the Phyrian who was swallowed by a smarth. We need a way to get Dare and Lunna and the skimmer, quick and quiet. I don't suppose you can find me an exit?"

*Find an exit, Third,* said a voice in Kel's memory. *I can hold them off if you find—*

Kel closed her eyes, fighting the roiling of her guts, and pictured the layout of the camp in her mind. The skimmers had been hidden on the eastern side of the island, with disguised gaps in the palisade. This tent was at the northern end, but there were at least four tents between them and freedom. Assuming they could sneak behind those tents in the dark, and assuming no one noticed them and sounded an alarm, they might make it out before Hegrun and Miza awoke. But that plan hung from a lot of straps that weren't well secured, and failure would mean an ugly fight.

"One of us should cause a distraction," Kel said. "The other should get to the skimmer, either behind the tents or in plain view, if it's not suspicious. Dare and Lunna are hopefully there already, otherwise the first to see them brings them along. Once we're all aboard, we pole away and head back toward the village, or find somewhere else to hide for the night."

"Simple," Savvy said. "I like simple. Do you have an idea for a distraction?" As she spoke, she methodically searched the unconscious men.

"You could say you need to get something from the boat," Kel said. "Or I could, if you're better at stealth. We could stage an argument with each other, and you could order me to get the others and wait in the skimmer."

"We could also give them a taste of their own smoke," she said. "Tear a hole in the tent, spread some propellant around and set the fence on fire."

"People could get hurt," Kel said.

"People have already gotten hurt," Savvy retorted. "And these two just threatened us, if you recall. They're not good people."

"Good isn't something you are. It's something you do. Death takes away that possibility permanently."

"It also stops a bad person from doing more bad things," Savvy said, her scowl returning. "I expect if we had the full story from Esrondaa, you might be less sympathetic to them."

"I'm more worried about the outcasts," Kel said.

"The ones who tried to burn down a village?"

Kel opened her mouth to protest, then closed it. *Why am I defending them?* she thought. *Why am I trying to protect them when they've already harmed others tonight, by their own choice?*

*Because that's who you are,* she told herself, her stomach tight and heavy. *You defend. You subdue. You try not to harm, even when someone's rushing at you with a weapon. You came into this camp under false pretenses, and now you have to get out before someone finds you and starts another fight. At least a fire can be put out, or people can escape.*

"Fine," Kel said. "If we cut a hole in the back of the tent, you should be able to toss a pair of those flares over the wall, where the brush is hiding the palisade. Might be too wet to catch fast, but it'll happen."

Savvy grabbed the devices from the table of weapons, giving the rest of the items there an appreciative examination. A few she quickly disappeared into parts of her clothing that Kel hadn't realized were concealed pockets until now. Others she shoved into a filched bag that she hefted onto her back.

"Don't suppose you want any new toys, Kel?" Savvy asked.

"Thank you, no," Kel replied curtly. A sword might have tempted her, but there wasn't one, and sometimes a weapon was just an excuse to reach for violence first.

She used the scythe to slice through the fabric of the tent. If anyone were patrolling the back of the camp, they might see a sudden light spilling out of the new gap and come investigate. But no cry of alarm sounded, no rush of footsteps approached, and when she poked her head out, only the shadows of trees and tents surrounded her.

"I'll toss the flares, then come back in," Savvy said, hunkering down next to Kel. "When someone yells fire, you run out the front and join the fire crew, same as you did at the village, then meet me at the skimmer. Grab Lunna or Dare if you see them."

"If no one yells fire?" Kel asked.

"I will," Savvy said.

"Hurry, then," Kel said. The longer they waited, the more likely someone would come to check on Hegrun, or the stun darts would wear off.

Savvy squeezed out through the hole and into the night. Kel positioned herself so she could keep an eye on the unconscious men and the door flap. The whine of the hummer made it difficult to hear anything beyond the murmur of conversation where the bandits congregated, and the occasional muted scuff of boots or scream of distant creatures in the sky or treetops.

Kel studied Hegrun. If he was a privateer, he had free license to work for the Pale, took orders from them, but was ultimately a higher-tier mercenary rather than a full citizen with all the privileges and obligations that entailed. He'd picked a side, he and his crew. And now he was masquerading as someone from the opposition force—if Defiants could be called a force.

By the time they began staging their various acts of disruption and resistance in her system, Kel was already hiding on Loth, learning how to survive. Her only news came from whatever she overheard when she traded in the village, or what Lunna told her. And all of that was as much rumor as reality, as it had been before the war: exaggerated tales of reckless battles and destruction of Pale properties, of scattered pockets of rebellion throughout the ever-expanding Anocracy territory. Like biters stinging a xoffedil, hoping to eventually kill it or drive it away.

Sad that the outcasts might believe they were part of something bigger than themselves, when they were the victims of a conman. But then, for all Kel knew, Savvy was just like Hegrun.

No, that wasn't fair. Until this moment, Savvy had been guarded, evasive even, had pumped Lunna and others for information when possible, but she'd done nothing wrong. Neither had Dare.

Savvy ducked back inside the tent, tugging at her gloves. "I tossed them both into a thick patch of scrub and waited until I saw smoke, so let's hope the flares are hot enough for wet, green wood to start a real fire."

Kel exhaled. Her training and experience were in different areas, not this clandestine spying and sabotage. With which, she noted, Savvy seemed quite comfortable.

Perhaps more lies were layered on this situation than she realized, and Savvy really was one of the Defiants?

They sat in tense silence, Kel counting down in her head. If she reached three hundred with no alarm raised outside, she'd check to be sure the fire was burning and then do it herself. And if the fire wasn't burning? They'd have to come up with some other plan, or she might have to use her bracers to—

"Fire!" came the cry, at last. Kel wasn't sure whether she was relieved or sorry to hear it. She nodded at Savvy, then dashed outside, looking around as if in confusion.

"Where's the fire?" she shouted. One of the bandits pointed to the back of the camp, where plumes of smoke rose above the palisade. Flames licked at holes in the wood and the gaps between logs that hadn't been secured tightly enough.

Kel inhaled deeply, reaching for the voice of command she'd refrained from using on Savvy and Dare before. "Everyone evacuate to the other side of the island," she bellowed. She pointed at two of the bandits who seemed about to argue. "You and you, grab a bucket and a skimmer and pole around to the outside. Start tossing mud on the fire, as fast as you can."

"Where's Hegrun?" someone asked.

Kel ignored them and pointed at another bandit. "You, are there any chemical fire suppressants?"

The bandit shook their head in confusion, and Kel dismissed them with a gesture. She looked back at the tent under the guise of checking the situation, but Savvy was nowhere to be seen. Hopefully she'd made it out and was on her way to their skimmer. Where were Dare and Lunna? Kel scanned the camp, but neither of them appeared. The moon overhead illuminated the area, but there were too many shadows.

"Are we under attack?" someone else asked.

"It's possible," Kel said. "You three, circle around the camp from the west. Look for unknown boats. I'll check the other end. Be careful."

With that, she moved toward the edge of the island, then made her way counterclockwise toward where the boats were moored. She didn't see her allies. She hoped they hadn't been detained inside a tent, unaware of what was occurring, or that they hadn't run off to help with the fire as she had back at the village.

A dark form stepped into her path as she was about to pass the first skimmer. Thin, sneering, skin the color of bleached stone mottled with sunburn.

"Where you going, eh?" they asked. Moonlight glinted off a hooked blade in their left hand.

"Checking for hostiles," she replied coolly. "Have you seen any boats come in?"

"Only yours," they said. "Don't suppose you brought a few more friends with you?"

Kel shook her head and feigned misunderstanding. "We couldn't have been followed. The route we took was winding and it's too dark."

"Ah, but you could have a location marker, so the law could catch up in their own time." They rolled their wrist as if to loosen it, the blade's point making a slow circle.

Kel opened her arms. "You could search me, but the camp might burn down by then. And even if I had such a device, it would be too late to do anything but kill me over it."

By the leer that spread across the bandit's face, the prospect of a search pleased them. Or perhaps the killing. Kel kept her arms open, a stance meant to look harmless, defenseless. But she watched their hands, their feet, their eyes, her muscles ready to act the instant they moved.

Their blade swung parallel to the ground, level with her neck. Kel leaned back, then stepped diagonally toward them and grabbed the outer edge of their arm, just above the elbow. She hooked a kick at the back of their head that knocked them facedown into the mud, then stomped on the hand that held their weapon. Without checking whether they remained conscious, she dashed toward the skimmers.

Another dark shape appeared, accompanied by a flicker of green at eye level. Dare.

"It's me," Kel said. "Did Savvy make it?"

"She and Lunna are on board," Dare replied. "The chip is secured. We only awaited your arrival." His sword was angled back with the point down, its color rendering it nearly invisible in the dark, its length impossible to judge, a posture designed to lure an attack he would no doubt quickly overcome.

Kel had never been fond of that maneuver. It felt like a

trap intended to provoke violence rather than quell it. But her instructor had said, *The provocation is in their perception, not in your action. They must still choose to take the first step, or you will remain as unmoving as a statue. A statue cannot harm anyone without their own interference.*

After a last glance to see if anyone followed, Kel leaped aboard the skimmer, offering Dare a hand up. He hesitated, then took it, his glove warm. His palms must be sweating and uncomfortable, she thought, unless the material was temperature controlled like her old uniform. Her gaze fell to his naked blade, and she felt a yearning unbecoming of her rank and training. She closed her eyes and drew a deep, ragged breath.

When she opened her eyes again, Dare had sheathed his sword and affixed it to his back, his eyes no longer glowing. Kel grabbed one of the skimmer's poles and pushed the boat away from the island, not waiting for Lunna to give her instructions on which way to go. She doubted there would be pursuit while Hegrun was incapacitated, and once he awoke, with any luck he wouldn't want to take his chances in the dark.

Smoke from the brush fire drifted into the sky, leaving a dirty film across the moon, the scent of ash thick on the air even as they fled into the warm, concealing embrace of the swamp.

# CHAPTER EIGHT

For several tense hours, Kel poled them through the swamp, not wanting to risk the sound of the engine giving away their position. Lunna activated their jammer to stop any drones the bandits might send out to damage their skimmer, and Dare kept a wary eye on the waterline for movement that couldn't be easily attributed to wildlife.

Savvy slept, having noted that at least one of them should be rested to take watch later, and she was presently the least useful member of the party. Kel respected that level of practicality; she'd always been advised to eat, sleep, or relieve herself anytime the opportunity arose. And Savvy had done most of the heavy lifting among the bandits, so to speak, in terms of getting them there and charming their leader. It wasn't her fault Hegrun was a grasping, selfish thief with his own ulterior motives. With any luck, they'd seen the last of him and his crew.

Kel wished she believed in luck, or even the precepts of balance many of her instructors and peers had accepted as truth. Too much harm came to pass and seemed to remain unanswered.

Dare patrolled the small boat in a tight circuit, his sword sheathed but his gloved hand opening and closing as if eager to reach for it. Kel could almost follow the pacing count in his head, and the rhythm of it, the familiarity, sharpened her own actions like a dull blade newly honed. It was as if she had been in stasis for five years and was slowly awakening, the long sleep receding from her senses, muscles shaking off the last of the burn that came from prolonged disuse.

Shadows drifted across the deck as they passed beneath trees, the scent of white and purple night-blooming flowers suffusing the air like spilled perfume. Creatures cried out in the dark, hungry or eager to rut. A swarm of glowbugs in the distance floated above the surface of the water, their dim green light reflected and multiplied into a ghostly cloud that seemed to reach into the bowels of the swamp, to touch the mud far below. Nothing attacked them, and no one pursued them, and still Dare kept his vigil and Kel raised and lowered her pole, pushing them forward.

They came ashore at Yonneron just before the sun crested the horizon, the sky streaked with magenta and violet. Fishers who hadn't left for the early catch greeted their arrival with a mixture of curiosity and concern. The village was too small to have even a guesthouse—travelers stayed with friends, family, a volunteer host or the local Speakers. It didn't matter now, as they had all agreed to stay on the skimmer. Lunna curled up inside the covered bench area, while Kel unrolled a loose tarp and secured it to the benches as well as cleats on opposite sides of the bow, giving her and Dare some shade even if it wouldn't alleviate the impending heat. Savvy promised to awaken them all by midday, sooner if they were needed.

"Don't lie awake worrying," Savvy said, tossing one of her new knives into the air and catching it easily. "We don't have enough stims to do more than top us all off."

Kel had never been fond of stims. They made her eyes feel gritty and her scalp itch. So she covered her face with her hat, controlled her breathing, and forced relaxation into her muscles one at a time, from heel to head. Dare seemingly did the same next to her, his rhythm matching hers intentionally or subconsciously, and within minutes she had meditated herself into a dreamless sleep.

THE SOUND OF FRANTIC MURMURING DREW KEL OUT OF THE DEPTHS OF unconsciousness, then a loud thump pulled her to the surface like a fish on a hook. She rolled onto her belly and pushed into as much of a crouch as the tarp allowed, a hand on her machete, when she met Savvy's worried gaze and froze to evaluate the situation.

Dare thrashed in his sleep, eyes squeezed shut, face twisted in rage or fear. He wasn't armed, but his hands curled into fists, which he flung wildly as if fending off an unseen foe. Sweat beaded on his face, his jaw locked so tightly Kel could almost hear his teeth grinding. His heels knocked the deck and his back arched as he loosed a groan of pain or sorrow or some other feeling only he could name.

"Don't touch him," Savvy whispered. "He'll hurt you or himself."

He's already hurting himself, Kel thought. "Does he have a projectile weapon or only blades?" she whispered.

"Blades," Savvy replied.

Not ideal, but Kel expected she could disarm him if necessary. A glance told her Lunna was safe, still sleeping if their posture was any indication. What fortune to be able to rest so tranquilly. Or more likely the frantic energy of so much danger the night before had led to subsequent exhaustion.

"How long do the nightmares usually last?" Kel asked.

"How do you know it's nightmares?"

Kel stared impassively at Savvy, who sighed.

"It varies," Savvy said. "Sometimes he wakes himself up quickly, sometimes it goes on for ten or twenty minutes before he comes out of it." She watched him move, far enough away to avoid his limbs, close enough to intervene if the situation turned for the worse.

Kel squinted up at the sky, then down at the length of the shadows dwindling on the deck. Approaching midday, which meant she'd slept enough to get by, even if she felt like the sun was too bright and her muscles were weighted down with mud. Still, they couldn't afford to rest longer. Once Dare and Lunna awoke, they should eat and head for the next village on their itinerary if they wanted to reach it before nightfall.

"I'm surprised you didn't try to hold him down or something," Savvy said. "We had an engineer who earned himself a black eye that way." Her tone aimed for light, teasing, but her worry bled through like ink on wet paper.

Any answer Kel gave would reveal too much, so she simply shrugged. Such afflictions could happen to anyone who endured traumatic violence, and she had been trained along with her cohort in the necessary steps to handle the situation. At worst, she would restrain Dare while Savvy disarmed him, or throw a bucket of water on him to bring him around quickly. But waking someone in the throes of nightmares could make them more violent and aggressive.

Memories were ghosts that haunted at all hours, appearing from nowhere and gripping the heart with frigid hands. In sleep, their forms were more immediate and tangible, for all that they were products of the mind rather than reality. Knowing a thing was merely imagined did little to deprive it of power and pain.

So they crouched, and they waited, and after a few minutes Dare awoke with a strangled gasp. His eyes were wide, pupils dilating the green of his irises to a sliver despite the blazing light. He took in his surroundings with darting glances, one hand reaching for the sheathed sword beside him, which he clutched as if it were a knotted rope saving him from a long fall. Slowly, his breathing calmed. Kel rolled out from under the tarp and stepped off the boat to perform her morning—now midday—ablutions and give him and Savvy some privacy. She elected to skip her usual run.

When she returned, Savvy and Lunna were discussing fastest routes, and they wandered off together to use the dock's washroom. Dare stood at the front of the skimmer, arms crossed, sword on his back. His hair was wet, from a quick dousing with some of their drinking water if she was any judge. She remembered his dark expression, the flailing and groans of his sleep perils. Kel wasn't sure what to say to him, if anything. But some part of her reached back to who she had been, almost reluctantly, and she found she couldn't stay silent.

Making enough noise that she wouldn't startle him, Kel stepped up behind Dare. He acknowledged her presence by inclining his head, but continued scanning the swamp. She considered her potential words, mentally perusing advice and anecdotes and long-ago lessons conveyed by much wiser people, and finally settled on one memory in particular.

"Some people," Kel said quietly, "are blessed with the unshakable conviction that their actions are just and righteous. Their lives are split into good and evil as surely as day and night. They are like worlds locked to their stars so only one face ever feels the light, and always turns away from the dark. But the rest of us, we know the borderlands of dawn and dusk, the twilight places. We carry a little of them with us wherever we go. Doubt grows fertile there, and regret. The fears of what could have been, and what still might be." She looked down at her boots, resisting the urge to rub her bracers beneath her shirt. "We cannot compel those thoughts to leave us, but we can learn to lie among them without despairing, and sometimes, find beauty in the gloaming."

Kel glanced at Dare, who stared at her with a startled expression, brow furrowed and mouth half-open. It quickly shifted into a scowl, and Dare's hand closed into a fist.

"What do you know about me?" he snarled. "Did Savvy tell you something, or do you have other means of gathering information?"

A flush crept up her neck, regret tightening her throat. She'd miscalculated. She shouldn't have spoken so openly. Now he thought she was privy to whatever secrets he kept, ones only Savvy knew. And judging by his reaction, they were entirely unpleasant.

"She only mentioned you sometimes have nightmares," Kel said carefully. "Nothing else. Not their source or their contents."

"And your pretty speech was meant kindly, I suppose?" he retorted. "No sidearms hidden behind your back, no veiled insinuations about my past?"

"No," Kel said. "The only past I'm aware of is what Savvy has said in stories of your adventures together. And I'm not requesting you bare your soul to me now. I was only—" She stopped, searching her feelings and finding sorrow and pain, and a loneliness she carried like a block of raw futhite, heavy and rough and scarred from the blows that mined it.

"You were only what?" Dare snapped.

Kel pressed her lips together. "I'm sorry," she murmured. "I overstepped. It won't happen again."

The sound of footsteps along the dock had them both turning toward the noise, Kel's muscles tensing. But it was only Lunna and Savvy returning. Lunna laughed at something Savvy said, and some of the worry in Kel's stomach dissipated.

Not all of it, not nearly. Any trust she had earned from Dare so far had been cut down like a sapling still trying to spread roots. All because of her ill-conceived desire to be helpful. It served her right for not keeping her mouth shut.

Not that it mattered. None of them needed to be friends to accomplish their task. All they needed to do was work together. They had to reach Lichi, then Handeen, and then they had to track and disable the demolisher. And they had to continue to keep one another safe, especially now they might have bandits after them, stalking them to get the control chip for their own ends. Kel made a note to ask about Hegrun when they stopped for the night and she reported back to Speaker Yiulea.

If nothing else, the people in Esrondaa needed to know they were dealing with offworlders masquerading as Defiants and not the real thing. The difference might not mean anything from a practical standpoint, but it might change how the authorities dealt with the problem.

Kel sighed and rolled her shoulders, trying to loosen them. In a few more days, this would all be over. Savvy and Dare would be gone, and she could go home.

Home. The word felt like a lie on her tongue, thick and bitter. She wondered if she would ever use it again without that instinctive recoil, or if she would feel uprooted and listless for the rest of her days. She wondered if she deserved more.

Savvy cast a speculative glance at Kel and Dare as she boarded the skimmer. "Anything happen that I should know about?" she asked.

No better time than now to practice silence, Kel thought, so she didn't respond.

AN HOUR INTO THEIR JOURNEY, THE RAIN STARTED. THICK CLOUDS MASSED overhead, blotting out sun and sky with shades of gray from light to dark. Kel mused that it had been unusually dry as far as local weather went, so they were due for a run of wet luck. And it suited her present mood. She stayed in the front of the skimmer while Lunna steered, their progress slowed as before by reduced visibility. Savvy lay beneath the tarp between the benches and grumbled about hair oils, while Dare crouched next to Lunna cradling his sword.

Two hours in, they reached the outskirts of the Endless Swamp and passed into the waters of Lake Ayakocha. The surrounding trees fell away, leaving only a long, flat stretch of flooded grass broken by scrub-covered islands. Kel knew from previous journeys and maps of the area that eventually the balance would shift, with the lake splitting into tributaries of rivers that branched north in all directions, and only one of those rivers would take them to Lichi. The rest led to other villages, or to the western sea, or into wilder parts of southern Loth where no humans dwelled. Lunna watched the skimmer's sensors to ensure they didn't ground the boat on an unseen swell of earth or mud or hardy plants; its bottom was flat so it navigated shallow waters easily, but it wasn't impervious to damage.

A flock of long-legged wading birds leaped into the air at the sound of the approaching engine, wings carrying them gracefully across the lake's surface to a place less prone to intruders. Still the rain fell, sometimes a sprinkle, other times so dense it pummeled Kel's head and shoulders and turned the deck into a river of its own. Her cloak kept the worst of it from soaking her upper body, but even with her hat, she had to squint every time a gust blew drops into her face. She almost lost her footing more than once, and finally gave up her post and crouched near Lunna.

"Should we take shelter somewhere and wait this out?" Savvy asked, her voice raised to be heard over the clatter of rain on the tarp.

"There's no shelter for marks," Kel said.

"At least this isn't a thunderstorm," Lunna added. "No zaps, only wet. We should be through the other end of it soon."

Kel looked forward to drying off, even if it meant she'd be sweating through her shirt instead. The air was saturated with humidity at the best of times, but there was sweat, and then there were soggy boots. She might shuck them and slip on her sandals for a change.

Lunna hadn't been wrong—not that Kel was expecting them to be—and from one moment to the next they went from downpour to nothing, as if they'd passed some invisible border. Scattered clouds stretched across the lavender sky, but the sun peeked through, promising a respite from the storms. The isolated islands dotting the lake's surface were covered in creatures sunning themselves, mostly throllax with their toothsome mouths hanging open, and a few of the strange dun-colored fish that lived both in and out of the water.

"I don't miss this nonsense, I tell you what," Savvy said, peering back at the curtain of rain receding behind them. "Liquid falling from the sky? Give me an ion storm over that any day."

The last time Kel had been through an ion storm, her starship had nearly lost all its navigation equipment and was barely able to make repairs to reach a safe port. As she recalled, the captain had given a vigorous tongue-lashing to the technician who had missed the instrument warnings until it was too late to reroute.

"Kel?" Savvy asked, interrupting Kel's thoughts.

"Yes?" Kel replied.

"I said, was the weather like this where you're from?"

Kel shrugged noncommittally. Still, memories flooded her mind. Summer storms so large everyone had to hide in special rooms until they had passed, the wind howling and tearing up trees outside. Lightning forking across a gray-black sky, followed by rumbles or boom-cracks of thunder. The patter of rain on roofs or against windows, and the smell of the soil it left behind, rich and full of life. Water pooled in orange flowers shaped like cups, birds the size of her thumb dunking themselves inside and shaking their feathers dry before bursting into song. This part of Loth was wilder, with fewer people and more untouched nature, but its similarities to a home long lost to her was one of the reasons she had decided to settle here. To hide here.

"What about you, Savvy?" Lunna asked. "You must not be from somewhere rainy, are you?"

Savvy's nearly permanent smile softened, sad or wistful or something else Kel couldn't read. "I was spaceborn, actually," she said. "Started my life screaming into the void and never stopped."

"Oh!" Lunna covered their mouth with a hand. "That's so exciting. It's like being from anywhere and everywhere at once."

A child of all-between, Kel thought, then bit her lip at another flood of memories, forcing her attention back to her surroundings with effort.

Something about the hum of the engines sounded strange. She carefully stepped to the back of the skimmer, peering at the air rings, apparently functioning normally. The rain shouldn't have affected them; they were built for all sorts of weather. Surely Lunna would have noticed if there were a problem. So what—

Movement in the distance. More skimmers, at least two—no, three. Kel watched them and dared to hope they might be fishers or fellow travelers making their way to Lichi. So many skimmers at once was unlikely, though, not in this part of the season.

Kel made her way back to Lunna's side. "Turn on the jammer," she said.

Lunna looked up at her, eyes wide with surprise. "You think the bandits followed us? All this way? There isn't a thing on sensors but weather and animals."

Savvy shaded her eyes, looking behind them. "Tell that to those sneaky rotters. Stealthed, I assume, which your locals wouldn't be doing for work or pleasure. Dare, get your long gun ready." He nodded and crawled under the wet tarp, rooting around in his pack.

One of the skimmer's engines sputtered, and Lunna had to fight the controls to keep the craft from spinning out. Savvy stumbled but caught herself on the roof, while Kel slid into a defensive stance, shifting her weight to stay balanced on the slippery deck. Dare rolled and thumped into one of the benches, spitting a curse that sounded Vethonian.

"The jammer, Lunna!" Kel shouted.

"It's not working!" Lunna yelled back.

Had the bandits sabotaged the skimmer somehow after stealing it? But why? It didn't matter now. What mattered was getting away from the boats coming after them, and keeping everyone safe.

With a wrenching groan, the second engine stalled. Their skimmer was dead in the water. And in a few minutes, they might be, too.

## CHAPTER NINE

**D**are emerged from cover holding a sniper rifle that must have been collapsed inside his pack. He ran it through some quick checks before propping it against his shoulder in a way that suggested easy familiarity. Savvy edged past him and retrieved the plasma rifle she'd stolen from Hegrun, which she activated with an uncharacteristically grim expression.

"No rest for the wicked," she said. "Let's see if we can't thin the ranks before they reach us."

Kel stared at their weapons, hoping her dismay wasn't plain on her face.

"You're going to kill them?" Lunna squeaked.

"Before they kill us, yes," Savvy replied. She raised an eyebrow. "I didn't take you for a pacifist."

"It's just . . . that's not . . . ," Lunna sputtered. "They're so far away! And you don't know whether they mean to kill us or capture us. Shouldn't we find out first?"

Savvy ran a hand over her face and sighed. "They were

already plotting to kill us back on the island, dear heart. I doubt they came up with a kinder plan after we knocked out their leader and stole this boat back."

She wasn't wrong. But self-defense should not be intended to kill, if killing could be avoided. Could it be, though? Had they passed the point where the conflict could be de-escalated? They were outnumbered, and while Hegrun's team of twelve were likely armed and trained, she doubted the outcasts he'd recruited would pose much of a challenge for her and Dare and Savvy.

Still, that was four-to-one odds at best, not counting Lunna, who'd never done more than train to defend themself from the wildlife of Loth—or more often, to run or hide. And the bandits had made sure they couldn't run or hide, so their only option was to fight.

They had to survive, to finish their mission. With that thought in mind, she began negotiating with herself. What would it take for her to activate her bracers? She would have to do it before she herself was killed, if the goal was to ensure everyone's safety. A dispassionate part of her noted that only Savvy had to be kept alive for them to succeed.

That would be her priority, then: protect Savvy with her life. Ideally Lunna as well, and Dare, though she expected he could manage on his own.

"Lunna," Kel said, and Lunna turned big blue eyes to her. "Can you repair the engines?"

"It depends on what stopped them," Lunna said. "I can try to manually restart."

"How long will that take?" Kel asked, eyeing the incoming skimmers.

Lunna grimaced. "If it can be done? A few minutes. But if it can't—"

"Do your best," Kel said. She grabbed an oar and realigned their vessel so Lunna would be partly shielded by the benches.

Dare, who had begun setting up his weapon, repositioned himself with a scowl. "Do you mind?" he asked.

Kel didn't dignify that with a response. Instead, she subtly put herself between Savvy and their enemies.

The bandits drew closer, four to a skimmer, their speed difficult to gauge because the receding storm wall made it seem they were moving faster. Part of her hoped it was only Hegrun's crew, that he'd left the outcasts behind to ensure the secrecy of his mission. Her conscience would rest more easily.

The crack of splintering wood had Kel tackling Savvy to the deck. Lunna yelped and covered their head with their hands.

If Kel activated her bracers, she could . . . no. Not yet. But what if she waited until it was too late? She got to one knee and peered over the top of the bench.

Dare calmly adjusted his targeting. His rifle boomed, but the bandits were too far away for Kel to see the outcome of the shot. He reloaded, adjusted his aim and fired again.

"How many shots does he have?" Kel asked Savvy.

"Five," Savvy replied. "He would have brought more ammo, but I didn't think we'd need it." In Iccati, she muttered, "Blazing stars, I told him we wouldn't need to bring the rifle at all, and look at us now."

Kel stiffened. Was Savvy from Icca? That planet was Pale occupied, unless things had changed.

Whatever Savvy was, she wasn't military. Not everyone wandered the galaxy with their own ship, though—that was expensive. So how had she been able to afford one . . . Unless she stole it? Pointless to speculate in the middle of this. Maybe she'd ask later.

"Can you shoot?" Savvy asked her.

"If I must," Kel replied.

For some reason, this made Savvy laugh. She shifted from lying prone on her stomach to crouching. "Here," she said, and handed Kel one of her pistols. Kel slid the disabler off smoothly despite being out of practice.

"What's your take on our predicament?" Savvy asked.

Kel hesitated, collecting her thoughts. "Skimmers aren't the most maneuverable vehicles," she said. "They'll have to stop to engage with us, or shoot as they pass and circle back. Our main problem is not being killed in the crossfire."

"Stay close to Dare," Savvy said. "He has a little surprise in store."

Kel's brow furrowed.

"Don't worry," Savvy said, winking. "I'm not planning to use him as a meat shield."

Dare snorted, not bothering to look away from the oncoming skimmers.

Something splashed in the water, then another shot cracked like thunder. The sniper had missed. Dare answered the shot with one of his own. Two more left.

Savvy still had the plasma rifle, and presumably various other weapons secreted in her pack or about her person that could be used to fire on their enemy from a distance. But those were shorter-range options, though unless all the bandits were killed on the approach, close combat might become necessary.

Unless the bandits finished them off first, Kel thought morosely. Another crunch signaled an attempt, at least, and Lunna yelped in fear as they continued to cower in place. The benches, sadly, were not a particularly good shield.

"I don't mean to pry," Kel said, "but if Dare can do something to keep us from being shot, it might be useful to know what it is in advance and plan for it. Tactically speaking." It might also mean she was safe not to reveal her own skills for a little longer.

"Best to light up the board and show our pieces, hmm?" Savvy asked. "Tell you what: you give us a detailed rundown of your available abilities, arms and armor, and we'll do the same."

Kel winced. Once she revealed who she was and what she could do, she could be putting all of them in more danger than before. If she didn't, they might not survive for it to make a difference.

"Oh, blazing stars," Savvy said, "you look like you're marching to your own execution. Don't worry, I was only being nosy."

"Savvy," Dare said, his tone a warning. But for what?

"You heard her," Savvy said. "She has a tactical mind, like you. So let's be tactical." She met Kel's gaze, her half smile more bravado than amusement. "Dare has a . . . toy he picked up in his travels."

Dare snorted derisively again but said nothing.

"Not a toy, fine," Savvy said. "It's highly illegal, and we

only save it for emergencies, primarily ones where we don't expect there to be anyone left at the end to tattle."

Despite the heat shimmering in the air, the sun blazing in a cloud flecked sky, Kel felt cold from skin to bone. What Savvy was saying came too close to her own situation for comfort.

"Do you not anticipate Lunna and I will survive this?" Kel asked quietly.

Savvy's smile vanished and her shoulders hunched. "You seem accomplished at keeping secrets. Lunna, not so much. But I'm more worried about any survivors on Hegrun's crew."

"Because of their Pale associations."

Savvy nodded.

That wasn't quite a promise that she and Lunna wouldn't be sacrificed for this secret to be maintained, but it would have to do for now. Savvy was an accomplished liar, and Kel didn't think making her swear an oath would make a difference. She had to hope the captain was truly a good person under all her charm.

Dare fired again, their enemy now close enough for Kel to see the burst of blood spray into the air, the body topple like a felled tree. Kel had thought herself accustomed to the sensation of killing, of being near the dying and dead, but that was a bold lie. Each time it happened, she was merely temporarily numbed, the pain and remorse buried so she could finish her task, but the wound to her soul bled freely until she attended to it with greater care.

Death was so easy, in the end. The strings of life seemed

so strong until they were cut. And once they were, no force in the universe could knot them back together.

"What is the device, then?" Kel asked.

An oppressive silence fell, no insects or birdsong, not even a rush of wind to fill it. Kel forced herself to inhale and held the breath.

"A bracer," Savvy said, quietly enough that only Kel could hear. "From the Order of the Nine."

Dare took his final shot. Kel exhaled as if she'd been punched.

Staying low, Dare briskly collapsed his sniper rifle until it was the size of a sidearm. Some distant part of her was relieved, or proud, that he was apparently a better shot than whoever had been firing on them from the bandit skimmers. The rest of her was in a daze, still trying to process what Savvy had said.

"Did you get their sniper?" Savvy asked.

"Yes," he replied. He wasn't smiling, but the way he said it conveyed a savage satisfaction.

Savvy passed the plasma rifle to him, then retrieved a pair of pistols from Kel didn't know where. The rifle would have a longer range, but at this rate, the bandit skimmers would be on them soon enough that it wouldn't matter.

"So, the bracer," Savvy continued, apparently not noticing Kel's reaction. "It can make a barrier around us that their weapons can't penetrate. It won't last forever, but we can use it to stay safe while we pick them off one by one, or until they give up and leave."

Kel struggled to form words, to gather thoughts that raced off in every direction or jumbled on top of one another like a pile of mrilli. She had so many questions, few of which were useful in the face of the enemies closing in. She tried to concentrate on what mattered, what would help them form a plan of defense, and what wouldn't reveal too much.

"How large is the barrier?" she asked, proud her voice didn't crack.

"Variable," Dare answered. "If we stay close, I can form a small shelter. It can also be a shield, as tall and wide as one might reasonably fight with."

It could also form part of a linked barricade if all of them had bracers, but Kel didn't tell him that. She closed her eyes to think, and when she opened them again, Dare was searching her face with his brows furrowed.

"Will Hegrun recognize the shield as illegal tech, do you think?" Kel asked.

Savvy shrugged. "It depends on where he's been working."

"The Pale cover a lot of territory," Dare said. "Privateers tend to reach out to the places they don't want to send their own people. They might not have been on that front."

Savvy bit her lip. "He'll likely know it by reputation, at least," she said. "The Pale have a bounty on former Order members."

"What are you talking about?" Lunna asked, their hands stilling. "What shield? Recognize what? Who are the Order?"

Before Savvy or Dare could attempt to explain, Kel intervened.

"The reboot," Kel said. "How goes it?"

Lunna flushed, their freckles a spray of brown against the sudden redness. "Honestly, Friend Kel, I've been doing more worrying than fixing."

Kel offered them a patient smile. "You can do this. Keep

trying." She still clung to the faint hope that if they could start moving, they might evade the bandits instead of cutting them all down or dying in the process. Then Dare wouldn't have to use the shield at all.

"Are they in range yet?" Savvy asked.

"No," Kel and Dare replied in unison. Dare smirked at her, but it quickly faded.

Kel leaned close to him. "I'll protect Savvy with my life," she murmured. "Do whatever you must."

Dare's eyes met hers, the green nearly iridescent, like a bird's feather. He nodded gravely, and Kel turned away.

A high-pitched whine alerted her to Dare readying his plasma rifle. A moment later he fired, the red beam searingly bright. In the closest skimmer, one of the bandits screamed and staggered, just enough to fall overboard and be quickly left behind. The craft veered to one side, then the other, but even Kel could see the pilot wasn't trained in evasive maneuvers. Dare lined up another shot and took it, muttering something under his breath that sounded like a curse.

"Lunna, the engines?" Kel asked, one last time.

"I don't know," Lunna said. "I think they're zapped. Why would the bandits do that?"

"They're probably planning to kill us and tow it back to their island," Savvy said.

"But why?" Lunna asked. They sounded dazed, disbelieving.

"We made a fool of their leader," Savvy replied. "We stole what they'd already taken and we escaped unharmed. More than just the skimmer, they want revenge, and to save face."

"They aren't going to turn back," Kel muttered. All hope of escape faded.

Within moments, they'd be in pistol range. Dare must have realized it, too, because he stopped shooting and touched the sleeve covering his left forearm. That must be where he had the bracer, though it was activated with mental commands rather than physical ones. He crouched between the pilot's seat and the covered benches, and Kel knelt beside him, while Savvy and Lunna huddled behind them.

"I'm going to raise the shield," Dare said. "Once they're in range, I'll deal with them. You stay here." He handed the rifle to Kel and pulled his sword off his back.

"Are you sure you can fight so many?" Lunna asked.

"Nothing is sure but the sunrise," Kel said.

"I like that," Savvy said. "Better than what Dare always says."

"What does Dare say?" Lunna asked, hugging their knees.

Savvy dropped her voice to a raspy grumble. "Only death is certain."

Lunna gave a nervous laugh, then covered their mouth with their hands.

A moment later, the shield rose around them, shimmering with a faint energy. It wasn't tall enough for them to stand in, but they could crouch or sit without hitting the edge. The color was pale green as the sea in daylight, which meant the bracer was from the Order of Sotera. Who had it belonged to, Kel wondered? And how had Dare obtained it? She studied his profile, thoughts racing. He couldn't be from Sotera himself, could he?

Was he a Shield? Maybe even a Knight?

"Incredible," Lunna murmured, reaching a finger out to touch the barrier.

"Don't," Kel said, and Lunna dropped their hand guiltily. Dare rested the sword against his shoulder and waited.

Sweat beaded on Kel's forehead, pooled in the small of her back and under her breasts. She forced herself to breathe evenly, in and out. In the storm, the calm eye. Above the storm, clear sky. Funny how the old mantra still came to her easily in the space before battle. Next she repeated the Litany of Peace to herself, even though it didn't soothe her as it once did.

*Where peace is lost, may we find it.*
*Where peace is broken, may we mend it.*
*Where we go, may peace follow.*
*Where we fall, may peace rise.*

So many had fallen, and for what? The peace that was brokered to end the war had led to more hardship and death and injustice. She'd hidden herself away to comply with the terms of the treaty, to protect herself and her comrades, but how many of them had been pursued by Dirges and killed for the crime of existing? For daring to serve as proof that the Pale weren't invincible? Was Kel truly protecting anyone with her actions? Was she helping peace to endure with her exile, or was she merely cowering as far from her failure as she could manage?

Those thoughts weren't new, and they were of no use to her now.

More shots rang out as the enemy skimmers entered pistol range. Fewer than she had expected; perhaps Savvy's theft had taken away more of their arms than she'd thought. At least two energy weapons sent ruby-colored streaks of plasma toward them, where they sizzled harmlessly against the green barrier surrounding them.

The bandits flew past, shooting all the way. They had slowed down, though, and didn't make it far before they began to ponderously turn. They could see their attacks had no effect, and were screaming and gesturing angrily at one another.

Kel found Hegrun at last, standing next to one of the skimmer pilots. His expression was unreadable, but he shouted, "Stop firing, fools! They can't be hit." The attacks ceased, and Kel's lips pressed together as she awaited his next order.

Hegrun stared at them, then grinned. "They're stuck," he said. "If they drop the shield, we shoot them. Take us along their sides. Fol, Raz, get the towlines ready. Everyone else keep your aim steady."

A quick count indicated there were nine bandits left, spread out across the three skimmers. Dare rolled his shoulders. Kel put her body between Savvy and the bandits as best she could.

She could still use her own bracer, to make absolutely sure Savvy and Lunna were safe. But while one shield could possibly be explained away—why had she never thought of saying she'd found or bought a bracer, like Dare?—two would be too much.

Unless she killed all witnesses. The thought was like a razor up her spine.

Hegrun's skimmer held back as the other two approached. Kel couldn't be sure the men would do exactly what he'd just said, or if there had been some other order given, hand signals or subvocal communicators perhaps. So she watched, and she waited, and she breathed. Nine people, three of them piloting, which left six weapons aimed at them.

Dare shifted minutely.

The first bandit skimmer pulled up alongside them, barely four paces away, and one of Hegrun's people lowered their weapon to grab a rope. They would need both hands to tie the crafts together. Kel kept the rest of the enemy in sight, but her attention fixed on that pistol, those hands, as her breathing slowed.

They slid their pistol into a holster and grabbed another part of the rope.

Dare moved, fast as a diving bladebeak.

The barrier vanished. He raced for the bandit skimmer, and with a small leap he was aboard. Surprised cursing and gunfire rang out, but the close quarters had everyone hesitating out of fear they might hit each other or be struck by a deflected projectile.

A hesitation Dare used to his advantage. He stepped forward and sideways, bringing his sword down in a slash from shoulder to hip. The sharp edge sliced through flesh and muscle and even armor. With a twist of his wrist, he let momentum carry the dark blade back up and around for another strike, driving his opponent down to the deck, where they lay unmoving.

The other bandit dropped the rope and fumbled for their pistol. Dare feinted to the left, then swung from the right toward the enemy's head. They ducked and Dare charged, knocking them down. The blade met them a moment later as they tried to rise.

Behind the skimmer controls, a third bandit huddled with their hands covering their—no, her head. Her clothes suggested she was local, outcast, a single short braid threaded only with the color for her gender. If she were armed, she seemed too afraid to draw her weapon. The tactical part of Kel's mind discounted the woman as a threat, and Dare seemed to agree, because he turned his attention to the other skimmers.

Hegrun still hung back, his craft too far to reach. "Get them!" he shouted at the others. But even as he said it, he whispered something to the pilot, and their engines hummed to life.

Kel and Savvy and Lunna were all but forgotten as everyone focused on the whirlwind of death that Dare had become. No, not a wind; his movements were too precise, too controlled. Still, his raw power and speed felt like some ungovernable force of nature.

The skimmer on the far side of theirs had been successfully tied on, but the knot was awkward, hurried, loosening as the two boats knocked into each other. One of the bandits fired their pistol as the other two rushed toward Dare with a double-spiked staff and two arcknives respectively. The staff wielder attempted to swing the weapon down at Dare's head. He batted it aside and stepped into them, sword point pressing straight into their neck. He didn't bother retreating or pulling his weapon back, simply moved sideways as the body collapsed.

The knife wielder scrambled backward, but the skimmer was small and had no walls like a starship. They overbalanced trying not to fall into the water. Dare reversed his attack and cut upward, hip to shoulder. With a harsh cry, the bandit crumpled and slipped overboard.

Hegrun's skimmer retreated into the distance. But the one tied to theirs still had a pilot, who held a cross between a sickle and a machete. Their eyes were wide with fear, and they swung their blade in a wild, untrained defensive maneuver. Another local.

Dare advanced on them, a trail of blood dripping from his sword.

"Mercy," the bandit croaked, dropping the weapon and falling to their knees. Dare showed no sign he'd heard them.

"Dare," Kel shouted. "Enough."

He froze, then pivoted to keep both her and his enemy in sight. His scowl either said he didn't agree, or was dealing with other feelings about the battle. Kel worried he would ignore her plea, but he nodded and lowered his sword.

In the ensuing quiet, Lunna groaned, stumbled to the side of the skimmer and threw up into the water. Savvy rubbed their back a few times, then pulled them to their feet with a tense, whispered command.

Kel shouldered her pack quickly, and Dare's. Still using her body to guard Savvy, she led them onto the skimmer that wasn't tied to theirs. The one they'd borrowed from Beelea, it seemed. That pilot had emerged from behind her seat and was kneeling next to the body of the other bandit, staring at it in horror. When she looked up, Savvy calmly pointed her pistol at the trembling woman.

"This is your stop, friend," Savvy said, gesturing to the other skimmer with her head.

With a sob, the bandit stood and raced away, avoiding Dare as best she could. She slipped and slid as she went, leaving bloody footprints across the deck.

Kel eyed Hegrun's now distant vessel, already out of pistol range. He might regroup and try for them again, but she doubted it. He seemed the kind to seek vengeance only when the odds favored him. Given his status on Loth, Kel didn't think it was likely in the near future.

Lunna started up their new skimmer with trembling hands while Savvy kept her weapon pointed at the two remaining bandits. Dare's chest rose and fell as he caught his breath, slowed it, dealt with the rush of whatever he felt now that the battle was over. His expression was eerily blank, as it had been when they faced the bladebeaks, and Kel wondered what nightmares he would have tonight.

Should she have protected him, or at least shared his burden? Fought beside him? Had her reticence caused him pain she could have prevented?

She knelt to close the dead bandit's sightless eyes. She had hoped never to be at the center of a storm of violence like this again. But then, her hopes could fill the void, and she'd suffocate before they came to pass.

She grabbed the bandit's body and pushed it into the lake.

## CHAPTER TEN

Kel stared down at her plate of food, surprised to see she'd eaten half of it without noticing. If she forced her attention to her mouth, she found the expected flavors—stewed vegetables, lightly charred flatbread, the sweet and savory blend of spices that found its way into many dishes at the guesthouses. She couldn't remember serving herself, and tried retracing her most recent steps, realizing she'd not only done so, but had also gotten food for Lunna, who sat on the bench across from her, mutely picking at their own meal. Savvy sat next to them, with Dare next to Kel, having chosen the spot that would let him watch the exits.

Around them, voices filled the room, rising and falling unevenly, with more than a few questioning looks sent in their direction. No doubt word had spread that the demolisher problem was being handled by offworlders, which Savvy and Dare clearly were, and Kel was borderline with her covered hair and lack of braids. The friendly air Savvy had cultivated with the locals was strained now, and Lunna's natural exuberance had shriveled like crops in a drought.

With an effort, Kel continued eating until her plate was empty. Strange to feel like a new initiate after her first battle, her meal sitting like rocks in her stomach. To hear the voice of her commander coaxing her to rest, to recuperate, to be ready for the next battle. If she closed her eyes, she could almost imagine she was back on Amorleth, waiting for her turn to speak with the mind-healer.

But Amorleth was dead to her, and she would be dead, too, if she wasn't careful.

Lunna put their spoon down, eyes watery with unshed tears. "How," they asked, voice catching. They swallowed. "How do you just . . . kill someone, and then eat dinner as if nothing happened?" Their freckles stood out starkly on their pale face.

"Should we starve to ease your conscience?" Dare asked. Kel resisted the urge to kick him under the table. Savvy did kick him.

"No, of course not," Lunna sputtered. "It's . . . shouldn't you . . . I don't know!" They tossed their spoon onto their plate in frustration.

Savvy patted their arm. "It gets easier," she said.

Lunna's wide eyes conveyed their dismay. They turned their gaze to Kel, who tried to search for an answer that would ease their heart, if only for a time.

"Hurting others also hurts oneself," Kel said finally. "If it did not, we would be inhuman. Over time, for some, that hurt becomes a scar that no longer feels pain in the same way. For others, it festers and rots and eventually kills them."

"Can't there be another way, then?" Lunna asked. "Did we have to . . . do what we did?"

*Violence is always a failure, Third,* whispered a voice long dead. *Fear is eager to rationalize and defend it, but make no mistake, it is always a failure. The challenge is not in avoiding failure, but in knowing which failures cannot be avoided.*

"We cannot change the past now," Kel continued. "We can only strive not to repeat it, and to accept when it must be repeated."

Lunna's brow furrowed, their mouth shrinking to a thin line. "I still have no appetite," they said, as if they wished it were otherwise.

"Grab some fruit for the road," Savvy suggested. "And get to sleep. We need all the rest we can get. In fact—" She rose and stretched, covering a yawn with her gloved hand. "I'll join you. Let's go see what the bed situation is here."

Lichi was large enough to have two guesthouses, so despite the influx of people from the south, north, and northwest, there was still room for them. Now that they'd reached the lake's edge, they'd be proceeding over land, so their skimmer was left in the care of the local boat-share attendant.

Lunna paused on their way out, a trace of their usual humor returning. "You know, Friend Kel," they said, "I think you just spoke more in one meal than you have in five years."

An exaggeration, certainly. Kel tried to smile. "I've reached my quota then," she said. "I'll be sure to stay quiet for the rest of the journey."

With a laugh as sudden as startled bird flight, Lunna trailed after Savvy, leaving Kel and Dare alone at the table.

Seconds stretched into minutes as they sat in silence. After her last disastrous attempt to speak to Dare, she had no desire to strain whatever fragile truce they might have reached, or renew open hostilities if he was still angry at her. They didn't need to be friendly; they only needed to trust each other enough to work together.

"Thank you for guarding Savvy," Dare said, polite but grudging.

"Thanks for your sword work," Kel replied. That praise felt too faint somehow, so she tried again. "It was prudent to bring the sniper rifle."

"Wish I'd brought more ammunition as well," he said, staring at his drink as if he could divine the future in the cup's bottom.

Silence fell again between them, filled only by the murmur of conversations and the clink of spoons on plates. A bug snuck in and made a nuisance of itself, flitting from table to table in a flurry of buzzing wings and flapping hands.

"Why don't you carry a sword?" Dare asked.

I carry it in my heart, Kel thought morosely.

"They attract too much attention," she replied.

Dare frowned. "Should I have left mine on the ship?"

Blessed stars, was she doomed to always say the wrong thing to this man? "You're not from Loth," Kel said. "Weapons like yours are considered impolite, but some allowances are made for offworlders, and you specifically have a task that may require such a sword. You're already noticeable, with or without it. You . . ." How could she explain he was handsome without the sentiment being misinterpreted? "You have a distinctive appearance," she said, realizing belatedly that was even worse.

He didn't seem offended, at least. His gloved hand went to his bandaged arm for some reason, then he lowered it to the table. "Perhaps I could cover my hair with a cloth, as you do," he mused.

"That isn't common, either," Kel said. "The hat, perhaps, would suit you. Most locals grow their hair out and braid it with colored strings, as you may have noticed. Bald people wear a kind of headpiece that shows their scalp. But offworlders are rare enough that anyone who knows of the demolisher problem will make the connection, so there's no sense in trying to hide."

"They don't seem to treat you as an oddity," Dare said.

"I'm a refugee," Kel said, picking at a loose thread on her pants. "They go out of their way to be kind to me. Hospitality is sacred here."

"But this will never be your home," Dare said softly.

Kel's hand stilled. "It's the only one I have, now," she said. "I have to protect it. I imagine you and Savvy feel the same way about your ship, or wherever you normally live when you aren't traveling."

"Just the ship. We move around often, go where we're needed." He paused, then added, "Where the money is."

Strangely, she got the feeling that last part was a lie. A partial one, at least.

"I used to love traveling," she said wistfully. "Do you enjoy it, or do it out of necessity?"

"I do enjoy it," he said, sounding almost surprised at

himself. "I didn't always. I suppose it depends on the circumstances."

"Or the companions," Kel said. "Some shipmates are more pleasant than others."

As soon as the words left her mouth, she realized they might sound suggestive. Flirtatious, even. What a fool she was, letting her mouth get away from her again. If the First could see her now, he would laugh. Too bad he was dead.

Dare's lips twitched up in a tiny smile. "Careful," he said. "You've already told Lunna you're over quota for conversation. If they see us talking for much longer, it may give them ideas."

Was he flirting back? He'd been so angry at her before, but he seemed friendlier now. Unless she was completely misreading the situation?

"I didn't mean to . . . ," Kel began, then couldn't think how to end. She simply stared at him helplessly.

Dare's cheeks darkened and his smile vanished. "Forget it," he said, directing his attention pointedly away from her.

"I'm sorry," Kel said. "I've lived alone for too long, and I don't . . . I am not as thoughtful as I once was." Not that I was ever the finest diplomat, she added to herself. She'd been a leader, a counselor to those ranked beneath her, but she'd been known as forthright; diplomacy had been left mostly to ambassadors and the First and Second. All of them dead, now.

Dare said nothing, and Kel found herself possessed of an irresistible urge to bang her head against the table. That wouldn't be dignified, though, so she rose to leave.

Dare's hand reached out, but he pulled back just as his gloved fingers brushed her arm. Kel stopped and waited, unable or unwilling to meet his eyes. When had she become so meek? A foolish question, easily answered.

"You didn't . . . I didn't . . . ," Dare began, then paused. He took a breath and expelled it in a rush before proceeding. "You've done nothing wrong. I'm the one who is sorry. About before. I am not accustomed to being the target of such niceties. Savvy tries to set people at ease with diverting chatter, not . . ." He trailed off, as if unable to find the right words.

And before Savvy? Kel wondered, but now she couldn't possibly ask.

"I was prepared to serve as Savvy's guard here, for whatever that entailed," Dare continued. "Not to suggest Savvy can't look after herself, but her skills are different from mine. Then with you and Lunna coming along, I thought I was now responsible for all of you. For protecting you three, I should say. I was . . . not pleased."

A smile touched the edge of Kel's mouth. That was an understatement.

"I know as little about you as you do about me," he said. "But you have not been the burden I thought you would be." Dare continued more quietly, his voice slightly huskier. "I have . . . enjoyed having someone to share that responsibility with again. It was unexpected. You are unexpected."

Kel's flush spread across her face and chest, hot and prickling. He was speaking of the situation in a professional capacity. Unless . . . ?

"The feeling is mutual," she said, unsure whether it truly was. But he might take that in whichever way pleased him, and Kel would . . . what? Endure, she supposed. One way or another.

She lifted her eyes to his face, and was surprised at how warm a half smile could look on someone, how eyes so green could exist. Less like the swamp or forest, and more like an ocean she'd loved on another world, in another time. Her heart wrenched at the thought that she would never see it again, and she struggled to keep the pain from showing, from sending an unspoken message she didn't intend.

"How is your arm?" she asked.

Dare's smile fell away, replaced with a faint scowl. "I can manage," he said. "I used the salve you suggested, for the toxin."

"Good," Kel said. "You may want to change the bandage again, if you haven't recently." She hadn't seen him do so, but that didn't mean he hadn't. Belatedly, she realized she must sound like a parent minding a wayward child. "Not that you don't know your own business," she added. "I'm sorry again. It's been a long day."

"It has," Dare said.

Say something, Kel thought. Do something. Fix this. There must be a way.

"Do you want to check the perimeter?" Kel asked. "Of the guesthouse, I mean. And the buildings around it, perhaps. With me." She winced inwardly at her own awkwardness and wondered if she'd gone temporarily mad. She should have just done it alone, and let him do it alone, which he had probably intended to do until she spoke. Maybe he wanted some time to himself. Maybe she needed to dunk her head in a bucket to see if she could find the sense she'd clearly lost at the bottom.

"That seems prudent," Dare said. If he noticed her inward

turmoil, he gave no sign of it. He stood and collected his plate, waiting for her to do the same.

The evening was as warm as any other, the air smelling of earth and trees and the herbs and berries growing nearby. Children played, tossing and kicking a ball, their excited yells wringing smiles and calls of encouragement from those watching. Local villagers and travelers fleeing the demolisher shared the streets, gossiping or commiserating or exchanging wordless support. There was worry, yes, but they all went about their lives as best they could, because what else could they do?

Kel wished she could have explained that better to Lunna, that one could either keep living or stop, whatever happened, and so far she'd chosen to keep living even when others didn't. Even when it was her fault they didn't.

She and Dare took it all in as they walked, drawing speculative glances wherever they went. They didn't speak further, for which Kel was immensely relieved and disappointed.

KEL TOOK FIRST WATCH AGAIN, THEN SLEPT MORE FITFULLY THAN USUAL because the room was so full of people. She'd grown accustomed to the sounds around her little house in the swamp, the night birds and bugs, the wind in the trees that sometimes sounded like rain, and the rain itself drumming against her roof. A storm that would have lulled her to sleep instead overlapped with the rustling of blankets, the creaking of bunks, and a dozen discordant breathing patterns. Everything was strange, despite the relative peace and comfort. It was as if she had found herself suddenly living someone else's life, and even though she had no understanding of who they were, she was meant to carry on as if nothing had changed. And yet, these things had once been familiar, so when she came across them it was almost more disorienting for their being found in an unfamiliar place.

Luckily for them all, Dare had no nightmares. Lunna, however, gasped themself awake more than once, and quietly sobbed back to sleep.

Morning dawned, damp and bright, the village bustling with locals off to fish the lake, or meet the farm volunteers bringing the morning deliveries, or take advantage of the influx of travelers to engage in off-season trade. Kel and the others ate a hearty breakfast—though Lunna's appetite was still slow to return—then made their way to the transport station and waited in an already lengthy line to borrow land vehicles for the next part of their journey. When they reached the front, they found their options were limited.

"It's called a what?" Savvy asked, half her face screwed up in an incredulous smile.

"A zhoomer," Lunna replied, unconsciously mirroring the expression. "It makes a noise, like, *zhoom*. But quiet?"

"It's like an EMSAT-V," Kel explained. "But the magnetic field of this planet is weaker, so it stays closer to the ground."

"What's an EMSAT-V?" Lunna asked.

"Apparently it's a zhoomer that can fly," Savvy replied. "These are single-rider, too?"

Kel nodded. "They can carry two if necessary, but it slows them down. They're not very fast to begin with."

"And you're sure they don't have something bigger?" Savvy asked. "With a roof, maybe?"

The attendant shook her head. "Loaned them all out

already. Some people went northeast instead of south, and no one's available to bring those vehicles back."

Likely no one wanted to risk the journey, either. Everyone was sheltering in place or trying to get out of the demolisher's potential future range, or the Pale base's if they believed that rumor. Kel was fairly sure she didn't.

"Fine, we'll take them," Savvy said. "Faster than walking."

The attendant left to retrieve the keystones, while Savvy plastered on a friendly expression that didn't match the tension in her posture.

Within minutes they were off, Lunna leading the way down the road to Handeen. It was divided by a grassy strip to prevent head-on collisions, with a separate footpath on each side so people could walk the distance if they chose. Lunna rode in the center of their lane, occasionally wobbling when the wind kicked up, while Savvy seemed comfortable despite her earlier complaints and lack of familiarity with the vehicle. Dare struggled with the controls at first, but soon picked them up, and Kel brought up the rear, her hat tied on more tightly to keep it from flying off.

Unlike the flatness of the Endless Swamp and Lake Ayakocha, the land north of Lichi featured gently rolling hills covered in patches of forest, many of the trees bearing thin needles instead of leaves. The tended areas near the road were lush with vines of ripening sunberries and furmelons, enough to feed any traveler who failed to carry food. Farther afield, rows and clusters of other crops grew, waiting for the first harvest season to arrive.

That this peace might be disturbed by death and destruction was unthinkable.

Kel kept her eyes on the road, and on Dare's zhoomer in front of her, but she also scanned their surroundings for any sign of trouble. Most outcasts weren't violent like the ones Hegrun had enticed into banditry, but other hazards might appear—wild animals, road-blocking accidents, fallen tree limbs or rocks. She watched the sky as well, ready to suggest they rest if the weather looked too foul to ride in.

In the back of her mind, she still wondered about the demolisher. Why was it lumbering toward the xoffedil breeding grounds? Had someone activated it on purpose, and if so, why? Would more war machines be coming?

Conversation was impossible while they traveled, which Kel decided was a mixed blessing. It was easier to keep her mouth shut, but she suspected Lunna still needed to talk through their jumble of thoughts and feelings about the bandit attack. Being a few steps away from death was a sobering experience, and people often found themselves unable to focus on what was, instead reliving the terror of what could have been.

Hindfear, the mind-healers had called it. The morass of worry and anxiety and dread about all the ways something could have gone wrong, but didn't. Better to have it after the fact than before, to let the stress of a situation rush in when there was time and space to manage it, and yet it was arguably more of a foolish waste of energy because it served no purpose. What had happened was in the past and couldn't be changed; why fret over it now?

Kel wanted to protect her friend from that, but there was only so much she could do. Lunna would have to find their own methods for coping and healing.

They had to stop twice when rain fell too thick to see the road, but otherwise the first stage of their journey passed uneventfully. An hour before sunset, they arrived at a guesthouse in the middle of nowhere, unattended but not empty. The other travelers greeted them politely, then kept to themselves, not even making the attempt to share stories or games. Only a quarter of the tables were taken, with other guests either cleaning up in the communal bathing rooms or already retired to the sleeping quarters, exhausted from their respective journeys.

The kitchen was stocked only with food that didn't require cooking, periodically replenished by the council responsible for the area. Kel helped Lunna prepare plates for them all—preserved fruits and berries with a flat salted bread that didn't spoil quickly, blocks of cheese cut and wrapped into manageable servings, and some smoked meat strips seasoned with peppery spices that made Savvy hum in appreciation.

"Better than cheap ship rations," Savvy said. She gestured at Dare with a slice of fruit. "Careful with that stuff. It's hotter than your taste buds can handle."

Dare snorted and took a bite of the meat, barely stifling a raw, choking sound, then casually wiping his eyes and nose when they started to run.

After they ate, Kel allowed herself the luxury of a warm shower instead of merely a quick scrub. A dunk in the lake wasn't as pleasant as this, and the guesthouses at Lichi had been too full for anyone to overstay their turn. Now she could indulge, let the water rinse away the day's sweat. She even washed her hair, toweling it as dry as possible before wrapping it up again, out of sight.

On the way out of the dressing room, she ran into Dare, tugging at his gloves as if he'd just put them back on. His silver hair was wet as well, tan skin flushed from the heat of his own shower. The gloves were a continuing curiosity; it wasn't her place to ask, though, so she put it out of her mind. Dare gave her head covering a glance as if he had his own questions, but he, too, kept them to himself.

Before she slept, she needed to report back to Speaker Yiulea. The communications room was tucked in the hallway that led between the common room and the sleeping quarters, surrounded by closets and soundproofed for privacy. Kel had left a message the day before, indicating that there had been trouble but they were all fine, and noting the approximate time she expected to call again. Part of her hoped she would be able to leave another message and go to bed, but as one of her comrades had once said, her luck only expended itself on large favors, leaving her to suffer the smaller inconveniences on her own. An enviable problem in its way.

Kel waited awkwardly in the hall as people passed her. She rehearsed what she needed to say in her mind, so she could leave a more detailed message this time, if nothing else. When her turn came, she shut herself in the room and told herself to relax, that this was no different from any other debrief. She scanned the code Yiulea had given her and waited, the eerie whistle of the connection pitched just high enough to make her ears ring.

An instant before the message recorder would have taken over, Speaker Yiulea's face appeared. She smiled at Kel, but her eyes held no friendliness or amusement, the wrinkles around them and the bags beneath them suggesting fatigue and ill temper.

"Friend Garda," Speaker Yiulea said politely. "I received your message and am eager for a fuller accounting."

Kel explained as much as she dared about the theft of the skimmer and the subsequent infiltration and escape, but she hesitated to disclose Dare's possession of the Order bracer. He didn't fight like an Order member, but she couldn't be certain of his history without asking. As long as she wasn't sure, she could honestly claim she didn't know, which protected both of them. So she gave details about the bandit identities, the base location, the estimated number of casualties, and so on—all true facts and reasonable speculation, hopefully enough to satisfy the shrewd woman so she didn't ask more probing questions.

When Speaker Yiulea didn't immediately respond to Kel's report, Kel took the opportunity to pose her own questions. "What crime did Hegrun commit, if I may know?"

The Speaker frowned. "He and his crew became violently inebriated at a guesthouse and attacked others. We stopped them and intended to ask them to leave the planet after paying restitution. They ran, so we impounded their starship. Then they attacked the spaceport, and we apprehended two of them while the others once again escaped. The ones we caught were sent off-world later, with some merchants who agreed to take them." Her frown turned to a smug grin. "We still have their ship. The statute of limitations for privateers to reclaim abandoned vessels will soon be over."

Kel closed her eyes and shook her head. Incredible. And

he thought he was the injured party in that situation, to the point that banditry was a reasonable recourse.

"Has the trajectory of the demolisher changed?" she asked. "Has it sped up or slowed down, or attacked anything along the way?"

"It has not," Speaker Yiulea replied. "Stay your own course and continue to Handeen."

"Understood. We should be there by tomorrow evening."

"Spirits willing," Speaker Yiulea said.

"Spirits willing," Kel repeated, a sudden shiver making the hairs on her arms rise.

"The captain and her guard have not behaved suspiciously?" Speaker Yiulea asked.

Kel shook her head. "They could have given up when the skimmer was stolen, or demanded aid from the local Speakers, but they didn't. They have conducted themselves professionally and seem committed to the mission." They killed for Loth, Kel thought, and that was no small thing.

Speaker Yiulea twined her fingers together and pressed them against her mouth for a moment, then tucked them under her chin. "The Prixori Anocracy still refuse to send help. We will not stop asking, but it appears the offworlders were correct: we cannot rely on their aid arriving in time."

Kel swallowed the frustration and dismay that surged through her. How had she ever trusted the Pale, after everything they'd done to her and her people? She was a fool. But now wasn't the time to relive old arguments, open old wounds. Enough scars had already split with the arrival of the demolisher, and Dare's bracer.

"We will succeed," Kel said. I swear on my life, she added internally. Lothians didn't take kindly to oaths.

"May it be so," Speaker Yiulea said. "Rest well, Friend Garda, and give my regards to the others." With a twinkle of mischief in her first real smile, she added, "Tell Lunna to call their family."

Kel smiled back, despite herself. "I will. Rest well, Speaker Yiulea." She ended the call, leaning back in her chair and rubbing her hands over her face.

When she left the room, Kel found Dare outside, leaning against the wall. His crossed arms suggested a feigned ease that his neutral expression did little to soften.

"What did you tell her?" Dare asked.

Kel knew what he meant. "Only what she needed to know."

"And did she need to know about . . . our tactics?" he asked.

"No," Kel said. "She did not."

Their gazes locked for several long moments, until a pair of giggling teens appeared and stepped between them. "Get some privacy," one said as they passed, and the other covered their mouth with a hand and erupted into titters.

Kel's cheeks flamed and she stared down at her boots. Dare said nothing, merely turned and headed toward the sleeping quarters, his footsteps surprisingly quiet on the wooden floors. At the last moment, Kel looked up, admiring his backside as he walked away. He glanced over his shoulder and she dropped her gaze again, hoping he hadn't realized what she was doing. She also hoped she imagined the huff of a laugh that escaped him as he disappeared into the other room.

## CHAPTER ELEVEN

Rolling hills became foothills as they traveled toward the Cloudrise Mountains, the sun-dappled road soon bordered by rows of trees. On their left, the ground rose, while on the right it fell; ahead of them their path wound and curved for reasons known only to whoever had meticulously sculpted it out of the terrain in the first place. The underbrush grew unfettered, less carefully tended, more drying straw and thorny bushes and saplings trying to earn a place for themselves in the reddish soil. Flowers found space, too, bright bursts of pink and red and yellow clustered in small clearings like carelessly strewn garments. Every so often, a glimpse of a side road would come and go, little more than a sudden break in the trees, leading off to isolated homesteads or villages too small to support a guesthouse. Eventually, Kel knew, they would reach a place with steeper terrain, with canyons and cliffs overlooking the Braided River. Then, finally, they'd come to Handeen, clustered around Lake Deecolea near the large waterfall they called Lakefall Point, and from there they'd continue on foot to the Gounaj Gulch.

But for now, they rode, the wind of their passing loud in Kel's ears, sometimes punctuated by the raucous calls of birds or the crash of a larger creature through the woods. The zhoomers were faster than walking, but not as fast as skimmers on open water. Occasionally other craft approached from the opposite direction, and they had to slow down further and move to the side to make room. They also had to pause once when a lumbering creature blocked the road, waiting until it moved along peacefully rather than charging at them. By the time they stopped for lunch at a rest spot, claiming one of the bare wood tables for themselves, Savvy had worked herself into a lather, sweat beading on her dark skin and her veneer of friendliness stripped to raw wood.

"We could have been to Handeen in a blink if it had a spaceport," Savvy grumbled, wiping her forehead on her sleeve as she sat on a stone bench next to Lunna. "Or if I could just land in an open space nearby. Even one of your flitters would have been a hundred times faster."

"We've never needed another spaceport," Lunna mused between bites of a tart fruit. "Best to keep the offworlders in one spot."

"What, you don't want anyone to experience the unique pleasures of your scenic vistas and aggressive insects?" Savvy swatted at a large fly buzzing around her.

Lunna shook their head. "If they want to travel, that's fine, so long as they don't make a mess. Ships are noisy and smelly and they upset the animals. The planet has a right to peace."

Kel didn't want to admit how much of Savvy's annoyance

she shared—not because of the heat or the wildlife, but the slowness. She'd dealt with tedious assignments before, ones where others in her company resorted to pinching themselves to keep alert and she had to increase rotations to stave off boredom. This, at least, had the benefit of a better view and less chance of being shot. Well, aside from the bandits.

"If we had more spaceports," Lunna said, "maybe the Pale wouldn't have left."

"You're fortunate they did," Dare muttered.

Lunna stopped chewing. "Why?" they asked, their mouth half full. "I don't disagree, but I think your reasons are not the same as mine."

"They have yet to meet the planet they couldn't exploit," Dare said. "They may still send someone here eventually to suck every bit of meat and marrow from your bones, then burn what remains so no one else can have it."

"No," Lunna said, eyes wide. "I can't believe they'd be that awful. They do good, too, don't they? Bringing in new trade, expanding opportunities—"

"—to places that don't want it," Savvy interjected. "You just finished saying you didn't want more offworlders here, didn't you?"

Lunna flushed, their freckles seeming to darken. "Well, I won't be here much longer, anyway. I might sign on to one of their cargo ships for a season or two when I go to Uchoren Station."

"Don't," Dare said, glaring at Lunna. "They're cold, calculating monsters who care for nothing but themselves. Look at the war machine they left behind, the very one we have to save your planet from, because they can't be bothered to exert the slightest effort for anyone who can do nothing for them in return." He stood and pointed at them, his gloved hand trembling slightly. "It's because of fools like you that they keep spreading, gaining more territory. By the time you realize you've let a monster into your home, they've already destroyed it and left you starving in the street."

Lunna flinched. Kel got to her feet, slowly so as not to provoke a startled reaction from the enraged man.

Savvy signed something at him with a frown. Dare made an exasperated noise and stormed off, past the washroom and into the trees.

Lunna covered their mouth with a hand. "I didn't mean to upset him," they said. "What did I say? I don't want to say it again, whatever it was."

Savvy continued to scowl at Dare's retreating form as she put an arm around Lunna.

"His secrets aren't mine to tell," Savvy said quietly. "But he isn't fond of hearing people speak well of the Pale." Then, more loudly, she added, "Since we have a few minutes, let me teach you another game. This one uses the Nova Cubes, but the rules are a little different . . ."

Kel considered whether to wait on Dare or follow him. Odds were he was the most dangerous thing in this forest, so concern for his safety was a minor factor. More pressing was their time constraint; they had only a few days remaining to reach the demolisher and disable it before the risk to Handeen and the xoffedil breeding grounds became exponentially greater. They needed to leave soon.

With a sigh, she stepped away from the table and went after him.

The trees here alternated between needles and three-pointed leaves, slim-trunked with corrugated bark, grooves filled by swaths of dark green moss. Smaller plants sprouted in patches from the red-brown soil, and mushrooms jutted out from rotting logs like steps for some tiny creature to reach the moldering summits. Gnarled roots made the ground more uneven than Kel expected, so she stepped carefully as she followed the sound of Dare's motion. That he wasn't bothering to move silently boded ill.

The noise stopped, quiet descending on the area as any remaining wildlife waited before resuming their own chirps and whistles and hums. Kel spotted a sunberry bush and paused to pick a few of its offerings, inspecting them for ripeness and pests before proceeding.

Dare sat on a mold-streaked stone in a small clearing filled with other rocks, likely tumbled there by some long-ago storm and mudslide. He leaned forward, elbows resting on his knees, palms pressing into his eyes as his gloved fingers spread through his silvery hair.

Kel selected another place to sit across from him, several paces between them so her presence would hopefully be less intrusive. She mimicked his hunched posture, cupping the berries in her hands, and began to count down from five hundred. It might not be enough time for him to calm completely, but hopefully it would be sufficient for her to convince him they needed to move on. He could brood on the road, and perhaps the motion and landscape and attention to a task would help him recover further.

She had reached two hundred and twelve when Dare broke the silence.

"I should not have lashed out," he grumbled. "I will apologize."

Kel hummed softly to acknowledge she'd heard. The golden flesh of the berries seemed to glow from within, though she knew it was only a trick of the light.

"Savvy is used to my moods," he continued. "Lunna could not have known—" He inhaled sharply. "As I said, I will apologize."

"I expect Lunna is more worried about you than hurt," Kel said. "They can be a little sheltered, naive, but they're kind and wish you no ill. Even so, you're not obligated to correct their ignorance, and your feelings are not unwarranted."

Dare put his hands down and stared at a small ring of bright red mushrooms. Kel began to count down again.

"You said you live alone," Dare said. "Is that by preference?"

Kel knew she should lie, and yet.

"No," she said. "But I'm . . . it's fine." But that wasn't true, either. It wasn't fine. It hadn't been fine for years, and the realization was a knife between her ribs. She looked up at Dare, who watched her with an expression she couldn't read.

"Is Savvy a pleasant captain?" Kel asked, desperate to shift the topic away from herself.

"Frustrating sometimes," Dare said ruefully, lips pursed. "But she has a keen mind. Too keen, according to some who've been cut by it."

"I admire that the two of you came all this way to help strangers," Kel said. "That you're doing something good, because you can."

"It's so little compared to the many who suffer in this

galaxy," Dare said. "The Defiants are making real progress. Back-channel relief missions, subtle economic manipulations. They managed to shut down an entire missile project just by increasing inspection times of outgoing cargo ships on a single occupied world." He smiled with his mouth closed, but his admiration shone through his eyes. "Even in areas where it seems hopeless, they're still trying."

And Kel, meanwhile, was doing nothing. Had done nothing for years. She'd chosen to hide instead, to make a new life on a planet far from her home, far from the war that had claimed her people and destroyed everything she loved. She had good reason, she told herself; thanks to the Treaty of Amorleth, the Order of Mercy could keep doing their humanitarian work if she and the rest of her comrades were gone. Her only option had been to run, to hide.

Hadn't it?

She could have done what Savvy and Dare were doing. Traveled the galaxy, righting wrongs, cleaning up messes left by those who refused to take responsibility. Helping others instead of merely surviving. She'd retreated so far into herself out of fear of being exposed that she'd denied herself the one thing she'd always wanted to do, the reason she'd left her own family in the first place.

No wonder she rose in the morning out of habit more than desire. Still, it was her responsibility to find things worth living for, rather than wallowing in self-imposed misery. The alternative was slow death by stagnation. If only it were as simple to do as it was to say.

"You seem an admirable person," Dare said suddenly, drawing her out of her thoughts. "If you ever found yourself with an urge to leave Loth, I suspect Savvy would be pleased to have you aboard."

Kel's breath caught in her throat. "Thank you for the offer," she said. "I will consider it."

You can't have me on board, she thought morosely. I'm too much of a danger to you. Anything I do, I must do alone.

Then again, Dare already had a bracer from the Order of Sotera. Savvy had explained it away as something he bought, or found—what had she said? Kel couldn't remember. Could she pretend she'd bought hers at some black-market trader? Likely not. That she had two bracers and a sword would be impossible to explain. Especially since she was hiding on Loth, so far from Amorleth and Lovalra.

Before she could begin counting again, Dare stiffened and swore under his breath.

"We need to go back," he said.

Kel nodded and followed him toward the rest spot. As they moved, she scanned the area around them, noticing nothing strange or dangerous. Dare kept glancing to the right, down the incline that eventually led to a tributary of the Braided River, but Kel couldn't see whatever he was looking at. That he could detect something she couldn't was unsettling enough that her jaw began to twitch from strain.

They returned to find Lunna and Savvy engaged in whatever game they'd begun when Kel left. Savvy saw Dare's expression and immediately swiped the cubes and stuffed them back into a pocket.

"What happened?" Savvy asked.

"There's a grimstalker patrolling nearby," Dare said.

Kel's blood turned to ice. First a demolisher, now a grimstalker? Surely this couldn't be a coincidence. Someone must be intentionally activating them, if only to set them to patrol. It couldn't be related to her, though; the Pale would send a Dirge if they knew she was here, wouldn't they? Unless this was a Dirge's plan to lure her out of hiding? No, too convoluted.

And how did Dare know the grimstalker was there? The bracer, perhaps. She yearned to activate hers, but if she did, and his was also active, he would know.

"What's a grimstalker?" Lunna asked, looking back and forth between Savvy and Dare.

"It's another Pale war machine," Savvy said. "Smaller than a demolisher. Four legs with wicked sharp claws, extremely fast. Their heads have a really painful clamping restraint with needle teeth, and a plasma weapon instead of a gullet."

That she mentioned how much the restraint hurt suggested Savvy had experienced it firsthand. Kel hadn't, but she knew people who had. She'd fought grimstalkers before, though, and they were quick and ferocious, able to tear through many types of armor with little resistance—certainly mere human flesh was fragile as a dry leaf in the face of their attacks.

"We can't simply leave it," Dare said. "Its destructive capabilities are more limited than a demolisher's, but otherwise the same logic applies."

"It could start killing people?" Lunna asked, their eyes wide with horror.

"Assuming it hasn't already," Savvy murmured. She looked toward the zhoomers, then back at Dare. "This isn't our job," she said quietly. "We have to stick to the plan."

Dare scowled. "By the time we return to this area, the forest could be littered with corpses."

"It could—" Kel stopped, altering her phrasing to hide how much she knew of grimstalkers. "If a caravan of villagers came this way, could the machine follow them to Lichi?"

"Without a doubt," Savvy said. "Or if anyone comes behind us heading for Handeen, it might trail after them."

"And your control chip doesn't work on them?" Kel asked.

"No," Dare said grimly. "It only works on demolishers. If we don't stop this grimstalker now, mark my words, someone will die."

He was right. But if something happened to Savvy now, if the control chip were damaged or couldn't be activated because she was killed, many more people would lose their lives or livelihoods. The planet was already being harmed, and Lothian law protected the rights of the planet as much as its people. There was only one solution that accomplished the most possible good.

"I'll do it," Kel said. "I'll take care of the grimstalker."

Lunna gasped. Savvy burst into laughter, but it was incredulous, almost shuddering, like the sound was escaping her against her will.

"Absolutely not," Dare growled. "If you think you can fight a Pale war machine with a machete and a staff—"

"I won't fight it," Kel said. "I'll lead it away while you get to Handeen and warn them."

"Lead it away?" Savvy asked, erupting into another fit of giggles. "You'll what, let it chase you for days while you hide in the trees?"

"They can climb trees," Dare said darkly.

Kel knew that, too, but she kept hoping they would cease their objections. She couldn't very well tell them she knew she could defeat it if no one was around to watch her.

"Can it survive a long fall?" Kel asked, curbing her rising exasperation.

"You're thinking to push it off a cliff?" Savvy asked, her lip curled up in an unbecoming sneer. Dare, however, narrowed his eyes in thought.

"Lure it, yes," Kel said. "If I can get it to chase me on a zhoomer, then pull up short—"

"Ride a zhoomer through the trees?" Lunna exclaimed. "You'll crash!"

Kel had plenty of experience threading obstacles at much higher speeds, but she couldn't say as much, so she shrugged.

"It could work," Dare said. "But it's incredibly dangerous. I should go with you."

"No," Kel and Savvy said in unison. Savvy gestured for Kel to speak, bowing sarcastically.

"You need to protect them," Kel said. "Savvy has to get to the demolisher with the chip. I may catch up with you quickly, or it may take some time. Perhaps the whole business will be finished by then." She didn't say she might not make it at all; anything was possible when fighting a grimstalker, but as long as no one saw her use her armor and shield, she should be fine.

How quickly you succumb to its lure now, she thought. You were prepared to die before letting the bandits see who you are, but a single grimstalker appears and you've all but leaped into the fray without hesitation.

This was different, she told herself. The grimstalker was

a threat to any innocents nearby, not just their group. She would be in the middle of the forest, with no homes or people in the immediate area—unless some wayward refugee or resident happened to wander by. She was the only one who could defeat a grimstalker—besides Dare, potentially, if she was right about the alloy of his sword. And if Kel really was able to stay ahead of the machine and lure it to a cliff's edge, she might not need her armor at all.

If the worst happened, she could always try to summon her soulsword. She hoped it wouldn't come to that, because she wasn't entirely certain she still could.

"How far is it?" Savvy asked Dare.

"A mark and a half that way," Dare said, pointing into the forest to the north. "Moving south. It may have been dormant in the area, or it may have come from the same place as the demolisher."

The road twined through the mountains to the northwest, so while it would briefly take them closer to the machine, they would ultimately be heading in the opposite direction. And if Kel lured it to the east, where she was most likely to reach a cliff, that would put even more distance between them.

"Come on, then," Savvy said. "Let's put this plan into action." Her blank smile said she didn't expect Kel would survive, but was willing to accept the sacrifice. Practical, if cold.

They mounted up and rode out, the zhoomers quickly reaching the point where Kel would diverge. Dare pointed her in the right direction, his handsome features twisted into a scowl that made him more fearsome than usual.

"I should go with you," he insisted again.

"I'll be fine," Kel said. "Trust me."

"Kel can handle herself, don't worry," Lunna said, then paused. "Well, I suppose we'll all worry, but that can't be helped. It's a worrisome thing, this machine, isn't it?"

A faint smile touched Kel's lips at her friend's faith. "Be good, Lunna," she said. "Keep to the path, and don't let Savvy run you off."

"Perish the thought," Savvy muttered. "Enough dawdling. I hate goodbyes." She eased back onto the road and sped away, Lunna squawking indignantly before chasing after her.

Dare's expression darkened further, but he left Kel there, not even glancing back as she peered into the forest with the early afternoon sun beginning its descent.

Off the road, Kel drove more slowly, slipping between trees and around rocks, the zhoomer sometimes lurching or bouncing when it passed over a jutting root or stones. She didn't attempt stealth; the whole purpose was to entice the grimstalker to chase her. The deeper she went, the more the underbrush thinned out, leaving the ground clear except for fallen leaves and branches and logs.

About half a mark in, she stopped and listened. This should have been far enough. And yet she hadn't found the machine, hadn't detected even a hint of its passing, or glimpsed it moving about. Surely it wouldn't be difficult to spot, since it was nearly twice her height from end to end. Had Dare miscalculated when he sent her this way? Was it already south of her?

Kel pursed her lips. She'd have to use her bracer after

all, to find it before it found someone else. The problem was, if Dare was still using his bracer when she activated hers, he would receive an alert and an automatic homing beacon would tell him her precise location.

That thought gave her pause; if she hadn't already known Dare wasn't part of the Order, this all but confirmed it. Using the bracer to track the grimstalker would let anyone else potentially home in on his location, including any other Order members—and, more importantly, Dirges. That he'd immediately felt it come into range meant he had it continuously scanning the area, which meant it was always on. Spirits, she needed to tell him to turn it off before someone came after him, but how to do that without explaining how she knew what she knew?

The cracking of twigs jerked her attention to her left. A glossy white form stalked between the trees like a vengeful spirit, striped by alternating sun and shade. It vaguely resembled an enormous cat, though it moved less quietly or fluidly, its four legs designed with joints in different locations and its head smaller and eerily round. Instead of eyes, it had a horizontal sensor strip that went all the way around, tiny lights inside blinking on and off quickly, hypnotically. The lights coalesced into a solid red bar in the front, and its maw opened to reveal multiple rows of tiny pin-like teeth.

"Where we go, may peace follow," Kel murmured. With an eerie shriek, the grimstalker charged.

Kel revved her zhoomer and sped away as fast as she dared. She'd examined the map of the area earlier, so she thought she was about a mark from the cliffs above the river. A crash behind her signaled that the grimstalker had taken down a tree, which she hoped would slow it enough to give her a lead.

If she looked back, she might end up in a tree herself, so she concentrated on driving. She weaved back and forth, ducking under low branches and around boulders. A rhythmic thumping followed her, the rapid tattoo of the grimstalker's steps nearly as fast as the beat of her own heart.

A faint breeze blew in from the east, warm but carrying a hint of moisture. She must be nearing the cliffs. The shrubs and other low plants would thicken again soon if she were right. Sure enough, more of the trees' trunks were swathed in leafy vines, and banks of purple flowers with long stalks gathered around the roots. Kel wasn't sure whether the trees went all the way to the edge where the land dropped off, but she couldn't afford to slow down.

The grimstalker shrieked again. A bolt of plasma blew apart a trunk so close to Kel that she threw up an arm to protect her eyes. The splinters tore into her shirt and exposed skin, stinging viciously. Another bolt toppled a huge tree, which fell in front of her with eerie slowness. She ducked beneath it just in time to feel the shock of air on her back as it landed.

She should activate her armor. One unlucky plasma shot would mean the end of her, and the machine was still in pursuit. Dare would be alerted to her presence if his bracer was still tracking the grimstalker, but maybe he wouldn't know what it meant. Maybe he wouldn't assume it was her. Maybe she could even pretend she'd seen someone else out here, and that person had taken care of the grimstalker while she watched from safety.

Kel snorted ruefully. She was a terrible liar.

A flash of motion on her left caught her eye. Kel struggled to keep navigating as she glanced to the side. Had the grimstalker flanked her? No, this was more shadow than light, dark against the bright green of the leaves.

Blessed stars, it was Dare. He'd come after her. Why?

She couldn't even yell to stop him; if he slowed down, the grimstalker would go after him instead. If he veered away, he might lead it back to the road. The only option was to let him drive toward the cliff, too, and hope they both survived this. Hope he wouldn't try to fight a razor-clawed, plasma-spewing war machine twice his size with only a shield for defense.

Hope he wouldn't see her activate her armor if she had to.

The grimstalker gained ground, its footfalls closer. But now it was no longer behind Kel; it had shifted to her left, running between her and Dare. Its programming would force it to track both targets simultaneously until the weaker one took precedence. Perhaps that would help them more easily send it over the cliff? Keep it undecided until the last moment, and it might have trouble slowing down or changing direction.

This could still work. She couldn't communicate any of this to Dare, so she stuck to the original plan. Kel controlled her breathing and sharpened her focus until only zhoomers and trees and the grimstalker existed.

Ahead of her, the light brightened as if a cloud moved away to reveal the sun. The tree line broke, and she brought her zhoomer to a skidding halt, close enough to the cliff's edge that soil and rock flew from her boot out into the open air. She leaped free of her vehicle, perched a step from oblivion, shifting into a defensive stance as she waited to see what the grimstalker would do. Ready to armor herself if needed.

Dare did the same, but one of his boots and part of the zhoomer went too far. Kel's breath caught as he used his other foot to push himself back toward the trees, pieces of the cliffside crumbling beneath his weight.

And then the grimstalker charged out with a shriek, barreling into Dare and sending them both over the edge.

# CHAPTER TWELVE

**K**el barely had time to register their position and trajectory—Dare's limp form, the grimstalker tangled around the zhoomer—before she dove after them. Years of training made her actions reflexive, instinctual. Hands stretched over her head, feet together, her body's profile narrowed to give her speed.

In a blink she reached Dare, wrapped her arms around him, gripped her wrist with her other hand as tightly as she could despite the sheath of his sword rubbing against her. The ground rushed toward them, hard and sharp, all jagged rocks from old landslides. The river was too far away for them to have any hope of reaching it.

Kel summoned her wings.

They unfurled at the speed of thought. Even so, she couldn't slow enough to land properly so close to the ground. Instead, she guided herself and Dare to the river. They plunged into the swirling water, and she had to deactivate the wings or risk being unable to swim. Their immediate loss, so soon after being used again, was almost a worse shock than the impact, the cold water, the breath driven from her lungs as she fought to kick herself and Dare to the surface.

How far the current carried them, and how Kel managed to drag them both ashore, she hardly knew. Dare was heavy and unwieldy, his sword awkward to maneuver around, and she had no idea whether he was unconscious or dead. An eternity after hitting the water, she gasped on the shore, cold and trembling with fatigue. She yearned to lie on her back and rest, let the sun dry her clothes and skin and drive the chill from her bones, but she had to check on Dare. She crawled to his side, wincing at a scratch on his forehead that bled down his face.

Dare wasn't breathing.

Kel dredged long-ago lessons about resuscitation from the depths of her memory. First, press on his chest to restart his heart. If he didn't breathe on his own, do it for him. He was soaking wet, so using her bracers to shock him might do more harm than good. She'd leave that as a last resort if nothing else worked. Finding the center of his chest, she placed the palms of her hands on his breastbone, one atop the other, and began to push down.

*Hard, but not so hard,* the quiet voice of the Order teacher said. *You're stronger than you look, aren't you? Don't worry, it's rare to break a rib doing this. A cracked rib is easier to fix than death. Count in your head, feel the rhythm. Fast and steady. Focus on the process, not the outcome.*

She tilted his head back, chin up, and opened his mouth.

Pinching his nose closed, she took a deep breath and sealed her lips around his, exhaling all her air. Another breath, another long exhale, then she started to push again.

Dare lurched and sputtered, water spilling down the side of his face and neck. Kel turned him sideways and he coughed, choked, vomited river and lunch on the muddy ground. Then he curled into a fetal position as he fought to regain control of his breathing. Kel sat on her heels with her knees tucked under her, watching, waiting. She could afford to be patient now, even if her own heart still beat like a wild bird trapped in a box.

Finally, his breath came steadily, though he was still unconscious. His tan skin had paled, lips tinged purple rather than blue, which suggested he hadn't been without air for long. Kel considered rolling him onto his back again, but his sword pressing against his shoulder blade and hip wouldn't be comfortable. At least he hadn't lost it in the water.

He could still die, she thought, then pushed that thought away. It helped neither of them.

Kel crouched next to him and grabbed the sword, struggling with the manual release mechanism, her fingers clumsy from the loss of adrenaline. Finally she removed it and set it aside, but not too far away, in case the grimstalker had survived. She repositioned Dare, who remained unresponsive, his chest rising and falling heavily.

Now was as fine a moment as any to see to her own injuries; she could check him more thoroughly for wounds after she ensured she wouldn't succumb and leave them both helpless. Kel started at her head and worked her way down to her feet, shifting or removing her clothes and boots to ensure no hidden cuts and scrapes might bleed her to oblivion. She was lucky; all she found were a few bruises that would no doubt ache later, and an unpleasant stretch of raw, weeping skin down the side of her leg and arm where she'd slid with her zhoomer. Her dunk in the water had more or less washed it all clean. Her shirt and pants had holes that would require patching, especially where her bracer was visible through the torn material.

She returned her attention to Dare. His forehead had stopped bleeding, so it probably didn't need stitching, which was good as her sewing kit was in her pack at the top of the cliff. She peeled back his eyelids to check for the expected concussion. The whites of his eyes were bloodshot, but the irises glowed, an unnatural bright emerald color. Kel furrowed her brow, wondering.

His clothes would need to come off. But he'd been so adamant about not being seen, right down to the gloves, that it felt like a violation of his privacy. Nothing seemed torn, which suggested only bruising was likely, but broken bones were also possible. As gently as she could, she ran her fingers over his neck, his collarbone, down each arm. Firm muscles. No apparent fractures, but that could be hard to tell by touch alone. Chest and stomach also seemed fine. A slow flush crept up her neck as she contemplated his legs and told herself she was a professional and he was an injured comrade. She swallowed heavily and continued, finding nothing.

No more delays. With a silent apology, Kel grabbed a handful of Dare's shirt where it was tucked into his pants and gingerly pulled it up. Two rows of abdominal muscles flexed as he breathed. Kel started to berate herself for acting like a fresh recruit who'd never seen an attractive human body before, when something else caught her eye. Not a bruise, or a wound.

On either side of Dare's stomach were white vertical lines, like old scars. Except they weren't. Kel knew precisely what they were, and with a stifled gasp she dropped his shirt and scrambled backward. No, it couldn't be.

She moved toward him again, gently easing off one of his gloves for confirmation. More white lines, traveling down the backs of each finger, up his hand and disappearing into his sleeve. They would go all the way up his arm, she knew, across his collarbone and chest. Down each leg as well, tracing paths of blood and bone.

Dare was one of the Pale.

Kel's breathing quickened as she fought panic. How had he found her? Had they always known she was here? Were they simply biding their time before they sent a Dirge after her? Was Dare a Dirge? It would explain why he had a bracer . . .

No. It didn't make sense. With an effort, Kel wrestled her shrieking thoughts into a semblance of order.

Savvy was a good liar, so it wasn't unreasonable to suspect their whole mission was a charade, that she had pretended to be critical of the Pale every time they'd come up. Who better to activate a demolisher than the people who regularly used them? Kel didn't think so, though. Dare's animosity toward them felt real and deep, not feigned. Thus far, the two of them had proven their good intentions repeatedly. It seemed more likely that Dare was a deserter, someone who had joined with

Savvy after he left the Pale. It was entirely possible he had been on the run from them ever since. Like her.

But then, perhaps that was simply what Kel wanted to believe.

No. If he were a Dirge, he could have let the grimstalker take her. Or had he followed to ensure it had? Again, no. If that had been his goal, he would have trailed behind them instead of racing to the front. He could sense the creature, after all. Not because of the bracer, she now realized, but through his own Pale tech, embedded in skin and muscle and skeleton. As far as he knew, she was facing a deadly machine with only her wits and a machete or staff, and she could have fallen off the cliff or been mauled or disintegrated by a plasma shot. When Dare could have left Kel to what he believed were impossible odds, he'd risked himself to save her life. He cared whether she lived or died. That had to mean something.

But it wasn't enough to make her trust him with her own past. Revealing one secret led to another, and if she wasn't careful, her entire life would be dashed to pieces on the rocks. And worse, the Order of Mercy would be in jeopardy. They were only permitted to continue to run hospitals and rescue missions so long as the martial Orders were dissolved. If the Pale got word that someone from the Order of Lovalra had destroyed a grimstalker, they might decide the treaty was no longer valid, regardless of the circumstances.

Blessed stars, what was she going to do?

Dare groaned, writhing as if awakening from a nightmare. He opened his glowing eyes, then closed them, then opened them again. They were back to normal, except for the redness staining the green a muddy brown around the edges.

Kel searched for something to say, words rising in her throat like acid. Would it be best to pretend she knew nothing, to stay quiet about his past? To warn him right away that she had seen the markings? She swallowed, and when she spoke, her voice was hoarse.

"As you may have surmised," Kel said, "you aren't dead." She paused, then added, "Yet."

Dare tilted his head to stare at her, brow furrowed. Then, for some odd reason, he began to laugh. It sounded rusty, grudging, as if he hadn't expected it and was only half willing to find humor in the situation.

"I hope that wasn't a threat," Dare said.

"More an acknowledgment that the day is young," Kel said. "I would hardly pull you from a river only to kill you." To her surprise, the thought hadn't crossed her mind. If anything, she'd planned to run.

*You care too much, Third; it will kill you someday.* The ambassador who had told her that was dead, though he might still be proven right.

"I suppose I am fortunate." Dare closed his eyes again, inhaling deeply and wincing in pain.

"Where are you injured?" Kel asked. "Your head, I assume?"

"Splitting in half," he replied. "But I heal quickly." He tested other parts as she watched, occasionally gritting his teeth.

"Shoulder, forearm, and calf?" Kel asked.

Dare nodded. "I expect there are bruises I'll find later,

but my bones and joints seem to be fine." He let out another harsh laugh. "And to think, I believed I was hurrying to your rescue."

Kel swallowed an angry retort. There was no changing the past. Berating him for doing what he thought was a good deed would help neither of them.

"I thank you for the consideration that motivated your actions," Kel said carefully.

Dare hissed out a breath between his teeth. "Are you naturally capable of delivering such stinging backhands or have you practiced?"

"I was trying to honor your intentions," Kel said, clenching her hands into fists atop her thighs. "Even if the outcome was not ideal. I am often . . . I have been misunderstood many times. Sarcasm doesn't come naturally to me."

"My apologies, then," Dare said. "Savvy wields words like a sharp knife, and before her . . ."

"Shouting, punctuated with occasional beatings, physical punishment, or unpleasant chores?" Kel asked.

Dare inclined his head in agreement.

Kel had heard of such things from recruits who joined the Order after being trained in other places. Some of them returned to those ways, deciding they were preferable to the more meditative tendencies of her people. She bore them no ill will, though they didn't always return that sentiment. Part of her hoped they took some peace with them when they left, but she had found that many such people carried too much lust for violence in their hearts to be satisfied with anything less than communal cruelty and pain.

The Order typically weeded out that tendency quickly.

The desire to hurt others was a weakness, not a strength. The Pale believed the opposite, however. Spirits, how could Dare be one of them?

"What happened to the grimstalker?" Dare asked.

"Crushed on the rocks, I hope," Kel replied. "If not, perhaps you'll get your chance to rescue me after all."

"I find that unlikely," Dare said. He rolled onto his side to face her and used his bent arm as a pillow. "How many grimstalkers did you say you've destroyed?"

Kel thought about it. "I didn't," she said finally.

"Didn't destroy any?"

"Didn't say."

Dare smirked. "You're right, you didn't. If you had, perhaps I wouldn't have come rushing to save you. I'll wager it's more than . . ."

For a moment, Kel wasn't sure why he'd trailed off. Then she realized he was staring at her head. Was she bleeding? No, she'd already checked, even run her fingers through her . . . Oh stars. Her hair covering was gone. She must have lost it in the river.

Her hair was long enough to touch her ears; she kept it short, more for ease of dealing with it than aesthetic preferences. Despite the march of time, it was still black, not graying yet. But spreading back from her forehead, above her right eyebrow, a streak of purple two fingers wide marked her as a Knight-Celestial of the Order of Lovalra. It couldn't be dyed, could only be hidden by wigs or mods that were impractical on Loth and vulnerable to detection by Pale tech. She'd tried shaving it off once, but her scalp was purple in the place where it grew, and it always came back the same.

Just as his markings had told her what he was, her hair had revealed her. How had she been so careless?

At least now we're even, she thought bitterly.

Kel didn't move, didn't blink, simply met his gaze directly. "Your sword is in arm's reach," she said.

"Is that a threat?" Dare asked, his eyes flickering. His expression had gone slack again. Cold.

"Your arm's reach," Kel said. "Not mine."

The gurgling rush of the water kept the silence from being complete, but it was still uncomfortable. Tense. Kel wished idly that she could reverse time, but like the river, it only moved in one direction.

"How long have you known about me?" Dare asked.

"Since just before you awoke," Kel replied. "I saw your stomach and hands."

"Are you armed?"

"I will not fight you."

Dare snorted. "So yes." He glanced at the cliff, then the river, his lips shrinking to a thin line. "The river is a long way from the cliff. I couldn't have made it to the water alone."

"No."

Kel could almost see Dare going through the same mental calculus she had, when she realized he was one of the Pale. His people had destroyed hers. They were the reason she was hiding on a planet far from her former home, why she'd spent the last five years pretending to be someone else. Did she bear a grudge? Would she take it out on him?

"I am no longer one of them," Dare said, pushing himself to a sitting position. "You must believe that."

She wanted to. She had to, or she didn't know what she

would do. She wanted to go back to fulfilling their mission, not sit by the side of a river, wet and worried and sick with old sorrows.

"They took my life, too," Dare said. "My family, my home—"

"Don't," Kel said. Her voice trembled, and Dare winced as if embarrassed.

"You were a Sword?" he asked.

Kel answered with a tight nod.

"Would it be intrusive to ask your rank?"

She'd been Third, at the start of the war. She'd watched the Second Sword of Lovalra die with her own eyes, and the First was killed when the Pale burned the skies over Taav to ash.

"You don't have to tell me," Dare said softly.

Kel wondered what emotions had been written on her face to make him say that. Did it matter, telling him now? Secrets may be keeping the Order of Mercy safe, but they could also get her companions killed. And even if it hadn't quite worked out, Dare had put himself in danger to help her. Didn't that mean she could trust him with something? Did she already trust him too much?

"I have no interest in collecting a bounty from the Pale," Dare said, nearly spitting the last word. "If that's what you're thinking."

"There's a bounty?" Kel asked, an ember of curiosity sparking in her cold heart. "How much?"

"Ten thousand domins for a Shield," he said, scowling. "Twenty thousand for a Knight. Fifty thousand for a Knight-Celestial. An extra ten thousand for every rank above Sixth."

A hundred thousand domins for her life. Blessed stars, that was enough to buy a starship. Maybe two. It was a fortune, far more than Savvy and Dare were earning to stop the demolisher.

"Would Savvy want it?" Kel asked.

"Yes," Dare said. "And no. Money makes her feel safe. But she has priorities. Her heart is softer than she wants to admit, and she hates the Pale as much as I do, so she wouldn't try anything."

"The bounty can't be legal," Kel said, aware of how absurd it sounded even as she said it.

"Since when do the Pale care about the law?" Dare asked, mouth twisted as he glared at the ground. "They use it when it suits them and ignore it when it doesn't." After a moment, he added softly, "I should know."

A question formed on Kel's lips, escaped before she could call it back. "Is the Order of Mercy gone?"

Dare looked up at her, and Kel knew the answer.

"They were disbanded two years ago," he said. "You didn't know?"

Kel's body felt boneless, like all her strength and tension was gone. Like he'd sliced her open and her blood had left her in a rush, sunk into the ground.

"But who took over their responsibilities?" Kel asked. "Who is running the hospitals? The schools? Handling crisis aid?"

"Sometimes the Pale," Dare replied. "Sometimes locals, or someone else who stepped into the vacuum. Sometimes Defiants. Often no one."

How had Kel ever been such a fool? She knew the Pale

were sending Dirges after her people even when the treaty was signed—trying to kill them quietly, or staging confrontations or accidents that left them and any bystanders dead. It was why she'd halted all contact with the outside, to protect herself and her former allies. She knew they would use any possible loophole to wipe the Order of the Nine from the galaxy as if they'd never existed. She knew—or why would she have hidden?—that they had never intended to honor the treaty, no matter how proper and diplomatic they pretended to be. Why had she lied to herself?

Five years of her life, wasted. And for what? The Prixori Anocracy continued their expansion, rolling over system after system like a vast summer storm. How many other planets had they drawn into their empire by coercion or force? How many more of her people had died?

If she hadn't been hiding like a coward, could she have saved any of them?

Horror and shame and despair gave way to harder feelings. A rage as cold as the void. She would be prudent, once they left this place. Other people were counting on her, other lives. But here and now, there would be no more secrets.

"Tell me who you are," Kel said.

Dare scowled. "I am no one's to command," he said. "Not anymore. Why don't you tell me who you are?"

Before Kel could snap a response, Dare's eyes flared green and he lunged for his sword. Kel raised her shield, the shimmering amethyst separating them like a translucent wall, then realized he was looking behind her.

Kel spun and knelt, angling her shield to deflect a plasma bolt harmlessly into the sky. The grimstalker limped toward her, a dozen paces away, its mouth open to deliver another searing blast. How had it snuck up on them?

"Lend me your sword," Kel said. Her staff was with her zhoomer, not that it or her machete would be any use.

Dare raised his own shield and staggered to his feet, ignoring her.

The grimstalker had sustained damage in the fall, its armor cracked and sparking along its flank. One rear leg glitched, straightening so it dragged in the dirt, then folding away like a wading bird's. But its plasma weapon worked fine, as it once again demonstrated. The heat of the burst flowed around the edges of Kel's shield like a desert wind.

Dare stumbled, leaning on his sword. He might be recovering quickly, but he remained weak. Why wasn't he sheltering beneath the shield as they had on the skimmer?

The grimstalker paused as its programming analyzed its opponents, decided on the easier foe and acted accordingly. It turned and bounded toward Dare, whose bright eyes flickered. Launching into motion, Kel intercepted the machine, knocking it sideways with her shield and assuming a defensive stance. Her own muscles trembled with fatigue, but they had come to stop this enemy, for the sake of the Lothians. She would not allow it to leave this place. She wouldn't let it kill Dare.

Kel considered summoning her armor, but it might encourage the grimstalker to continue pursuing Dare, the weaker opponent. Now at least she had its attention.

She deflected another plasma bolt, then slid as the machine raked its claws against her shield. Its leg glitched again, and a spasm wracked its body, but it recovered quickly. Sparks flickered from cracks in its carapace, points she could possibly exploit with her machete?

Strategy eluded her as she reacted, fending off one attack after another, the grimstalker moving quickly despite its damage. The longer she fought, the more likely she would exhaust herself. The machine had no such problem.

A glance told her Dare was moving toward the river, trying to flank. His sword point hovered just above the ground, occasionally dropping to draw a line in the earth. A surge of frustration flooded her. If he had given her the sword, this would be over already. She would have dispatched the machine, and they'd be on their way to Handeen.

But he didn't trust her. Or perhaps he still underestimated her. That, at least, she could rectify.

My body is my shield, she thought. My soul is my weapon. With my body, I defend. With my soul, I strike.

Kel's focus sharpened to a keen edge. She summoned, not her complete suit of armor, but the gauntlets, protecting her hands. Positioning herself between the grimstalker and Dare, she feinted left, then whirled to the right as the machine lunged at her. She slipped past it to the side, and its programming stuttered briefly as Dare once again caught its sensors.

Dropping her shield, Kel leaped onto the grimstalker's back. Before it could buck her off, she drove her fist into one of the cracks in its white exterior. The crack widened and she shoved her hand inside, gripping sinewy cables and tearing them out like clingers in the swamp.

Now the machine tried to fling her off, first kicking up its hind legs, then rearing the front. Its back leg broke under the weight, and it dropped to the ground. Rather than attempt to stand, it rotated its head completely around and opened its maw to fire its plasma weapon at Kel.

She shoved her shield against the grimstalker's mouth. The plasma fired, and the machine's head exploded in a shower of plasteel and metal, fragments flying toward the river and raining down on the soil.

The body collapsed, its mechanical brain destroyed. It still sparked as the last of its functions died, but the villagers— and Dare—would be safe from this threat now.

Kel climbed off its back and glared at Dare. His skin was tinged green from his shield, which he deactivated as he lowered his sword. He regarded her warily, gaze flicking back and forth between her and the destroyed grimstalker, his mouth set in a grim line.

Had she strolled out of his nightmares like a spirit of vengeance? So be it, then. He had met Kel Garda, refugee, kexeet harvester. Had perhaps even liked her. Now, he would become acquainted with the self she hid beneath.

The power of her bracers rippled up her arms, tightened her skin, and though she couldn't see it, she knew her hair now rose from her head as if in a silent wind. When she spoke, her voice was richer, more resonant, all timidity and temperance forgotten.

"I am Kelana Gardavros," she said. "First Sword of Lovalra. Knight-Celestial of the Order of the Nine and protector of the City of Stars. I ask you again: who are you?"

# CHAPTER THIRTEEN

**D**are raised his sword instinctively, eyes brightening. "First?" he said, his voice briefly cracking, whether from fear or surprise she couldn't be sure.

Kel lifted her chin and waited.

He shook his head as if to clear it, eyes dimming, and lowered the weapon again.

"I go by Darennir Tanseith, among other names as needed," he said. "I had another name before, but I don't answer to it anymore. I won't." He met her gaze, a trace of bravado returning as he continued. "I was last transported on board the battlecruiser *Liberation*, but I wasn't crew. I was . . ." He sighed and looked down. "I was a Scourge."

He was altered, then, with accelerated healing in addition to temporary strength and speed. The Scourge were a brutal force, a punishment and a warning: defy the Pale and the retribution would be merciless. Their reputation was half their power, but it was earned. One skirmish, one Scourge, as the saying went. Kel had encountered them more than once; the memory of their bone-white armor and eerie, faceless helmets sent a brief shudder through her. They had fought as if pain had no meaning, as if death were their god and fought alongside them.

"Not that it changes anything," Dare said, "but I was never deployed against you. I . . ." He hesitated, his eyes closing. "I was on Izlan for most of the war."

Izlan had been the first planet in the Order of the Nine to fall. The occupation was supposed to be calm, civilized, but Kel had quickly learned the Pale's concept of civility left much to be desired. Where the rest of the Order had expected the people there to be treated with a measure of dignity, instead the Pale had blockaded the planet. Hunger was widespread, illness took hold when medicine ran out, and a violent resistance led to daily clashes, assassinations, and retaliation from both sides.

Kel was swept away by memories of her own helplessness every time she heard about Izlan. She had been on Lovalra first, then Prylda, and ultimately Amorleth, guarding the capital with units assembled from all the other planets. By the end, Izlan, Sotera, and Taav had fallen, but the Order was loath to endure more destruction when diplomacy might prevent it. Indastral and the Kaolaras Collective had refused support, and without additional allies, victory would have come at a cost most were unwilling to pay.

Kel had supported the treaty, curse her soul to oblivion. Knowing the Order of Mercy had been dismantled anyway, that the Order of the Nine was gone or scattered across the galaxy in hiding, and no good had come of it? It took all her restraint not to bellow at the skies, to activate her armor and fly into the void and consign herself to vengeance or oblivion. Either was equally appealing.

"How many of us did you kill?" Dare asked, his voice pained, as if he were tonguing an aching tooth but couldn't help himself.

"I don't know," Kel said, closing her eyes. "Too many. There were times I wondered how the Pale persuaded so many people to give their lives for such a terrible cause, how they could build so many machines for the sole purpose of killing. Whether they felt anything but annoyance for the cost and trouble as we left their armies broken in our wake." She glanced at the inert grimstalker. "At least fighting the machines was better than fighting the people."

"Yes," Dare said. "Not that the Pale see a difference. It's all numbers to them, and sometimes people are cheaper to replace."

Kel trembled as rage surged through her like a jolt from a shockstick. "I could never believe that," she said. "Perhaps because my people weren't soldiers as most understand it. We were protectors. Guardians. Mediators. We traveled with trade ships and diplomats to keep them safe from attack or subterfuge. We assisted the Order of Mercy when they sent aid to a place suffering from famine or disaster. We sought to preserve life, not to take it."

Dare gave a minute shrug. "Sometimes the former requires the latter."

"Don't," Kel said, waving sharply as if to deflect his

words. "I have endured that argument enough to last me ten lifetimes. I would prefer not to repeat it now."

"I wasn't trying to provoke you."

"I didn't think you were. I am . . . I am weary."

They fell silent again. On the other side of the river, a flock of birds wheeled into the sky. Their small bodies were dark against lavender, disappearing into a low, solitary cloud briefly and then swerving down into some other tree farther away. Kel's life had been so much simpler for years, like theirs. Eat and sleep and try not to die. How did humans manage to make everything so complicated?

"I was fine, you know," Dare said.

"Hmm?"

"I was trying to lure the grimstalker into attacking me by pretending to be more hurt than I am." He rotated his wrist, spinning the sword in a quick circle. "I've fought them before, and my sword can cut through their armor plating. As far as I knew, you only had a machete."

He had certainly played his part well. She'd been completely fooled. Good to know that about his sword, though.

"What now?" Dare asked.

Kel knew what he was asking, but her mind turned to practical things first. Much as she craved rest, and Dare no doubt needed it despite his protestations, they had to find her zhoomer and continue on to Handeen. Kel eyed the climb to the top of the cliff with an inner sigh. She expected she could manage, even tired as she was, but Dare might not have her experience. They could keep walking until they found somewhere easier, more sloping, but then they'd have to double back. Walking all the way to Handeen was out of the question, and if they hoped to find a ride with someone along the road, they might be waiting in perpetuity.

At least Savvy could keep going with Lunna, complete the mission without her and Dare. Unless . . .

"Please tell me the control chip wasn't in your bag," Kel said.

Dare chuckled again, a low rumble. "No, Savvy has it. She wouldn't let me bring it. Said she'd find someone else who could use it eventually if I—" He stopped abruptly, clearing his throat. "Anyway, it's safe, assuming she and Lunna are."

Kel's relief turned to confusion as she repeated what he'd said in her mind. Why would Savvy need to find someone else to use the control chip?

Ah, of course: Dare was the only one who could, because he was a former Pale. The chip must be tuned to their troops, perhaps even to specific ranks or units. Kel couldn't remember what Savvy had said, how she'd worded it, whether she had lied or simply used careful phrasing to suggest the chip was hers and Dare was merely her crewmate and bodyguard. People often drew their own conclusions based on expectations.

It was just as well Kel hadn't been fed a steady diet of vengeance, either before joining the Order or after. If she'd killed him without a thought, she'd have been forced to destroy the demolisher herself, too. The only way to do that would be to fully utilize her Knight-Celestial armor and weapons. As it was, only Dare knew her secret, and she knew his, which made them both less likely to act on that knowledge. The original plan could still proceed.

"Savvy didn't approve of you charging over here, I presume," Kel said.

"She said she looked forward to blowing my ashes out the airlock," Dare said. "That it was bad enough I risked myself with the bandits, and you weren't worth it with so many other lives at stake. But if she really thought I was going to die, she would have tried harder to stop me." He sounded oddly relieved, as if he'd been expecting Kel to say something else, but an edge of tension remained.

"Well, it wouldn't do to deprive Savvy of a good fuss at our expense," Kel said. "Now that the grimstalker is taken care of, we should get started."

"You won't try to kill me, then?" Dare asked warily.

"Not if you don't try to kill me," Kel said. "We have work to do."

Dare searched her face for something she couldn't name, then sheathed his sword and fixed it to his back.

"You're stronger than you look," he said finally.

Kel regarded him impassively.

His green eyes softened, and his lip twitched up. "I hope you're much stronger, in case you have to carry me."

Kel smirked and began to walk. After a moment, Dare followed, the sounds of their boots scraping against the rock and sand barely audible over the river, which almost seemed to be chuckling at them in its own way.


KEL AND DARE REACHED THE SHATTERED WRECK OF DARE'S ZHOOMER faster than she expected. It had landed on a pile of boulders, smashed into a sad scattering of component parts. While Kel knew a wrecked zhoomer was preferable to an operational war machine and the havoc it might cause, she still felt bad for diminishing the public fleet yet again. First a skimmer, now this. Though technically they had come back with a skimmer, just not the one they'd left with.

"Yours is still at the top?" Dare asked, looking up the cliffside.

"Yes," Kel said. "It will carry us both, faster than walking, but slower than with only a single rider."

"And your plan for getting back up?" He raised a dark eyebrow.

"We climb," Kel said. "Unless you can't. Which I trust you to honestly tell me, please."

Dare hummed in acknowledgment and studied the rocks. "If I can't, will you fly us up?"

"No," Kel said. "You have your climbing gear, yes? For the demolisher? I'll climb it myself and lower a rope."

"And then lift me up. Is there anything you can't do?"

Kel heaved a sigh. "If I started that list, we'd be here for days. Climbing, however, I can manage."

Dare decided not to take the risk, so Kel went alone, a coil of climbing line lying across her chest like a sash. She resisted the urge to look down, not because she was afraid of vertigo or falling, but because assuring herself that Dare wasn't attempting to escape or shoot at her would only cement the lack of trust that had sprung up between them again. One false move would lead to an ugly fall, literally and figuratively, and they needed to work together to deactivate the demolisher. Or rather, Dare needed to do that work, and Kel needed to make sure it was done. They were allies for as long as it took, and after that, they could figure out what they were exactly, if anything.

By the time Kel reached the top of the cliff, sweating and trembling with fatigue, the sun had begun its descent toward the horizon. They had a few hours left of light at best, which meant they wouldn't make it to Handeen. She tried to remember where the next rest spot was, whether it had sleeping quarters or simply a washroom, then decided they'd cross that stream when they found it. She located her abandoned zhoomer and searched for the best place to anchor the line.

When she looked down at Dare, she half expected him to be gone. But he waited patiently, scanning the area as he always did. She whistled at him to get his attention, then tossed him the end of the rope.

Dare took less time to get up than she had, partly because he had a rope and pulley where she was free climbing, and partly because she helped haul him up. Even so, it was a laborious process, and they were both exhausted and out of breath by the end. A wound Kel hadn't noticed on her back, just inside her right shoulder blade, stung in a way that suggested it had reopened.

"I'm surprised you preferred that method to the alternative," Dare said, resting his arm on a bent knee. "It would have been faster."

"I took a chance using my wings once today," Kel said. "I would rather not double the odds of being detected if I can avoid it." Even if the Order of Mercy was gone, and she no longer had any compulsion to remain hidden for the treaty's sake, she didn't want to risk luring Dirges to Loth and putting its people in danger.

Once they had rested, they climbed aboard Kel's zhoomer and began driving back through the forest toward the road, Kel in front and Dare behind her. They moved more slowly due to the added weight, but it also felt like an eternity now that she wasn't on edge and trying to find a wayward grim-stalker. Tree after tree whipped past them, and was she imagining it or were there more obstacles along the way? At last they reached the path, which was as deserted as it had been earlier, and Kel turned their vehicle northward.

As she expected, they had to stop for the night, marks from their destination. It wasn't safe to continue through the hills in the dark, and tongues of lightning flickered across the sky with promises of a late storm. Thankfully the rest spot had a single small guest room that wasn't in use. After a quiet meal, they each claimed a bed, and then the arguments began.

"I am capable of staying awake through the night with no ill effects," Kel said, her tone mild but firm.

"And I am capable of splitting the watch with you," Dare said gruffly. His tone acquired more venom as he added, "My modifications already repaired the worst of my injuries. I won't succumb to a concussion overnight, so you don't need to nurse me."

"Waking you every hour is standard procedure for—"

"Is it that you don't trust me?" Dare demanded. "You won't sleep because you want to keep an eye on me?"

"No! I'd do the same for anyone under my command." Even as she said that, she wished she could swallow the words or pluck them out of the air.

"I am not yours to command," Dare said, eyes flashing.

"I didn't mean it that way," Kel said. "I'm sorry. I only meant I am not treating you differently from any other ally." She absently rubbed her forehead, wincing when her fingertips found the wound there. At least she'd covered her hair again.

"I certainly hope you don't intend to hover over me like you do Lunna," he muttered.

Kel lowered her hand. "Do I hover?"

"Like a landing pod waiting for a docking bay."

After years of guarding diplomats on their travels, she had thought she was doing a decent job of letting Lunna go their own way while she kept an unobtrusive but wary eye out. Perhaps that was another skill she'd lost. The notion that the only skills she'd retained were the martial ones made her stomach turn.

"Would you prefer first watch or second?" Kel asked.

"Either is fine," Dare said.

"Take first then." She could let him sleep longer in the morning if he did. Kel hesitated, considering whether to broach the next topic or let it go. How to phrase the question if she did ask. She decided to leave it entirely in Dare's hands.

Kel cleared her throat, carefully avoiding his gaze. "Do you want me to check your injuries?"

"I can check them myself," Dare replied.

Kel nodded. That's what she had expected him to say. The small mirror in the washroom didn't allow for a full view of all their respective body parts, so it would be prudent for them each to examine the other, but she wasn't going to press the issue. Regardless of whether she knew his secret now, there might be other things he didn't want her to see, out of shyness if nothing else.

"Did you want me to check yours?" Dare asked, his tone utterly flat.

Kel smothered her impulse to refuse. Her original logic still held even if Dare didn't want to participate. While she'd be able to wash any wounds clean, applying medicine to cuts that needed it might be a challenge on her own. As if she'd made it worse by thinking about it, her unseen injury near her shoulder blade began to sting again.

"If you don't mind," Kel replied, "I'll bathe first, so if I need bandaging or ointments, the skin and wounds will be clean."

Dare grunted assent. Kel gathered her change of clothes and medkit and left him there, staring out the window at the shadowy trees. She wondered if he could see them with his augmented vision, or if he wasn't seeing their dark shapes at all.

While she might have lingered to soothe her aching muscles, Kel decided to shower as quickly as she could. How warm water and soap seemed to find every minor cut and scrape and magnify their pain was a mystery of the universe she had never unraveled. Certainly she knew how nerve endings worked, but surely they weren't meant to send such intense flashes of fire straight to her brain. The only positive thing she could say was the discomfort made it harder for her to think about the complete shambles her life had become over the course of a few days.

When she returned to the sleeping quarters, Dare was sitting on the floor, examining his sniper rifle. He barely glanced up when she entered, as if to assure himself it was merely her and not some new threat.

"Did the fall damage anything?" Kel asked.

Dare shook his head. "Not as far as I can tell," he said. "It's a miracle considering the state of the zhoomer."

Kel sat on the bed across from him. "Zhoomers are sturdy, but I don't think they're intended to be driven off cliffs. Your weapons at least are built for battle conditions."

"I suppose," Dare said. "I would have said grimstalkers were nearly indestructible, too, but you didn't even need a weapon to handle it."

My body is my weapon and shield, Kel thought.

"Everything has its weak point," she said. "It's not so hard to pop the head off a grimstalker with a sword if you—" She realized what she was saying and stopped, appalled. "Sorry. I didn't . . ." She inhaled and blew it out her nose in a rush. What did one even say to someone who used to be on the other end of your blade?

Dare shrugged, his lips thin. "I've been in conversations with people describing their favorite methods of torturing Pale soldiers so they would die as slowly as possible. At least a grimstalker is only a machine."

That didn't make Kel feel better. Torture was a horrible practice. She dragged herself out of a spiral of dark thoughts as Dare finished putting his things away and stood.

"Do you still want me to check your back?" he asked.

"It can wait until you're clean," Kel said. There had been a few traces of blood and ooze on the cloth when she'd dried herself, despite how careful she'd been.

With a curt nod, he departed, and Kel's thoughts intruded

again. That Dare had left the Pale didn't absolve him from joining them in the first place. But he had used the word "escaped" as if the Pale held him prisoner. Had they? He had been a Scourge, not a common conscript. He had been modified to make him stronger, tougher. Could such a thing be forced? Why do it against someone's will? Did it give the Pale some form of control over their troops?

While she had been taught, and firmly believed, that acts done by a person against their will were not their responsibility, there was a difference between being forced or coerced and simply following orders without any concern for their morality. Where did Dare's experience fall? Was he a willing recruit who reveled in his power over his enemies, who wielded that power cruelly and without just cause? Or was he compelled to fight by some sway the Pale held over him?

Kel couldn't judge him without knowing more about him. He had gone from reluctant ally to former enemy, yet their situation had not otherwise changed. Here they were, alone together in the middle of the forest, and spirits help her, she still looked at him and saw a man rather than a monster.

She wondered whether he felt the same way.

It shouldn't matter. Let him think what he wanted. So long as he didn't tell anyone who or what she was. She repeated what had become a mantra: they didn't need to like each other; they only needed to work together for a few more days. Then he would be gone, and she would be back to hiding in the swamp.

Or she could leave. The thought occurred to her, sudden as a clap of thunder, that if the Order of Mercy was gone, the only thing keeping her on Loth besides kexeet harvesting was her fear of attracting a Dirge's attention. It was certainly not an unreasonable fear; any place that regularly traded with the Pale would be dangerous for her, assuming the reputation of the Dirges was to be believed.

The stories she had heard before she went into hiding . . . how the Fourth Hammer of Veoh was garroted in the middle of a crowd on a space station, and yet no one seemed to have witnessed anything. How the Seventh Glaive of Izlan was shot in the head while ordering breakfast from a street vendor. How the Fifth Scythe of Ganapool died when the building he was staying in blew up in a supposed freak accident that killed everyone inside. There was even a rumor that the Second Fist of Taav was murdered in her sleep on her own starship, though to Kel's knowledge, her body was never found.

Dirges went beyond the confines of battle, hiding among civilians and striking in places that were meant to be safe. Then again, given the situation on Izlan, why would it surprise her that the Pale had no compunctions about violating the rules of sanctuary and hospitality?

Kel smiled bitterly, thinking of how much searching she had done before settling on Loth as her refuge. A place where the Pale were unlikely to take root, where community was sacrosanct and nature was granted legal rights and privileges. When she first arrived, she would catch herself thinking how she couldn't wait to tell certain people about one thing or another. The fruits the xoffedil plucked from trees and ate whole, their seeds sown in huge fertile piles of excrement. The clouds of insects whose rattling echoed until Kel felt she was living within some vast gourd instrument.

The mushrooms that grew inside dying trees and lit them up from inside, attracting birds with beaks designed to pull out the fungus, their feathers eventually glowing as well.

But the people she wanted to share it with were gone, dead, or in hiding like her. Each time the urge to reach for them arose, she was instead harshly reminded she was alone.

Was it like that for Dare, too? He had Savvy, but did he miss anyone within the Pale? There she was again, assuming he wasn't still one of them, assuming he was being honest. Could she trust him, or did she need to feign sleep during his watch?

Before she could answer her own tumult of questions, Dare returned. His hair was still wet, pushed back from his face, a few strands falling across his forehead. He had applied medpaste to his wounds, the clear gel giving his skin a faint shine. He had also changed clothes, the new ones as dark as the old, covering him from neck to boot. The memory of his ridged stomach muscles flashed through Kel's mind, and she pushed it away with an internal scowl.

"You have your own medkit, yes?" Dare asked. He hadn't put his gloves back on yet. Easier to manage wound care that way, she supposed, but it felt intentional. A show of faith? Or simply an acknowledgment that he no longer needed to be so guarded around her?

"I do," Kel replied. It waited on the bed. She frowned at the jar of muscle ointment, almost empty; she had intended to trade for more after her last kexeet run and hadn't gotten around to it. But she still had medpaste and compression bandages and a few other items for emergencies.

"Let's see the damage, then," Dare said gruffly, crossing his arms over his chest.

Kel turned away and pulled her shirt up, baring her back. Her breast-band covered some of her body, but the cut was above it.

Dare studied her in silence and she resisted the urge to fidget or look at him over her shoulder. Her skin prickled, though the room wasn't any colder than the outdoors.

"I'm surprised you have so many scars," he said. "I thought your armor was impermeable."

"It is," Kel replied. "But it doesn't stay active forever, and sometimes its mere presence constituted a threat we didn't want to make. And I wasn't always a Knight-Celestial."

"What did this?" he asked, his fingers brushing a place above her left kidney. She pictured it in her mind, a wrinkled starburst the size of her palm.

"Acid shot," she said. "I was guarding an ambassador's son from—" She stopped, lips twisting into a rueful smile. "You don't want to hear about it. Foolish old tales."

"Savvy claims that's all we are, in the end," Dare said. "A miserable pile of stories."

"Perhaps that's why she enjoys telling hers so much. She leaves pieces of herself wherever she goes, so they'll live on after she's gone."

"I don't expect she does that intentionally. She would prefer to consider herself immortal, all evidence to the contrary."

"Well, she hasn't died yet," Kel said. "So she hasn't been proven wrong."

Dare chuckled. "And to think, poor Lunna is missing all this chatter from the great, silent Kel."

"I won't tell them if you won't," Kel said, glancing over her shoulder with a grin. She flushed at the look in Dare's eyes and turned away again, staring at the dark square of window and the shifting shadows outside.

How did this keep happening? This strange intimacy between them. She had sealed herself away in a cave and now she stood in daylight once again. It was disorienting, and warm, and spirits help her, she didn't want to go back. It was like her secret was a weight she'd been carrying for all these years, and now she had been able to put it down, at least for a little while. She hadn't realized how heavy it was, though even a small weight became heavier the longer it was carried.

And yet it wasn't simply that, because she and Dare had been connecting before they knew what they each were. Kel had watched a spider once spin threads and toss them between the leaves of a bush until a shining web was built. This felt the same, as if they'd been quietly weaving something between them, and the more time they spent together, the fuller the web became.

It didn't make sense. They were enemies. Had been enemies. The war was over. But it would never be over. It lived on in their scars and nightmares. It lived on in broken landscapes and redrawn star charts. It lived on in the disrupted and destabilized existences of millions of people forced to learn new ways of being. A miserable pile of stories, indeed.

But her story wasn't over. Neither was Dare's. They were still being written. And perhaps they could end better than either of them had once hoped.

"The cut on your back is deep," Dare said, breaking the silence. "I think that's the only one that needs medpaste for now. The rest are scratches and scrapes and bruises. Nothing serious that won't heal in its own time."

Kel heard him open the medpaste container, and a few moments later, rough fingers smeared cool gel across her wound. She closed her eyes and forced herself to breathe normally. It was only medical care. Nothing to get so worked up over.

When he finished, she thanked him and they bid each other a good night. Kel struggled to find sleep until the storm reached them, the rhythm of the rain against the roof soothing the beat of her own anxious heart.

# CHAPTER FOURTEEN

Morning found Kel seated in front of the door, a square of sunlight against the far wall sliding down toward the floor. The deep purple bruise of sky lightened to lavender, and the songs of night birds and bugs fell silent as their crepuscular counterparts appeared, then gave way to the denizens of day. The air was cooler than the swamp, but still carried the heat of summer, thick with the promise of rain. No new travelers had appeared overnight, no bandits nor any more deadly machines, for which Kel found herself exceedingly grateful.

And yet, the tranquility unsettled her. Kel's internal landscape had shifted, as if struck by a mudslide or earthquake, but Loth was the same as it had always been.

No, that wasn't true; the demolisher still moved inexorably through the wilds. Now that she knew Dare was the one who could stop it, her mission was to protect him and get him where he needed to be. That at least was familiar, after so many years of guarding others with her life. She had simply never expected to be doing it for a person like this, under such circumstances.

Being left to her own thoughts for half the night hadn't helped. The vast stewpot of her brain filled with a muddled mess of ingredients, different ones floating to the top every time she stirred. Some were sweet, some bitter; some pickled her tongue with salt, and some burned like fire. Only time would tell how the final meal would taste.

It all boiled down to trust. Did she trust Savvy and Dare? She had to, or the mission was doomed. They each had their own secrets and truths written like scars on their skins and souls. Perhaps they would share more of them with each other; perhaps they would continue to hide them underneath sleeves and gloves and hats. Truth was a gem with many facets, and not all of them caught the light at once.

Dare might have been feigning sleep, but Kel didn't think so. His breath came evenly, his lips parted slightly. His face sometimes twitched as he dreamed. If he had nightmares, they didn't force him into motion like the other one had. He looked younger, and she wondered how old he was, how long he had been a soldier, how long he had been something else beforehand.

Kel smiled as she remembered her first day of training to become a Shield. She'd been fourteen years old, from a town on a world not unlike Loth, raised in a family home with four parents and a half dozen siblings. By comparison, the Academy on Amorleth had felt huge and empty, her every footstep echoing beneath the high ceilings of the main hall. Her uniform had been slightly big, and her assigned Knight-Trainer had told her she'd grow into it. They'd been right. She hadn't gotten much taller, but her muscles had filled out the sleeves and pants within a year.

Nearly twenty years ago. And a quarter of that spent on Loth. Time truly dilated and shrank in unfathomable ways.

Balancing the need for haste against the need for rest, Kel decided an extra hour wouldn't hinder them and let Dare sleep in. He awoke just before she planned to rouse him, tensing with a gasp as his green eyes flew open. One hand unconsciously tightened around the grip of his sword before relaxing along with the rest of his body.

"Morning," Kel said. "Nothing to report from my shift."

Dare grunted and sat up, swinging his legs over the edge of the bed and running his hands over his face.

"I'll get us food, then we can go," Kel said. She uncrossed her legs and got to her feet, stretching her stiff muscles. Foolish to let them tighten like that. What would she have done if they'd been attacked? Pulled something, probably.

"I'll go with you," Dare said. He stood, completing a quick series of stretches before shouldering his pack and sliding his sword into place.

They raided the kitchen, finding smoked meat along with some granola mixed with dried fruit. Practically a feast compared to some of Kel's meals. They didn't bother with plates or utensils, simply stuffing their faces and pocketing some for the road. They also replenished their supplies of the daily pills that made the food digestible.

"And here I thought Savvy was being smart, asking for our meals to be provided," Dare said between bites. "That Speaker must have thought we were fools."

Kel shrugged. "Or she thought you were being prudent.

She knows not everywhere is like Loth. They may only have one spaceport here, but the people aren't completely unaware of what the rest of the galaxy is up to."

"And yet you didn't know the Order of Mercy had been disbanded?" Dare asked.

Kel flinched as if struck. "No," she said softly. "No one told me, and I never asked." She forced herself to finish eating, even though her stomach rebelled.

"I still can't believe you thought the Pale would honor the treaty." Dare shook his head. "As soon as they had a shred of justification, they claimed the Order had reneged and swooped in like scavengers."

"Regrettably, I didn't know them as well as you," Kel said bitterly.

Now it was Dare's turn to recoil. He crushed his cup, juice spilling over his gloved hand and onto the table. Kel silently cleaned the mess with a damp cloth.

"That was cruel of me," Kel said. "I apologize." She paused, then added, "I have no intention of telling Lunna anything, much less anyone else, in case that wasn't clear. I'll guard my words more carefully."

Dare opened his hand and examined the cup's remains, as well as the sticky moisture on his glove. Kel offered him the cloth, waiting for him to accept or reject it.

He took it, wiping himself clean.

"I'm sorry as well," Dare said, not looking at her. "It isn't your fault the Pale prioritize victory over honor or decency. It must be shocking to deal with people who have so little conscience."

Different cultures grew from different seeds, were shaped

by different climates and catastrophes. Some bore sweet fruit, others bitter poison. By flattery or force, the Pale took what they wanted and chewed it up and spat it out again, leaving others to collect what was left and attempt to make something from it.

And yet, they erected monuments to themselves across their empire, as if their statues weren't standing on pedestals of bone and blood. And whatever had come before was removed like so many forests, leaving only splinters and, eventually, not even the memory of trees. It turned Kel's stomach.

"Nothing is simple," Kel said. "Perhaps I was naive enough to think it was, but even as I hid, I think I knew it was nonsense. A child's story to help me sleep. A person can only hold so much despair before it overflows."

"And now?" Dare asked, the soiled cloth hanging from his hand. "Has your plan changed?"

"I don't know," Kel said. "But whatever else happens, we need to stop that demolisher."

A pained smile flashed across Dare's face. "An easy challenge for the First Sword of Lovalra, surely."

And yet here I am, Kel thought. And Lovalra is gone. If defeating war machines was that easy, I would still be Third.

"One thing at least has not changed," Kel said. "No one can know who I am."

"They'd send a Dirge if they found out," Dare said soberly. "They might send one anyway, if Hegrun manages to get word to someone about my bracer."

Kel had nearly forgotten amid everything else that had happened since that battle. She started to say it wouldn't matter, that by the time Hegrun managed to get access to an interstellar communicator, Savvy and Dare would likely be gone. But then she realized: a Dirge would still come to investigate the reports. And if they did, they would likely seek out both Lunna and Kel for testimony.

A Dirge would know right away that Kel didn't belong on Loth. That she was a refugee. But perhaps they wouldn't be able to tell she was a Knight-Celestial? Kel knew little about their abilities or methods; the Pale deliberately maintained secrecy to add to their fearsome reputation.

"You're worried about the Dirges," Dare said, interrupting her thoughts. Kel nodded, and he looked down at the cloth he held. "It's my fault if they come," he said. "I'm sorry."

"If you hadn't used your shield, I might have used mine," Kel said. "Or worse."

"Worse?" Dare asked.

"I had almost talked myself into using my full armor. At least this way, if someone asks, I can honestly say the shield was yours, and that you claimed the bracer was bought secondhand."

"You wouldn't lie to cover for me?" Dare asked, his green eyes narrowing.

"Not to a Dirge," Kel said. "It would serve no purpose. Lying would only make them suspicious of me and wouldn't help you in the slightest."

Dare's bleak smile returned. "Sensible. And here I wondered if it was some moral concern about lying."

"I've been lying about myself for years," Kel muttered. "Mostly by omission. If such a thing were against my moral code, I broke it long ago."

"That bothers you, doesn't it?"

Kel couldn't find the words to express the depth of her shame and sorrow, especially knowing now that it had all been for nothing. The Order was gone, and she hadn't even had the courage of her convictions to die for it like so many others had. She was alive, and a liar, and if she didn't have a mission to complete, she didn't know what she'd be doing with herself.

Silently, she held her hand out for Dare's dirty cloth. He gave it to her, and she dropped it into a laundry bin. One mess at a time.

THEY REACHED HANDEEN WITHIN A FEW HOURS, THEIR PACE SLOWED BY rain and riding double. The town was smaller than Esrondaa but larger than Lichi, built near the banks of Lake Deecolea at the top of Lakefall Point, with taller mountains to the north, sweeping views of the Braided River's valley to the east, and the rocky, tree-filled scar of the Gounaj Gulch to the west. Homes were made mostly from stone with some wood, those materials being closest to hand; the guesthouse in particular was a towering gray structure of rectangular blocks cemented together, adorned with carvings of plants and animals and small glinting gemstones or shining white pebbles. It was large enough to hold two hundred people or more, with multiple sleeping quarters and a vast eating room that doubled as the assembly space.

About a mark inside the edge of town, Dare went stiff as a board and clutched Kel's waist more tightly. When they stopped to return their zhoomer, he stared toward the center of town with an expression that promised death.

Savvy and Lunna had arrived safely the day before, according to the guesthouse attendant. To Kel's surprise, Savvy was keeping quiet about herself and their mission; she had claimed to be a friend of Lunna's from off-world who came to visit at a bad time. The attendant had accepted this story with some suspicion, but no one had come forward to contradict it.

Kel and Dare finally found their companions in the trade area, where people laid surplus goods or handcrafted wares out on blankets or tables for perusal by the other residents. The last time Kel had been to Handeen, it was much more crowded, bright with pottery and adornments and complex braid work; now, only a half dozen offerings tempted the few people milling around the public fountain. Most attention was fixed on a scene playing out near the north side of the square, in front of the small offices where at least one Speaker was always on hand to provide assistance or counsel. Savvy and Lunna stood under the awning of a nearby building, Savvy's gaze appearing to wander even if she was focused on what was unfolding. Lunna simply stared.

Kel had to force herself not to reach for her machete, and Dare seemed to have a similar struggle before folding his arms across his chest.

A trio of Pale soldiers argued with not one, but two Speakers, as well as their assistants. The soldiers were in full uniform, bone-white armor like the grimstalker's covering their bodies, white voidsuit underneath peeking through the gaps. All wore helmets, rendering their faces flat and featureless apart from the red glow of their optics. One man, presumably their leader, had retracted his faceplate, perhaps an attempt to balance intimidation and friendliness. His skin was creamy, cheeks flushed slightly from heat or emotion, and his forced smile didn't fool Kel in the slightest. All of them were armed.

"Whoever told you that is lying," he said in Dominari. "Only a member of the Prixori Anocracy military can deactivate a demolisher. Without our help, this village will be a smoking crater soon." He'd pitched his flat-accented voice to carry, earning a worried ripple of discussion from those in the crowd who spoke his language.

"I believe that you believe that," said one of the Speakers, a short, fat man whose braids were coiled atop his head. "But we have already negotiated in good faith with others who assure us they will handle the problem."

"You won't tell us who these mystery saviors are, though," the soldier said. He held up his hands to stop the other man from speaking. "I get it, you don't want to accept you've been swindled. But you're running out of time. And if you don't make a deal with us now, the price will go up when things get more serious."

Dare's hand went to the hilt of his sword. Without looking at him, Kel gently touched his other shoulder and shook her head. He lowered his arm, but his muscles remained tense.

The Speaker peered up at the Pale soldier, eyes wide. "What do you mean by more serious?"

One of the masked soldiers made a scoffing sound. Almost a laugh. Kel's eyes narrowed.

"It's a dangerous machine," the first soldier said. "You know that, or you wouldn't have hired someone to deal with it." He raised an eyebrow. "Strange that they showed up just in time to help, isn't it?"

Stranger that you did, Kel thought. She doubted she was the only one thinking it, but no one said it aloud.

"You're lucky we were passing through," the soldier continued, as if realizing the suspicion he had tried to sow had muddied his boots instead. "But we need to get back to our patrol route. If you won't pay us, we don't have a reason to stay."

The Speaker blinked as if surprised. "We were not told there would be a cost if someone was sent," he said. "We were simply told no one was available."

"We're not available," the soldier replied smoothly. "We would be doing this off duty, so we have to charge for it." His smile widened. "Or you can keep waiting for a technician. Might be too late to save you by then."

Kel's face was as expressionless as the Pale's masks, but inside she felt a cold rage. At least now she knew how the demolisher had been activated. Likely the grimstalker as well; had they intended that as a surprise bonus, perhaps, an incentive to raise their price after a few people died? They had certainly waited for the demolisher to be found and build up fear, cause destruction, before they stepped in to extort the Lothians. And this was extortion, beyond a doubt. She hated that she had ever believed this might be an accident, that the Pale had nothing to do with it besides having left the machines behind. The only question now was whether these soldiers were acting on their own, or whether their superiors were complicit.

Kel removed her hand from Dare's shoulder, and without another word, he retreated and vanished. She hoped he didn't plan to do anything that might cause trouble. If the Pale were here under orders, or with someone's blessing, attacking them could bring down more troops to retaliate, or even start a full-scale takeover. Their best chance now was to quietly deactivate the demolisher and see what came of it.

The Pale continued talking to the Speakers, but they were invited into the office and the crowd dispersed quickly afterward. Kel approached Savvy finally, trying not to attract too much attention.

"Quite a show," Savvy said when she noticed Kel.

Lunna started in surprise, then flung their arms around Kel. "You're alive!" they exclaimed. "I was so worried. Not that I didn't trust you, but you took so long."

Kel stiffened, then awkwardly returned the hug. "We should go somewhere more private before we talk."

"Agreed," Savvy said. "Where's Dare?"

Kel shrugged. "He's around. If we go to the guesthouse, I expect he'll find us."

If that made Savvy worry, she didn't show it. She simply nodded and led them on a circuitous route back to the building. That she knew the town's layout so well suggested she had either studied it carefully in advance, or had explored it while she and Lunna waited to find out what had happened to her and Dare. Perhaps both.

The eating room of the guesthouse was bright and open, a breeze drifting through to circulate the warm air. Thick wooden beams crisscrossed the high ceiling, colorful strands of braided cloth hanging between them to soften the space, the walls painted in the same rich reds and greens and yellows. Beyond the windows, Lake Deecolea stretched between rocky banks lined with trees, a spectacular view that made Kel yearn for her wings. Only a few people waited inside. It made the appearance of three strangers more remarkable, but after what the Pale soldiers had said and done, the locals probably wouldn't share any information with them.

"Are you hungry, Kel?" Lunna asked.

"Food would be welcome," Kel said. "And something to drink. With my thanks."

Lunna looked to Savvy, who nodded agreement, then left to arrange for meals.

"What happened?" Savvy asked quietly.

"Too much," Kel muttered. "Suffice it to say the . . . problem was taken care of. Dare and I are fine. And we need to finish what we're doing before someone tries anything else." It was neither the time nor the place to explain more, and while she wouldn't have worried as much about eavesdroppers previously, with Pale soldiers in town, she was taking no chances.

Savvy studied her face with a smirk, as if trying to read into what Kel had told her. "I agree," she said finally. "Lunna explained that we have to go on foot from here, so if you're not injured, we should leave when you finish eating."

There was no sense in delaying for weather or a full day of light. They'd camp when the sun set, then keep going until they reached the demolisher. Dare could do whatever needed doing, and they could leave.

"How will we all get close enough without risking attack?" Kel asked. Dare would no doubt be fine, but everyone else—

"We have a beacon that broadcasts the necessary friend-or-foe codes," Savvy replied. "If it scans us, we should be marked as safe."

Possibly true, or possibly a cover for what Dare could do innately. Before Kel could ask more questions about the device's range and mechanism, Lunna returned, balancing two trays while an attendant helped with two others. They smiled shyly at Kel as they put a tray down in front of her.

"An extra dessert for me?" Savvy batted her eyelashes at Lunna, who blushed.

"I got something for Dare as well," they said. "Do you think he'll be hungry?"

"I suspect he will," Kel said. "Thank you for taking care of us."

Lunna's freckles stood out against their light cheeks. "Of course. Your comfort is my comfort."

"Speaking of Dare," Savvy said, smiling mischievously at Kel. "Did you two have a good time alone?"

It took Kel a moment to recognize the innuendo, and when she did, her face and neck warmed. She chose not to dignify the question with a response, instead concentrating on her food.

Lunna's mouth fell open as they also caught the not-so-subtle hint. "Kel!" they exclaimed. "Are you and Dare sweet on each other?"

Kel remembered his gentle touch as he applied the med-paste to her back. It hadn't meant anything. And after what they knew of each other, it never would.

Movement caught her eye, and Dare stalked in, a smug

grin lighting up his face, an extra swagger in his step. For some reason, it put Kel on edge.

Savvy seemed to share that sentiment. "What did you do?" she asked.

"Nothing," Dare said, taking the empty seat at the table. He gestured at the fourth tray of food. "Is that for me?"

"Yes," Lunna said, their mouth half full with a nutty roll. "Are you sweet on Kel? She won't tell us. She never tells me anything, not even when I feed her."

Shock flashed across Dare's face before he schooled his expression into neutrality.

"Never mind that," Savvy said. "Something happened. Spill it."

Dare rested his elbows on the table, his sword angled over the edge of the seat. "I heard a rumor," he said. "It seems someone sabotaged the Prixori soldiers' transport. They're quite upset."

Lunna gasped. "Have the Speakers been notified? They'll have to form a committee to investigate! Did anyone see who did it?"

I certainly hope not, Kel thought.

"Oh dear," Savvy said, her serious tone at odds with her smiling eyes. "I do hope the damage isn't too extensive."

"I expect it might take several days to fix," Dare drawled. "It was one of the larger vehicles. Perhaps years of delayed repairs caused problems all at once?"

Kel stifled a snicker. Handeen had a fabricator, but getting the right patterns and materials might take a while, especially with all air traffic grounded because of the demolisher. The

Pale had violated the no-fly restrictions, which they probably weren't aware of until they arrived in the village; since they were the ones controlling the war machine, they would have known they had nothing to fear from it anyway. They might be able to convince the locals of their immunity and borrow flitters, but if the Speakers refused, and the soldiers didn't want to commandeer vehicles at gunpoint, they were stuck.

More importantly, this might buy Kel and the others the time they needed to ensure they deactivated the demolisher without the Pale's intervention.

Kel quirked an eyebrow at Dare, who grinned back unrepentantly. Without breaking eye contact, he sucked a smear of juice off his thumb, slowly enough to make Kel's neck prickle with heat again, then took another bite of fruit.

Savvy snorted a laugh, at what Kel wasn't sure. "Hurry up, then, my sweets," she said. "We have work to do."

# CHAPTER FIFTEEN

The higher elevation of the Cloudrise Mountains, combined with the shade of the forest, made for breezes that cooled the sweat beading on Kel's skin. Dry leaves and needles crunched and twigs snapped beneath her boots as she ducked under or around low-hanging branches. The ground was surprisingly rocky in places, ranging from stones as small as her palm to ones larger than her outstretched arms. Most of the trees grew tall and thin, far enough from each other that they seemed sparse, no trouble to walk between except where the underbrush thickened; but from a distance, the green and brown formed a vast wall rising up and down with the slope of the land. The canopy high off the ground filtered the fading sunlight, and every breeze was like a breath through rustling lungs, smelling of soil and sap and moss. A pair of mrilli chased each other, fighting over a mushroom, with the victor triumphantly racing away while the loser squealed its frustration.

Lunna chattered almost incessantly since they left Handeen, which was both comforting and exasperating to Kel in her current mood. They commented on the beauty of the day and the natural world surrounding them, pointing out specific plants and creatures as they walked. They professed a hope that it wouldn't rain and excitement that they would be camping out in the wilds all night, and would it be safe to make a fire to roast a fish if they caught one? Roasted fresh fish was a treat, or perhaps some toasted barknuts if they could find any. It was the season for rasples, too, which were tart, though their flowers were supposed to be sweet . . . On and on they went, with Savvy occasionally asking questions and Kel humming to show she was paying attention. Dare listened without comment, or ignored them in favor of his own thoughts.

"I wonder what might have happened to the Pale soldiers' transport," Lunna said, entirely unironically.

"Truly a mystery," Savvy said mischievously. Dare grinned.

"Perhaps some witnesses saw something and will submit a report to the Speakers," Lunna continued. "Or perhaps it really was just a maintenance problem. Why were the Pale here, though? And with a big transport like that? They said they were passing through, but then why did the Pale say no one was available to help? And why were the soldiers trying to charge to take care of their own machine?"

Kel sighed internally.

Lunna gasped. "You don't think they're the ones who activated the demolisher, do you?"

"It's likely," Savvy said gently.

It occurred to Kel that Savvy might have known the

whole time, that her contact within the Pale could be privy to more information than she initially shared. But if so, how did she intend to deal with possible retaliation from the soldiers if their plan was thwarted?

"I can't believe it," Lunna said, staring mournfully at Savvy, then Kel. "How can anyone be so heartless?"

"Practice," Dare muttered. Kel wasn't sure if Lunna heard him, but she shot him a warning look anyway. Lunna, for their part, was shocked into silence.

After a few hours, they took a break beside a pool at the bottom of a small waterfall. The cool spray of the water refreshed Kel, even as it reminded her of the previous day's drop into the river. The sun's rays striking the mist formed a rainbow, and she willed herself to appreciate it as Lunna did, instead of reliving the grimstalker chase and fall, Dare's near drowning and the fight after. What would she have done if he had died? How would she have explained it to Savvy? What would have happened with the Pale soldiers? Would she have let the Lothians pay the extortion fee to stop the war machine, or would she have shed her long-guarded secrecy to take care of it herself?

Hindfear again. The fear of what might have gone wrong could swallow a person alive, leaving behind only bones.

Dare stood atop a rock next to the water, peering into its depths. Kel wondered what he was thinking. He glanced up at her as if he could feel her scrutiny, and she quickly looked away. A few moments later, he was at her side.

"What?" he asked, his tone wary.

Kel swallowed, not wanting to explain herself. "Can you sense it?" she asked quietly, though Lunna had wandered off to relieve themself privately and shouldn't be close enough to hear.

"Not yet," Dare said. "Tomorrow, probably."

"And the soldiers?" Kel asked.

Dare shook his head. "I doubt they'll come out here on foot to find their toy."

"You sensed them in Handeen, didn't you? Can they sense you as well?"

"No. I had that subroutine deactivated."

"That must have been a relief," Kel murmured. "They can't track you, but you can still find them."

"Just so. But it also means we have to use the friend-or-foe beacon to approach safely." Dare opened his mouth as if to say something else, then closed it.

"I can only feel my people if my bracer is active," Kel said, guessing at his unasked question. By the look on his face, she'd been wrong. "Sorry," she said. "Was there something else you wanted to know?"

He took a step closer to her, but before he could answer, Savvy strolled over, shading her eyes with a gloved hand and grinning. "Come on, lovebirds, let's get moving."

"Savvy," Dare said, his voice gruff with ire. He stepped away from Kel, arms crossing over his chest.

"Sorry, did I interrupt something?" Savvy asked innocently, her dark eyes twinkling.

"No, you didn't." He sounded almost disappointed, though that might have been Kel's imagination.

"You can serenade each other under the stars later," Savvy called over her shoulder as she walked toward Lunna. Dare rolled his eyes, his tan face taking on the barest hint of a flush that might have been from the sun.

"I don't know about you," Kel muttered, "but I'm not serenading anyone. I can't sing worth a domin. Though some might pay me to stop, I suppose." She cast a sideways glance at Dare, who looked startled for a moment, then gave a throaty chuckle. She grinned back, then picked up her pace to catch up with Savvy.

Above them, a pair of birds erupted into their own song, a trilling call and response as old as the forest itself.

THEY CAMPED A FEW MARKS FROM THE GULCH, IN A CLEARING LUNNA found thanks to trail signs carved into the rough bark of the trees. The setting sun cast long shadows across the ground as the sky darkened, stars winking into view on the western horizon. The roughly circular space hadn't been used in a long time, if the clusters of clover and saplings sprouting inside were any indication. But it was still mostly clear, free of the fallen logs or large stones that would make lying down uncomfortable. A spring nearby provided water they could filter and purify with the bottles Kel and Lunna carried, and sunberry vines wrapped around several of the trees, likely planted deliberately and left for nature to encourage or ignore.

Kel emptied leaves out of a firepit, then helped Lunna and Dare gather wood, none of them wandering far enough to lose sight of one another. Savvy spread her sleeping roll out and sat on it, checking and rechecking the climbing gear Dare would use to get onboard the demolisher. She seemed satisfied that the contraption of lines and grips was in working order.

To be so close to completing this mission gave Kel a curious feeling in the pit of her stomach. As if she'd swallowed a black hole and it was trying to suck the rest of her into itself, but her skin strained from the effort of holding everything in place.

She had expected to return to the village with Lunna when this was all over, but was that still safe? And safe for whom? If only she'd been able to come up with a plan to escape the bandits that didn't require Dare to use his shield. Then Hegrun wouldn't be out there with the knowledge that someone had an Order bracer, possibly someone with a huge bounty on their head.

You should have killed him before he could tell anyone, a cold voice in her mind whispered. The thought discomfited her, practical though it might be. It was bad enough Dare had killed the other bandits in self-defense, but to find Hegrun and murder him outside the bounds of battle? She'd be no better than the Dirges who did the Pale's assassinations.

What is the point of being better than them? the voice asked. What good has it done you? How has it helped anyone but the Pale?

That much was a fact. If the Pale expected everyone else to play by the rules except for them, it put them at an advantage every time. Even so, Kel knew there were some rules she wouldn't break. If she did, she wouldn't be able to live with herself afterward.

But which rules were those? Her certainty guttered like a candle's flame.

A twinge of pain shot through Kel's back as she stretched for a stick. She hoped it hadn't torn open her wound, but a faint throbbing suggested she wasn't so lucky. The memory of Dare applying medpaste there, his gentle touch, made her flush. He likely needed help as well, though she suspected he wouldn't ask for it, and would simply suffer quietly. But unlike yesterday, she had a potential ally in handling that.

"Savvy," Kel said, hunkering down next to the woman.

Savvy smiled, but her gaze was distant, distracted. "Need something?" she asked.

Kel shook her head. "Not me. Dare might have injuries somewhere he can't see or reach. Could you . . . persuade him to let you check?"

The strained smile vanished. "That void-huffing star shit. I tried to ask him earlier and he said you were probably hurt worse." She laughed without humor. "He's getting better at my brand of dodging questions. Serves me right, I suppose."

"It may be true," Kel said.

"Exactly," Savvy replied. "Or it may be a blazing lie." She stretched her legs, then tucked them underneath her and stood. "Keep Lunna occupied for me?"

"Lunna," Kel called. "Come help me with the fire?"

Lunna bounded back with a spring in their step that Kel envied. "You need help?" they asked, puzzled. "You know how to make a fire as well as I do."

Kel smiled with closed lips. Bad liar, as always. "How are you?"

Lunna deftly arranged their store of twigs and branches and dry leaves as they spoke. "I'm a little tired, but it's such an adventure, isn't it? And tomorrow we'll see the demolisher."

Their voice dropped to a whisper. "Have you ever seen one? How big is it? Will it attack us? What if we can't stop it? Does it have guns? Or a shield like Dare's? Do you think he could stab it with his sword?" They shuddered and their hands stilled as they stared blankly at the firepit.

"It's all right to be afraid," Kel said quietly.

"I'm not afraid of the machine," Lunna said. "Or I am, but that isn't it. I'm afraid for you."

Kel looked at them in surprise. "For me?"

Lunna's light eyes were hard to read in the gloaming. "You've been here so long," they said. "You never told me what you left behind when you came here, but I knew it had to be bad. All you wanted from Loth was peace. I'm sorry it was taken from you."

"That was the Pale's doing, not yours," Kel said.

"It was my fault for making you bring me to Esrondaa, then volunteering for this." They picked up strands of kindling and braided them together, mouth twisted into a miserable frown.

"I would have gone anyway," Kel said. "I was worried, and I wanted to help." She was surprised to find that was the truth, for all that she'd wavered, wanting to avoid the responsibility. She would have talked herself into it if Lunna hadn't intervened.

"Truly?" Lunna asked.

"Truly," Kel replied. "And you've been an excellent guide. This would have been a lovely journey if not for the dangers we've faced."

Lunna tossed the braid of kindling into the fire pit and

gave her a weak smile. "I'm happy not to be returned to the sky and soil just yet."

"So am I," Kel said.

They finished building the fire in silence as full darkness took them. With the sun down, the temperature fell, the mountains colder than the swamp at night. Kel wondered how Dare and Savvy were holding up; life on a ship typically meant a single season and artificial light, and she didn't know how warm or cool they kept themselves.

A flash of movement caught her eye: Savvy returning, wearing her usual smile with an extra layer of something Kel couldn't quite catch in the dim glow of the flames.

"Question for you, Kel," Savvy said. "Do you have training as a medic, by any chance?"

Kel's brow furrowed as she stood. "I do," she said. "Is there a problem?"

"There might be," Savvy said. "Could you go look at Dare's back for me? He's moved farther off for privacy."

"Of course," Kel said, retrieving her medkit from her pack. Was Dare more hurt than she'd thought? That stubborn fool. If he had let her check him yesterday—

Stop speculating and move, Kel told herself. This isn't a battlefield or a bargaining table.

The firelight faded behind her, while her own shadow lengthened in front of her until it disappeared among the trees. The insects chirped and hummed in near-constant chorus, louder than the swamp, and the occasional rustling at ground level signaled the appearance of the bristle-tailed mrilli or other small creatures who foraged or hunted while others slept.

Not sure where he was, and not wanting to startle him, Kel softly called out, "Dare?"

"Here," he said, just ahead of her and to the right. As soon as he spoke, she was able to pick him out as a black shape against the lighter trees. His hair was its own beacon, silver as the moon that would soon rise over the distant peaks.

"Savvy sent me," Kel said, stepping closer.

"Why?" Dare asked. He sounded more puzzled than annoyed.

"She asked me to look at your back," Kel said. "But I don't—"

"Why would she—?"

They stopped at the same time, and each loosed a sigh.

"This is my fault," Kel said. "I asked her to see if you'd let her check you for injuries. I shouldn't have meddled."

Dare didn't answer, and Kel thought he might be trying to swallow his irritation, so she took a quiet step backward. She wasn't the only one meddling, perhaps. Savvy's smile took on a different cast in her memory.

"No, you're right," Dare said gruffly. "I couldn't get a good look in the washroom at the rest spot. I think . . . I told Savvy I might have a gash between my shoulders, and I thought she was going to the camp for medpaste."

Kel gripped her medkit and looked down. "I brought some," she said. "But I can tell her—"

"It's fine," Dare said. "You're already here. Let's get this over with."

"It wasn't fine yesterday," Kel said. "I can't see how it's suddenly fine today. I should have realized as much when she sent me over."

"I said it's fine," Dare snapped, then pulled his shirt over his head.

Kel froze like a raw initiate in her first training simulation. Dare's upper body was limned in starlight, his skin faintly glistening from a sheen of sweat. He was all lean, hard muscle, from the firm curves of his shoulders to his broad chest and ridged abdomen. It was nothing she hadn't seen before, living and training with people whose bodies were honed to sculpted fitness by their duty, but apparently five years of celibacy had affected her in ways she was only now discovering.

"If the scars disgust you that much, you can leave," Dare said. His voice held pain, and tightly leashed anger.

Kel had no idea how to begin to respond. He had utterly misread her expression, whatever he could see of it, but confessing what she had actually felt—

"I already told you I was a conscript," Dare said, eyes flashing green in the dark. "I'm not like those men in Handeen. Vile thieves, risking innocent lives, and for what? Money." He spat the word like a curse. Kel supposed it was. She shifted her grip on her medkit.

"Savvy helped me get free, you know," Dare continued. "I was on leave after the treaty was signed, my first time off Izlan in two trade years." He braced himself against a tree with his arm and rested his head on it. "I went to Zeopra, because I'd heard a rumor that someone there was able to deactivate the tracking protocols in Pale soldiers. It was the only chance I had of not being imprisoned or worse if I deserted."

"This person helped you?" Kel asked softly.

"No. It was a trap. Savvy warned me before I fell into it."

He rubbed part of the scarring on his left forearm, just above the Order bracer. "I didn't believe her at first. But instead of walking in like a fool and asking for the man's help, I pretended I was a good little Scourge coming to ask how well the trick was working. He'd caught six soldiers in as many days, he said, up and down the ranks. He was so damn proud of himself, the rotting maggot-food."

"That many people desert?" Kel asked numbly. Across the entire Order, there were nine times nine Knight-Celestials, their ranks replenished when retirement or death made it necessary. Nine Knights per Knight-Celestial, nine Shields per Knight . . . The idea of even six Shields deserting at once was astonishing, much less a Knight or a Knight-Celestial.

"The Pale don't make it easy," Dare muttered. "I expect more would run if they believed they wouldn't be caught. Lucky for me, Savvy knew someone who really could help me." His eyes flashed green again, meeting Kel's in the dark.

"Defiants?" Kel asked.

Dare snorted. "The term hardly has meaning. Anyone who opposes the Pale is a Defiant, by their definition. But yes, they were among those who call themselves Defiants. And thanks to them, I'm free except for my scars, which they couldn't remove."

And those only the scars one could see, Kel thought. "You stayed with Savvy after that?" she asked.

"It was meant to be temporary," Dare said. "She offered me a ride; I took it. She asked for my help along the way; I agreed. We've been watching each other's backs ever since."

"That must have been . . . nice," Kel said. The villagers near her house helped her, cared for her, but only rarely—by her own choice. She had alienated herself from everyone she could, like cauterizing a self-inflicted wound. Until this whole mess of a journey had started, she had fooled herself into thinking she liked being alone. Yet another lie she'd made herself swallow, bitter and nauseating, and twice as foul coming back up.

"She's stubborn," Dare said, but his tone held grudging affection. "She's talked us into almost as much trouble as she's talked us out of. She pretends to be utterly mercenary, but she has a good heart. And thanks to her, I can try to . . . make amends. For all I did, or failed to do."

Kel hesitated, then stepped forward and rested a hand on Dare's arm. He flinched, but didn't pull away.

"I'm sorry," he said, his voice a low rumble. "I don't want your pity, and I don't deserve your forgiveness, after everything I've done. Especially to your people."

"It's not my place to forgive you," Kel said. "But for what it's worth, I'm glad you were able to get away from them." She paused, then added, "Your scars don't disgust me. You don't disgust me. I was just . . . I haven't . . ." She cleared her throat, still unable to find the words to explain. "I have been alone a long time," she said finally. It sounded worse out loud than in her head, and it had sounded bad there. Her insides writhed with embarrassment.

Dare didn't respond, and Kel dropped her hand to clutch her medkit, trying to decide whether she should leave. She shouldn't have said anything. She just didn't want him to think . . . Oh, why did she care what he thought?

"I'll send Savvy over here to help you," Kel muttered.

"Don't," Dare said. "It's fine. Here." He turned around,

exposing his back to her. The same scars on his front were mirrored here, starting just below his neck and disappearing down into the top of his pants. Other lines and welts crossed them in places, from battle wounds rather than the alterations inflicted by the Pale. A long scratch down his spine had mostly scabbed over, the flesh around it swollen and darker; probably red in the light, but the night bled out most color.

Kel opened her medkit and pulled out the jar of paste, then tucked the kit back under her arm. She swiped out a dab with her finger and carefully applied it to the cut. Dare's skin was warm despite the growing chill, or perhaps because of it. A quick scan showed another scrape above his hip, but as soon as she touched him there, he recoiled and spun around.

"I'm sorry," Kel said. "I should have warned you first."

"It's all right," Dare said. "I'm . . ." He huffed out a breath. "I'm ticklish there."

Kel snorted a laugh. "You? Ticklish? Does Savvy know?"

"Regrettably, yes," Dare said. "Not that we, that is, we've never—"

"What you and Savvy do is your business," Kel said, raising her free hand.

"We don't do anything but business," Dare said. "She found out the same way you did."

Kel could imagine that. "I suppose I could keep that secret as well," she said. "It wouldn't do for Lunna to think you're capable of being tickled. And if word got out to the bandits, well. I'm sure they'd exploit the situation mercilessly."

Dare snorted, but a flash of teeth told her he had grinned. "I am in your debt, great goddess of mercy."

"Goddess?" Kel scoffed. "I think not. I'm a simple human."

"There's nothing simple about you," Dare said. Some roughness in his voice made Kel look down again, her face hot.

"We should—" Kel began, her voice breaking. She inhaled sharply. "We should get back before they get any ideas about what we're doing here."

"Perhaps," Dare said. "I suspect there'll be talk either way."

Kel sighed. "You're probably right." She didn't look forward to the teasing from Savvy, and Lunna—

Dare loomed in front of her, all silver and shadow. "We could give them something to talk about."

Kel's heart lurched. Was he serious? She had thought he was angry with her. Afraid of her. That for all the ways they had connected since they met, their fresh knowledge of each other had erected a wall between them that neither could climb over. And she, curse her soul, was too afraid to use her wings again.

"If I've misunderstood . . . ," Dare said.

Had he? She had leaped off a cliff for him already without hesitation. What was one more?

"No," she said, laying a hand on his chest and looking up at him. "I mean, yes? Spirits, what was the question?"

Dare gave a deep, rumbling chuckle, and then he kissed her.

He tasted like sunberries, sweet and a little tart, his lips surprisingly soft and gentle. After a few moments he pulled back, still close enough that their breath mingled. With a sharp inhale, Kel slid her hands up his neck and kissed him more firmly, burying her fingers in his thick hair. Dare caressed her back, then gripped her hips and pulled her toward

him, a low moan escaping him as their bodies pressed together, deliciously warm in the cool night air. He pushed
her against the tree, miraculously missing her wound, the
bark rasping against her spine through her shirt. All of Kel's
nerves flamed, until she wondered how she could possibly be
alive rather than a wisp of ash. And yet she was alive, more
than she had been, and a sudden understanding blew through
her like a winter storm, sharp and cold.

As if sensing something had changed, Dare drew away
again. "Is this not—?" he began, stopping when Kel tightened her grip.

"I am afraid," Kel said softly, resting her forehead on his
chest. "Of so many things. I had thought I lost everything
but myself. And yet I had lost myself, too. I was gone, and
you found me. And now . . . Now I have something to lose
again, and I'm afraid."

Dare's arms tightened around her as he laid his cheek on
her head. "It gets easier," he said. "Especially with practice."
He kissed her, light and sweet, almost playful.

"This is . . ." Kel sighed. "You'll be gone tomorrow if we
succeed. I'll never see you again."

"I told you before," Dare said, "you could come with us."
His eyes flashed, green and bright.

The offer was tempting, more tempting than it had been
when she thought her self-imposed exile still served a greater
purpose. Now she knew the only person she was saving by
staying on Loth was herself. If anything, her existence en-
dangered everyone around her.

"I would make you and Savvy the target of Dirges," Kel
murmured. "I can't do that to you."

"Let them come," Dare said, his voice thick with vitriol. "I would be more than happy to consign a few of them to the void."

"No," Kel said. "Let them chase shadows until the light takes them." Still, his offer was tempting, deeply so, now that she had a taste of what could be. "I will think about it," she said.

"Will you?" Dare asked.

Kel kissed him again in reply, savoring him like a sweet she had never hoped to taste again. After this, maybe she never would.

She lost track, then, of how long they spent together under the stars. His lips tracing a path down her neck. Her hands wandering up and down his arms and chest and back. His tight grip on her waist, her shoulders, clenching and unclenching as if he couldn't decide whether to hold her or let her go. Her body throbbing with needs she had suppressed, desires she had only acknowledged alone in moments of quiet desperation. They took and gave from each other until they were both full and empty, panting in the dark as if they'd fought a long battle and won. Or perhaps lost.

A brightness overhead startled Kel into awareness, and she put enough room between her and Dare for a shaft of moonlight to separate them.

"It's late," she said.

"Is it?" Dare asked.

Kel nodded, glancing up at the risen moon. "I'm surprised Lunna hasn't come looking for us."

"I imagine Savvy is entertaining them thoroughly," Dare said wryly.

Kel sighed. "We should rest. Tomorrow will be . . ." She trailed off, unable to contain the vastness of what the next day might bring.

"Tomorrow will be tomorrow," Dare said. "We have tonight. It's enough."

"It's enough," Kel agreed. She held him close, lost in the scent of his skin and the forest, hoping she would have the strength to fly instead of being dashed to pieces on the rocks.

# CHAPTER SIXTEEN

The Gounaj Gulch stretched out in front of them, a long pass between mountains filled with green, except for the wide stomped-down path the xoffedil took to reach their breeding grounds. It wound southward from the Cloudrise Mountains until it reached the Verdwell Basin, where the land flattened out and became mere forest, northwest of the Endless Swamp. Since the breeding season approached, the trees and bushes had begun to bear their huge fruits to tempt any migrating megafauna, plump stinkmelons and furmelons and rasples ripening in the warm sun. Birds flocked to the offerings as well, and insects buzzed around the piles of xoffedil droppings left in their wake.

Kel blinked away bleariness, feeling the effects of so many nights of insufficient, interrupted sleep. Her skin crawled, hot and tight, and her lungs pulled in air that seemed crisp and sharp as smoke or snow. Her muscles at least were accustomed to long treks on uneven ground, her boots broken in and comfortable, which was more than she could say for poor Savvy.

The captain hadn't said anything when Kel and Dare returned from their tryst, perhaps because Lunna's flushed face and tousled hair suggested similar activities had occurred at camp. Kel had been more surprised than Dare; either Savvy was notorious for her seductions or simply more clear in her preferences to someone who knew her. And Lunna was not without experience of their own, might even have initiated the proceedings in their usual straightforward, enthusiastic fashion. Whatever the circumstances, it was nice to avoid the teasing she had expected, but now she had to worry about her young friend's heart being broken.

Guard your own, she told herself sternly. It's not your business. Lunna and Savvy are adults and can manage for themselves.

They'd altered their original trajectory to account for lost time, angling southwest to get ahead of the demolisher, which had passed their position in the night. They reached the rendezvous point at midmorning, their vantage giving them a sweeping view of the gulch, deep and broad as it was. The war machine towered over the trees, visible even without the help of a farscope, about a mark north and moving slowly. Its white bulk left a trail of crushed debris in its wake, every step sending tiny tremors through the ground that grew stronger the closer it came. It could be operated remotely or piloted from inside, with room for a dozen crew and as many additional passengers. A dark sensor bar circled the squat, oblong body—no head, not even the suggestion of one, just a smooth pod on legs with gun turrets on its armored back and underside.

"Will it attack us when it gets close?" Lunna asked, their voice trembling. They pulled the ends of their heat-masking cloak around themself more tightly.

"If it was going to, it would have already," Savvy said. "Our friend-or-foe codes should keep us safe until this is over." She glanced at Dare as if for confirmation. He nodded imperceptibly.

"If it does attack, remember the plan," Kel said, trying not to single Lunna out with her gaze. Her own cloak lay heavy on her shoulders.

"Yes," Savvy said. "Dare and I will get in through the emergency access hatch while you and Lunna wait out of sight. If all goes well, we'll maneuver the demolisher out of the way and then shut it down for good."

"If anything happens," Kel said, "we'll make a run for Handeen to warn them." The hummer Savvy had stolen from Hegrun would mask their footsteps, and the cloaks would hide their heat signatures. If those didn't work, they were unlikely to make it far; the demolisher would almost certainly gun them down unless Kel raised her shield to save them. Or if she took it down herself, with all the implications that would entail.

"Nothing will happen," Dare said gruffly. Kel wondered who he was trying to reassure.

Lunna shuddered. "It's unfortunate you have to leave it here. I wish you could send it back to the north."

"So do I," Savvy said, her tone surprisingly gentle. "It's

not worth the risk, though. It'll be ugly, for sure, but it won't be able to hurt anyone or anything once we're done with it."

That was the best they could hope for at this point. Maybe someday the Pale would send someone to remove it, but after all that had happened, all she now knew, Kel highly doubted it. Her main concern, assuming all went well, was the soldiers in Handeen. She took Dare aside.

"Do you think the machine could be reactivated later?" she asked quietly.

"It's possible," Dare said, scowling. "Whether they would make the journey to find it and bring it back online, I don't know. Their vehicle is damaged and they strike me as lazy vermin."

"You think they'll abuse the local hospitality until their transport is repaired, then leave?" Kel asked.

"That seems more likely," he said. "With luck, they'll receive another assignment from command that keeps them away until they find a new scheme to line their pockets."

A light breeze ruffled Kel's shirt as she thought it through. "I wonder why they were here in the first place," she said.

"Blackmail," Dare replied immediately.

Kel raised a hand and shrugged assent, but furrowed her brow. "Why here, though? It's a long trek, hardly worth the cost of fuel and the time spent. If they'd done any research, they would know the people here barely trade in domins. Surely there's a more lucrative take out there somewhere? And how is it they haven't been missed yet? What are their orders meant to be?"

Dare mulled that over, his frown deepening. "They may have known any requests for assistance would be ignored, making the scheme all but certain to succeed. It's possible they were sent to the abandoned base for some other purpose, and contrived the plan when they arrived. It may even be that this is pure mischief on their part."

"They could be doing this for fun?" Kel exclaimed, loud enough that Savvy and Lunna stopped talking to stare at her.

"It makes as much sense as any other explanation," Dare said. He smiled at her crookedly. "You're as innocent as Lunna sometimes, aren't you?"

"To know people can be so casually cruel and to see it happen like this are very different things." Kel huffed out a breath. "We may never know the truth. And I hope for everyone's sake that the soldiers don't force more direct confrontation."

Dare's smile vanished. "I'd happily gut the demolisher's controls to be sure it can't be used again, but that might bring in more Pale soldiers, asking unfortunate questions and making unpleasant choices."

"They might move in again," Kel murmured. "Decide this planet needs to be watched more closely. Perhaps managed by their benevolent hands. They could do it even if we do succeed. Spirits, that might be the entire purpose of this situation." A chill rippled through her that had nothing to do with the wind, and she hugged herself, wishing for a moment that she'd brought her sword instead of leaving it under her house. But no, that would be too tempting, and she'd already used her wings. Best to let Savvy and Dare handle this and keep to her position as Lunna's guard.

So she watched, and she waited, and the demolisher slowly stomped closer. Savvy and Dare prepared their climbing gear, bickering amiably to relieve the tension building like a storm. Sweat pooled in Kel's armpits and the small of her back, and she flexed her hands every time she caught herself clenching them into fists. Lunna had fallen entirely quiet, crouched low to the ground, staring into the distance with a tight expression on their usually open face.

Any wildlife in the area had long since hidden or fled, driven away by the growing tremors and the crash of trees pushed aside or crushed by the war machine. Once it was deactivated, teams would be dispatched to handle cleanup, clearing away splintered wood and collecting fallen fruit for consumption at best, fertilizer at worst. There would be planting, and tending, and mourning of what was lost, of the failure to protect the rights of the gulch to exist free of such unnatural harm. The damage the demolisher had already done was appalling, and Kel wondered if it would have been better to risk using a flitter to get to it faster.

Too late to second-guess those decisions. Too late to take back what had happened. All they could do now was try to make the best of it, to ensure no one else would be hurt.

The war machine was almost upon them. White lights flickered on and off in its sensor bar, mostly in front, in a pattern that meant nothing to Kel. Its guns were tucked away close to its body, blessedly inactive. Its internal mechanisms groaned and whined as if it hadn't been properly maintained. Perhaps that had slowed it down. Worse, it was leaking some fluid, leaving a nasty trail of blackness like blood, except it caught the sunlight and shimmered with eerie rainbows in nauseating colors. Cleaning that up was going to be a trial. Maybe Kel would stay and help with that, too.

Don't think about that now, she told herself. Don't think

about the future. One thing at a time. Concentrate on the present, on finishing this task before the next one comes.

She crossed the distance to where the others were preparing to head down into the gulch and stood next to Dare, his expression grim, shoulders tense. Savvy looked past him, a lazy grin hiding whatever she was thinking.

"Come to give us some last words of encouragement?" Savvy asked. "Maybe a kiss for luck?"

"Did you want one?" Kel deadpanned. Dare snorted. More seriously, she added, "You know the dangers and you've prepared yourselves. Take care and we'll see you when it's done." No lies, no empty promises. She squeezed Dare's arm, flushing as memories surged through her. His soft, tentative smile before she turned away was worth any amount of teasing.

"Go on, then," Savvy said. "I hate goodbyes."

Kel returned to Lunna's side, her roiling emotions compelling her to engage in her increasingly regular breathing exercises. In the storm, the calm eye. Above the storm, clear sky. Lunna silently tapped their forefinger against their knee, hardly blinking as they watched the machine's feet rise and fall in slow rhythm. The wait between steps was interminable, like a pendulum swinging through some viscous substance.

Savvy and Dare went down into the gulch. Their steps occasionally sent pebbles rolling, and once Savvy slid a few paces when her foot found an especially slimy pile of leaves, but otherwise their hike was controlled and careful. Sometimes they disappeared behind a stand of trees, only to reappear farther down. When they made it to the bottom, they took up a position near the area kept clear by years of xoffedil

migration, a natural path carpeted with vegetation that toler-
ated giant feet. They looked so small from far away, so still,
and Kel wished more than anything that she could be beside
them, helping them with this trial, rather than simply watching from relative safety.

The demolisher reached Savvy and Dare's position, then
passed it. The pair surged forward. Savvy shot a line up the
machine's leg to the access hatch on its underside. It held,
and she passed it to Dare, who began to climb. Savvy followed him. They had said they'd done this before, and seeing
how swiftly they moved, Kel believed them. How many of
these machines were reactivated across the galaxy like this?
Or perhaps their other experiences were in more hostile
situations . . .

On what fronts was the Pale waging war, now that the
Order was gone?

Dare opened the access hatch, and Kel held her breath,
legs tensed beneath her, half expecting the demolisher to become hostile as soon as it was breached. If it did, she'd have
to ensure Lunna escaped to warn the Lothians. The plasma
weapons were likely to hit nothing but layers of rock since
they only fired in a straight line, but the missiles were another
story; their range was long enough that it would be a hard
run. Thankfully, the machine moved slowly, and they were
hidden from the sensors by their cooling cloaks and the hummer. On the other hand, if the Pale base really was armed
with long-range weapons and launched an attack, she and
Lunna might not make it very far before they were vaporized.

Stop worrying, Kel thought. It does no good. Stay sharp.

She began to count up. How long would she wait before

assuming something had gone wrong? Her experience was in destroying demolishers, not operating them. She should have asked what the expected timeline would be. Spirits, she was rustier than a machete left in the swamp. She wasn't fit to be Third, much less First. Not that it mattered anymore. She was no one and nothing.

"How much longer?" Lunna asked when Kel reached three hundred and twelve.

"I'm not sure," Kel said. "It could be a while, or—"

The demolisher stopped moving. The lights on its sensor bar blinked rapidly, chasing each other around.

"Did they do it?" Lunna whispered.

The sensor lights turned red, and the machine gave an ear-piercing wail. A thick cloud of gas drifted from hidden vents, a sickly yellow color Kel remembered all too well from previous encounters.

"No," Kel whispered. Her heart thumped hard as her stomach tried to climb into her throat.

The demolisher was in attack mode, and it had flooded the interior with poisonous gas to quickly eliminate intruders. Savvy and Dare hadn't been wearing masks when they entered . . .

Kel and Lunna had to get back to Handeen and warn everyone, or at least try. Those damn Pale soldiers would get their money after all, if there was anyone left to pay them.

And yet, she hesitated. What if she didn't run? What if she used her armor and soulsword to fight the machine? She had done so before. Not alone, but it could be done. She might be able to rescue Savvy and Dare before the poison took them, and Loth would be safe.

Or she might die along with them, and then Lunna would probably follow, and Handeen would have no warning of the war machine lumbering toward them intent on destruction. She might even trigger the long-range attack she hoped to prevent, if it hadn't already happened.

And if she did defeat it? The Pale would want to know who had done it and how. They would find Kel, or if they didn't, they might retaliate, thinking the Lothians had knowingly harbored a fugitive with a bounty on her head.

But how could she abandon Savvy and Dare? They had known the risks, true, but if Kel could still save them—

"What do we do?" Lunna asked, their voice trembling with urgency.

The demolisher's cannon swiveled toward the sound. Kel tackled Lunna to the ground, away from the edge of the gulch. An instant later, a bolt of plasma tore a hole in the side of the hill. Trees exploded into splinters, some catching fire while others disintegrated. Lunna screamed, and Kel clamped a hand over their mouth as the cannon shifted.

Reaching into her pocket, Kel fumbled for the hummer and activated it. The teeth-aching sensation of the noise cancellation started immediately, but she stayed on top of Lunna for a ten count, longer than it should have taken the demolisher to spin up its next shot.

Nothing happened, though the machine's siren wailed again, and more gas drifted into the air. The hummer and the cloaks were working. But as the demolisher's giant legs rose and fell, moving it in their direction, Kel had to accept that Savvy and Dare weren't coming out, and she had a duty to fulfill.

Her eyes hot with unshed tears, Kel hauled Lunna to their feet and pulled her cloak shut. "We need to go," she said. "We need to get out of range before it launches any missiles." She didn't add that it might be pointless if the whole area was bombarded, because what good would it do?

Lunna mimicked Kel in closing their cloak, and together they began to run.

They kept a brutal speed, faster than they'd attempted before. Kel was used to running, a bitter truth with sharp edges under the circumstances, but Lunna couldn't maintain the same loping pace. The pair moved in bursts, sometimes jogging, sometimes sprinting over a stretch of level earth, sometimes slowing to a walk so Lunna could catch their breath. When Lunna tripped, Kel caught them, pulling them forward relentlessly even when they cried in protest. The inside of the cloak grew hot as an oven, and Kel wondered if she were already dead, if this was the afterlife and justice demanded that she be punished for her failings by roasting to a cinder.

They followed the trail signs back to their camp, but didn't stop to rest for fear that death was only a whistling projectile away. On they went, retracing their steps, the sun blazing overhead, the shadows of the trees around them slowly shrinking. Kel could no longer hear the wail of the demolisher, but she left the hummer on, kept the cloak pulled tight, until finally Lunna stumbled and couldn't rise.

"Water," Lunna gasped. "I can't."

"You must," Kel said. She fumbled in her pack for water and passed it to Lunna, who drank so fast they began to cough. Kel drank, too, the liquid warm and heavy in her guts.

The farther they got from the gulch, the more Kel hoped they wouldn't be targeted, hoped the threat of the base's weapons was as idle as she believed, but she still kept up as rapid a pace as Lunna could manage. Her muscles began to ache, so when Lunna developed a limp and a painful, persistent stitch in their side, Kel finally slowed to a walk. For all the good it did them, they caught their breath. The sounds of the forest eased back into her awareness; the insects and birdsong, once soothing, now grated like shearing metal. Their footsteps were audible within the sphere of the hummer's effect, but outside that, it was as if they didn't exist. The only sign of their passing was the trail of disturbed brush and fallen leaves in their wake.

"What happened to Dare and Savvy?" Lunna asked, their hand clutching their side.

"I'm not sure," Kel replied.

"How will they get out of the demolisher?"

"I don't know that either."

Lunna fell silent for a minute, then whispered, "Are they dead?"

Kel swallowed, despite her mouth being painfully dry. "Maybe. Probably. Assuming the poison gas didn't . . . They could have found a way out, but even if they did, they would have had to escape the demolisher in its attack mode, as we did."

Lunna gave a hoarse laugh. "You could have lied to me, Friend Kel."

Kel closed her eyes. "I'm not a very good liar. It does not come naturally to me."

"That explains why you never talk at home."

"Yes," Kel said softly, opening her eyes again.

Lunna studied her face, then shook their head. "I'm not a fool," they said. "I know there is more to you than you pretend. And I know you can't tell me. Don't worry, I won't ask."

Kel's brow furrowed. "It's not that I don't trust you—"

"I know," Lunna said. "It's all right."

I don't know if it is, Kel thought miserably. If the Pale came looking for her, if they interrogated the people in Lunna's village, ignorance might not shield them. Kel had believed it would, had believed all she had to do was hide and be quiet and no one around her would come to harm. But the ignorance wasn't a shield, it was simply ignorance. It wouldn't protect them from anything if the Pale descended, would potentially even prolong any hardship.

Kel had believed her exile to be a form of control over her destiny, and that of her Order. It was an abdication, a negation, a relinquishing of herself, and the benefit she derived from it was safety. But it was ephemeral. It would not persist. It could not, so long as her enemy continued to spread across the stars.

And yet, Kel was one person. What could she possibly hope to accomplish? The sea could not be emptied with one pair of hands.

For now, she could get back to Handeen and warn them. That lay within her power, and by all the stars and the void between, she would see it done.

So they continued, exhausted through muscle and bone and deep into their souls. The sun slid down the sky and the shadows lengthened. The chorus of birdsong changed, and the wind stirred fallen leaves into swirls and skips of motion.

Small creatures avoided them by scent despite their silence, and larger animals watched them warily before bounding away or continuing with their own concerns. By the time they reached Handeen, Lunna was stumbling more than walking, and Kel would have traded every secret she knew for one night of dreamless sleep.

Instead, she trudged to the Speakers' building, Lunna in tow, and knocked politely. Around them, the few people trading for the day had already gone home or to the guesthouse, leaving the area mostly deserted. Kel wondered how many were on their way to another place, farther from the demolisher, and the reminder of their failure made her stifle a sob.

Control yourself, she thought sternly. A few deep breaths later, she was calmer, and then someone opened the door.

"Can I help you, friend?" the person asked.

Kel couldn't honestly answer that question, so instead, she stepped inside to deliver the bad news.

# CHAPTER SEVENTEEN

K el waited in the antechamber of the public building, the smug voices of the Pale soldiers carrying from the other room. Her low-backed wooden chair forced her to lean forward or rest her head against the wall with a slat digging into her spine. She almost chose to sit on the floor instead, but she wasn't sure she'd be able to get back up. Not with any grace, at least.

She'd sent Lunna to the guesthouse to eat and bathe and rest, promising to tell them about anything that happened. They'd wanted to get a closer look at the soldiers, but Kel had no desire for anyone from the Pale to know her friend by sight. Not that she wanted to be memorable, either, but one of them had to be on hand to answer questions if necessary. Perhaps most importantly, she wanted to know what the extortionists intended to do now, whether they would take care of the demolisher as agreed or leave the Lothians to rot and ruin out of sheer spite. If her stars-forsaken luck would deign to make an appearance, they might also let slip useful intelligence about the capabilities of their base and at least put that fear to rest.

The answer to one of her questions came a minute later as the door to the inner room burst open and the Pale soldiers stalked out. As before, two were masked and one had lifted his visor to show his face. He wore an expression of cold amusement, all toothless smile and mirthless eyes as he followed his companions to the exit.

"I did warn you the price would go up," he called over his shoulder. "The Prixori Anocracy doesn't take payment in fruit or future favors."

The Speaker on duty trailed after him, followed by another who had been pulled from other duties. Kel fought the urge to stand and go to them, instead watching the scene unfold.

"We simply don't have that many domins," the Speaker said. "It's not a matter of refusing to pay, or not wanting to accept your terms. We do not have it."

"Then you'll die, I suppose," the soldier said with a shrug. "A pity."

Kel's skin flashed cold, then hot. Was this man serious?

"We can try to get it," the other Speaker said, a tall, thin woman with nearly black eyes. "Esrondaa keeps the communal funds, so we can petition them for a release. But it will take time."

"Time you don't have." The Pale soldier leered, oily as engine grease. "Better clear everyone out of here quickly, or there won't be anyone left to save."

"Please, friend—"

"We're not your friends, alien," another soldier said. In

the stunned silence that followed, the trio stepped outside, letting the door swing open in the wind.

It took every shred of control Kel had left not to go after the man and shake him until his teeth fell out. But that wouldn't help anyone.

The Speakers stared out the open door, wearing nearly identical expressions of shock, mouths half-open and brows furrowed. To be treated so disrespectfully was bad enough, and by strangers to whom the laws of hospitality were sacrosanct. The ramifications of the refusal to help would ripple out to the rest of Loth unless something was done, and quickly.

"How much did he ask in payment?" Kel asked.

The short, heavy Speaker flinched when she spoke, as if he'd forgotten she was there. The other one pressed her palms together, fingertips under her chin, and inhaled deeply.

"Fifty thousand domins," she said.

Kel struggled to form words. "That's outrageous."

The Speaker gave a sideways nod, her head angled. "The alternative is too monstrous to fathom. We will do what we must." That the woman didn't hesitate eased some of the horror Kel felt, but she remained tense with anger and frustration and despair.

Savvy and Dare had only asked five hundred, plus food and fuel. Fifty thousand was a huge portion of Loth's yearly trade revenue, what they used to buy off-world goods for all the towns and villages collectively. To lose that money now would mean putting off machinery repairs indefinitely, skimping on spaceport maintenance, and—perhaps worst of all—being unable to replenish medicinal supplies. And with the Order of Mercy gone, there were few groups they could petition for emergency aid, possibly none who would risk piracy and other travel pitfalls to bring valuable resources to a single, isolated planet.

Especially not a place having problems with the Pale.

It wouldn't have stopped the Order, Kel thought bitterly. The Lothians could have petitioned her people to help. Someone would have been sent to destroy the demolisher, and the grimstalker, perhaps the entire Pale base if necessary. And the Pale might have stayed their hand, refrained from retaliating because the threat of the Order would have made the proposition too expensive to be worthwhile.

Wasted thoughts, Kel told herself. The Order was gone, the Pale soldiers were blackmailing the Lothians, and now she had to—what?

She could stop the demolisher. But instead of fifty thousand domins, the price might be Loth's freedom, its people's lives. Worries spun out in her mind like strands of a weaving, tangling to form a jumbled image of fear and violence and subjugation.

But worry was also a rope for her to hang herself with, and she could feel the noose tightening the longer she fretted over what might or might not be.

Curse it all to the void, why hadn't she helped Savvy and Dare instead of running? If she was going to have to fight the blighted machine anyway, she might as well have saved them, too.

"Friend Kel," the woman Speaker said, "you look exhausted. Perhaps you should rest while you can?"

Before you have to run again, she meant. Kel pressed a

trembling finger against the wound on her forehead, letting the pain center her before she lost herself entirely.

"Yes, Speaker," Kel replied dully. "My thanks for your consideration."

"Your comfort is my comfort," the Speaker said absently. "I am sorry, but I must contact Esrondaa." She flicked her fingers from her lips in farewell.

Kel mimicked the gesture, then forced herself to rise and leave. Her muscles ached less than she expected given the hard run, but perhaps the rising tide of anger gave her strength. She still wasn't sure what to do, but she knew who to blame, who to name as an enemy. The speech she'd given Dare about being unable to split actions into good and evil, right and wrong, returned to her mind, but today her convictions were solid.

The Pale soldiers were evil. Not because of who they were, but because of what they were doing. Whatever happened with the demolisher, Kel had to stop them, to keep them from ever doing such a thing again.

But how, when anything she did to them would bring down the same consequences on Loth as destroying the demolisher herself?

At least the soldiers hadn't said anything about the base's defenses, mentioning only the war machine. They might be keeping that threat in reserve, but she had a feeling they would have been happy to spitefully deploy it already if the option were available. As one of her parents had once said, sometimes when you were soaked in sweat, the spirits sent you a cool breeze.

One thing was sure: the Speaker was right. Kel needed to rest. Back to the guesthouse she went, one step at a time, one foot in front of the other. The dim glow of lights on building walls illuminated the darkening street. None were bright enough to chase away the shadows lurking in every corner, and yet they still lured insects to them, swirling around in a pale cloud of hope. She tried not to consider how many creatures lay stunned or dead from futilely pounding themselves against the untouchable blaze.

LUNNA LAY IN ONE OF THE BEDS IN THE SLEEPING QUARTERS, AN ARM FLUNG over their tearstained face. The steady rise and fall of their chest told Kel they had succumbed to sleep despite their despair, or perhaps because of it. As much as she wanted to join her young friend, Kel instead bathed, then returned to the eating room. She wasn't hungry, but her body needed nourishment almost as much as rest. It would be best if she took care of it now rather than waiting until she woke up.

The room was surprisingly full, and after watching the flurry of activity, Kel realized the Speakers must have called everyone together to prepare for a mass exodus or retreat to the mountain shelters within the next few hours. Every cooking implement in the kitchens seemed to be in use, steam rising from huge pots as dense fruity nut breads came out of the ovens and were replaced by more of the same. Meals were being prepared and packed for transport rather than immediate consumption, and people filed in and out bringing whatever they had at home to contribute to the communal stores. After all, if they didn't eat it, anything left behind would go bad.

More people arrived as she loitered, unsure of what to do. Word no doubt spread slowly to the farthest reaches of the town, and the isolated homes beyond. Children were organized into groups by age, overseen by adults and the oldest among them, who struggled to manage the bursts of energy and emotion arising from the strangeness of the situation. Some helped with the food, their small hands already practiced at their work from previous shifts in the guesthouse with their families. Others played dance games, singing and clapping and squealing in delight, or bursting into quickly dried tears before returning to their circles. Still others fell asleep despite the bustle and noise, and were laid out on mats on the floor or wrapped into slings and carried.

The crowd, the sense of unity and community, suddenly overcame her, and Kel stumbled back outside, struggling to get enough air. The night was cooler than in the swamp, but still warmer than many nights in the Order barracks on Lovalra, and it closed around her like a fist. She wanted to help, to go back inside and present herself to whoever was organizing tasks and volunteer to do what needed doing. Even after she'd become a Sword, she spent enough time on various aid missions that surely she could do something now.

But she was hungry and exhausted, and worse—this was her fault. None of this would be happening if she had dealt with the demolisher.

True as that might be, blaming herself was another way to grasp for control that eluded her. This was the Pale soldiers' fault. If they hadn't activated the demolisher—and she was sure they had—Loth would have continued onward in its orbit, in the peace it had earned through obscurity and the hard work of its denizens. She would have stayed in her house in the swamp until death came for her, perhaps in her bed, perhaps while she gathered kexeet.

Where peace is lost, may we find it, she repeated to herself. Where peace is broken, may we mend it. Where we go, may peace follow. Where we fall, may peace rise.

And yet, she had been so focused on keeping the peace that justice had slipped through her fingers. It had been the rift that tore the Order apart: some had wanted to attack the Pale, others to defend as they always did. The Pale outnumbered the Order, and the Shields couldn't be everywhere at once.

Kel had supported the treaty, had believed a small measure of subjugation would be preferable to more death. How she wished she could return to that time and scream at her comrades to fight. They were gone anyway, dead to Dirges or their own self-inflicted isolation or immolation of self. The Order of the Nine was gone, the Order of Mercy was gone, and who knew how many more people had died on their worlds in the aftermath.

What good was a blood-soaked peace to the ashes of the lost?

A movement in the distance dragged her from her thoughts. A burst of furtive motion followed by stillness, someone sneaking from shadow to shadow rather than walking along the street normally. Strange, and suspicious.

Kel pressed her back against the wall of the guesthouse and watched. It was two people, not one, making their way from building to building. One tall and broad, the other shorter and stocky. Their footsteps were not the slap of sandals or the soft pad of leather, but the thump of thick-soled boots.

As slowly and quietly as she could manage, she strode forward until she reached the edge of the nearest cone of light. The people she followed held a brief, whispered conference, their words swallowed by the wind. They continued onward, shifting direction; were they lost? Once they left her field of vision, she braved the lamp's glow and made her way to the corner of the building, peeking around it to track her quarry. Seeing nothing, she wondered if she had lost them. A moment later, they crossed an area that forced them close enough to the light for her to see their faces.

It was Hegrun and his second in command, Miza.

How had they come all the way to Handeen? Stolen zhoomers, no doubt. More importantly, why were they here? Revenge? After suffering such profound losses, Kel had expected them to retreat and lick their wounds until well after Savvy and Dare left. Clearly, she'd been mistaken.

To learn their purpose, she had to follow them, so she did.

Kel didn't have much experience in covert activity. She had been a Sword, not a spy. She tried to move when they moved, stop when they stopped, hoping their footsteps would cover hers, that the wind would muffle the sound or it would be mistaken for something else. Twice they came across residents on their way to or from the guesthouse, waiting for the unsuspecting people to pass before continuing. The air cooled enough that her nervous sweat left her clammy and uncomfortable, and she was painfully aware that she had only her machete and her own two fists as defense unless she summoned her shield or armor.

She'd done more with less, but it wasn't ideal.

They reached the edge of Lake Deecolea near Lakefall Point, the rush of the waterfall quieter at the top than the bottom. The moon rose, its pale curve cresting the distant trees like a baleful eye, the sprinkle of stars a reminder of what had transpired between her and Dare the night before. She couldn't think about that now, couldn't let it overcome her.

The two men stood alone in the grass and waited for something or someone. Kel wished she had brought the hummer, but it was in her pack, which she'd left in the sleeping quarters with Lunna. She circled around them as widely as she could without losing sight of them, keeping to the shadows, wishing there were more things to hide behind on this side of the lake. A cluster of bushes had to suffice, the moonlight falling on them as she crouched in its shade.

"You sure they'll come?" Miza asked after a few minutes of silence. He spoke in Dominari now instead of Rekari.

"If they don't, we'll have a shitting long wait until someone else does," Hegrun replied crossly.

Kel barely had time to wonder who they meant when a trio of white-armored forms stomped up to the men, utterly unconcerned with secrecy. She watched them around the edge of the bushes, ready to shift back behind cover and bolt if they noticed her.

"Lazarun," Hegrun said, saluting one of the soldiers, arm horizontal under his chin with his fist near his shoulder. Something about the way he did it seemed sarcastic.

"Hegrun," Lazarun replied. Kel wasn't surprised it was the one who'd been serving as spokesperson. She was, however, surprised the two were on a personal-name basis. Then the light caught them both in profile, and she realized they resembled each other. Brothers? Cousins?

"I appreciate you meeting me," Hegrun said, his tone just dry enough that Kel's sense of his sarcasm persisted.

Lazarun apparently hadn't missed it, either. "I certainly hope you do," he said coldly. "I assume you want something?"

"A ride off-world, for me and my people," Hegrun said, gesturing at Miza.

"How many?" Lazarun asked.

"Four."

Kel winced. Had Dare killed so many of them?

"I can manage you two," Lazarun said. "Four might be pushing it. What happened to your ship?"

"Impounded," Hegrun said.

Lazarun gave a dry, harsh laugh. "Who did you fuck?"

"Myself, mostly," Hegrun replied. "These people are soft fools, but they know how to use a stun net on a drunk."

"You never did know your limits," Lazarun said. He fell silent, then turned to face the lake and said something that was lost to the wind.

"What do you mean?" Hegrun asked indignantly. "I'm a privateer. You're meant to provide aid as needed. It's in the contract."

"Ah, but does this qualify as a need?" Lazarun retorted. "Seems there's some leeway in the interpretation. What will you give me if I take you with us when we leave?"

Silence fell as Hegrun and Lazarun faced off. Kel's legs ached from the fatigue of crouching piled onto her already exhausted body.

"How about information?" Hegrun asked. "I know something you don't about the people who were sent to stop the demolisher."

"What do I care about them?" Lazarun asked. His tone implied a smile that Kel yearned to wipe off his face.

"Tell me you'll give me a ride, and I'll tell you what I know," Hegrun said. "I promise it could be extremely lucrative for you."

Kel stilled, her heart slamming into her ribs. Curse him to the void. There were only a few things he could mean, and none were good.

"Could be or will be?" Lazarun asked.

"Depends on whether you can find them."

"Oh, I can," Lazarun said. "They failed to stop the demolisher, so I assume I can search their bodies for any fun surprises at my leisure."

"The surprise may be more trouble than you're imagining," Hegrun said, and now he almost sounded smug. "Come on, Laz, it's just four extra people from here to the nearest hub. You're in a Vigor-class cutter. You can bunk sixteen and you're only three."

"Four," Lazarun said. "We left our pilot with the *Brimstone*."

Kel's brow furrowed. If the Pale soldiers had come in a cutter, optimal capacity was at least eight, not four. This couldn't be an official mission, not unless the Pale were stretched thinner than she thought. Or this was a special assignment. But to what end?

"Maybe you help me," Hegrun said, "or I tell the locals

all about your little scam and let them turn you in to your superiors."

"As if they care," Lazarun replied. "You don't think they're getting a cut? One of them even helped us falsify logs to make this all look like a tragic accident. Not as if anyone was ever coming back for this stockpile anyway. Might as well get something out of it."

And there it was. The whole sordid tale in a few words. No grand conspiracies, just the greed of a half dozen monsters. Kel's blood burned like ice.

"Fine," Hegrun said. "This was all a waste, then. At least let me use your pulsecom so I can sell the information to someone else?"

"Why bother?" Laz asked. "Will it still be valuable once I find the bodies?"

"If you find them," Hegrun corrected. "And you won't find them all, anyway. I'll tell you that for free, because you'd know it yourself if you thought for longer than a second."

Lazarun paused, and the two men faced off, limned in moonlight. Their expressions weren't clear from where Kel crouched, but Lazarun's eyes narrowed to a sliver.

"Someone survived," Lazarun said finally. "To report back. Of course."

"Moving at sublight, but you got there eventually," Hegrun said mockingly. "I'll tell you something else for free, since you'd figure that out, too: I didn't land on this wealth-forsaken planet with only three other crew members. Your competition took care of that."

Lazarun fell silent again, and one of his helmeted associates spoke up. "They just want a ride," he said. "We don't want to walk into a shitstorm with our visors off."

"Fine," Lazarun said. "Tell me what you know, and I'll take you to Uchoren Station."

Hegrun slapped Lazarun on the shoulder. "Now we're talking. I'll start at the beginning." He gave the Pale soldiers a longer version of the story she'd heard from Speaker Yiulea, making himself and his crew out to be the victims. Her disgust toward him increased; he could have paid his fine and left, but here he was, down to three crewmates and no starship.

"I don't have all night, Heg," Lazarun grumbled. "Get to the point."

"Fine," Hegrun grumbled back. "The point is, my people grabbed one of the local boats, and it turned out to be the one your competition was using. The woman said they had a control chip for the demolisher."

"Meaning one of them is a deserter," Lazarun said. "Interesting."

"Maybe not," Hegrun said. "Maybe they killed one of you and stole the chip."

Lazarun was quiet, his lips pursed, pensive. "That would explain why they failed to control the demolisher," he said. "But not why you seem to think they might have survived."

Hegrun grinned, lips peeled back from his teeth, mirthless. "They stole the boat back, and we went after them. Twelve against four. They'd taken some of our weapons, too, but we thought they had no chance."

"And now there are only four of you?" Lazarun asked, and for the first time, an edge of concern crept into his voice.

"One of them had a shield, Laz," Hegrun said. "An Order bracer. He cut through my people like a garrote through soft cheese."

Kel bowed her head and forced herself to continue breathing slowly and quietly, even as all her hiding, all her careful distancing from everyone, all her abandonment of herself was rendered worthless. As soon as Lazarun reported this information to his superiors, or Hegrun sold it, Loth would be infested with bounty hunters at best, Dirges at worst. Five years of caution, utterly wasted. And it hadn't even been her shield, or her sword.

I will not weep, she thought distantly. I will not lose myself to despair.

But with Savvy and Dare gone, and the demolisher still out there, now actively seeking hostile targets instead of passively patrolling, it was difficult to hope.

"Well steal my spit and clone me twice," Lazarun said slowly. "You know how much a Shield is worth? Or even just a bracer?"

"It's not worth my life," Hegrun said, raising his hands, palms out. "If you're in the mood to try for them, it's your eulogy, but they almost got me once. Just leave word with your pilot to take me with them even if you don't make it."

"Wish I could, but the tech on this planet is nonexistent. We can't even control the demolisher from a distance unless we're at the base or on the ship. Have to be in sensor range otherwise. Best I can give you is a coded holo."

"I'll have that, then," Hegrun said.

"Come on, man," Lazarun said, exasperated. "They're not invincible, no matter what you've heard. They folded like cheap tin as soon as the diplomats dangled a cease-fire. They're cowards."

"Spoken like someone who's never seen one in action," Hegrun said. "He killed four of my people in less than a minute. With a sword, Laz."

Kel's face flushed with disgust at the memory, and a trace of something darker. Pride that this vile man was afraid of Dare.

Lazarun gave Hegrun a dismissive flicking gesture with his right hand. "They lost to the demolisher. It's done. Now we're just waiting for the funds to manifest so we can swoop in and save the day."

"And if the funds don't manifest?" Hegrun asked.

"They will." The certainty in his voice tossed fuel on the flame of Kel's anger again. "Go on back to whatever hole you crawled out of for now. Meet me here tomorrow night, same time. If I'm not here, come back the next night."

"How will I know if you're never coming back?" Hegrun asked sarcastically.

Lazarun didn't respond, simply snorted and walked away. Hegrun and Miza watched the soldiers go, their faces shadowed.

"Send me that holo!" Hegrun called after him. Again, there was no response.

"Do we wait?" Miza asked.

Hegrun turned to his second, his expression fixed in a venomous scowl. "That fool's going to get himself killed. As soon as he sends the holo, we steal flitters and head toward their base up north. If he doesn't, we get Jenz to fake something and do the same. I don't want to be here when this place goes to shit."

Kel almost wished she could tell him not to worry, that she didn't intend to harm the Pale soldiers, nor did she have the means. But she might. She could. If they were going to spread the news of local Order activity far and wide, the only reason for her to continue to hide would be to keep the Dirges an extra step behind her. But if they came, they would catch up eventually. She couldn't stay on Loth.

Unless the soldiers and Hegrun didn't get the chance to report their information to anyone. And their deaths were made to look accidental.

Grim thoughts grew in Kel's mind like the busy sounds of the lake at night, jumbling together until all she could hear was the rush of her own blood, like the thunder of water tumbling down to the rocks beneath her. She watched the men depart before quietly returning to the guesthouse, no longer staying in the shadows.

# CHAPTER EIGHTEEN

When Kel arrived, the guesthouse was in an uproar. All semblance of order had fled, people now wildly rushing to and fro instead of staying at their food-packing stations or sedately carrying supplies between tables. Some sat on loosely arranged chairs or long benches, and clusters of children shrieked and spun, and—was that music? Clapping? It took her several blinks to register that everyone was smiling, happy, even excited, and that they were dancing, some with their braids loose and streaming behind them.

Had they finished with the meals already? No, some pots and pans still steamed in the kitchens, and the smells of spiced vegetables and baking bread filled the room. And yet this had apparently become a celebration rather than a stoic group labor. Were they simply making the best of a bad situation? Certainly everyone who wasn't up and about seemed to be eating. A break for the evening meal, perhaps?

How could anyone think of frivolities when the demolisher would be in range within hours?

A few people tried to draw her into the dance, but Kel stepped away, pressing herself against the wall next to the door. If the throng had been overwhelming before, now it was suffocating. She had to get to the hallway that led to the sleeping quarters and check on Lunna.

As if summoned by her thoughts, Lunna jumped to be seen over the crowd, their bright red hair bouncing as they waved their arm frantically to get Kel's attention. Kel waved back, gesturing for them to come to her; she didn't think she'd be able to navigate her way over, not the way her breath was coming fast and her vision was going sparkly.

Get ahold of yourself, she thought sternly. Unfortunately, her body had other ideas. A hysterical laugh bubbled up from deep inside. She'd been in countless battles against human and machine, guarded people with her own body even after her shield and armor had failed and her wounds soaked into her uniform, launched herself into the void between starships with no hesitation; yet here, in the midst of kind, pleasant people who meant her no harm whatsoever, she was obstinately panicked for no apparent reason.

"Friend Kel?" Lunna asked, their voice hard to hear over the din of the room. They sounded puzzled, concerned, and oddly distant.

"Out," Kel managed to say, and then her legs were moving. In a blink she was leaning against the side wall of the building away from the main street, forehead resting on her arm as she sucked in great lungfuls of night air, smelling faintly of stone and water and green things. A few laughing people exited after her, singing something about the moon and stars and a traveler's eyes, their stumbling steps suggesting they were half drunk. It was difficult to focus on them, on anything, and the longer she struggled, the harder it became.

Smooth-planed wall under my hand, Kel thought. Hard ground. Feet sweating in my boots. Machete straps tight on my thigh. Insects circling the light. No crowds, no bodies. Thick green air. The open hand catches the closed fist. The cool water quenches the raging fire. In the storm, the calm eye. Above the storm, clear sky. Life is breath. Inhale. Exhale. Let it pass.

Gradually, Kel's pulse slowed and she regained control over her trembling limbs. She unclenched her jaw and relaxed her shoulders, the ache in her neck attesting to how tight her muscles had been only moments earlier.

"Kel, with every respect, you do not look well," Lunna said. They stood nearby, hugging themself as if unsure whether to offer the comfort of touch.

"I will recover," Kel said. She wiped her forehead with her sleeve, the smooth metal of her bracer beneath reminding her of the conversation she had just witnessed. What would she tell Lunna? The Speakers? She had to warn them.

"I would invite you back in to the feast," Lunna said, "but I think it's best if you rest. If that's what you wish, of course. Where have you been? Did you—?" Their gaze flicked up, past Kel, eyes widening as their mouth fell open in what looked like a warning.

Fingers brushed Kel's shoulder and she instinctively moved to defend herself. By the time her mind caught up with her body, she held a muscled arm in a lock behind a broad back with a sword crossing it, pressing a familiar face against the wall.

"Blessed stars!" she exclaimed, releasing her grip and stepping away, hands raised in apology. If she hadn't just been holding him, she'd have thought he was a ghost.

Dare clutched his shoulder, rotating his arm carefully. "Hello to you as well," he said with a wry smile. His black shirt was gray-streaked with dried sweat, his lower lip split but scabbed over.

"I think he was expecting a friendlier welcome," Savvy said, stepping out of the shadows. Her face was smudged with dirt, her curly hair coated in a thin layer of grime, but her eyes crinkled with amusement.

"You're not dead," Kel said faintly.

"Disappointed?" Savvy joked, but her smile vanished. "We're fine," she continued. "The demolisher is deactivated. Everything can go back to normal now."

Kel grimaced and shook her head. "We need to talk," she said. "Lunna, can you get my staff and pack, please? And yours, too."

"Of course, Kel," Lunna said. Instead of going in through the front door, they darted around the opposite corner to the back.

Privacy. They needed a place they wouldn't be observed easily. The Speakers' office would do, as it was likely to be empty. Kel had no doubt the party in the guesthouse was to celebrate the news she'd just received, which meant Savvy and Dare must have returned after she left, and someone had spread word of their success. The Speakers would report back to Esrondaa, then they would join the celebration themselves, and anyone with essential business could find them there. If the feast ended before dawn, Kel would be surprised. Everyone would enjoy their impromptu holiday tomorrow.

Except for the Pale soldiers. They would be furious.

"Any chance we can clean up before we chat?" Savvy asked, a single eyebrow raised.

Kel considered it. "Not here," she said. "The fewer people who see you two, the better."

Savvy and Dare exchanged a glance and retreated out of the light. Savvy leaned casually, one leg bent, boot pressed against the far wall. Dare pulled his sword off his back and rested the point on the ground, the pommel on his chest. His gaze swept methodically up and down the alley in which they stood. Kel did the same, and they all silently waited for Lunna to return.

The patter of footsteps signaled their arrival, but until Lunna's familiar red hair appeared, tension suffused the air like static. Their freckled cheeks, rounded from smiling, flattened out as they realized no one else was happy.

"What—?" Lunna began.

"Later," Kel said, holding out her hand for her things. "Come with us so we can discuss the situation, please."

Lunna nodded solemnly and passed Kel the bag and staff. Without another word, they made for the Speakers' building. The entire way there, Kel rehearsed what she was going to say, and hoped one of them would see some path out of this mess that wouldn't end in pain and death.

One of the Speakers was leaving as they arrived, and she

offered Kel a tense smile and a thumb to her chin. "Good to see you again, friend," she said. "The news has reached you?"

"It has," Kel replied. "May we use your offices? You do not need to stay," she added quickly, as the woman's expression pinched with dismay.

"Of course," the Speaker said. "The building is communal." She held the door open and gestured for them all to enter, which they did, Dare's gaze sweeping the area one last time. The Speaker closed the door behind them, no doubt off to the celebration.

They set up in a side room used for meetings, with high windows and a dozen chairs neatly tucked under a long wooden table. Dare took a seat that let him see all the entry points, while Savvy slumped down across from him. Kel stayed close to the door, and Lunna sat stiffly next to Savvy, their brows furrowed and lips thinned in confusion and concern.

Without preamble, Kel pulled the hummer out of her pack and set it on the table, turning it on. The whine sank into her teeth; gritting them didn't help, so she forced her jaw to relax.

"Do you want to clean up first?" Kel asked.

Savvy and Dare shared a look, then shook their heads in unison.

"Might as well get this over with," Savvy said. "We're the good news, obviously, so I presume you have the bad news."

"Is it that the soldiers activated the demolisher?" Dare asked.

Kel nodded, but before she could continue, Savvy interrupted.

"We already suspected that," Savvy said. "It's an annoyance, to be sure, but as long as we keep shutting down their nasty little scheme, eventually they'll give up and move on. Or get called back to their duties. Or get themselves killed, if we're lucky." Her smile at that was sinister.

Something about her tone put Kel on edge. Was Savvy lying? If so, what about?

"The risk is if we have to leave before they do," Savvy continued. "The Speakers can report them to the Pale and see what comes of it, but . . ." She shrugged.

"The Pale won't help, will they?" Lunna asked, a frown marring their usually open face. "Not even to stop their own people from doing something so wrong?"

"They might," Dare said grudgingly. "But at most they would likely recall the soldiers, not send anyone to collect them. They wouldn't punish them, especially if some of them are colluding."

"Which they are," Kel interjected. "They said as much."

"Their superiors might just let the soldiers finish the job," Savvy muttered, staring into space. "Claim bureaucratic slowdowns prevented the right person from hearing about it until it was too late, how very sad, and would Loth like to become a colony world now for the low price of everyone's freedom?"

"But we already told them no!" Lunna exclaimed, rising to their feet in a clatter of chair motion. "They can't make us do it! We'll . . . we'll fight them!" Thoughts flitted across Lunna's expressive face, their brow furrowing and their mouth half-forming words, until finally they sat back down, shoulders slumped.

"You can't fight them," Kel said quietly.

"Of course they can," Dare said. "They'll simply die."

"I don't want to die," Lunna said. "You killed those people in the lake, and it was horrible. I don't want that. Not for me, or my family, or my friends." They looked beseechingly at Savvy. "What can we do?"

Before Savvy could answer, Kel said, "I have other news."

"I don't suppose it's good," Savvy said, pinching the bridge of her nose and sliding her fingers up to rub her grit-covered forehead.

"Hegrun is here," Kel said. Lunna gasped, but she ignored it and continued. "He's a privateer, and he brought his surviving crew to negotiate passage with the Pale soldiers when they leave. As payment, he told them about Dare's bracer and they all drew their own conclusions."

Dare cursed under his breath, and Savvy raised a hand to silence him. "What exactly do they think?" she asked.

"They aren't certain," Kel said. "They suspect he's a former Order member, but the tech alone is valuable enough for them to want it. We'll have to stay hidden while Hegrun is here, or the soldiers may come after us all. Even when you're gone, if word gets out—"

"The Pale will send someone to investigate," Savvy said. "And they'll be after us, too." With a groan, she let her head fall back until she was facing the ceiling. "I hate having to ditch perfectly good identities."

Lunna wrinkled their nose. "What do you mean, they'll send someone to investigate?"

"A few years ago, it might have meant only that," Dare said, staring at the door as if seeing something else. "They would send a spy first, someone trained in diplomacy or embedded in the bureaucratic system, on some pretense that had nothing to do with the Order of the Nine. The spy would ask questions, sniff around, then leave and write a report to their superiors. It might escalate, or it might not. But when the Order of Mercy was disbanded, all pretenses were dropped. They'll send a Dirge. They can't afford for their victory over the Order of the Nine to be seen as less than absolute."

He looked up at Kel, who nodded. She had expected as much. The fear and despair she'd felt before slowly drained away as she struggled to figure out a plan, any plan, that would save Loth from Pale control.

"Lazarun said their pulsecom wasn't working," she said. "They would have to go back to their base to contact anyone off-planet."

Dare's eyes narrowed while Savvy smiled and sat up straighter in her chair.

"Well bless my boots," she said. "That does give us a fair chance, doesn't it?"

"A chance to what?" Lunna asked.

"Kill them before they tattle," Savvy said.

Having it said so bluntly made Kel wince, even though she'd all but said it herself.

Were their deaths an acceptable price for Loth's freedom? Kel considered the cold way the Pale soldiers had planned and implemented their blackmail scheme, how they were prepared to allow Handeen to fall and any people in it to die if it meant being paid to stop the machine they themselves had activated. And Hegrun's crimes spoke for themselves. Surely if anyone was worth killing, it would be them.

But doing so might only delay the inevitable. Someone could come searching for them and decide Loth was suspicious enough to warrant closer observation, And . . . Kel struggled to imagine killing someone in cold blood. When guarding someone, yes, or when fighting soldiers who knew the risks and chose to take them in the hopes of winning the day. But even that felt ugly and empty, the failure of discussion and diplomacy to solve a problem both sides believed in strongly enough to compel them to action.

*Is violence inevitable?* Kel had asked one of the Order's Sages once. The Sage's reply came to her again, bringing the warm scent of summer flowers through an open window.

*Nothing is sure but the sunrise. Those who believe violence is a useful tool are often quicker to reach for it. Those who believe violence is the answer will be first to ask the question.*

"Kel?" Savvy asked.

"I'm sorry, I was far away," Kel said. "What did you say?"

"I asked if you knew where the Pale soldiers were staying," Savvy repeated.

Kel's gaze shifted to Dare, who gave the barest shake of his head. His implants should allow him to track them the way he had tracked the grimstalker, then the demolisher. If he couldn't, it meant they were either out of his range, or they'd found a way to disable or mask their own tracking subroutines.

"I know where they'll be tomorrow night," Kel said, "assuming they keep their appointment with Hegrun. When they made it, they didn't know you'd stopped the demolisher. They still might not."

Dare leaned forward, his green eyes cold and hard.

"Hegrun will be there, even if they aren't. We can end him as we should have back at the lake."

"Leave no witnesses," Savvy agreed.

Lunna stared at them all, aghast, their mouth half-open. "How can you sit here and casually plan to kill people?"

Dare glanced at Kel, then looked squarely at Lunna. "Let me tell you about how the Pale occupy worlds," he said. "It starts with a few of them visiting. They heap praises on everything they see, but buried within the praise is a seed of scorn that begins to poison you from inside. Next, they send merchants who wish to trade with you, diplomats to negotiate treaties. They make you feel special," he spat, "and yet still insufficient. If only you were part of the Pale, they say, you would be so much more. Better. Stronger. Their poisoned words grow in you until you want nothing so much as to become one of them. You demand it of your leaders, and so you are consumed."

"What if it doesn't work?" Lunna asked, their voice barely above a horrified whisper. "What if the people don't believe their lies?"

"That," Dare said, "is why they have armies."

Savvy reached out to pat Lunna's hand. "It's them or you, sweetling," she said. Lunna twitched away, wrapping their arms around their upper waist as they stared down at the table.

This was another death, Kel thought, of the innocence that came from a life of love and safety. If Lunna had stayed home with their family, they might never have had to suffer this loss. Other losses, perhaps, but they might have continued until they had children or grandchildren or niblings, all of them growing up and old without the fear and sorrow and frustration Lunna was feeling now. It was too late to save them. They could never return to that and be who they had been.

To her surprise, Lunna collected themself, sitting taller next to Savvy. Their freckles stood out sharply against their creamy skin, blue eyes dark as the shields of the Order of Mare.

"If a throllax attacks a hunter, the hunter may defend themself without guilt," Lunna said. "The death of the throllax is regrettable but necessary if the hunter can't escape or subdue the creature otherwise. Anyone who will kill innocents on purpose is no better than a throllax, and their demolisher already attacked us once. And the bandits tried to kill us, too, when all we did was take back what was ours to begin with. We're defending ourselves, and they would do worse to us in our place." They nodded as if satisfied, a small smile returning to their face.

Savvy stared at Lunna, then barked out a laugh. "There you have it, then. That's one vote for the plan."

"What plan?" Dare asked. "We have a goal, not a plan."

Savvy gestured at Kel. "We know where they'll be, she said. We wait, we spring a trap."

Dare and Kel shared a deadpan look, then simultaneously returned their gazes to Savvy.

"Oh, sure," Savvy said. "You want to know how we do it. Typical." More quietly, she muttered, "What did I do to deserve two Dares at once?"

Kel flushed at the comparison, then said, "We can scout the area, then discuss more concrete strategies. Dare and I

have the most experience with this, so we can take the lead."
As soon as she said it, she realized the potential implications
of her words. She looked first at Lunna, who was simply nodding in agreement; they hadn't ascribed any deeper meaning
to what she'd said. Savvy, however, raised an eyebrow, and
Dare's mouth thinned to a grim line.

"If that's all right with you, Captain," Kel said, acutely
aware of how formal she sounded now. That did make Lunna
blink and furrow their brow slightly, looking to Savvy for an
answer.

"I don't mind leading from the back," Savvy said dryly,
her lip curled at the corner. "In fact, why don't you and Dare
go scout the area, then give Lunna and me a report on your
recommendations?"

Dare snorted. "Shall we submit it in writing? Perhaps a
formal presentation with holos?"

"Whatever you think is best," Savvy said, flapping her
hand dismissively. But her smile widened, and she winked at
Kel before standing. "While you're out getting dirtier, Lunna
can show me where to clean up. Is there somewhere to rest in
here other than the floor?"

Lunna sprang to their feet. "Yes, there's an extra sleeping
quarters and washroom like in Beelea, for guests or locals
who need privacy. No food, though, I'm so sorry," they added,
embarrassed.

"I still have some in my pack," Savvy replied, patting
their arm gently.

"I can sneak over to the guesthouse if—" Lunna began.

"Let's not take chances," Savvy replied quickly. "Better

to stay away from the crowds in case they recognize us and start a fuss."

"Oh, you're right," Lunna said. "Here, the washroom is this way." They opened the door and held it for Savvy, who moved slowly, gingerly, a slight limp in her right leg.

She and Dare hadn't said how they survived the poison gas, or what happened with the demolisher to make it shift to attack mode. Perhaps it had been a quick, temporary change? If so, and Kel hadn't insisted on fleeing, a lot of pain might have been avoided. It had seemed like the right choice at the time, though. So many things did.

She'd ask Dare once they got to the lake. A flush rose from her neck to her face as she realized why Savvy had winked at her, and why they had been sent off alone.

Dare's green eyes stared impassively at her as she rose. Neither of them spoke as they left the room, then the building, the darkness closing around them like a gloved hand.

# CHAPTER NINETEEN

With the moon fully risen, it was easier for Kel to find her way back to the lakeside meeting spot, but harder to stay hidden from anyone who might be watching her and Dare. They stuck to the shadows where possible, but the darkness was softer now, less deep and sharp. The homes around them were mostly silent, with everyone at the guesthouse to celebrate the demolisher's deactivation. Instead of the quiet noises of domesticity, the rattle and hum of insects permeated the area, punctuated by the occasional call of a night bird or the sudden flutter of wings. Sometimes a wind sprung up and shook the trees with a shushing noise like heavy rain. It was almost like being back at her house, but the texture of the sound and silence were different, as were the smells of the homes and trees and the water beyond.

Kel pointed out the place she'd hidden before, which could probably accommodate two of them if they were careful. Together, she and Dare walked the perimeter, discussing potential tactics, checking distances between various landscape features and identifying obvious escape routes for themselves or their enemies. Her experience was more in observing her surroundings and determining how to best guard someone given the circumstances, but as she had expected, Dare was no stranger to ambush tactics from his time on Izlan, and beyond.

The reminder of her lost home rang through Kel's heart like a bell, but she pushed the feeling away.

"Can you sense the soldiers?" Kel asked.

"They're either out of range or they have some means of remaining undetected." He picked up a smooth stone and hefted it in his hand, glaring at it as if it had offended him.

"This isn't a standard mission for you and Savvy, I take it?" Kel asked.

Dare shook his head as he tossed the stone toward the water. "We've been in our share of fights, but we're typically hired for courier or transport purposes. Or shutting down stray demolishers, or helping to move ones left in awkward places. Occasionally causing trouble for units left behind to occupy isolated areas." He smiled at that one before his expression returned to careful neutrality. "The Defiants include a fair number of former Order members, to my knowledge. They're trying to step in and do what you used to do. Medical aid, crisis management, protection against pirates . . . whatever they can."

Kel inhaled sharply. "I imagine the Dirges don't make it easy," she said.

"There are only so many Dirges. They can't be everywhere at once, and it's a large galaxy. The Pale aren't welcome in some places, which makes it harder for them to operate."

"Small graces," Kel murmured, looking out over the lake at the risen moon. It carved a path across the water that shimmered as the wind and current turned the surface to small waves. The tall grass around them rustled, the stalks brushing against their boots.

Dare moved closer, standing within arm's reach. "You know you cannot stay here after this," he said gently. "Even if we end these soldiers, stop them from reporting back and fake their deaths by some other means, your presence is a danger to Loth."

Kel wanted to protest, to insist it wasn't so dire assuming they covered their trail, but she had her doubts. All it would take was a single survivor, a single account of her existence or Dare's bracer reaching the wrong ears or eyes, to bring the Pale down harder on this planet. The Lothians had worked to build their own culture over hundreds of years, starting with the foundations they brought from their original home-world, and while a few of them grew tired of it and returned to the rest of the galaxy, the others loved it. They deserved peace and autonomy.

If Kel's absence guaranteed that freedom for even a little longer, she would be selfish to stay.

"Perhaps I can—" Find another place like Loth, she had started to say, but the same would be true of anywhere she went. And anyone she traveled with would be exposing themselves to similar problems.

"Can what?" Dare asked.

Kel shook her head. "I don't know. I thought all I had to do was hide, but that isn't good enough." She smiled bitterly.

"I wonder how many of my people realized how futile this all was in the end, and chose the manner of their own deaths so they would burn as brightly as they could before being snuffed out."

"Some did," Dare said, grimacing. "I was already free when the Order was fully disbanded, but Savvy and I would still hear stories." He hesitated, searching Kel's face. "I can tell you what I know, if you want me to."

A hard question to answer. The knowledge would give her nothing but pain, since the events of the past were fixed, immutable. But perhaps she would find closure, rather than endlessly wondering who was still alive, who dead. Perhaps she could take solace in the fact that not all her people had chosen to live and die alone, in shadow and secret.

Perhaps it would give her the strength to follow their path. Better to have something to die for than nothing to live for.

Dare gripped her shoulder suddenly. "Don't," he said. "You are not an easy one to read, Kel, but I saw that much. You owe your life to no one but yourself."

Kel shifted away, anguish rushing in to fill the pitted ruins of her heart. "I owed the Order everything," she said. "They were my family, my friends, my cause. Without them, I am no one and nothing. Less than nothing. A hollow void without a true name. Even a black hole was once a star."

Her legs trembled beneath her and she sat down in the tall grass, the tips of the stalks brushing her arms and back. She bent one leg and tucked her foot close to her thigh, resting her forehead on her knee.

"Why did you join the Order?" Dare asked. "They weren't like the Pale. They didn't force anyone to fight for them. Why did you?"

"I wanted to help," Kel said. "My own family suffered from hard times when I was young, and the Order saved us."

"Hard times?" Dare asked. He sat down next to her, close enough to speak quietly, but not touching.

"An earthquake left us homeless and hungry," Kel said. "There were so many of us, and so little food and clean water." The entire generation building she'd lived in had come down, killing some of its residents, trapping others beneath rubble. She remembered that time in ugly shards—helping shift stones with her hands, her nails tearing, palms and fingertips scraped and bleeding; her siblings crying in fear and confusion as one mother soothed them and the other argued with an uncle about rations; sleeping under the brilliant star-filled sky, huddled close to the rest of her family for warmth; the triumphant shouts of abandoned grief as a survivor was found after hope had been lost. The wails when the opposite was true.

"And the Order arrived with supplies and medical care?" Dare asked.

"Among other things," Kel said. She began to break off pieces of grass and weave them together. "Immediate supplies first, and medics. They helped search the ruins for anyone still trapped, with instruments I'd never seen or heard of. They organized people, gave them purpose. And after the situation was stable, they helped us rebuild. They lived with us, worked with us."

"And unlike the Pale, they left when the work was finished."

Kel nodded, staring down at the braided length of grass in her hands. "They gave so much and took so little in return. They only asked that we do what we could to repay the kindness when we were able."

"Did you?"

"It took a few years, but yes." Kel smiled wistfully. "I was already part of the Order myself by then. I had thought I wanted to be in the Order of Mercy, focus on healing perhaps. That was before I saw a Knight-Celestial for the first time."

"Impressed, were you?" Dare gave her a hesitant grin.

"More like dazzled," Kel replied. "Have you ever seen a Knight-Celestial in full armor?"

"Not in person," Dare said, looking away. "Only in holos." More quietly, he added, "In debriefings and warnings."

"It is . . . incredible." That memory, too, raced through her. A shimmering figure limned by the sun descending from the top of a tall building, wings folded back, then snapping out like strands of white flame as they glided to a halt and landed gracefully in front of Kel and her fellow students. Pearlescent armor encased them from head to foot, the smooth crystalline energy seeming to both catch the light and give off its own inner glow. Then the armor vanished, and a mere human stood before them, smiling radiantly, wearing a tight-fitting uniform with a nine-pointed star on their chest. The instructor had blushed as the Knight-Celestial bowed over his hand, and Kel had only learned later that the two were lovers who hadn't seen each other in months.

In that moment, all she had cared about was the thought of soaring through the sky like a bird. It felt embarrassing now to admit that to herself, that for all her noble intentions, she'd been swayed to another path for selfish reasons. The more she had learned about the Order of the Nine, though, the more they sounded like figures from myth or legend. Another way to help those who needed it, to protect them when their lives were threatened directly by violence. To guard those who tried to preserve peace through diplomacy or aid.

Where peace is lost, may we find it, she thought, realizing that while she had thought she'd found peace on Loth, she never truly had. She had been too alienated from everyone around her, too afraid of making a mistake that would cascade and cause the end of the Order somehow, too worried about a Dirge finding her and not only killing her, but harming someone nearby as well.

"I had thought peace meant simply avoiding conflict," Kel murmured, "and I thought I could manage that by being alone. But I will never be at peace so long as my circumstances are controlled, even indirectly, by an unjust regime."

"That is not peace," Dare agreed. "That is only a temporary cease-fire."

"I need to do something," she said, clenching the grass braid in her fist. "I need to fight back, even if I never raise a sword again. There are other ways to seek justice; I simply have to find them."

Dare hesitated, then put a hand on her knee. "I already said you could come with us," he said. "Even if you don't want to stay on board, we can take you somewhere else. Find Defiants to help you do whatever you're meant to."

"The offer is tempting," Kel said, meeting his green eyes, which flashed in the dark. It was hard to tell whether he flushed, but the hand on her knee grew warmer.

"I don't want you to think I'm trying to—" He looked away, clearing his throat. "I am not attempting to trade favors, or coerce you into doing anything you don't want. Nor am I making any promises I can't be sure of keeping regarding my feelings."

"What feelings are those?" Kel asked.

His roguish smile returned. "I thought we went over that in some detail yesterday." He rubbed her knee lightly with his thumb, and the memories of what they'd done in the forest sparked a flash of pleasure.

"So this is merely physical attraction?" Kel asked, closing her eyes to better enjoy the caress.

"I admire you greatly," Dare said carefully. "But I would be lying if I claimed some unbreakable bond with a woman I met less than a week ago." His hand slid down her thigh, slowly, giving her time to pull away. She didn't.

Kel huffed out a laugh. "Not a romantic, then?"

"Are you?"

"Perhaps I am. I would have said I'm a realist, having seen what love can do and be. To generalize that experience would be foolish, though, wouldn't it? Not everyone is so fortunate."

Dare's hand stopped, then he took it back. "No, not everyone is," he said. "Some of us wouldn't know love if it slid through our ribs like a knife."

Kel's stomach lurched at the implications of what they'd both said. "The Pale were bad, I'm sure, but even before that, you didn't—"

"I remember little of it," Dare said curtly. "I was ten standard years old. My family got a fair number of domins for me, as a signing bonus, and had one less mouth to feed after."

"Is that how their conscription works?" Kel asked, a sour taste in her mouth.

"More or less," Dare said. "Sometimes the incentives aren't monetary. Sometimes it's join or die. At least my sisters got a few meals out of it. I saw others ripped from their homes screaming, or sedated and tossed in a box like so much cargo." He tore up a patch of grass as he spoke, tossing it away almost immediately after in apparent disgust.

"How have they not all defected?" Kel murmured, half to herself.

"The implants," Dare said. "They keep us compliant. Why else bait a trap with the promise of having them deactivated? But don't imagine there are no voluntary recruits. Plenty of good little citizens are happy to spread the civilizing influence of the Anocracy to every star in the galaxy."

He fell silent, lost in his own memories, and Kel didn't disturb him further with painful questions. Would it always be like this with him, if she accepted his offer to travel with him and Savvy? There was an attraction, yes, but how much of the growing pull she felt toward Dare was the first stirrings of something deeper, and how much was her natural impulse to help someone in need? Was it possible to overcome their own separate histories, to heal their wounds enough to find

more than temporary passion? Could they ever truly be more
to each other than former enemies?

Once, she would have said all things were possible. Now,
she wondered.

The night breeze ruffled Dare's silver hair as he stared at
the lake. Kel checked around them for any sign of someone
possibly watching, then pulled off her head covering and ran
her hands through her own hair with a soft sigh. It was a
sweaty mess, no doubt, but she wanted to feel the cool air on
her scalp, if only for a little while.

"You always wear that thing, don't you?" Dare asked.

"As you always wear your gloves, I imagine," Kel replied.
She untied the knot in the cloth and spread it out so she could
refold it and put it back on.

Dare pressed a hand on the cloth to stop her. One by
one, he took off his gloves and tucked them into his pocket.
Then he shifted closer and raised a hand to her face, caress-
ing her cheek with his thumb before running his bare fingers
through her hair. They stopped at the base of her neck, nearly
burning her despite the gentleness of the pressure.

"It's a mess," Kel muttered apologetically. Blessed stars, his
eyes were beautiful.

"What, your hair?" Dare asked.

"Among other things, I suppose." The situation. Her life.
The galaxy.

"And?" Dare leaned in, his lips hovering above hers.

"And we're talking too much again." She closed the distance, kissing him as if it solved all their problems.

Maybe, for a little while, it did. Maybe love, even just
the spark of its becoming, was the only good solution to any

problem. Maybe it was another kind of cease-fire, an armistice between people and the fates, waiting to be broken.

The future was uncertain, now more than ever. But the present could be managed, one kiss at a time.

EVENTUALLY, EXHAUSTION CREPT PAST THE WALLS OF PLEASURE KEL AND Dare built around themselves, and they reluctantly agreed to return to the meeting room with its private sleeping quarters. Tension seeped back in as they moved from shadow to shadow, Dare wearing his gloves, Kel's hair hidden under its covering. She wondered briefly if she might be able to get a new hat before she left, having lost hers to the river, then winced at the thought that leaving meant she would have no need to blend in on Loth anymore.

The sounds of far-off celebration rose and fell in irregular waves, a reminder that for now, the people of Handeen were safe. Kel wasn't sure whether the Speakers, including Speaker Yiulea, truly believed the situation was resolved; if not, they must have decided even temporary success was worth a little revelry. The question of how the Pale soldiers would react to the knowledge that their plan had failed, well, that was a problem for another time.

Outside the building, Dare gave a soft, fluttery whistle, then waited. An answering call came after a ten count, and he led Kel inside. Everything was quiet as they entered, smelling faintly of mushroom wine. A peek into the sleeping quarters showed Lunna in one of the two beds, curled up on their side with an arm flung over their face, more relaxed than they'd

been at the guesthouse earlier. Kel smiled, glad for this respite for her friend, brief though it might be.

Savvy rose from her seated position on the other bed,
holding a finger to her lips. With the other hand, she mo-
tioned them into the other room, where the hummer still
waited on the table. Kel raised an eyebrow and inclined her
head at it, and Savvy nodded, so she flicked it on. It would
be a wonder if the whine didn't wake Lunna up sooner than
their voices would have.

"So," Savvy said, falling into a chair and gesturing for
Dare to talk.

"We'd have to be fast," Dare said. He didn't sit, pacing
instead. "The area is too open for any kind of bottleneck, but
we can pin them on one side against the lake. If we flank them,
their only choices would be to run toward the village, jump in
the water or take cover behind a few trees and boulders."

"You're out of ammo for your sniper rifle," Savvy reminded him.

"We have the other weapons we took from Hegrun," he
countered.

"Yes, but that means we have to be close enough to use
them, and the Pale have armor." Savvy sighed and peered up
at Kel, who stood with her hands loosely clasped behind her
back. "Think it would be easier for Dare to let loose like he
did back on the boat?"

"It might work," Kel said. "You and I flank and he attacks
up the middle."

"We have to be sure we've eliminated all of them before
they can run," Dare said.

"We need to do that anyway," Savvy said. "The question is, which method would make that easier?" She propped her head up with a hand to her forehead, her face lined with fatigue.

Kel forced herself to relax her shoulders, which were slowly creeping toward her ears. "We can finish this discussion in the morning," she said. "You need to rest, and I doubt the soldiers will return before then. I'll keep watch the first half of the night and wake Dare for the rest."

Savvy laughed, more bitter than amused. "I'll sleep when the void takes me. But thanks for the polite reminder that I look like warm smarth shit."

"That's not what I—" Kel swallowed the rest of her words. She'd fallen into old habits again. Every time she wasn't careful, it seemed to happen.

"Savvy," Dare said, his tone split between chiding and annoyed.

"Was there something else you wanted to discuss?" Savvy asked innocently. "Perhaps you could tell me how your recon went in more explicit detail."

Kel flushed and cleared her throat, but Dare simply glared at Savvy, who smiled unrepentantly.

"I do have one question," Kel said, and they both turned wary gazes to her. "What happened with the demolisher? Why did it switch to attack mode? How did you survive the poison?"

"That's three questions," Savvy said. "It didn't change modes. You misunderstood what had happened. Everything was under control the whole time."

"Is that what you told the Speakers?" Kel asked.

"Of course," Savvy said, meeting Kel's eyes directly. "It's the truth."

Kel maintained as neutral an expression as she could manage. Savvy really was an excellent liar. That she could spin such a falsehood suggested not only a great deal of practice but a natural aptitude. If Kel hadn't known it was a lie from the start, she would have been hard-pressed to tell.

Dare sighed and pressed his palms against the top of the table. "Savvy, you don't have to feed her that story."

Savvy glanced sideways at Kel and switched to Canzoran, which Kel understood though she spoke it haltingly. "When did you get so trusting?"

"When she saved my life even after she saw the scars." Dare enunciated each word sharply.

Savvy groaned, her head lolling back as she rolled her eyes. "Flaming shits, man, if I'd known you were this hard up, I'd have paid for—"

Dare made a rude hand sign and Savvy snorted.

"You don't get to decide who knows what," Savvy said. "We're a team, not a pair of freelancers. What exactly have you told her?"

"She knows I'm the one using the chip. She knows I was a Scourge."

"So you spilled your guts, and she still let you juice her? What do you think that says about her, precisely? That she's so forgiving and merciful?" Savvy spat the last word and turned her glare to Kel, who shifted into a defensive stance. This was a side Savvy hadn't shown before, hard and vicious.

Dare, to her surprise, recoiled and clenched his hands into fists, his eyes closed. His hunched back suggested he was suppressing thoughts, emotions, all roiling inside him like a storm in his gut. She didn't like that, either. As she looked between him and Savvy, she realized something ugly they both shared, something she felt in her own way.

"Savvy," she said quietly.

"What?" Savvy snapped.

"Dare will never stop hating himself if you don't let him," Kel said in Canzoran.

"If I don't—" Savvy began angrily, then stopped. Her eyes widened, her mouth fell open for an instant, and then in a flash she was smiling with her mouth closed. "I suppose you think you understand everything," she said. "But you don't know my secrets. I, on the other hand, can guess yours."

"And?" Kel asked, wearier than any physical exertion could make her.

"You're pathetic," Savvy said. "You told yourself you were alone so often, you began to believe it, when it was never true." She slammed a hand on the table and pointed at Kel. "You could have helped someone. Anyone. You could have used your skills to do something good. Instead, you've hidden on this rim world and let the galaxy fend for itself."

"Savvy—" Dare said.

"I'm not finished!" Savvy roared, standing so fast the chair fell behind her. "We've all lost people, and places, and lives we hoped to have. We've all done things we regret, or failed to do things we wish we had. Maybe the specific shit stuck to your boots smells worse than mine, or Dare's—which I highly doubt—but by all the void between stars, we are none of us clean. So crawl out of your cave of self-righteousness and do something useful for a change. Or don't, but either way, don't you even think of talking down to me like that ever again. Do we understand each other?"

Kel nodded. Savvy was right. She'd been wallowing for ages and it helped no one. It still stung to hear it.

Savvy calmly righted her chair as if she hadn't lost her temper and sat down again. "The demolisher attacked because the control chip Dare used on it was running an outdated version of the command module. We had thought it was the most recent available, but it seems the Pale soldiers ran their own updates before they started this little scheme."

"Thankfully the patch for the chip was also in the system," Dare added. "It took a few minutes to force the upgrade, and then the machine accepted the codes as usual. We masked up before we started the procedure, so the gas didn't harm us."

"If the Pale examine the machine, will they be able to tell what happened?" Kel asked.

"There will be a log, yes," Dare said.

"Normally it wouldn't matter," Savvy said. "But if the soldiers reach the machine before we find them, they could undo all our work and lock out Dare's chip."

So what Savvy said before, about being able to deactivate the demolisher until the soldiers got bored, wasn't a certainty. It explained why she was so keen to kill them quickly. Kel's lips pressed together in displeasure.

"One more reason they can't be allowed to live," Dare said grimly, as if he heard her thoughts. "If the demolisher manages to interface with the Pale uplink in the north, or if the soldiers obtain the log and upload it themselves, my chip would become useless. Not just here, but everywhere."

"And that means no more helping people like this," Savvy said, staring at Kel fixedly. "So you can see why this matters to us. We don't want Dirges and bounty hunters after us for Order tech, and we don't want to lose a chunk of our livelihood, and we don't want future Loths to be left to the nonexistent mercy of the Pale. You don't want to be tainted by association, or to have the Pale descend on this perfect paradise of yours. I ask you again, do we understand each other?"

"We do," Kel said. "You can rely on me to do what must be done."

Dare seemed to be trying to tell her something with his gaze, but she looked away, her ears still ringing from Savvy's blistering rebuke.

One thing was certain: she wouldn't be traveling anywhere with Savvy and Dare after this was over. She wished she had held her tongue, but it was too late, and perhaps it was for the best that she knew how Savvy felt about her. She'd find another way to leave Loth as soon as possible, once she knew it was safe from the demolisher.

# CHAPTER TWENTY

Kel, Savvy, and Dare spent an awkward, long day hiding in the back room of the Speakers' office. Lunna brought them meals from the guesthouse, since they were the least likely to be recognized as an outsider by either the Pale soldiers or Hegrun's people. Savvy alternated between napping, making notes on a handheld scriber she dug out of her pack, and, to Kel's consternation, juggling knives. Lunna, between errands, studied the starship manuals they'd brought with them from home. Dare exercised, which Kel found most interesting because his methods differed from hers, and they discussed the benefits and drawbacks of the various techniques while performing them together.

"Two Dares," Savvy muttered to Lunna at one point. "At least now he has someone to practice grappling on instead of dragging me into it."

When not exercising, Kel meditated and cogitated. Sometimes she was able to focus on her breathing and let her busy mind recede enough to fall into a peaceful trance, but more often she thought about their journey, all they had gone through to reach this point, and everything Savvy had said the night before. If she once again set herself the task of helping others, what would be the best way to accomplish it, once this mission was over? Different answers presented themselves, all of them carrying an element of uncertainty. But then, when had anything in life ever been certain?

Night finally fell, and Savvy got rid of Lunna by sending them to the guesthouse with orders to keep a low profile, listen in to any chatter there and report back. Kel guided Savvy and Dare quickly and quietly to the lake and set up their trap, with Kel and Savvy at two points of a triangle and Dare at the center to catch anyone who ran toward the village. Kel and Savvy carried pistols, while Dare wielded his sword, ready to deploy his shield if needed.

All their plans, in the end, were foiled by the simple problem of the Pale not showing up.

The Pale's leader, Lazarun, had said this might happen, but it was still disappointing. Hegrun didn't come, either, or he and his people never revealed themselves. After a few hours of waiting, with no sign of anyone either visually or with Dare's tracking sensors, Savvy signaled for them to give up and return to the Speakers' office. Lunna hadn't come back yet, so they mutually agreed to stay up to hear that report before going to bed. They sat around the meeting table, Kel straight-backed near the door, Savvy with her feet propped up on one of the chairs, Dare leaning against a wall with his arms crossed.

"Where did the soldiers say they were going?" Savvy asked Kel.

"They didn't," Kel said, gloomily picking at a late snack

of dried fruit and meat. "They said if they weren't there, to come back the next night. But Hegrun told his crewmate they should leave as soon as they had the holo they needed, so he might already be on his way to their base in the north."

Savvy sighed, tugging at her gloves. "So we might lose them anyway if we keep waiting. Damn it all to the void."

"Should we split up?" Kel asked. "Two of us could try to track them, and the other two can stay here to see if they return."

"Not an ideal plan," Dare said, "but potentially necessary if our goal is to ensure none of them live to send a communication off-world."

"How far can they get without a functioning transport?"

Instead of answering, Dare tensed, his eyes brightening. "They're here."

He threw the door open and dashed out of the room, then into the night. Kel and Savvy chased after him, though Savvy fell behind quickly, breathing hard. Kel's boots pounded against the dirt and stone of the streets as she tried to keep the flash of Dare's silver hair in sight. His longer legs gave him an edge, and while he recovered more quickly thanks to his augmentations, Kel still fought days of accumulated exhaustion. Buildings passed in a blur of wood and stone, light and darkness.

She caught up to him a few streets from the guesthouse, turning in circles. He let out a string of curses in Vethonian that was almost poetic in its rhythm and complexity.

"Gone?" Kel asked as her breath steadied.

"They must be cloaking," Dare said. "They appeared out of nowhere, then vanished. If I'd been a little faster—"

"I can't think the Lothians would approve of you killing them in cold blood in the middle of the village."

With a disgusted growl, he turned and began to retrace his steps. Kel followed silently, giving him space. Eventually they found Savvy, who also fell in, and together they returned to the Speakers' office.

Not long after they settled back into their places in the meeting room, Lunna burst in, their wide-eyed expression somewhere between delight and horror. "The Pale came to the guesthouse!" they exclaimed. "They walked in and the one in charge smiled at everyone in a mean way, and they made fun of our food, and then they heard the demolisher had been deactivated and they left!"

Savvy and Dare exchanged a dark look, then Savvy smiled at Lunna. "So they hadn't heard yet? Must have been an unpleasant shock to them."

"They looked mad," Lunna said. "I mean, only the leader had his face showing, but he stopped smiling and said he was glad to hear the problem had been solved. He wasn't glad at all, though." They made a rude gesture with one hand. "Serves them right, the mudsuckers."

"What did they say exactly?" Savvy asked. "More importantly, did they say where they were going?"

Lunna wrinkled their nose. "I think his exact words were, 'I suppose our services aren't needed after all. How fortunate for you.' Then he said something quieter to the Speaker who was there. I couldn't hear that."

"What they did for money, they might now do for spite," Kel muttered.

Dare nodded agreement. "They have incentive to either

reactivate the demolisher or return to their base for additional war machines."

"Would they fire any long-range weapons?" Kel asked.

"Our last intelligence said nothing about those, whatever the Speakers might believe." Savvy steepled her fingers and tucked them under her chin. "There are a half dozen demolishers still at the base, and about fifty grimstalkers, less the one you already encountered."

"So many?" Lunna asked, blue eyes wide with shock.

"There used to be more," Kel said. "Not all of them operational." She pressed her lips together as soon as the words left her mouth. She'd meant to reassure Lunna, but instead she'd told Savvy that she'd known more than she let on previously.

Savvy smiled, her eyes cold. "Kel is right. When this base was decommissioned, they took most of the smaller units with them and let the rest rot. I'm sure they expected to come back eventually, and eventually hasn't happened yet."

"Well, they're here now," Lunna said morosely. "But you don't think they're going to take them and leave, do you? You think this will get worse."

"Don't lose hope," Kel said. "Not while you still live."

"Of course not," Lunna said, tucking a stray hair back into their braid. "You three can handle anything, I'm sure, and if you couldn't, we Lothians aren't entirely helpless."

Certainly they weren't—their dealings with Hegrun alone showed as much—but that didn't mean they were equipped to defend themselves against the Pale's war machines. They had experience preparing for disasters, extensive protocols in place to guide them, but those protocols were mainly designed for natural disasters. Sheltering from a storm or flood wasn't the same as hiding from a giant automaton trying to find and kill you.

But as she'd told Lunna, she wouldn't lose hope. If she was alive, she could help. Whatever was in her power to do, she would, for the sake of these people who had unwittingly hidden her for so long.

Savvy tapped the table with the hilt of a knife that had magically appeared in her hand. "The question now becomes: do we let the Pale go through with whatever new plan their twisted little minds are concocting and deal with it as it comes, or do we try to find them and stop them?"

Dare grunted. "We already planned to kill them. I don't see why this changes anything."

"It changes the strategy," Savvy said. "What if we can't find them in time? They'll have to come back here if they want to get any money out of this debacle. We could set a trap."

"That worked so well for us earlier," Dare muttered.

Savvy pointed her knife at him and dragged the blade theatrically in front of her throat.

"Or they might try to go to Esrondaa after reactivating the demolisher," Kel said. "They know the Speakers here can't pay them. The journey would take them about a sennight with vehicles, as we know from experience, but reaching their base would take longer. Unless they manage to commandeer flitters." She leaned back in her chair. "Dare, what do you think?"

Dare pursed his lips, sensing the undercurrent of her question: what did he think as someone who knew their procedures from following them, who could think like them because he had been one of them?

"They'll likely seek out the demolisher in the gulch to learn how it was deactivated," he said, "which will take them at least a day on foot, and they won't travel at night. Unless, as you said, they obtain flitters. As I see it, that will be the deciding factor for any of their actions going forward."

"I can't imagine they'll subject themselves to a long journey like we did," Savvy said. "They won't walk away with nothing to show for it, but they want their money to be as easy as possible."

"So the flitters will be their top priority. Do we know where they're being kept?"

"In the shelters, I suppose," Lunna mused. "There are some rooms that only Speakers can open."

"And they won't open them tonight, not even for locals." Savvy tossed the knife into the air and caught it by the tip. "They're going to continue celebrating, then they're going to sleep. We should do the same."

"We need to warn the Speakers first," Lunna said, leaping to their feet. "About the Pale. They might be harmed if we don't."

"After making such a dramatic exit, I doubt the soldiers will return so soon to demand vehicles or make threats. They'll be licking their wounds and plotting."

Dare shook his head. "We cannot take the risk of assuming that. If they make it to within pulsecom reach of their base, we've lost."

"So perhaps two of us should go to the demolisher now, and the other two should watch the flitters?" Kel asked.

Savvy narrowed her eyes. "You seem keen to split up, Kel."

Kel blinked at her, wondering whether her confusion showed on her face. "I would not say I'm keen on it," she replied. "I would prefer not to. But given the uncertainty of what the Pale might do next, and whether we'll succeed in catching them, I'm simply trying to cover multiple contingencies."

"We're making best guesses," Dare said. "For all we know, if they obtained vehicles, they might head right to their base to unleash the remaining war machines all at once."

"Even if they did that, it would take time for any machines, aside from the deactivated demolisher, to reach populated areas."

"Not," Savvy said, "if they have access to another transport vehicle."

They fell silent as they considered the full implications of that. A Pale transport like the one Dare had damaged couldn't hold a demolisher, but it could carry all the remaining grimstalkers in their compact travel form. If the soldiers reactivated the demolisher and loosed the other machines? So much of the forest would be destroyed, and the lake, and the area surrounding Lakefall Point, and Handeen itself. If the people didn't evacuate in time, or didn't go far enough away, they could be caught in an ugly storm of laser, plasma, and missile fire. And while the demolishers moved slowly, designed to work at a distance or as siege weapons, the grimstalkers were quick and tireless, and would easily chase down any individuals or groups that didn't barricade themselves inside an impregnable shelter.

"Why are they doing this to us?" Lunna asked, their voice nearly a whisper.

"For money," Dare replied, his ire making his tone raspier than usual. "I tried to warn you before. Perhaps you believe me now."

Lunna nodded mutely, and Kel wished she could offer them some comfort.

The thing she could offer was a resolution that didn't involve the deaths of thousands of Lothians. Even if it meant sacrificing her own life, her anonymity, and consigning herself to the Pale's Dirges. If the animosity and vigilance of her enemy would be turned toward Loth no matter what she did, better to save people now and give them a chance to escape or fight another day.

AFTER DEBATING THE MERITS OF THEIR DIFFERENT OPTIONS, THEY DE-cided to warn the Speakers of the potential for flitter theft, with Kel and Dare offering their services as guards while Lunna and Savvy slept. If the soldiers didn't make things easy by coming to them, they would head to the demolisher together in the morning in the hopes of finding their quarry on the way or beating them to the spot and laying a trap. If they found the machine once again active and advancing, they could shut it down—or, Kel thought privately, she could use Dare's sword and her armor to defeat it for good. If it was still inactive, and the soldiers didn't make an appearance by the next day, they'd return to Handeen and come up with a new plan.

If the worst happened and more war machines had been deployed, their hunt would begin.

Dare would be able to track them remotely if he got within a certain range, thanks to his Pale modifications, which he still hid from Lunna. It was fair to assume they would travel in a more or less straight line toward Handeen, but it wasn't certain.

And they didn't know how many Lothian scouts might be stationed at different points in the forests, or how many people or families lived there because they wanted the solitude. All of them were in danger.

Seated with her back against a boulder, paces away from the entrance to the mountain shelter where the flitters were housed, Kel alternated between watching for the Pale soldiers and sleeping like a stone from sheer fatigue. Just before dawn, Lunna arrived to check on them, and was once again tasked with replenishing their food stores; this time, they were also told to ask anyone at the guesthouse whether the soldiers had been seen again. The hope was that the Pale wouldn't have a head start, that they'd still be resting wherever they'd holed up nearby while Kel and the others were proceeding to the demolisher's location. But anger might push the Pale to hurry, and the farther away they were, the harder it would be to catch them.

Lunna returned with Savvy, plenty of rations and nothing to report. The Pale hadn't been sighted again, but they might still be in Handeen, or halfway to the machine, or sleeping in whatever hole they kept crawling out of. Regardless, packs were shouldered and, with the air crisp as a dry

leaf, they once again began walking through the forest toward the Gounaj Gulch.

All the natural beauty Kel had admired on their first
journey felt muted now, as if the colors had been drained
from the ground and trees and sky. Her boots seemed to be
made of futhite instead of leather, every step heavier than
before, and her pack might have been loaded with stones. She
had stayed fit after she left the Order, but not to the same
degree, and this pushed the limits of her endurance.

Kel quietly coordinated with Dare to ensure their pace
didn't become unreasonable. Sometimes they reached a stretch
of level ground and sped up, other times the terrain tilted
sharply enough to make Kel's muscles burn, or the earth was
strewn with rocks or roots that forced them to be more careful
of their footing. Kel didn't have a mechanical timing device,
but she counted in her head, and the count became its own
form of meditation that allowed her to ease into a focused
yet relaxed flow of movement. Once she reached a certain
number, she called for a rest or signaled that Dare should do
so, and they all replenished their fluids and ate enough to give
them more energy without making their stomachs churn.

The sun traced its usual path across the sky, the shadows
shortened, and the sounds of insects and birds and other animals shifted as some took shelter and others awoke to their
daily rituals. Leaves once more crunched underfoot, and the
alternately rhythmic and ragged sounds of labored breathing
marked the time as surely as Kel's counting.

The midday meal was somber, none of them inclined to
make conversation the way they had during their first trip.

Even Savvy was uncharacteristically brooding, as if she had siphoned some of Dare's demeanor or Kel's mood. Lunna knew intellectually what could happen, but Kel and the others had lived it to varying degrees—at least, Kel assumed Savvy had personal experience with the Pale and their machines and machinations, given how much animosity she felt toward them. While Kel had accidentally stumbled on Dare's secrets, she still didn't know Savvy's, and the captain clearly preferred it that way.

Midday slanted to afternoon, and before the light faded, they reached the demolisher.

It hadn't been activated, to Kel's surprise and relief. It was still immense, taller than every building on Loth except for the spaceport, and in its wake it had left a trail of broken trees and footprints large enough to bathe in if they filled with rain. A team would eventually be sent to repair as much damage as possible, to haul the wood back to town or mulch it, to fill the holes with soil and seeds so nature could gradually be restored. But the demolisher would have to remain, a testament to the greed and selfishness of its users, because to return it to the Pale base would cause more damage.

Lunna, who had tracking experience, found evidence of someone—at least two people—walking around the machine. But no trail led away, either toward Handeen or the northern base.

"It doesn't make sense," they said, brow furrowed as they knelt beside a clear boot print in a pile of soggy leaves. "It's like they weren't here, and then they were, and then they weren't again."

Just like the night before. A terrible suspicion rooted in Kel as she stood next to Lunna and looked up. The trees around them appeared untouched, but then, there was plenty of space for someone to land easily without running into anything, assuming they were competent flyers.

"Do you see any trace of a flitter?" she asked.

Lunna retraced their steps, frowning in concentration. "No," they said finally. "It likely would have made a mark here somewhere, since this seems to be where the prints begin. Though these do seem deeper and sort of stretched, like the soldiers . . . jumped?"

"Sparks and ashes," Savvy said in Iccati.

"Shit on my tongue," Dare added in Vethonian.

"What?" Lunna asked, alarmed.

"They must have rocket packs," Dare said. He stormed over to Lunna and crouched next to them, swiping a gloved finger across the soil and sniffing it. "Do you smell that?"

Lunna leaned down and inhaled. "Is that . . . grease?"

"Fuel," Dare replied. "The packs are always leaking." He wiped his glove and stood. "This changes everything."

"Yes," Savvy said. "Now, we're well and truly fucked."

"We are?" Lunna exclaimed. "How?"

"If they have rocket packs, they might already be at the Pale base," Dare said. "They could have arrived here in at most a few minutes from Handeen, and they would have been able to fly at night with little trouble thanks to the sensors in their helmets."

Yet they'd left the demolisher inactive. What were they planning? Something worse? Visions of grimstalkers running free across southern Loth chilled her to the bone.

"So what do we do?" Lunna asked. "Does this mean we're too late to stop them?"

Dare glanced at Kel, then looked away. She knew precisely what he was thinking. She could make it to the Pale base quickly, too, if she flew.

But if she did that, there was no turning back. While right now there was uncertainty as to whether Hegrun's attackers were Order members or merely people in possession of illegal technology, the truth would be revealed to anyone who saw her in the sky, especially the Pale.

Unless she was very fast, and very lucky, they would report this information to someone off-planet. Loth would suffer even if she killed every soldier and destroyed every war machine they unleashed.

A realization struck her with the force of a fist. There was another option. One that would likely save everyone, and ensure the Pale didn't return to Loth seeking wayward Order members.

"I'll stop them," Kel said softly.

"You'll what?" Lunna asked.

"So you do have wings," Savvy said. "I had wondered, given Dare's miraculous survival falling off a cliff. He was stubbornly quiet about it, though."

"Wings?" Lunna asked, bewildered. "What wings?"

Before Kel could respond, Dare spoke. "You're sure you can kill them all before they get a pulsecom message out? You won't be tempted to be merciful?"

Kel met Dare's gaze, straightening to her full height. "No mercy," she said. "Only justice. For the Lothians, and for me. With luck, you'll never hear from any of us again." She looked away, afraid of what she might see in his eyes when he realized what she meant to do.

Savvy squinted, lips moving slightly as if she were repeating what Kel had just said to herself. Then her eyes widened and she shook her head incredulously.

"You damn fool," Savvy said, but there was a hint of approval in her tone.

"I don't understand," Lunna asked. "How will she even get there without a flitter?"

Dare loomed in front of Kel as she removed her pack and held it out to him, along with her staff. She wouldn't need them anymore. He didn't move to take her offering. She pushed both against his chest and let go, and he grabbed them to keep them from falling.

"Divvy it all up," she said. "If you feel inclined, you're welcome to my sword. It's buried underneath my house. Lunna can show you the way."

"What are you talking about?" Lunna asked. They threw up their hands in frustration. "What sword, and why did you bury it, and why are you acting as if you're about to die?"

"Because I am," Kel said. "Not right now, but as soon as they turn me in for the bounty." She smiled bitterly. "I'm sure the execution will be well attended."

Lunna grabbed Kel's arms, peering up into her face. "You're going to give yourself over to the soldiers?" they asked. Kel nodded, and they sucked in a breath. "But why would they want you?"

"Because she's a Knight-Celestial of the Order of the Nine," Savvy said. "The Pale have been hunting them for years, and there's a bounty on her head bigger than whatever

the soldiers are trying to get from this little scheme of theirs."
She crossed her arms over her chest, tapping a gloved finger
against her bicep. "How much?"

"Enough," Kel said, gently extricating herself from
Lunna's grasp. "You've been a good friend, Lunna. Even when
I wouldn't let you be. You respected my boundaries even as
you tried to lure me beyond them with kindness."

"Kel—"

"Whatever happens, try to retain that generosity of spirit.
Some people will find it naive, but others will recognize its
value. You've been a credit to your family and your village,
and your hospitality has been faultless."

"Kel, don't talk like that. Don't—"

"You'll find your way to the stars when you're ready," Kel
continued, her eyes burning. "And when you do, you'll shine
brighter than any of them. Where you go, may peace follow."

Lunna's mouth opened and closed, like they were a fish
gasping for air.

"We can find another way," Dare said desperately, but
even he was only looking at her now, not trying to touch her,
hold her, convince her to stay. He clutched her pack and staff,
his green eyes flashing like a broken light. He knew this was
right, but he didn't want it to be.

"Let her be a martyr," Savvy said, arms still crossed.
"She's spent years practicing. At least this time it will help
someone."

Kel nodded, despite the venom of the words. "It has
been my honor to travel with you," she said, then turned and
walked toward the broken clearing behind the demolisher.
Whatever happened to the rest of them now was beyond her

power. If this plan worked, Lunna might be home within the week, and Savvy and Dare would be out in the void again, flying to their next good deed. The thought of that made her smile.

"Kel," Savvy called from behind her.

Kel stopped and looked back. "Yes?"

"I assume Dare knows," Savvy said, "but I want to hear how much of a bounty I'm about to let fly off. Who are you, really?"

Kel closed her eyes, the breeze brushing her skin for what might be the last time. The air smelled green and alive, making her think of Dare, who even now was still rooted in place like one of the trees.

With a thought, she summoned her armor, iridescent purple like an amethyst glowing from within. It encased her from head to sole, weightless and translucent, tinting everything the same color as the sky until her helm's optics resolved and clarified. The suit began interfacing directly with her mind, expanding her senses, providing her with intuitive information about her surroundings: temperature and humidity, air composition, seismic activity, even planetary rotation and orbit. She could hear every leaf whispering around her, every creak of a branch. It warned her about nearby humans and creatures, and with a thought she confirmed which ones were friendly or nonthreatening, which warranted vigilance.

Once that was done, she opened her wings, stretching them to their full length with a blissful sigh. Vast purple constructs of pure radiance, three pairs spreading out to nearly triple her height, each wing diaphanous and shimmering. In her dreams, in nightmares, in flashes of waking memory as she walked the swamp or lay awake in her lonely bed, Kel had seen them, felt them, light and strong, carrying her atop wind currents and through the airless void. As they would carry her now to her fate.

Lunna gasped and stumbled back.

"I am Knight-Celestial Kelana Gardavros," Kel said, her voice more resonant, amplified by her helm. "By right of trial and ascension, I am the First Sword of Lovalra. Where I fall, may peace rise." She crouched, touching the ground, then leaped into the sky.

Distantly, she heard Savvy give a low, throaty laugh. "A hundred thousand domins," she said. "I'll be damned."

# CHAPTER TWENTY-ONE

**K**el had wondered over the years if she would ever fly like this again, except in her dreams. If she would someday forget how it felt. If she had already forgotten, on some level.

She hadn't. She would never, could never, forget the sensation of the air rushing past her, the freedom from the comparative tyranny of her own clumsy body. She wasn't weightless like in the void, with the associated stomach-churning discomfort. Instead, gravity tugged at her while the compensating force of her armor pushed her away from the ground, and her wings and feet helped her rise and fall and change direction. The horizon curved away from her in all directions, the giddy joy of open sky surrounding her with its vastness.

Her suit warned her of any oncoming birds or beasts of the air so she could avoid them. Even better, it pinpointed the location of the Pale base, and she set a course that took advantage of currents and weather variations while being as direct as possible. Beyond that, she let herself sink into the sensations of her first flight in years—aside from the slower, more restrictive flitters and the few moments when she saved Dare—and what might be her last one ever. The past was immutable, receding behind her. The future barreled toward her like a dreadnought at full warp speed. But for now, she could enjoy the present for the bright blessing it was.

The sun shone overhead, brilliant and warm, though her armor mitigated the full brunt of its radiance. Below her, mountains spread out like folds of cloth embroidered with forests, rivers, and lakes shimmering with silver. The petty aches in her muscles eased, though they'd return after she landed.

Don't worry about any of that now, she told herself sternly. Stay in the moment.

She flew into a storm. Water flowed off her helmet in rivulets as lightning flashed around her, thunder rumbling and cracking, the force of it vibrating deep into the marrow of her bones. Then she climbed higher, above the clouds raining down on the distant earth and into placid air. It was as if she had entered another world built atop the world, with its own topography of white and gold, pristine and perfect.

In the storm, the calm eye. Above the storm, clear sky. This was the place she came to when she meditated. Her feelings weren't gone, and she had no doubt she would feel them again soon. But every storm, no matter how brutal, passed in time. And above every storm, peace persisted, a respite from the tumult below for any who managed to rise up.

Kel indulged herself with spins and loops and dives, like a fledgling Knight-Celestial first learning to use their wings.

A poor comparison, really, because even the most seasoned veterans still found pleasure in the sheer thrill of flight. She sought out those good memories—of races against her comrades, obstacle courses set up to test their skills, even games of tag and skyball. Of her first time in space, the fear of the void pressing in around her, tempered by awe at the endless arc of the universe. The stars and galaxies silently moving in their unceasing paths, Amorleth floating nearby like a tumbled blue jasper streaked with green and brown.

Tears welled up in her eyes and she blinked, willing them away, not wanting to sully this moment with sorrow. Again she gently refocused her attention, dipping down to skim the surface of a cloud, rising higher until she was as far from the clouds as she had been from the ground.

On a whim, she rolled to her back and let herself drop, spreading her arms as she plummeted. Down, down she went, like a falling star, through wisps of white and back into the world beneath, wings tucked against her back, wind whistling past until it nearly howled.

There was a tempting madness, a vertiginous lure inviting her to simply keep going, to let herself lose all sense and succumb to a sudden, sharp end. The strange seduction had taken other Knight-Celestials before her, but she had too compelling a reason to live, and well before she neared the ground, she unfurled her wings and turned the dive into a glide.

The landscape changed as she left the southern reaches of Loth. Mountains gave way to foothills, then to flat plains, wild wheats and flowers and grasses stretching before her, the horizon an unbroken line.

And yet it wasn't untouched. The demolisher had left its tracks here as well, its broad, deep footprints forming a pitted road that led inexorably back to the Parched Fields and the Pale base beyond. It offended Kel to see it, this scar on a planet whose human inhabitants had worked so carefully to defend nature's rights and preserve its integrity. All it took was a handful of greedy, grasping fools with just enough power and access to weapons of destruction, and the peace of generations was despoiled.

To the northwest, a flock of straw-colored birds wheeled into the sky like a massive swirl of golden smoke. There were so many they nearly blocked the sun, rays breaking through the gaps in their feathers and bodies as they hurried westward. It felt like an omen, but of what, Kel wasn't sure.

A bare grayish stripe grew and spread as she closed in on her destination, until everything below her was dull, dead earth. The Parched Fields. In some places cracks lined the dirt, in others the wind had stripped and smoothed the surface into a level expanse of sand. Here and there she found strange whorled piles of dust that reminded her of meditation gardens she'd seen on a moon in Indastral territory. Those at least were an act of thoughtfulness, intention. Not even weeds grew here, and Kel's suit dispassionately warned her that wind conditions would diminish visibility and impact her sensors. She flew higher, and despite her helmet's air cycling, she could almost taste the dry grit.

When she was a mark from the Pale base, Kel landed and deactivated her armor. The soldiers were unlikely to open fire on a single unarmed Lothian, but she suspected a Knight-Celestial landing among them would receive a very different reception. That she hadn't already encountered any transports, demolishers, or grimstalkers on the way suggested she had either arrived before her enemy, or they hadn't immediately sent more war machines lumbering and racing toward Handeen.

She might still have a chance to convince them to leave without harming anyone. That hope gave her another kind of wings.

Walking felt wrong after her brief taste of the flight she had denied herself for so many years. If only she had more time—but she didn't. Each heavy step took her closer to her fate, and all her aches and wounds bore down on her as surely as gravity. Dust swirled around her, until she was forced to wrap her nose and mouth with one of her head cloths to keep from choking on it. Even with her eyes narrowed to slits, it was difficult to see, and every time the wind rose, she had to close her eyes entirely and either stop walking or hope she didn't trip or run into something.

The air settled abruptly. Kel found herself standing in front of a gate taller than a demolisher. The walls connected to it were of the same height, and stretched for what seemed like a quarter-mark in either direction. The whitish color suggested they were made of mononite, what some outside the Pale called sludge, because it was formed by throwing virtually anything into a molecular reprocessor that then dumped out a mud-like material suitable for building. It wasn't as sturdy as some alternatives, but it sufficed against anything the Lothians might bring to bear. Gray patterns across the walls suggested the dust storms hit them regularly, and were only rarely washed away by rain.

Kel hesitated at the threshold. She could turn away now. If she did, no one would ever know. Savvy and Dare would draw their own conclusions—that the Pale were faithless liars, that they had set the war machines loose despite having her in custody. They might, even with her on hand to more than cover their ransom. She hoped they would be so eager to collect the bounty that they would leave immediately; a domin paid was better than a domin promised, as she'd heard they said. But who knew what greed would drive them to do, when they'd already done so much? She would be justified in leaving, rather than sacrificing herself for nothing.

No. This was Loth's best chance. If she didn't do this, the Pale would certainly loose more machines, and mercenaries or Dirges might be drawn to the prospect of finding an Order member. This way, the potential for preserving the sanctity of the planet and its people, beyond the harm already done, was greater than the alternative.

She just hadn't expected to find such a strong desire to continue living, now when her death could at last have meaning. With a long, shuddering breath through the cloth covering her face, Kel strode toward the communication interface on the door and tapped the alert panel.

The wind kicked up again. She waited several minutes for a reply, caught between fear and hope. Had they already left? Were they even now reporting back to their superiors that a renegade Order member was hiding on Loth? Had Hegrun escaped to sell that information to every bounty hunter he came across, or to the Collections League for a cut of whatever they earned if they caught her? Or had Dare misinterpreted the signs left at the demolisher, and the soldiers were nowhere near the base, meaning she'd come all this way for nothing?

The interface crackled. "What do you want?" asked a surly voice in Dominari.

"Is your commanding officer present?" Kel asked. "If so, I wish to parley."

The voice gave a short, sharp laugh. "Did they send you here from Esrondaa to check on us? Yes, we're still here. And we don't want your hospitality. We have our own supplies. We don't need your nasty pills and food." The interface disconnected with another crackle, leaving only silence.

Curse them to the void, Kel thought. They really were unpleasant, on top of everything else. She tapped the alert panel again, and again it crackled.

"Are you going to stand there all day?" the voice asked. "I'm busy."

"Do you intend to send more machines out to attack the villages?" Kel asked coldly.

There was a pause before the next answer. "What makes you think we sent the machines? We came to shut them down."

"Of course you did," Kel said. "And I'm here to ensure there aren't going to be any others that will require your attention. Is your commanding officer here or not?"

Silence replied again, this time for a longer stretch. "Are you threatening us? You aren't even armed."

"No," Kel said. "I wasn't sent by the Speakers, either. I have an offer for you that will be very lucrative, assuming you get off Loth quickly."

She waited nearly ten minutes after that, itching to activate at least her helm so she could access sensor information, to give her some idea of what the Pale were doing. The wind died down, leaving an eerie stillness across the dry land behind her. She hadn't realized until now how accustomed she had grown to the constant chatter between Lunna and Savvy. Even Dare's silence had a palpable quality compared to this emptiness, and its absence left her unmoored, adrift, even though she stood on solid ground.

Finally, the voice returned. "Step over to the processing entrance on the right and don't try anything foolish."

Kel refrained from asking what they might consider foolish, since she doubted a sharp tongue would convince them to take her offer. Instead, she simply followed the instructions, finding a door in the far wall where there hadn't been one before. The sunlight behind her slanted into a small, shadowy room with what looked like a sensor bar along one side. As soon as she stepped in, the door closed behind her, and she stood in total darkness.

The sensor bar activated, a series of small lights racing up and down the length of the device as it scanned Kel for weapons. Naturally, as soon as it found her bracers, an alarm began screeching. After a few seconds, it stopped with an unpleasant squeal.

"What in the deathless Anocracy's name are you up to?" the voice asked through an interface near the far door. "Did you honestly think you could sneak in here with those bracers and attack us?"

Kel kept her expression and tone flat, neutral. "If I wanted to attack you, I would have come in from the air." Realizing her rebuke would do her no favors, she quickly repeated, "I am here to parley. That's all."

"Remove the bracers, then."

"I'll remove them as soon as we have an agreement," she replied coolly.

"You'll remove them or I'll gas you."

Kel sighed. "I can get my armor on before you can gas me, or shoot me, or attack me with a blade. Must we continue this posturing, or can I present my offer to whomever is in charge here sometime today?"

The door next to the interface opened, revealing a Pale soldier with a shockstick pointed at her. "Come on, then," they said. "Make any sudden moves and I'll kill you."

"Kill me and you'll be much less wealthy," Kel replied. That seemed to get their attention, because they cocked their head before gesturing with their weapon and backing away.

The interior of the base was similar to others Kel had seen, in person or in reconnaissance holos and images. Squat mononite buildings clustered together, identical and un-adorned, each with a single door and no windows. Barracks for the troops, enough to house at least a hundred. Beyond them, a larger edifice rose, tall enough to fit a demolisher—the maintenance and fabrication hangar, where the war machines were stored and serviced. The door to that was open, but only a handful of the dreaded devices stood inside in rows, inert as they awaited the commands of their masters. Other ancillary buildings and fixtures were arranged nearby—a mess hall, refueling station, the landing pad for small ships and shuttles ferrying troops to and from larger transports.

The Pale's starship, she noticed, was still there.

At a far corner of the yard, near a depowered missile turret, one place stood apart from the others. It was low-roofed and dug into the ground, and instead of mononite, it was made from futhite-reinforced steel. The lockup, for captured enemies. Or for soldiers with insubordination issues, possibly. She imagined Dare being thrown into such a place, confined to a tiny cell without windows and with barely enough room to lie down. Then again, from what she knew, the barracks weren't a vast improvement.

Kel was marched toward a long building behind the barracks. The door opened as she approached, so she stepped inside and waited for her guard to follow. The room was unusually cool, the air temperature altered by machines like the ones they used in space. She had forgotten how the Pale prided themselves on this kind of uniformity and control across their territories, how it could either be a comfort or a strangeness. For her, for now, it was the latter; she had grown accustomed to taking the weather as it came, inside and out.

The others positioned around the room stared at her with mixed expressions of hostility and suspicion. She recognized the one called Lazarun, who wore a vaguely interested smile; next to him was Hegrun, and if he could have killed her in that moment, she expected he would have.

"We don't get much entertainment around here," Lazarun said. "Given that your bracers set off our sensors, I assume you're either a former Order member or you somehow acquired their tech."

"Correct," Kel said.

"Which is it?" Hegrun spat.

Kel ignored him. "You activated the demolisher and sent it toward the Lothian villages to extort money from them. A foolish plan, as they have little of it to spare."

All trace of Lazarun's good humor vanished. "You can't prove anything," he said, which all but confirmed it.

"It doesn't matter," she said. "You want money, and the method you chose won't yield it. I have a better alternative, if you'll agree to stop threatening the people here."

"She's a liar," Hegrun said. "Her ally killed my people in cold blood, after she sat in my tent and lied to my face. Don't bargain with her, or you'll be sorry."

Lazarun's throat moved—he was subvocalizing something. One of his soldiers laid a hand on Hegrun's shoulder.

"Let her finish," Lazarun said mildly. "Don't interrupt again or I'll have you escorted out."

Hegrun fell silent, but his hands shifted below the top of the table he sat behind. Kel assumed at least one weapon was now pointed at her. She hoped his greed was greater than his thirst for vengeance.

"You can take me," she said. "If you leave the people of this planet alone, I'll go willingly into your custody."

The soldier who'd brought her in made a scoffing noise, audible through their helmet. Kel held Lazarun's gaze. He was the only one she needed to convince. His watery blue eyes contemplated her as if she were an interesting gadget he was considering for purchase.

"You know how much we were requesting in payment?" Lazarun asked finally. "You think you're worth more?"

"I am," Kel said. "Unless the bounties have changed." She hoped they hadn't, for Loth's sake.

"If she's Order, the bounties are dead or alive," Hegrun remarked, his hands still hidden.

"They're more alive than dead," Lazarun said. "I hope you're not planning to owe me for the loss of an extremely lucrative prisoner, given that I'm already doing you a favor." He half turned toward Hegrun. "Come to think of it, her presence makes our entire bargain rather unnecessary, doesn't it? So if you still want a ride, you'd best learn some manners quickly."

Hegrun snorted and leaned back in his chair. The angle of his arms suggested he'd released his weapon.

Kel maintained her relaxed posture, arms at her sides. If she made any sudden movements, she had no doubt they would kill her and deal with the consequences. She couldn't afford to give them an excuse.

"Do you have any intelligence to offer, by any chance?" Lazarun asked, his attention once more on Kel.

"None," she replied. "I offer only myself. I expect your superiors have their own . . . information extraction methods." She didn't elaborate, because she was aware of some of them, and none were good. Her superiors had held that such approaches rarely yielded actionable intelligence.

Lazarun laughed, a surprisingly pleasant sound. No doubt he was charming among his own people. "As delightful as it would be to break a Knight or Knight-Celestial, money is of far greater use to me. What were your rank and title?"

"Will you swear to leave the Lothians alone?" Kel asked. Not that the word of a Pale soldier should hold much weight, given all she knew.

"If you're worth more than we were asking, certainly,"

Lazarun replied. "Our plan has already proven more trouble than it was worth, and we'd be fools to turn away easy money."

Before Kel could respond, Hegrun leaned forward. "You already have her," he said. "Why are you bothering to negotiate? You can take her and finish blackmailing the people here. Make twice the domins for the same work."

Kel forcibly stretched her hands, which wanted to clench into fists. This was precisely the outcome she hoped to avoid. In the back of her mind, she began calculating how fast she could manifest her armor, whether she could kill everyone in the room before one of them could escape or send a distress signal that would bring more Pale troops rushing to their aid—

"I believe I asked you not to interrupt," Lazarun said. His throat moved again, and the hand on Hegrun's shoulder tightened.

"You're making me leave?" Hegrun asked incredulously.

"I'll still give you a ride," Lazarun said, studying his gauntlets. "You were right that it's in the charter for privateers, and I expect you already sent word to someone off-planet in case I reneged. Get ready to leave and keep your damned mouth shut for a change."

Hegrun stood, his shoulders tight with barely controlled anger. Once again, he shot a look at Kel that would have melted futhite, then allowed the Pale soldier to escort him out the back door.

"Now then," Lazarun said, blue eyes narrowing. "You were about to give me your rank and title?"

Kel stood motionless, hardly daring to breathe. This was

it. If this didn't work, Loth was lost, and she couldn't help them be found.

"I was—" she began, then stopped and inhaled sharply. "I am the First Sword of Lovalra."

All traces of humor vanished from Lazarun's face, and his body stiffened. The soldier that had brought Kel in scrambled backward, and she felt more than saw his weapon come up to point at her head. She continued to remain still, controlling her breathing.

I am the cool water to quench the raging fire, she thought. But she was only one person, and this was a very large fire.

"Well," Lazarun said finally. "That is a bold claim. You can prove this, I presume?"

"I can," she said. "But I hope you understand that I want my death to serve a purpose. I would prefer not to be killed by your soldier out of nervousness."

Lazarun gestured, and the sound of shifting armor behind Kel suggested the soldier had lowered his weapon.

"You have your bracers?" Lazarun asked.

"I do," she replied. "My sword is regrettably not with me, but it can be retrieved if necessary."

Lazarun shrugged. "The bracers are more valuable by far." His eyes narrowed again. "They might even fetch a good price if we divest you of them now and sell them separately."

"I suppose," Kel said. "But that would make it harder for me to prove my identity. Which I imagine would delay your payment."

"Sir," said the soldier behind her. "She's not wrong. Remember how our last bonus was scuttled?"

Lazarun pursed his lips sourly. "They might frag this one,

too, if we're not careful. We need a solid story that doesn't involve a First Sword strolling up to our door and knocking."

"Perhaps loop in the privateer?" the soldier offered.

"Perhaps," Lazarun replied. "But then he'd expect a cut. The question is whether giving him a share will cost less than us doing it ourselves."

Kel remained still as they discussed the logistics of trading her in like an old starship. Strange to feel so hopeful while fear gnawed at her insides. She had finally done something useful, something that would help. The cost was her life, but it was her choice to pay it.

"Whatever we decide," Lazarun said, "we need to get her off-planet as soon as possible." He rose to his feet and stretched, taking his time as if savoring it, or trying to make Kel nervous. "Come then, First Sword. Give me your bracers and we'll stow you in the ship's brig."

"Is that secure enough?" the soldier asked.

"Without her bracers, it should be," Lazarun replied. He smiled, but it looked like more of a sneer. "Besides, she's here of her own volition. If she decided to escape, we'd simply consider our deal null and void, and activate the grimstalkers immediately."

Kel inclined her head in a slow nod.

"Let's have them, then," Lazarun said, and held out his empty hand.

After so many years without wearing them, Kel found herself loath to remove them again. But she had to. For Loth. Slowly, she pushed up her sleeves to reveal her ellunium bracers. The dark silvery material could be buffed to a mirror shine, but hers were matte, catching the light without reflecting her surroundings. She slid her thumb down the length of the metal, opening a seam that hadn't been there before. The bracer loosened enough that she could slide it off, and then she repeated the procedure on the other one. Her forearms felt naked, the hair pressed down and the skin prickling as the room's cold air sank into it.

Without a word, she gave the bracers to Lazarun. His smile widened to genuine delight as he examined them.

"Incredible," he said. "Your people have such advanced technology, and yet you still bent your knee when the Anocracy willed it so. Pathetic."

Once, Kel hadn't found it so unreasonable that the Order of the Nine had chosen to negotiate for peace rather than continue a painful war. It was true the Pale had lost more soldiers and more ships, had spent a vast fortune to perpetuate the conflict beyond all reason; they had also shown no sign whatsoever of stopping despite that. They seemed content to throw legions into battle with little regard for their survival, replace them as needed and continue. They used machines where they could, warm bodies where they couldn't. Their funds were nearly endless, and every war against them was one of attrition. No one yet had faced them and emerged victorious, because even a victory against them came at a horrifying cost.

She wondered now whether it would have been worth paying it.

But she knew better than to start an argument, and so she remained silent as he gloated. She said nothing when she was led to the Pale ship, long and white-hulled like a slice of rib bone, nor when she was taken inside and marched down a long, dimly lit corridor. When he shoved her into a bare cell, emboldened by her meekness and apparent lack of defenses, she accepted that this, too, was part of the price she paid, the cost of Loth's safety. And Lunna's, and Savvy's, and Dare's.

The barred door slid closed, leaving Kel alone again, as she had been alone in the swamp. But this time, she was at peace. She sat on the ground with her legs folded beneath her, breathed in the cool, recycled air of the ship's interior, and waited for the inevitable.

# CHAPTER TWENTY-TWO

**K**el sat alone in the cell for an indeterminate time. The room had no furniture, not even a mat for sleeping. A scuffed sanitation unit rested in the corner, but she didn't need to use it yet. All she had were her thoughts, just as she'd had for years in the swamp.

It wasn't to last, of course.

Beyond the soft hiss of the air circulators, other sounds intruded, some louder than others. The whine of the engines powering up. The artificial voices of the nav computers calling out system checks. Heavy boots stomping up and down the corridor, along with periodic thumps that might be crates of supplies dropped into the cargo bay, and muted, distance-distorted talk of whatever duties they were performing. Gear being stowed in the bunks. Muffled cursing as people argued over who would get which bed.

All of it relieved Kel, who had worried they would renege on their deal. The storm churning beneath her calm—the seed of fear she still carried—was that this would all be for naught, and she'd be killed or left to rot while the Pale soldiers continued with their plan to send war machines to decimate the villages. But given the speed with which they prepared to depart, she doubted they had the time to go forward with whatever was necessary to deploy the grimstalkers, much less a demolisher. The more noise surrounded her, the more she relaxed.

When the launch engines roared to life, Kel even mustered up a smile. She had never expected to leave Loth, and without a doubt the circumstances could be better. But she wasn't living in quiet misery, smothered by her own sense of honor and obligation, afraid to befriend anyone because she might inadvertently cause them harm or bring the Pale down on their heads and hers.

She wasn't hiding anymore. Sure, she was going to die, but no situation was perfect.

The starship lifted off, artificial gravity preventing the discomfort of acceleration and the stomach churn of the void. In a few minutes, they would pass beyond the boundary of the planet's atmosphere. The pilot would activate the warp drive, the computers would calculate the appropriate trajectory, and they would be on their way to whichever Pale station or world Lazarun had decided would serve as her final destination.

But some time later, instead of the thrum of the warp engines engaging, a different noise startled Kel from her idleness. A series of bumps and clanks, then a strangled shout, followed by silence. Kel began to count, and when she reached forty-six, the door to the cell block opened. Miza, Hegrun's towering right-hand man, staggered inside, hauling one of the Pale soldiers beneath their arms. He opened the cell next to Kel's and dropped his load inside, then closed the door and left. A pool of blood spread under the body, though the wound wasn't immediately visible.

Kel didn't bother demanding to know what was happening, because it was clear enough: Hegrun had taken over the starship. Her impression was confirmed when Miza brought in two more bodies, including Lazarun, one of his eyes a mass of blood while the other stared unseeing at the far wall.

Hadn't there been four soldiers? The three on the planet and the pilot? Perhaps they were still looking for the last one.

A pang of conscience struck her. She had no love for her enemies, be they former or present, but she had struck a bargain with Lazarun. Neither of them could honor it if he was dead.

Hegrun swaggered in, hands behind his back. He wore a Pale uniform he'd likely swiped from their storage closet and a smug, close-lipped smile. The confidence he'd shown back on his island on Loth was restored, perhaps increased now that he was once again in command of a ship, regardless of its provenance. But surely he had some fear of being found out by the Pale and placed on their bounty list?

"I would say it's a pleasure to see you again," Hegrun rumbled in Dominari, "but I'd just as soon kill you and space you."

Kel stared at him. If he was going to kill her, nothing she could say would change it, and she had no interest in groveling.

"Honestly, I had intended to do this before you even arrived," Hegrun continued. "Steal the ship, that is. And now

I have you as well, which is a lovely bonus since I thought I'd only be selling your location for a fraction of the full bounty. Even better, I can blame you for the deaths of those fools instead of faking a pirate attack. Plus, I have these." He brought his hands around to his front, showing what he had been hiding.

Kel's bracers. He wore them on his own forearms, meaning he could activate more than just a shield, like Dare did. He could encase himself in her full armor at any time.

Her stomach lurched, and it had nothing to do with the ship, whose engines had stopped entirely. It had been bad enough that she gave the bracers to the Pale. She didn't want to think of what someone like Hegrun might do with such tech.

"I'm not planning to keep them, if that's what you're wondering," Hegrun said, as if her face had betrayed her thoughts. "Too risky to hold on to Order tech, for all the good a shield and armor might do me. But I'm betting I can find a buyer before I turn you over to the Pale. I may even sell you to the highest bidder and cut the Pale out entirely." He clanked the bracers together rhythmically, one arm atop the other, watching her eyes for a response. "Sad to think I might not have my revenge on the rest of your merry crew, but we take the gifts we're presented."

Miza loomed behind Hegrun, who glanced back at him. "It's done," Miza said. "The codes worked."

Hegrun's smile widened. "Or maybe my revenge will be complete after all."

Kel remained silent. Clearly he wanted to gloat, to see her suffer, so she wasn't about to give him the satisfaction.

"Your little friends are going to receive a gift of their own," Hegrun said, running a bracer along the bars, taunting her. "Thankfully your new cellmates had already done most of the work. The grimstalkers were in position in that canyon near Handeen, in case more pressure was needed to ensure a quick payout. You arrived just before they were activated, so all I had to do was finish the job." He leered at her, his eyes dark with malice. "You somehow managed to deactivate a single demolisher before, and a grimstalker. I wonder how well the Lothians will cope with three dozen grimstalkers?"

The urge to scream rose inside Kel like some hideous beast, a slurx lurking below the surface of the swamp who now yearned to leap out and snatch its dinner from the air. Violence had always been a tool of last resort for her, a failure of available alternatives. Now, she sat locked in this cell, facing a man who had refused to submit to reasonable justice, who had turned bandit to punish the very people he had harmed to begin with, and who had unleashed further maliciousness against them in revenge. She wanted to grab Hegrun through the bars and slam his head into them until he bled. She wanted to tear out his throat with her teeth. The sheer strength of her reaction, her maniacal desire to harm him, to kill him, scared her almost as much as the horror Hegrun had set in motion.

"Nothing to say to that, hmm?" Hegrun asked. "No wise words from the great and merciful Knight-Celestial of the Order? Don't you have some mantra about peace and how you're going to bring it to everyone?"

Where peace is lost, may we find it, Kel thought. Where

peace is broken, may we mend it. I will mend this, and I will break you.

Hegrun gave the bars one last tap with a bracer. "Your friends will find the peace of the grave soon, like these fools here." He gestured dismissively at the pile of bodies in the other cell. "The whole shit-sucking lot of them will be torn apart in days. I wonder how long it will take you to join them. Perhaps you'll end up in a palladium mine, or scouring debris fields for scrap. If you're lucky, you'll get a very public execution. I'll think of it fondly while I'm flying around in the starship I'll buy with the bounty on your head." He turned to leave, chuckling to himself as if at some private joke.

Miza, who had watched the whole scene unfold silently near the door, scratched his nose. "You want someone in here to guard her?"

"No need," Hegrun said, waving dismissively. "Those bars are futhite, like the door, and she's unarmed. Let's go crack open their liquor rations and have ourselves a little celebration before we jump to Uchoren."

Both men departed, closing the door to the cell block behind them with a loud whoosh. The room was silent, but outside a raucous cheer went up among Hegrun's small remaining crew. Presumably someone had repeated the order to get the drinks flowing.

Hegrun was wrong about one thing: Kel was never unarmed. Her body was a weapon, and moreover, so was her spirit.

If he hadn't come in to gloat, she might not have realized what he had done until it was too late to act. But they were still close enough to Loth that if she took her bracers back, she could activate her armor and fly down to the surface, then deal with the grimstalkers herself before they reached Handeen or the other villages. No one would be harmed, except perhaps her. And, of course, Hegrun and his crew.

All she had to do was summon her soulsword.

It was the rite of passage for every Knight-Celestial. It set them apart from the Knights and Shields they commanded; the latter possessed only a shield, as their name suggested, while the former were trained in every weapon available to the Order, and typically expressed a preference eventually, or were assigned to a unit based on need.

But to become a Knight-Celestial, one had to be able to manifest a soulweapon, to draw it from one's own body and spirit as if from a sheath. Such a weapon could cut through anything, and it could be sustained indefinitely, in theory; in practice, the toll it took limited its use. Its size could change, though making it too large could cause it to vanish or render the wielder unconscious, because it was too draining. She'd seen a Glaive once summon a soulglaive that sliced an entire starship in half, and the man collapsed and died almost immediately afterward from the strain.

It had been so long since she'd truly been a Knight-Celestial, in name or in deed. Could she still do it? A week earlier, she had believed herself too lost, too ill at ease with her own spirit. But after her flight through the skies of Loth, after the sense of peace she had regained from her surrender to the Pale, perhaps she was not so lost after all.

Kel shifted her legs beneath her and slowly rose to her feet, reaching her fingertips toward the ceiling. Some of her joints cracked and popped as the muscles in her arms and stomach stretched, and then she reached down to touch the toes of her boots, feeling the same delicious burn in her back and legs. She straightened and rolled her shoulders, then her head. Her clothes shed dust as she moved, and she shook out her whole body like a dog, then sneezed. The banality of it almost made her laugh.

Moving her feet until they were hip width apart, she pressed her right fist to the center of her chest. She rested her left fist behind it, her knuckles facing up in a straight line. Then she raised her chin, closed her eyes, and took a deep, cleansing breath.

At first, she felt nothing but the cool air on her face. But with each exhalation, her fist seemed to push deeper into her shirt, until her heartbeat thumped steadily against the circle of her fingers. And with each inhalation, something inside her shifted, pooling at her core, until her entire rib cage filled nearly to bursting with energy. Kel visualized that energy coalescing further, until it was all gathered where her fist touched her breastbone.

My body is my shield, she thought. My soul is my weapon. With my body, I defend. With my soul, I strike.

Kel unsheathed her soulsword from her chest.

It glowed a bright purple like her armor, but where that was smooth and solid, her soulweapon rippled in time with her breath and pulse, flickering almost like a flame. The blade was nearly weightless and felt as if it were tethered to her, from its tip down its length and into her hand, up her arm until it anchored itself in her nerves and veins. It was an extension of her will, her spirit, and what she bid it do would be done.

With three quick slices, she cut a triangular hole in the door of her cell. It fell to the floor with a loud clang, the sound echoing in the small room. Hegrun and his men might have heard it, but she couldn't imagine they would recognize what it was until it was too late. No alarms sounded. Carefully, avoiding the sharp edges of the bars, she stepped out and moved to the room's exit, listening for any sign that the privateers were coming. Nothing except the muffled, distant noises of them moving around and drinking.

The door wouldn't open at her touch—likely locked from the outside. She once again made a hole for herself, the hunk of futhite she carved away clanging against the floor as it fell. She stepped through, but this time she didn't linger. Rumblings of confusion emanated from farther down the corridor, a room her distant memories assured her was the mess. She ran toward the noise, her steps light as her soul, which blazed before her with a vengeance.

Miza lumbered out of the mess, not watching where he was going as he said something to whoever was still inside. His gaze flicked up at her and then away, then back again with a slow blink. Before his mouth could do more than open, Kel's soulsword flashed diagonally from his shoulder to his hip. He collapsed to the floor with a hiss of pain that ended in his final breath.

A startled yell came from inside the room. Kel flattened herself against the wall next to the door, waiting. A moment later, an arm emerged holding a shockstick. She sliced through it just above the wrist and the weapon fell, the person's hand still wrapped around it. Another cut sideways and the hand's owner fell, too.

"Is that the missing pilot?" Hegrun asked, answering her question about whether he was in there. Interesting that the Pale's pilot was missing. Perhaps they had survived.

"How's a pilot gonna do that?" an unfamiliar voice asked.

"Show yourself!" Hegrun shouted.

She was past taking orders from anyone, least of all him. "Deactivate the Pale war machines and return my bracers. Then escort yourself to the brig so I can lock you in."

A shocked silence replied, broken quickly by a series of curses. "How did you get out, and where did you get a weapon? I knew I should have killed you when I had the chance."

"Your chance is gone," she said. "If you want to live, do as I say."

A chair scuffed against the floor, followed by a cry and a flurry of motion. Another bandit stumbled through the doorway as if pushed—the man who'd tried to stop her escape on the island, the one she'd kicked into the swamp. She cut him down now, and he collapsed with a gurgle.

"You want these bracers back?" Hegrun asked. "Take them if you can!"

He burst through the doorway in full Order armor.

With a roar, he launched a flurry of punches at her, faster than she expected. He was a skilled fighter, not so light on his feet as some, but he knew his advantages and used them. She danced away, moving like water, a smile touching her lips. She knew something he didn't. It was cruel of her, perhaps, to let him take swings, foolish when he might land a blow that would turn the fight to his favor. And yet each time she stepped under his purple-encased fist, she felt stronger. When she maneuvered him into knocking off a piece of the bulkhead, her smile widened. Every missed grapple and evaded lunge made her stand taller, because she had offered him peace, and he had rejected it out of hubris and spite. He had chosen, and his choice would be his downfall.

"Enough!" Kel shouted, retreating nearly to the brig. "I give you one more chance. Surrender or die."

"Surrender?" he spat. "I have your armor! I am invincible!"

"No," Kel said. "No one is invincible."

Hegrun charged at her with a hoarse shout. Kel let him come.

As soon as he was within her reach, her soulsword flashed in an arc of light, blazing with the purity of her purpose. It slid through Hegrun's armor—her armor—as if he wore none, cleaving him from head to stomach. She stepped away and let his body fall, still encased in the suit. His blood spilled inside it, filling it, tainting its shimmering purple with a foul, dark stain. Out of a respect he didn't deserve, Kel watched the life leave him, and prayed for his spirit to find wisdom and mercy wherever it went.

No, not mercy. Justice.

The armor vanished, leaving only the faint afterimage of its glow. All the blood that had pooled inside dropped at once to the floor around Hegrun's body. He lay in an eerie halo, its boundaries soon blurred as the rest of his fluids leaked out.

She crouched beside him and removed her bracers from his forearms. "You should have listened," she said. "No one is invincible."

Hegrun had clearly used Order tech before, which meant she wasn't his first such bounty, or he'd scavenged it from one of her dead comrades. However, no one had told him about the armor's one fatal weakness: a soulweapon could penetrate it without fail. It rarely mattered, since Knight-Celestials weren't prone to attacking each other, but today that knowledge had saved her.

She slid her sleeves up and awkwardly put on her bracers, still holding her soulsword. She would need it for what came next.

Returning to the brig, she found the missing Pale soldier—the pilot, she presumed—kneeling by the bodies of the others. They stared up at her with their faceless helmet, frozen in place.

"Are you going to kill me?" they asked tonelessly.

"Do you think I should?" Kel asked.

The soldier paused as if they hadn't expected such a question. "I would if I were you," they replied. "But I don't want to die."

Lazarun had mentioned the pilot had been left on the ship, so at least they weren't directly responsible for what had happened on the planet. That didn't mean they hadn't contributed to the plan or approved of it. If her existence hadn't been reported to their superiors, eliminating them could protect everyone on Loth. This death could even be blamed on Hegrun if the Pale sent someone to investigate, as he had intended to blame the rest on her.

The privateers' wounds were clearly not from a pistol or shockstick, though. And if she had to kill the grimstalkers, the mark of her presence would be much harder to erase. Moreover, if the Pale had reported her existence, killing this pilot served only vengeance, and perhaps kept them from harming others in future. In the present, they might still do some good.

"Can you deactivate the war machines the privateers set loose?" she asked.

"I'm not sure," the soldier said. "They might be locked in to Lazarun's codes, which I don't have."

And Lazarun was dead. Every passing minute put more Lothians in danger.

"Find out," Kel said, gesturing for them to go. They scrambled to their feet and ran past her. She followed them to the cockpit, stepping carefully around the bodies in the corridor.

The room fit only a pilot and navigator in a pair of padded seats, surrounded by blinking consoles and projected interfaces. The forward blast shield was up and the cameras were inactive, so there was no view of the ship's exterior. The pilot slid into their seat and, after a series of terse gestures, reluctantly faced Kel.

"I'm sorry," they said. They slammed a fist against the side of the chair, then slid down into a slouch. "I knew this was burnt trash from the start," they murmured in Iccati. "Drag me through the sand and leave me for the beetles."

"Would you prefer the black between worlds?" Kel asked in the same tongue.

The soldier stiffened, then shook their head. "I would prefer to see my home sky before I die, but the ancestors turned their faces from me long ago."

Kel understood that sentiment. Would their spirit return there, she wondered, if she killed them now?

"Take me with you," the soldier said, quietly, fervently. "Please. I don't want to be here. I don't want to do this."

"Do what?" Kel asked.

"Any of this. Be a soldier. Hurt people. I hate it." It was difficult to tell whether they were being truthful, because their voice was so flat, empty, as if all life had been sucked out of them and left only void.

"Are you a conscript?" Kel asked, thinking of Dare.

The soldier didn't speak, only nodded.

"Then you know you are trapped," Kel said. "The technology in your body and blood won't allow you to leave. But if you truly want to escape, perhaps the Defiants could help."

"As if I could find them," the soldier said, their voice carrying a trace of bitterness. Knowing what she knew of the traps laid by the Pale to catch their own, Kel understood their dismay.

"Perhaps they will find you," Kel replied. "If I can reach my friends in time. What is your name?"

"Belarun," they said. "Fiar Belarun." Their visor retracted, revealing an olive-skinned face with narrow brown eyes and angular cheekbones. Kel used her bracers to store an image, repeating the name to herself as she did.

"What will I tell my superiors?" Fiar asked. "If I have to go back to them?"

"Did Lazarun already inform them I was on board?"

"No, he wanted to reach Uchoren first, and get his story straight."

Relief struck her like a cold wind. Relief, and hope. Kel regarded the mess she'd made of the ship, Hegrun's body still cooling nearby, and the other bandits beyond it. No easy lie came to her. She wished Savvy were there.

Perhaps that could be arranged.

"Wait a few hours," Kel said. "Before you do anything. Monitor the grimstalker movements. If their signals stop, someone may contact you to help you soon after."

"What will you do?" Fiar asked.

"There has been enough death today," she said. "I intend to see there is no more."

Kel activated her armor and walked down the corridor toward the escape pods. The controls were unfamiliar, but she soon managed, stepping into the small unit and waiting for the doors to seal closed behind her. They did so with a clang, and she wrapped herself in the protective webbing lining the cushioned walls, banking the flame of her soulsword so it wouldn't damage any of the equipment. She pressed another button and the pod's exterior cameras activated, showing dimly lit airlock doors. These opened to reveal the vast sweep of space and, about ten thousand marks away, Loth turning in the void like a bright holo encased in crystal.

The engines whined to life. With a crack-boom like thunder, the pod was ejected. It would take at least a half hour to reach the Pale base, and from there Kel would have to track the released war machines. If Hegrun was right, they were heading for Handeen, and were already near enough and fast enough that she could be too late to do more than stop them from spreading to the next village.

Where peace is lost, may we find it, she repeated to herself as she hurtled toward the planet. Where peace is broken, may we mend it. Where we go, may peace follow. Where we fall, may peace rise.

# CHAPTER TWENTY-THREE

The trajectory of the escape pod took it above Handeen on its way to the Pale base, thanks to the planet's rotation and the original position of the ship. As soon as she was close enough, Kel slowed the craft and used her soulsword to cut the door open like a ripe fruit. She launched herself out, activating her wings, and barreled toward Handeen with her heart in her throat.

The village was as she'd left it, the buildings quiet, the guesthouse rising above the rest like a watchful parent. Her suit began tracking numerous machines converging on the area, racing through the forest from the Gounaj Gulch in the northwest. Three dozen grimstalkers, as Hegrun had promised. Any guilt she might have felt over killing him was lost to rage over his vindictiveness. Innocent people could die because of his petty grievances, caused by his own cruel actions in the first place.

Her suit didn't find anyone huddled in their homes, or hiding in the Speakers' offices or the guesthouse. Relief flooded her veins as she began to hope someone had realized the imminent danger early enough to evacuate everyone to safety in the mountains. The shelters there were strong and hard to find, but they weren't impermeable, not to Pale war machines. Eventually, they would be breached, unless she succeeded.

Her relief faded as her suit detected movement. Human, running up the eastern road. Someone who lived outside the main village? It didn't matter. The grimstalkers' sensors would be sweeping for enemies, and until they noticed her or the approaching target, they would engage in standard reconnaissance protocols. She had to protect whoever was coming, hide them or move them far enough away that they would be safe while she defeated the machines.

Kel swooped toward that lone spark of life. She flared her wings to decelerate, hitting the ground in a crouch, then straightening. The figure raced toward her, his heat-masking cloak flaring behind him, his silver hair darkened by sweat to the color of the distant storm clouds.

Dare. He slowed and gripped his sword, eyeing her warily.

"What do you want?" Dare asked.

Confusion and dismay yielded to understanding. He thought she was one of the Pale, making good use of their newly acquired Order armor. With the machines about to arrive, it was a fair assumption.

Kel deactivated her helmet. Dare took a hesitant step forward, then another. She watched him, unable to move, the tip of her soulsword pointing at the ground. He crossed the distance between them in a flash and dropped his own weapon. Strong arms encircled her, and with a giddy laugh, Dare kissed her until she was breathless.

He finally broke the silence, his voice rasping with suppressed emotion. "You're alive."

"So are you," she replied.

"I thought you would be halfway to Uchoren Station by now."

"So did I," Kel said. "It's a long story."

"I knew the Pale would do this." Dare's jaw tightened. "I knew they would—"

"It was Hegrun," Kel interrupted. "The Pale were happy to get off-world and collect the bounty. He wanted revenge, and now the grimstalkers are almost—well, you can feel how close they are. I have to stop them."

Dare gripped her upper arms. "We have to stop them. I'm not letting you go alone. Not again."

Kel swallowed her instinctive protest. The mission parameters had changed. This was no longer a covert control override or a desperate sacrifice in the hopes of avoiding direct confrontation. The machines had to be destroyed, all of them, or they would rip through the rest of the homes and villages across Loth until no one was left. Dare didn't have full armor, but he did have a shield, a sword, and the training to fight entire enemy squads alone. One skirmish, one Scourge.

"We need a strategy," she said.

Dare released her and picked up his sword. "Initial assessment?"

"My wings have a broad span," she said. "The narrow streets make diving on individual grimstalkers difficult. So would the forest, if I tried to head them off before they reach Handeen."

"Narrow makes it easier for me to fight them one on one, though," Dare mused.

"True." She projected a map of the village from her left bracer. "The market square would be a useful bottle trap that would give me room to maneuver, but we could end up sacrificing the buildings to plasma fire."

"Better buildings than us. I'm not eager to add to my scar collection."

Kel flashed him a grin. "A joke? If Savvy heard you, she'd expire."

"Fortunate for both of us that she's guarding the villagers in the bunker with Lunna."

The wedge of grimstalkers would reach the first row of buildings in minutes. If only they had more time to plan . . . But they didn't. They needed to move.

"I'll stage near the lake," she said. "Where we were supposed to ambush the Pale before. It gives me a broad killing field, one where I can minimize damage to the village if not the trees."

"They'll surround you," Dare said, shaking his head.

"I'm armored. I can withstand it. Will they attack you on sight?"

"I gave the friend-or-foe beacon to Savvy, but I have the heat-masking cloak and the hummer. Unless I move, they'll ignore me. As soon as I strike one of them, I'll be a target."

"I'll lure them in," she said. "Find a position where you can surprise them once they're all clear of the village. Don't die," she added, her voice firm.

"As you command," Dare said, and kissed her again.

Kel launched herself into the air, spreading her wings to catch an updraft and glided toward the setting sun. The village passed beneath her, bringing her to the edge of the forest that stretched toward the long scar of the Gounaj Gulch in the distance. Grimstalker sensors were shorter range than demolisher ones, but they'd notice her soon enough. She dipped lower, letting her crystalline armor and her shimmering wings catch the light, pausing to raise her soulsword as a beacon.

After years of hiding, now she was ready to be found.

A streak of crimson lanced toward her from between the trees, then another, accompanied by a cacophony of shrieks. Gentle alarms chimed in her suit to warn her that her enemy had deigned to notice her. Kel rose and dove, avoiding their plasma beams as she lured them through the village, toward the lake. She deactivated her wings at the last possible moment and rolled to her feet, coming up with her shield and soulsword raised in front of her.

Two—no, three grimstalkers would converge on her location almost simultaneously, with the rest trailing after in a staggered formation. Their razor-clawed feet struck the narrow street with a syncopated, staccato rhythm that echoed through the empty buildings. The wind from an oncoming storm ripped through the trees on the far side of the lake like an omen, and Kel hoped it promised defeat for her enemy rather than for her.

The first grimstalker emerged from between two buildings, bounding toward her with its plasma weapon primed. It fired and leaped almost at the same time, the shot going wide as Kel sidestepped and ran to meet it with her blade. Claws scraped against her shield, pushing her back. She pivoted and sliced through its front leg, sparks spitting from the wound. Before it could attack again, she passed forward and cut through its neck. With a mechanical whine, it fell to the ground, inert.

The next two grimstalkers attacked simultaneously, flanking her and firing. She leaped straight up, activating her wings to carry her higher. One plasma shot blew a distant tree to splinters while the other arced over the edge of the waterfall and into the distance. They repositioned to shoot her out of the sky, but she looped backward and plunged toward the grimstalker closer to the water. She flared her wings and raked the machine with her blade, cleaving it in half and returning to the air to circle back toward the other one.

More enemies loped into the grassy space, their glossy white forms ghostly and unnatural, the solid red of their sensor bars a malevolent contrast. Kel searched the road and the shadows of the buildings for Dare, but he hid well enough that even she couldn't find him.

Her suit flashed a warning. A streak of plasma hit her largest left-hand wing, sending her spinning into the lake.

While she had no trouble breathing thanks to her suit, the fluid was denser than air or void, harder to move in. A gentle current pulled her toward the waterfall that gave Lakefall Point its name. She deactivated her wings and sank to the bottom, the surface half her height away, sensing rather than seeing two machines approaching the shore. As soon as they reached the lake's edge, she gathered her legs beneath her and pushed up as hard as she could.

Thanks to her armor's augmentations, she burst from the water in a spray, just above the grimstalkers. Her soulsword flashed, and two more heads rolled away, two more bodies fell to the ground in a shower of sparks.

Three new grimstalkers arrived, drawn to the deaths of their kin. They fired as they approached, and Kel's suit took a hit squarely in the chest. The shielding dissipated the worst of the impact, but she staggered from the blow nonetheless. The machines closed in. One of them leaped, knocking her down and pinning her to the ground. Its claws raked along the length of her shield, its jaw opening and closing with a muted clang.

Kel cut through one of its legs. Unbalanced, the machine tipped toward her soulsword, and she finished the job. She shoved the body toward her other two enemies as she launched into her next attack. Battle sang in her blood, in chorus with her suit's sensors. Protect, it sang. She lost herself to its rhythm, striking and evading, advancing and retreating, dancing along the sharpened edge of life and death.

The last of the grimstalker horde passed the line of buildings. Before it had taken a handful of steps, a blade appeared as if from nowhere and bit deep into its neck. The red strip of lights on its head blinked wildly, then went dark, and the machine fell stiffly to the ground. Dare's cloak swirled around him as he spun toward his next target, his sword fast despite its size. Where his fight against the bandits had been careful, his motions economical, now he unleashed his full strength and ferocity.

Kel summoned her wings again and launched herself into the sky, plasma bursting around her. Swooping down, dodging blasts, Kel cut through dirt-spattered machine plating with her soulsword. When she next rose, the volley of fire thickened, and she took multiple hits to her body and shield. The impacts jarred her, sent her reeling; she was unused to shrugging off damage after years of living without armor.

Below, Dare carved his way through the enemy. The huge sword was an extension of his body, its futhite alloy honed to a sharpness that cut easily through plasteel. He moved with liquid grace, avoiding claws and plasma shots as if he knew where the machines were aiming before they did. Kel wished she could simply watch him, admire his form and skill, but their fight was far from over.

Too many grimstalkers turned away from her, judging him to be the preferable target. He didn't activate the Order shield, perhaps because he wasn't accustomed to fighting with it, or because the plasma bursts diminished as the machines calculated firing trajectories that wouldn't damage their own kind. Either way, she had to take advantage of the machines' programming to protect Dare and end this fight.

Kel landed and dismissed her wings. The nearest enemy charged and swiped at her. She dodged sideways, bringing her soulsword down in a smooth cut that took the grimstalker's head. Another one tried the same tactic, yielding the same result.

Five machines converged on her at once, unleashing a dizzying flurry of strikes coordinated through their networked consciousness. She retaliated in kind, her sword leaving a trail of purple light in the air as it scored pieces from the machines. They tried to pin her, to push her into the ground and keep her there with their heavy weight, to pass her between them like pets playing with a toy. But she had found her center, she had found the peace she lost, and with it came the certainty that she and Dare would prevail. Her death might come soon, or in a far-off place and time, but Loth would be protected.

Kel pivoted, sweeping her blade in an arc that drove the nearest grimstalkers back. She advanced, ducking beneath a clawed limb and taking it off below the knee joint. Using the momentum of the swing, she brought her blade down and cleaved its head in half, the internal components flickering and dying as it depowered.

Another grimstalker struck her in the back, the impact driving the breath out of her lungs. She turned the motion into a roll and came up blade first, one knee bent, the other leg splayed behind her. The machine leaped directly onto her soulsword, knocking her to the side but impaling itself. Its motion dragged the blade through its innards, sparks falling from the open wound. With a flick of her wrist, Kel finished the cut, then stood.

Three machines flanked her, the lake at her back. She retreated, shield raised, until her armor-covered boots nearly brushed the water. The grimstalkers paused as if recalibrating, determining optimal trajectories and attack patterns, the lights in the sensor bars on their flat white heads blinking on and off. Their programming included encounters with her kind, she was sure; the engineers of the Pale were thorough. That didn't mean she was out of surprises.

A moment later, they all pounced in a burst of speed. Kel's suit indicated they would reach her in seconds. If she went up, they'd fire. If she went low, they'd bury her.

So instead, she leaped backward into the lake.

As before, she sank quickly. But now she was joined by two of the grimstalkers, who tried to slide to a halt and failed. They were designed to be waterproof, but that didn't make their movements any more graceful than hers. Even better, their programming parameters weren't optimized for underwater combat.

Kel pushed herself off the lakebed, toward the furiously paddling machines. One fired a bolt of plasma at her, but the shot went wide, turning the water into hissing steam and blowing apart a piece of the far bank.

Her sword was her spirit, unaffected by the medium in which it was used. She cut through the grimstalker's flank, then traced a line up its body to its head. As its pieces sank, she used them to push herself toward the other machine, whose claws scrambled to find purchase so it could climb out. She carved off its hind legs, then opened a deep gash in its back. Water poured into its unprotected inner components. It shuddered and stilled, the fibrous cables drifting with the current like lake plants or filter feeding creatures.

Her suit's sensors told her the third unit paced along the shoreline, following her as she moved. She had surprised two of them before, so she attempted the same maneuver. Launching herself out of the water, she thrust her soulsword at the machine.

She miscalculated and her blade met empty air. The grimstalker knocked her into a boulder, pinning her to the stone. Her shield was uselessly splayed to one side, her sword arm wedged at an awkward angle with her wrist unable to rotate enough to strike a blow. Even with her augmented strength, she couldn't force the machine off her, could only wince as it fired plasma bolts point-blank at her head. The impact drove her helmet against the boulder like a flurry of punches, each more painful than the last. The sound reverberated in her skull until the armor compensated, dulling her senses to protect her hearing. When it realized the plasma hadn't killed its target, the grimstalker clamped its jaws on her helm like a vise and squeezed.

A blur from her right was her only warning of Dare's arrival. The tip of his sword sprouted from the other side of the machine's neck. Its mouth opened as if in surprise at being skewered. Kel wedged her back against the stone and used both legs to push the grimstalker away, freeing herself. Dare moved with it, tugging his sword loose with a grunt.

Behind him, Kel saw the red glow of a plasma weapon priming and leaped to intercept. The shot glanced off her shield, but was quickly followed by several more from multiple sources. A sustained torrent, suggesting the remaining machines had formed a line and would hold it until a better option presented itself. She widened her shield and planted her feet so she wouldn't stagger from the impacts, buying Dare time to decide his next move. His green eyes met hers, flat and fearless, then shifted as he performed his own silent calculations.

The trajectories of the barrage changed; the grimstalkers were moving, trying to encircle them. If they succeeded, they would hit Dare. He could use his Order shield, too, and either his or hers could expand into a shelter, but that would simply leave them surrounded and unable to strike back.

*Find an exit, Third,* Kel's memory repeated. The pain of

that loss surged again, a wound that would always be raw, easily torn open at the slightest provocation. But she couldn't wallow in that pain. If she did, the past would be repeated. She refused to allow it. This fight wouldn't end with her cradling Dare's corpse.

There was one thing she could try: increasing the length of her soulsword. She had been able to do it once in training and never again. Her teacher had explained it patiently, delved into the theory and the practice and the danger, cautioned that it should be done as a last resort and with a partner on hand to perform first aid if needed. Only a handful of Knight-Celestials could manage it, and those who did were unable to sustain it for more than a few moments.

That would have to be enough.

"Get ready to drop flat on my mark," Kel said.

"Should I shield?" Dare asked.

"It won't help. If this doesn't work, you might have to finish the battle alone."

"What? What are you—?"

"Please, don't argue. Be ready."

He nodded and crouched, looking up at her intently as the shots continued to batter her shield. Not tense, but alert. Waiting.

Taking a cleansing breath, Kel focused on her soulsword. She pictured it lengthening, imagined the sensation of it stretching until it could reach their foes. The weapon was a manifestation of her spirit, after all, an extension of her will and her essence. If she was strong enough, determined enough . . .

The sword remained stubbornly fixed at the same size. The wall of fire rapidly became a semicircle.

Kel ordered herself to relax. As if one could do such a thing while being pelted with plasma bolts. Then she remembered: she couldn't force the peace she needed, she could only open herself to it. Instead of trying to fight the frantic beating of her heart, she let it claim her, let it buffet her like wind in a storm. And then, when she was fully immersed in the sensation, she rose above it to where the calm sky awaited.

Her soulsword blazed out to ten times its usual length, purple and searingly bright. She felt light-headed, as if the air in her lungs had thinned, and her fingertips and toes tingled alarmingly. She had to hurry.

"Down!" she shouted. Dare threw himself to the ground just as a red shot streaked through the space where he had been a moment earlier.

With a triumphant cry, Kel swung her soulsword in an arc. The amethyst blade sliced through one grimstalker after another, so quickly they didn't have time to dodge. In a span of heartbeats, a dozen machines fell apart, sparking and twitching as their components died.

Silence followed. Kel's pulse hammered in her ears and her vision darkened and sparkled around the edges. She fell to her knees, the soulsword disappearing like a candle flame blown out. Her shield and armor sputtered next, leaving her clad in her Lothian clothes, just as she'd begun this journey. And yet, there was no sense in hiding her bracers beneath her sleeves anymore. There was no disguising who she had been, and who she still was.

The ground rose up to meet her. As if from a great distance, she heard Dare shout her name, then felt his hands on her face and neck.

Dark clouds rolled in, heralded by the scent of rich earth and growing things. Her body trembled, heart lurching, breath coming in ragged gasps. Her handiwork lay before her, the shattered bones of machines sent to bring death to an innocent populace, who now only had to fear what retaliation the makers of the demolishers might visit upon them.

But the Lothians would live to deal with that problem. Better to try achieving justice for the living than the dead.

Gradually, Kel's pulse strengthened, her extremities aching as blood returned to them. Her breathing steadied and her vision cleared. Dare peered into her eyes, his own lit from within like beacons to guide her back to herself.

"I overextended," Kel croaked. "I'll recover. Just give me a few . . . eons."

Dare huffed a laugh and pulled her into his lap, burying his face in her hair, which fell loose without her head cloth to contain it. After a time, Kel raised shaky arms and held him, too. They stayed that way until the rain began to fall, first a sparse patter, then a rush, as if even the planet itself was eager to wash away the foulness besmirching its surface.

"Come," Dare said, taking Kel's hands in his. "Let's get out of the storm."

## CHAPTER TWENTY-FOUR

Kel and Dare walked toward the village guesthouse, bedraggled and soggy. By silent mutual agreement, they didn't lean on each other, but their slow pace made the extent of their exhaustion clear. Dare's sword was once more sheathed against his back, his black clothes hiding any bloodstains except where his wounds showed through gashes in the fabric. Kel's boots squelched with each step, and she blinked away the raindrops running down her face and clinging to her lashes.

The lamps inside the building had turned off automatically, leaving only the thin cloud-filtered light of the sun to illuminate the room. The place bore signs of hasty abandonment: cups and plates sat on tables, the scent of burned food drifted from the kitchen, and the occasional dropped bag or cloak had been shoved aside or trampled into a shapeless mass. They retreated to the bathing room and took turns caring for each other's wounds, though Dare had incurred far more since he wasn't wearing full armor. When they finished, they returned to the eating room, where Kel collapsed into a chair by the window. Dare sat beside her, leaning his sword against the table. She stared toward the mountains, wondering how long it would take for the Lothians to realize the battle was over and they could emerge from their shelter.

A blurred form cutting through the rain resolved into Lunna, dodging the growing puddles as they scampered toward the guesthouse. Savvy trailed behind them, her pace more measured. Kel could just barely make out the metallic glint of the cleverly hidden bunker door in the distance behind them, one of several that led deeper into the earth and stone.

Lunna barreled into the building, their freckled cheeks pink from exertion. "Sky and soil," they said. "We were watching you fight on the monitors inside the shelter, and I still can't believe it. That was incredible."

Better to kill war machines than people, Kel thought, remembering Hegrun's blood soaking the starship's floor, and the corpses of the bandits sinking into Lake Ayakocha.

"Is everyone safe?" Kel asked.

"They are now," Lunna said. "What happened to you? Why did you come back?"

Kel explained briefly, Lunna gasping in outrage even as Savvy shook her head ruefully. Dare's face was a neutral mask, but the squint of his green eyes hinted at his wrath.

"We should have killed all of them when we had the chance," Savvy muttered.

"We couldn't have known," Lunna said. "Mercy isn't a mistake or a weakness. It's a show of trust, and hope."

"That show of trust nearly got all your people slaughtered."

"What a mess this all is," Dare muttered, crossing his arms over his broad chest. "The Lothians will be hard-pressed to explain it to whoever the Pale sends to investigate."

Kel had solved one problem, but created another, just as she had known would happen from the beginning if she interceded.

"I can still turn myself in to whoever comes," Kel said. "I can take the blame for the grimstalkers and the ship. Maybe they'll leave Loth alone."

"No!" Dare pounded his fist on the table, his green eyes blazing. "I should have stopped you the first time you did it. I won't let you throw your life away for nothing."

"Loth isn't nothing," Kel replied. "And you are not my commander to order me about. I'm only one person. My life is not more valuable than theirs."

"I'd say your life is worth quite a lot," Savvy said. "It's not every day a hundred thousand domins falls out of the sky."

"Don't," Dare said in a warning tone. "Don't take her side in this."

"I take my own side in everything," Savvy said sharply. "As you well know." Dare snorted, but she ignored him, turning her full attention to Kel. "Dare isn't thinking clearly right now, bless him. You don't seem to be either."

Kel swallowed her retort and listened, controlling her breath.

"You were right before," Savvy said, pacing as she spoke. "About the Pale soldiers being greedy enough to take a sure bounty over an unlikely and much lower payout. Dare is right now, that you'd be throwing yourself away for nothing if you stayed."

"Thank you," Dare said, throwing an arm out in exasperation.

"You can destroy a squadron of grimstalkers by yourself." Savvy gestured in the direction of the machine remains. "How many more people could you save if you took that power to one of the Pale's enemies? How many more planets?"

"I must put out the fire in front of me," Kel said. "Not save my water for distant smoke."

"Yes, you're very noble," Savvy said, her tone and raised eyebrow lightly mocking. "That's how they keep you from fighting back. They don't have enough Dirges to investigate every possible report of an errant Order member, or a Defiant engaging in sabotage, or whatever new threat they create. Instead, they spread rumors, kill enough people to give those rumors substance, then let you put yourself into a prison of your own making. You could have spent the last five years helping people, and instead you holed up here and rotted like a bad tooth."

Lunna put their hands on their hips, brows drawing together. "That's not very nice," they said. "I know you're angry with Kel and she disappoints you, but she does care. She could have stayed home in Niulsa from the start of this. She could have left when I volunteered to guide you in Esrondaa. She could have let us find the bandits alone, or ignored that grimstalker in the forest, or the ones here. She could run away now, but she won't. She's trying. She's not a bad person."

"I'm not a hero, either," Kel protested.

"We don't need heroes," Lunna said, staring up at her with their wide blue eyes. "We need helpers. You're helping, and that's enough."

To Kel's shock, Savvy laughed. "Finally, someone gets it. Maybe I can recruit you if Dare doesn't object to sharing our limited space."

Lunna flashed her a smile. "You can do it anyway. I saw your ship land. It's a Chonian Flexdash 305IPT. You have plenty of room for all of us unless you've completely remodeled the interior."

"I'm impressed you knew that just from looking at it," Savvy said, but all trace of humor vanished with her next words. "My life isn't for you, Lunna. You have a home here, and a family who loves you. Don't throw that away for nothing."

"Helping people isn't nothing," Lunna replied. "It's the opposite. If you don't want me along, that's your choice as captain. I respect it. But I want to go with you."

"And do what? I'm running a business, not a charity."

"Fix your ship," Lunna said with a shrug. "It's what I was planning to do anyway, on someone's ship. I'd be happy if it were yours."

Something unreadable sparked in Savvy's eyes. "Are you certified?"

Was she trying to dissuade Lunna? Kel wondered. Or was it a genuine question?

Lunna shook their head. "I can't get the practical hours here on Loth. Not enough ships to fix. But I've passed the exams through SMT Rank 7, and I've put in enough virtual time that I would qualify if that were accepted."

"Your parents, Lunna," Kel protested. Maybe she was trying to dissuade Lunna, too. A little.

"They knew this was coming. It's only a little sooner than

we thought. Sometimes life offers you a chance at something special, and it would be foolish not to take it." Lunna grinned at Savvy, the light burnishing their red-gold hair and the spray of freckles on their face like a smattering of copper.

Savvy lowered her gaze to the table, then raised it again. She and Dare exchanged a flurry of hand signs, an argument based on the vehemence of their movements. Kel, meanwhile, tried to sort through the tangle of her own thoughts.

Was there anything she could do to help, beyond sacrificing herself again? What if she decided to run or hide? The next seasonal traders wouldn't be arriving for months yet. The Lothians kept several starships on hand for emergencies; they might be willing to escort her to the nearest independent space station or planet. But that would leave a record of them helping her escape, which the Pale could use against them. If they still had Hegrun's starship, they might let her take it, but it would mean the loss of a potential source of income or parts. And Hegrun had been a privateer, which might complicate matters further if his ship vanished.

If the Pale pilot returned to their superiors, it would be impossible to hide the evidence of Kel's presence. If they didn't, the missing ship would no doubt draw attention at some point, and a team would be dispatched to investigate. Would a Dirge join them? Perhaps not at first, but once the field of broken grimstalkers was discovered, surely one would be summoned. They would scour the planet for any sign of the Order, any speck of dissent among the Speakers and the general populace, any flimsy evidence they could use to justify bringing Loth to heel—or cleansing it of supposed enemies. Would anyone strong enough to push back against the

Pale bother to defend a single unaffiliated planet far from the galactic core?

Then again, all the reasons the Pale had to leave Loth to its own devices hadn't changed. Once they were satisfied that there was no profit to be had from bringing Loth into their empire more deeply, they might depart again, and the Lothians could recover.

Kel wished she could believe that, but as possibilities went, it had all the seductive promise of a beautiful lie.

"It's incredible," Savvy said, leaning over to peer into Kel's eyes. "I can see that you're thinking, but your face has gone utterly quiet. Even Dare can't stop himself from getting this little crease between his eyebrows."

Kel glanced at Dare, who glared at her with precisely the expression Savvy described. Her own lips turned up in an involuntary smile, and his furrow gave way to a barely noticeable pout.

"I'm still trying to figure out what to do," Kel said.

"You should come with us," Dare said immediately.

"Yes, you should," Savvy agreed. "I told you I hate goodbyes, didn't I? Easiest way to avoid them is to stick together."

"And me?" Lunna asked innocently.

Savvy rolled her eyes but nodded, and Lunna's smile broadened. They showed admirable restraint otherwise, as Kel had known them to dance when especially pleased.

Kel gripped her forearm and ran a thumb over her hidden bracer, trying to find a polite way to question whether that was the best idea under the circumstances.

"You think I don't want you on my ship," Savvy interrupted. "Because of what I said before."

Kel nodded.

"I don't hold grudges," Savvy said. "Life is too short, and I have enough heavy grievances that adding light ones will unbalance me."

"Wise of you," Kel said, and meant it.

Savvy gestured at her with an upturned hand, accepting the compliment. "My wisdom extends to recognizing talent and skill when I see it, and being selfish enough to want yours despite the drawbacks. We're your best chance to get out now and get away clean. You can't help the Lothians deal with this mess."

"You're saying I should trust their abilities and resources?" Kel asked. "I do, it's just—"

"The Pale are overwhelming and amoral," Savvy finished. When Kel nodded agreement, she continued. "The Speakers are more capable of dealing with them than you might expect. Yiulea alone has done more than you know to keep them at bay for years, primarily by making Loth an unattractive investment."

"It's all down to money," Dare said bitterly.

"Many things are, in many places," Savvy replied. "Even Indastral and the Kaolaras Collective rely on it, for all that they're less grasping than the Prixori Anocracy. But you've been hiding for years now, and in even that short time, the Pale has been overextending itself one planet after another. Small-scale rebellions are breaking out in systems far from their core, and they're having a lot of bad luck with their supply chains and tax collections and whatnot."

"Through no fault of the Defiants, I suppose?" Kel asked.

Savvy's grin widened. "What is a Defiant, but someone who isn't one of the Pale?"

Dare snorted, but his mouth turned up at the corners as well.

"More to the point," Savvy said, "Dare and I know a few people who can render assistance here. I may have apprised them of our prolonged timetable and suggested they find themselves in this area soon, just in case." She pressed both hands against the table and leaned closer. "You mentioned a Pale pilot who wants to get out? It strikes me as tragic how they perished when Hegrun and his people mutinied, and the ensuing scuffle led to the stolen starship crashing into the Pale base. So many grimstalkers destroyed in the catastrophic explosion."

Kel opened her mouth, then closed it. Such a plan wouldn't have been possible before, with so many variables to account for, but now . . .

"You can do that?" Lunna asked.

"Who, me?" Savvy grinned. "I'm just a humble starship captain, aided by my trusty sidekick, working odd jobs wherever the stars call me."

Dare snorted in derision.

"And before you ask," Savvy added with a glance at Kel, "despite the enormously tempting bounty on your head, I also have no intention of turning you in. I do have some scruples."

Dare made a show of looking under the table, his eyebrows raised.

"What are you doing?" Lunna asked, puzzled.

"He's trying to find my scruples," Savvy replied dryly. "See how funny he is once you get to know him?"

"You do have scruples," Lunna declared, patting Savvy's hand affectionately. "You also said you think Kel would be useful for your cause, and you care about that more than money."

Savvy turned Lunna's hand over and traced a pattern on their palm, smiling enigmatically.

Kel stared at the glinting surface of the lake and the mountain peaks outside, green and brown and gray, limned in shadow and light from the setting sun. If they could reach the pilot in time, and if Savvy's mystery allies—Defiants, no doubt—could clean everything up and stage the wreck convincingly, that just might solve all their pressing problems. She could leave Loth with a clean conscience, start fresh, help people. Truly live instead of simply existing day to day.

"So that's it, then," she murmured. "We need to report this mess to the Speakers, if only so they'll be prepared for when help arrives. And then Lunna and I will need to pack."

"Fine," Savvy said. "Now we only have one logistical issue left: how precisely will we all get to Esrondaa? Because if we have to take the long way back, I need a small room to scream in for a little while first."

"Make sure you use the hummer," Lunna said. "Unless you want us to hear you."

"We'll all be sharing in each other's misery soon enough," Dare said, the corners of his mouth twitching as if he was suppressing a smile.

I don't believe we'll be miserable at all, Kel thought, but she decided perhaps she should keep it to herself. She'd talked enough for one day.

# CHAPTER TWENTY-FIVE

Up close, the CS *Brazen Solace* was more battered and worn than it had looked from a distance. Ablation damage pockmarked the gray hull, either from debris or projectile weapons, or both. Scorch marks scarred the coating, in need of buffing out and painting over. The blue and gold markings that had appeared to be dots from afar were delicate flowers, some with three petals, others with four, some twined together with thin scrolling vines while others simply floated alone. These, too, were scuffed and scratched and burned, but their persistence despite whatever had tried to erase them felt like its own form of resilience and defiance.

Kel stood on the platform in front of the main deck entry door, holding the box that contained the remnants of her former life. Patches of drying mud and muck covered her clothes, obtained from digging underneath her house to reach her hidden cache. She'd washed up as best she could, but they were in a hurry, and she hoped Savvy wouldn't mind if she finished the job after they departed.

This was her last chance to change her mind. Speaker Yiulea had quietly offered to smuggle her off-world in one of the spare Lothian ships, but had agreed that doing so would come at a cost to Loth in both money and labor. This way, Kel ensured the Lothians could honestly say they weren't involved in her departure if for some reason they were asked.

The door opened suddenly, and Kel stepped back, clutching her box more tightly. Savvy peered out at her, an eyebrow raised, amiable smile plastered on her face.

"I just won a bet," she said. "Dare was worried you'd use the excuse of clearing out your place to get away from us. Or change your mind along the way. I said you were like an old freighter and you'd come."

"An old freighter?" Kel asked.

"Hard to bring around, but steady once you do."

Kel wasn't sure whether to feel flattered or insulted. "What did you win?"

"You'll find out later," Savvy said. "Get in here. The galaxy waits for no one. Time is money." She sniffed the air. "You smell like you rolled in farts."

"I'm sorry," Kel said, shifting awkwardly. "I thought haste was essential, so I didn't wash completely. I can go to one of the guesthouses and—"

"Just come in already. It's no worse than Dare after a bowl of beans."

"I heard that!" Dare shouted from somewhere inside, accompanied by Lunna's cheerful laughter. Kel snorted and followed Savvy in.

The interior was in better repair than the outside. The front room was like the vestibule of a building, small and narrow, with blast doors leading fore and aft. Easy to seal off if someone tried to break in.

"Bridge is that way," Savvy said, gesturing to the fore door. "But it's a Chonian craft, as Lunna so aptly pointed out, so the corridor goes all the way around. Keep walking and you'll end up back here."

"Do your automated defenses flood the halls with toxic gas during an incursion?" Kel asked.

"They won't have to, if you don't shower and change soon." Savvy grinned. "But yes, they do, so stay in the interior and mask up if that happens. If the situation goes skin to void, all the doors will seal off and it will fill with expanding foam instead of gas."

Savvy led the way through the aft door, which revealed a corridor lined with various shelves and storage closets. Some were filled with plants and lit from above—hydroponic units of some sort.

"We keep mostly nonessential stuff here," Savvy said. "Anything replaceable, redundant backups, you know."

"Whatever you can bear to lose if someone gets in," Kel said.

Savvy pointed a finger gun at her and made a shooting noise. "The real goods are in the interior, along with our bunks, the pretty good room, and the head."

Kel's brow furrowed. "What is the 'pretty good room'?"

"It's actually the great room," Savvy said. "Combination living area and mess. I forget which of us started calling it the pretty good room instead, but it stuck."

"It was you," Dare shouted.

Savvy wagged her head noncommittally.

A dozen steps later, a doorway appeared to the left, through which was the aforementioned pretty good room. It looked surprisingly comfortable, even homey. The ceiling was low enough that Kel could reach it if she jumped, but it didn't feel confining. It contained a battered teal sofa, a low table in front of it covered in scattered objects, and a plush chair in a corner next to a lamp. A metal dining table big enough for six people, but with only four chairs, took up another area near the kitchen, which was old-fashioned enough to contain an oven and burner. A cabinet had been replaced with a foodsynth unit, though Kel couldn't tell whether it was the kind that used individual component packets or preset codes and powder containers.

"What do you think?" Savvy asked.

"If I say it's pretty good," Kel said, "I expect Dare will manifest behind me to deliver a scathing rebuttal."

"So?" Savvy asked.

Kel smiled. "It's pretty good."

Savvy barked out a laugh, which turned into a broad smile as her gaze flicked past Kel's shoulder.

"If I had known you'd share her sense of humor," Dare said from the doorway, "I would have voted to leave you on Loth."

"No, this is good," Savvy said, her eyes twinkling. "Maybe you can figure out how to remove the sticks from each other's asses."

"Ah, but then we might turn them on you and take over the ship," Kel said.

"You and what army, butterfly," Savvy replied. "Now if you'll excuse me, I need to start running system checks so we can leave sometime this year." She jutted her chin at Dare. "Why don't you be a dear and give her the rest of the tour, hmm?"

They exchanged a series of minute facial expressions and hand signs Kel couldn't read, until Savvy laughed and Dare sighed, gesturing for Kel to go ahead of him through the doorway. She made it a few steps before Savvy yelled from inside the room.

"Dare, one more thing."

Dare ducked back inside and made a strange twitching motion, as if he'd caught something Savvy threw at him. Kel envied their easy manner, the rapport she'd once known with others and had lost when she'd lost the Order. Maybe now she'd have such a connection again. If not here, then somewhere, with someone.

"The bunks are this way," Dare said, continuing down the corridor. "First one is the largest, with three beds. Second one is mine; it has two beds. Then there's the head and shower, then Savvy's quarters. She's closest to the bridge since she also pilots. Small room, but it's private."

The empty bunk's beds were standard issue Chonian comfort capsules, self-cleaning, a calming pale green. They looked as if they hadn't been used in ages, the privacy shields closed but translucent to show they were empty. Kel wondered how long the ship had been short on crew; she knew Savvy and Dare had met a few years earlier, but had Savvy been alone before that? The captain was like a scriber with the brightness turned so low it was impossible to read her.

"I should sleep in here?" Kel asked hesitantly. Then she realized what she might have implied with that and stuttered,

"That is to say, if Lunna already asked to share your room, I do not want to cause an issue."

Dare linked his hands behind his back and gestured with his chin at a pile of bags and boxes half-hidden by the closest bed. "Lunna's things are in here. It's entirely your preference." He paused, then said, "You could at least put that box down here for now. It will be awkward to carry around the ship."

A reasonable observation. Kel laid her possessions against the wall, aware again of how grubby she was. Even if she'd stopped smelling herself, Dare likely hadn't. She tried to give her shirt a subtle sniff and got a whiff of sulfur, mold, and rotting vegetation.

"I could show you the head next," Dare said. "The cargo bay might not be a problem, but the engineering room is . . . small."

Kel smiled weakly. "That bad, hmm? I'll have mercy on you both then and clean up. There will be plenty of time for touring on the way to . . ." She paused. "Where are we going, precisely?"

"Aderth," Dare said. "It's unaffiliated, but closer to Indastral space than Pale. Should be able to make it in a day of warp-skipping."

Kel didn't know the place, but then, the galaxy was vast. She'd borrow a scriber to read up on it, or perhaps simply ask. Make conversation. Spirits, when was the last time she'd done that? She hardly remembered how. Lunna would laugh if they could hear Kel's thoughts now.

Dare led her to the head, self-cleaning like the sleeping pods, with the usual sanitation features. An aftermarket shower had been installed, one that could switch between sonic and wet options; she wondered if it was Savvy's doing, or if the ship's previous owner had been prone to decadence. Still, an enviable luxury. A laundry drop led to the cargo bay or wherever the wash machine was installed, and a nearby shelf could hold her clean clothing.

"I'll let you clean up," Dare said. "If you need me, shout. I'll be in engineering with Lunna."

"Thank you," Kel said. She meant for the offer, and the tour, but she realized she had much more to be thankful for than that.

"Don't thank me yet," Dare said. "I'm making dinner."

Kel squinted. "Is that because you lost the bet with Savvy?"

He smiled ruefully and looked away. "You heard about that? I'm sorry I didn't trust you. I should have known better."

"I know neither of us started on a truthful footing. And we've both had to live with lying to others routinely. It's hard to extend trust when your survival relies on the opposite."

"Savvy believed you, though," Dare muttered. "She trusted you to come."

"No," Kel said. "Savvy calculated that I would decide it was the best option. It wasn't a matter of trust; it was knowing how I think."

"She's good at that," Dare said. "Not my strong suit."

Kel shrugged. "There is more than one course to the core. Everyone has their strengths, and it's best to play to them rather than endlessly fighting against them."

"Am I to be treated to these pithy wisdoms daily now?" Dare teased.

"Perhaps twice a day, if you're fortunate," Kel replied, grinning back.

Dare leaned forward, then shook his head and stepped away. "Get cleaned up so we can finish the tour."

Kel gave him a mock salute, fist to heart, with a perfectly proper bow. "So I am charged. Your will be done."

Dare groaned, but when he turned away, he was smiling.

Kel returned to the bunk for her gear. She'd forgotten to ask Savvy where her other things were, since she'd handed them off before surrendering to the Pale. Dare might know, but she was embarrassed to ask when he'd just said he had work to do, and Lunna was busy in engineering. Everything in her pack was dirty anyway.

She did have one other outfit to wear, assuming it still fit. More likely it would be loose rather than tight, which was fine. And she could change it as soon as she'd washed the rest of her clothes. How bad would it smell after years in a sealed box?

Only one way to find out.

REFRESHED FROM HER SHOWER, KEL LEFT HER HAIR UNCOVERED ON PUR-pose for the first time since she'd been exiled from Amorleth. She brushed it to the side as best she could; it was getting long for her tastes, long enough to fall into her eyes if she didn't manage it properly. Easier to hide it in a cloth, but something about seeing it again in a mirror, seeing the purple streak bright among the black, was warm and familiar. And yet it was a rebellion at the same time, a refusal to continue hiding. She felt at peace, comfortable, more like herself now that she was among people she didn't have to lie to, or pretend to be someone else around. Her Kel Garda persona still waited, like the clothing she'd dropped down the laundry chute: temporarily shed but available when needed.

Even so, she lingered in the head. As soon as she stepped outside, all pretenses would be stripped. There was no returning to this moment. She could only move forward.

Where peace is lost, may we find it, she thought. Where peace is broken, may we mend it.

There were a lot of places across the galaxy where peace was broken. She might not be able to fix them all, but she could try to fix some of them. Help where she could. The Order of the Nine was gone, but its essence lived inside her. So long as she followed its precepts, it would never truly fade away.

Kel rested her palm on her diaphragm, letting it rise and fall with every inhalation and exhalation. Time to go.

The corridor was quiet when she stepped out, aside from the usual sounds: the engines spinning up, the air cyclers hissing. She waited and listened, and was rewarded with a low murmur of voices informing her that her companions were in the great room—the pretty good room, she corrected herself with amusement. She headed in that direction, passing the bunks and coming to the open doorway. Dare stood in front of the small table, facing away from her as he spoke, while Savvy lounged on the sofa, one leg propped up on the back, Lunna cross-legged beside her.

"—lucky the reclaimers are running smoothly for a change, otherwise we'd have to—" Dare stopped, apparently realizing Savvy and Lunna were distracted by something behind him. He turned to look.

Kel tried to imagine how the others saw her now. Before, she'd been dressed like a Lothian: long-sleeved shirt and pants to ward off sun and bugs, the cloth a simple weave that dried quickly. No embroidery to indicate family or village allegiances, not even the rainbow-colored thread of a kexeet harvester. Hair hidden under a cloth and a broad-brimmed straw hat, which shaded her eyes as well, let her cover her face and disappear into the background.

Now she wore a tight-fitting suit, in a deep violet color trimmed with silver to indicate her affiliation with Lovalra. The collar rose halfway up her neck, the tunic falling to mid-thigh, slit open on the sides for greater freedom of movement. The sleeves ended just below her elbows, above her bracers, now exposed where before she'd taken pains to hide them. Her pants were form-fitting and tucked into her black boots, which she'd cleaned as best she could but didn't have the tools to shine properly. Across her chest, the nine-pointed star of the Order of the Nine shimmered, an upturned sword flanked by wings in the center to indicate that Kel was a Knight-Celestial of the Sword.

Savvy raised an eyebrow speculatively. Lunna covered their mouth. Dare's jaw tightened, eyes flashing bright green for a moment before fading to their usual color.

Kel winced. She should have realized how her appearance would affect Dare.

"My other clothes need cleaning," she said. "My apologies. If you'd show me to the wash area, I can—"

"It's fine," Savvy said. "Just a surprise to see you in uniform." She smiled wryly. "A bit like seeing a ghost."

"You look very formal," Lunna added solemnly. "It suits you."

Dare still said nothing, just stared. His shoulders had

tightened, his cheeks flushed, his breath hitching. He hadn't needed the reminder that they'd fought each other in the war, not when he'd worked so hard to put his past behind him. How many of her people had killed his squadmates? He'd said he never fought a Knight-Celestial, that he was sent to Izlan after it was occupied by the Pale, but that didn't mean he hadn't been given reason to fear the emblem on her chest.

Then again, he'd already seen her in armor. How was this so much worse? Was it because she was faceless in armor, her features obscured by the helm?

Or was she misreading him entirely?

Savvy cleared her throat and rolled off the sofa to her feet. "Now that we're all smelling pleasant, I'll get back to the bridge and take us out of here. Come on, Lunna."

"What about the Pale pilot?" Kel asked. "Were you able to—?"

"It's all been handled as promised," Savvy said. "If I hear more, I'll share it. Enjoy the rest of the tour with Dare, and I'll see you in a few hours." She cast one last smile over her shoulder as she and Lunna left, signing something at Dare. His response was a rude gesture even Kel could interpret.

"I really am sorry," Kel said, as soon as Savvy and Lunna were gone. "Show me where to wash my clothes and I'll put this back in the box as soon as I can. I won't wear it again."

Dare calmly reached into his pocket and took something out. The hummer Savvy had stolen from Hegrun. Why did he have it? Moreover, why was he activating it and putting it on the table in front of the sofa?

"What—?" Kel began.

Dare crossed the room and kissed the words out of her mouth.

"Your uniform," he said, "is a problem." He punctuated his words with more kisses, which made it difficult to concentrate on them, but Kel did her best. "It's a problem because, as attractive as you were before, this has unfortunately managed to emphasize some of your finest qualities."

"And what are those?" Kel asked breathlessly, sliding her hands up his chest.

Dare growled at her touch. "All of them," he rumbled, wrapping his arms around her.

Kel huffed out an incredulous laugh and Dare smiled. Blessed stars, he had a nice smile. Lunna's was like a sunbeam, warm and bright. Savvy's was a cool breeze on a hot day, easily turning to frost. But Dare's was rare and unexpected, a fiery meteor streaking across a dark sky. She cleared her throat, staring down at her boots.

He lifted Kel's chin with a finger, leaned in and pressed his lips against hers, gently this time, sweetly. She lingered in his deep green eyes, the pupils ringed with a hint of amber. Her hands reached up his neck, into his silver hair, nearly the same color as the threading on her uniform.

"Aren't you supposed to be giving me a tour of the rest of the ship?" Kel asked. "I still haven't seen the cargo bay, or engineering. I don't think I'll stink up the room now."

Dare pressed another kiss to the corner of her mouth. "Has anyone ever told you that you talk too much?" he asked.

Kel looked up at him and grinned, and for perhaps longer than was strictly advisable, they did no talking whatsoever.

# ACKNOWLEDGMENTS

Every book is its own challenge and ordeal, especially in these pandemic times. Humble and sincere thanks to:

Eric, my husband, for being the Orpheus to my Eurydice. Or is that the other way around? Home is not where you live, but who cares when you're gone.

My agent, Quressa Robinson, for being my shield when I need it, and my sword when someone else needs it.

My editor, Tessa Woodward, for letting me pivot to this quieter story than the one I first intended to tell, and for helping me make it better than I had hoped.

My mother, Nayra, for texting me weather reports and memes and cat pictures, and for sending me the good cookies from Costco, among many other things.

Jay Wolf, for unwavering friendship, support, and feedback, and for patiently enduring my brain dumps, even when they don't smell so good.

Matthew, Rick, and Amalia, for laughing with me and at me, and for keeping me afloat when we're all wallowing in the world's muck.

My Isle of Write friends, for every shared yay, even the secret ones, and for consistently relocating brain weasels to a lovely farm upstate.

My Strange Friends, for being endlessly kind, thoughtful, and committed to creating worlds where being kind and thoughtful are the truest sources of power.

Clint, Clarissa, Sean, Meg, GamerGramp, ShadowsProxy, and all my other Twitch friends, for mocking my aversion to mounts and encouraging my writing rants. Bring forth the snackrifice!

Mur, for being the best coeditor and supporting me in so many ways, big and small, on Discord and elsewhere.

My NaNoWriMo folks, for making the sometimes-lonely toil of writing a little less lonely.

My sister, Laura, for the dog pictures and jokes and salty political takes; stay warm, hermanita!

My family-in-law, Aimee and Luis and Vanessa and Ashley and Erik and Nate, for bread and childcare and holidays and Minecraft support and JRPG jokes.

My dad, Keith, and stepmom, Jackie, and my siblings and step-siblings, Tasha and Kirk and Jennifer and John, and all their excellent spouses, past and present, for unwavering support.

My many other friends and family, for all the ways you show your love, which I am doing my very best to honor and deserve and return.

And finally, all the readers picking up this book: if you loved my other books, I hope you like Kel and company as much as Eva and the crew of *La Sirena Negra*. If my work is new to you, thanks for taking a chance on me, and I hope it pays off!

# ABOUT THE AUTHOR

**Valerie Valdes** is a coeditor of *Escape Pod* and the author of the Chilling Effect trilogy. Her short fiction and poetry have been featured in Uncanny Magazine, Nightmare Magazine, and several anthologies. In her spare time, she streams video games on Twitch and role-plays with the Strange Friends crew. She lives in Georgia with her husband, children, and cats.